BORDERLINE

THE ARCADIA PROJECT

BOOK ONE

BORDERLINE

MISHELL BAKER

SAGA PRESS

LONDON SYDNEY **NEW YORK** TORONTO NEW DELHI

SAGA *S* PRESS
AN IMPRINT OF SIMON & SCHUSTER, INC.

1230 AVENUE OF THE AMERICAS, NEW YORK, NEW YORK 10020

Text copyright © 2016 by Mishell Baker

SAGA PRESS and colophon are trademarks of Simon & Schuster, Inc.

For information about special discounts for bulk purchases, please contact Simon & Schuster Special Sales at 1-866-506-1949 or business@simonandschuster.com.

The Simon & Schuster Speakers Bureau can bring authors to your live event. For more information or to book an event, contact the Simon & Schuster Speakers Bureau at 1-866-248-3049 or visit our website at www.simonspeakers.com.

Also available in a Saga Press hardcover edition

Cover photograph of woman copyright © 2016 by Jill Wachter; cover stock photography copyright © 2016 by Thinkstock

The text for this book was set in Chaparral Pro.

Manufactured in the United States of America

First Saga Press paperback edition 2016

4 6 8 10 9 7 5 3

Library of Congress Cataloging-in-Publication Data
Baker, Mishell.
Borderline / Mishell Baker. — First edition.
pages cm
ISBN 978-1-4814-5306-6 (hc)
ISBN 978-1-4814-2978-8 (pbk)
ISBN 978-1-4814-2979-5 (eBook)
1. Women with disabilities—Fiction. 2. Government investigators—Fiction. I. Title.
PS3602.A58665B67 2016
813'.6—dc23
2015009176

In memory of Paul David Briggs,

who was going to get this dedication, anyway

1

It was midmorning on a Monday when magic walked into my life wearing a beige Ann Taylor suit and sensible flats. At the time I had more money than sense, and so I had been languishing at the Leishman Psychiatric Center in Silver Lake for just over six months.

The Center had a rigid routine, and there was a perverse comfort in knowing what misery of boredom to expect and when. Breakfast: grayish sausage, carbohydrate mush, and the kind of eggs that are poured from a carton, all eaten with plastic utensils. Physical therapy: a rotating assortment of blue-shirted people who urgently pressured me to feel happy about accomplishing things a three-year-old could do. Patio break: a chain-link enclosed concrete yard where everyone else flocked to light up coffin nails and trade confessions. Knowing they'd all be gone in three to fourteen days and wouldn't stay in touch, I elected to sit in the fluorescent-lit common room and run reel after reel of movies in my head.

When a well-dressed woman stopped with purpose beside my chair that Monday, I assumed she was one of the Center's bureaucracy. She was of average height and build, with a conservative suit and ethnically ambiguous features. Her face was drab and powdered matte; her hair and eyes were a muddle of colors that defied category. If she had drawn a revolver, shot me in the kneecap, and walked out, I'd have had a hell of a time describing her to security.

Although her appearance put her in the ballpark of my age, she addressed me in a flat, husky alto that had forty years of smoke and whiskey in it. "Millicent Roper," she said.

"Yeah?" I was hesitant because when people in the movies say a name in that tone, the next line is usually, "You're under arrest." Instead she extended a gloved hand.

People do not wear gloves in Los Angeles. These weren't cold-weather gloves either, but light dress gloves the same shell pink as her blouse, their cuffs disappearing beneath the sleeves of her jacket.

"I'm Caryl Vallo with the Arcadia Project," she said.

"I don't know what that is," I said, leaving my hands in my lap.

She withdrew the gesture with no change of expression. "We are a nonprofit organization partially funded by the Los Angeles County Department of Mental Health. I would be pleased to tell you more if we can speak confidentially. Could we retire briefly to another area?"

Her formality nudged my brain into a rusty gear that I eventually recognized as curiosity. "Fine," I said. "We can go back to my room."

I grabbed the wheels of my chair and rolled myself down the hall with practiced economy. The chair was a squeaky piece of crap, and I found myself embarrassed by it.

"I was under the impression that you used prosthetics for walking," Caryl said.

"Only when I have somewhere to go. The AK socket starts to dig into my ass if I'm just sitting around."

"Are your prosthetics in your room?"

"Yeah."

"Will you put them on for me?"

"Sure."

Before you ask why I was so docile about an invasive request from a complete stranger, keep in mind that I'd spent the past year of my life following the orders of a procession of doctors, therapists, and other random concerned people whose names I sometimes didn't even bother to learn.

I was paying extra for privacy, so there was a desk in my room where a second twin bed would have been. When we arrived, Caryl seated herself at it, pushing back the chair.

"Are you happy here?" she asked me, looking around. She seemed an extension of the bland decor.

"If I were happy," I grunted, wheeling myself over to the locked chest containing my prosthetics, "I wouldn't be here."

Caryl, declining to comment, skimmed gloved fingertips over her tightly bound hair. I tried not to think about my own cowlicked mess, a few inches long all over except for a mostly hidden seam on the left side where hair didn't grow at all.

"Forgive my poor choice of words," she said. "Do you feel this is the best living situation for you at this time?"

"With my job and credit history," I said as I braked my chair, "I think my only other option is a refrigerator box." I took the key from around my neck, leaned over to unlock the chest, and pulled out my bottle of Dry-Lite, applying a generous amount to the stump of my right shin. I glanced at Caryl and found her watching me with the politely attentive expression of someone in the front row of a lecture hall.

"So," I said, lifting my BK prosthesis out of the trunk. "You were about to tell me about the Arcadia Project." I aligned the suction suspension and slid my shin into it. Once the carbon foot was solidly on the floor, I pushed myself to a stand with both hands, balancing one-legged and forcing the rest of the air out of the valve with a moist, embarrassing sound.

"The Arcadia Project," said Caryl, "is funded partially by the Los Angeles County Department of Mental Health and partially by private donations from members of the entertainment industry. We seek mentally ill adults who meet certain qualifications and provide them with meaningful employment, housing, and ongoing—"

"What sort of employment?" I interrupted as I pivoted to sit down on the edge of my bed.

"Employment opportunities vary depending upon the qualifications of the individual, but the majority are part-time or freelance creative positions in the film and television industry."

I blinked at her a few times, an assortment of sarcastic replies clotting together in my brain like cars on the 405. I tried to remember my former Hollywood manners, then remembered that as a mental patient I had a license to say whatever the hell I wanted.

"Let me be sure I understand," I said, reaching into the chest for the silicone suspension liner of my AK prosthetic and starting to powder the inside of it. "I flipped burgers for five years putting myself through community college, got fifteen grand into debt making a bunch of pretentious indie films about people trapped in rooms together, then bullshitted my way into what's arguably the most prestigious film school in the world, when all I really needed to do to break into the industry was jump off a building?"

Caryl looked at me with the kind of aplomb that comes from dealing with the mentally ill on a daily basis. "No," she said flatly. "You needed to do all that and *then* jump off a building." There was nothing in her demeanor to suggest that she was making a joke, or even knew what one was.

I snorted at her, hiking up the leg of my shorts. I slipped the powdered liner onto the stump of my thigh as far as it would go.

"You used lotion to make the first seal and powder to make the second," Caryl observed. "Why?"

I stopped and looked at her, but her face held only the same detached curiosity. "You just learn to do whatever works," I said with a shrug. "Every amputation is different."

I reached into the chest for the AK. AK stands for above-knee, but I liked that it sounded like an assault rifle. The silicone-only suspension fit like flesh, and with a twist of a knob the hydraulic knee gave the right resistance at anything from a stroll to a sprint. There are some occasions when a girl just has to splurge a little.

"So you think I fit some kind of qualifications?" I said, shoving my thigh and its silicone sheath into the socket of the prosthesis. "Now there's a list I'd love to see."

"Most of the list is confidential, but I can tell you some of it. I am looking for people with management potential, and your success as an independent filmmaker points to leadership skill and creative thinking. Then there is your diagnosis of borderline personality disorder and your willingness to accept and manage that condition, as well as your noted aversion to psychoactive drugs, legal or otherwise."

"Drugs don't work on BPD," I said defensively, squirming my way more firmly into the socket and wondering how the hell she knew I'd never tried recreational drugs. "It's not a chemical imbalance."

"Nonetheless, many Borderlines choose to medicate comorbid conditions such as anxiety or depression. Our project only accepts those who can function, at least minimally, without the use of controlled substances."

I paused to sweep a hand pointedly around the room. "Is there something that makes you think I can function?"

"The twenty-five years of your life that elapsed *before* you did something colossally stupid."

Indignation flared, and my thighs responded by trying to push me to a stand. But that's exactly the sort of thing a prosthetic knee can*not* do, and my weight was centered over both legs. So I just ended up lurching a few crooked inches off the seat and crashing right back down.

"Be careful," said Caryl mildly.

One of the fun bits about BPD is a phenomenon shrinks like to call "splitting." When under stress, Borderlines forget the existence of gray. Life is a beautiful miracle, or a cesspool of despair. The film you're making is a Best Picture candidate, or it's garbage. People are either saints, or they're scheming to destroy you.

Caryl Vallo, thanks to the shards of pain jangling through my pelvis, had just found her way onto the latter list. But she was dangling a hell of a prize, so I pushed aside my sudden surge of paranoid hatred and tried to keep my voice as calm as hers.

"There has to be a catch," I said. "Otherwise every starving wannabe in Los Angeles would be faking BPD to get this gig. So why aren't they?"

"Because they do not know about it."

She gave the words no more gravity than anything else she had said, but some intuition made the hairs rise on the back of my neck. I considered her stony face and her trimly tailored jacket. Aside from wardrobe color, she fit the Man in Black profile perfectly, and I didn't have much to lose by sounding crazy.

"Does this job involve aliens in any way?"

"Not in the way you mean," she said without asking what I meant. "There are, however, some aspects of the job that strain credulity, and they are better demonstrated than explained. Would you meet me tomorrow for an interview?"

"Sure, why not."

"You can find me at the corner of Fourth Street and Hollister, in Santa Monica. There is a small park there."

I felt a cold rush of fear that I quickly paved over with irritation. "I'm supposed to take a cab all the way from Silver Lake to Santa Monica?"

Caryl ignored my tone. "Tomorrow at noon. Pack and proceed as though you will not be returning to the hospital."

"I beg your pardon?" I gaped at her. "How am I supposed to get a suitcase, a wheelchair, crutches, and a cane in and out of a taxi on my own?"

"The choice is yours. The terms are mine. If you do not attend the meeting, I will move to the next candidate on my list. You are welcome to refuse the opportunity, but you will be the first to do so in the ten years I have been with the Project."

Ten years. She was definitely older than she looked. "What if you decide you don't want to hire me?"

"Then you may return to the hospital, or not, as you like. But if I weren't confident of your character, I would not have gone to the trouble to reach you."

"How much trouble is it, exactly, to call the—"

Wait a second. No one had introduced her. And shouldn't she have been wearing a name tag or something?

Carefully I pushed myself to a stand. Caryl remained seated, making no move to stop me. I forced the remaining air out of my AK suspension, then slowly walked to the door.

I called down the hallway toward the nurses' station, and then glanced back over my shoulder into the room, half expecting to find myself staring down the barrel of a gun. But not even my hyperbolic filmmaker's imagination could prepare me for what I saw.

Nothing. The woman I had been talking to was gone.

2

Dr. Amanda Davis must have been intelligent to get three degrees, but sometimes in our sessions I felt as though I were talking to a brick wall. Her lack of humor made our conversations halting and awkward; between that and her dogged, persistent faith in me, I'd jumped to the conclusion early on that she didn't understand me and couldn't help me. Jumping to conclusions is another thing Borderlines are great at.

At this point I was not very far along in my dialectical behavior therapy, and unmanaged Borderlines have a partially deserved reputation for manipulating others. I knew how to make Dr. Davis feel she was doing well, and I had learned which of my tangents fascinated her enough to keep her off the topics I didn't want to discuss. On that particular Monday, however, I wished I'd used all that energy to find out if I could really trust her.

"This seems a little sudden," Dr. Davis said, her chin-length hair slipping forward as she leaned on her knees. She made me think of Snow White at fifty: lips' faded bloom painted over, alabaster skin mottled by decades of sun damage.

"I'm not sure what you want from me," I said. "A couple of

weeks ago you were on me for staying here so long, and now you're on me for leaving."

"I'm just trying to understand what precipitated this," she said. "Obviously you can leave whenever you want, but given how long you've been under hospital care, it might be helpful for you to go to a transitional facility first, at least until you're more comfortable living on your own."

I considered bringing up the Arcadia Project and the disappearing lady, but then I quickly thought better of it. I knew Caryl hadn't been a hallucination, but Dr. Davis hadn't seen her, and I didn't have a great theory to counter "Millie's last marble finally rolled under the fridge somewhere." Assuming Caryl was real, the woman obviously wanted to stay off the staff's radar, and I wasn't sure it would be a good idea to burn my bridges with a potential employer, given how fast my inheritance was dwindling.

"I found someone willing to put me up for a while," I said.

Dr. Davis failed to conceal her surprise. "Someone from school?"

I tensed at the mention of school, but it wasn't a bad guess, since she knew I had no living family aside from some creepy rural grandparents I'd met once when I was eight.

"It's no one you know," I said.

"I'm sure it isn't, but you understand I'm curious about your future and concerned that you don't want to talk about it."

"Have I ever really been all that forthcoming with you?"

"That's part of why I'm confused. You've been here for six months and shown no sign of wanting to rehabilitate yourself for life outside the Center, you've refused medication, your DBT skill practice has been spotty at best, you've refused to talk about your father's suicide or the events that precipitated your own attempt, and we've all tried to strike a balance between patience and persistence—now suddenly you tell me that you're leaving tomorrow. I do care about you, Millie, as hard as you may find that to believe, and I would like some reassurance that you're ready for this step."

"What kind of reassurance do you need?"

"You could start by telling me about your plans. Are you going to go back to school?"

I set my teeth against a familiar sharp throb of pain, like an old war wound. "Of course not."

"Why 'of course' not?"

"You're not a film person, so you don't get it. Getting into UCLA was a huge deal."

"But you did get in."

I felt my blood pressure rising. I hated optimism; it served only to remind me how inconceivable the depth of my failure was to normal people.

"Yes, I got in, and then I blew it. Even if they would take me back—which they would not—he's still there."

"Who is?" She frowned. "Are we talking about the nameless professor?"

"He has a name. Just because I won't tell it to you, that doesn't mean I'm making him up."

"Millie, if he's real, and he assaulted you, someone needs to—"

"Stop." I held up a warning hand; I could feel something ugly threatening to open up just under my solar plexus, like a door to a spider-infested crypt. "I am not talking about this."

"If not with me, you need to tell someone. Let the authorities decide the appropri—"

"I said stop it!" I grabbed the box of tissues from the table between us and flung it at the wall. Not helping my case for being functional. My heart was racing; my jaw was locked; my breath was coming fast and loud through my nose. The woman across from me was no longer Snow White but an old hag hawking apples.

"You're angry," the hag said.

It was like a seizure, something that swept over me unopposed and turned my blood to venom.

"Shut up," I said between clenched teeth. "Just shut up right now or I swear to God I will punch you in the mouth."

"Millie, let's do what we talked about. What number are you at right now?"

"Fuck you."

"If you can do this, it will be easier for me to believe that you are able to manage on your own."

Once again I was reminded that Dr. Davis was smarter than I generally gave her credit for. "Eight," I said.

"And what word did you assign to eight?"

It was hard to think through the fog of rage. But I had never been able to resist an urge to prove myself, and I knew she knew it too. "Furious," I said. "I'm furious."

"Can you tell me your 'up thoughts'? If they are private, you can write them down."

Any emotion, good or bad, lasts only a few moments unless we feed it. We are especially good at feeding anger, and Dr. Davis called the bits of kindling we toss onto the fire "anger up thoughts." We use them without thinking, and it takes practice to pick them out.

"It's not that simple," I said.

"I know it's hard to—"

"I'm doing it!" I snapped. "That was one of them."

"I'm sorry."

I stared at the wall, unable to address the thoughts directly to her, unable to look her in the eye with the full force of my fury, because the better part of me knew she was the only reason I'd made any progress at all.

"Leave it alone," I said to the wall, struggling to make words out of the rage-doughnuts I was doing in the parking lot of my mind. "I told you to leave it alone and you ignored me. I'm sick of it. I'm not some poor little lamb with broken legs. Everyone here thinks they know me better than I do. I am not a fucking *child*."

I went on like that for a while; then we sat in silence for half a minute. When a fresh wave of anger hit, it was only a 4: "frustrated." I was able to do some mindfulness exercises, following my breathing in and out of my lungs. My pulse slowed, and my fists loosened. I turned the corners of my mouth up in a slight smile, as I'd been taught, but it felt ridiculous and I stopped.

"Are you angering down?" she asked.

"You can't just verb any noun you want. But yes."

"Can you share your 'down thoughts'?"

I heaved a sigh and complied. "She didn't mean it, she doesn't understand the situation, she means well even if she doesn't have a clue what she's talking about."

I shot her a glance, but if she was hurt, it didn't show; I imagine therapists get good at that.

Maybe it was the aftermath of adrenaline; maybe it was a surge of contrition. But something made me blurt out, "Do you know anything about the Arcadia Project?"

After a moment of incomprehension, Dr. Davis's face suddenly hardened into an expression I'd never seen. "No," she said, like a snuffer on a candle. Not the *no* of ignorance, the *no* of *don't even think about it.*

"So . . . you have heard of it."

"I assume Caryl Vallo came to see you."

I blinked. "You know her?" I said instead of, *She's real?*

"Did she claim to be affiliated with the Center?" At the very thought, she seemed to be rapidly approaching anger level six: Incensed.

"Not at all. She said something about the Department of Mental Health. She didn't mention this place."

Dr. Davis exhaled.

"Who is she?" I prodded. "Is it some kind of scam?" Icy fingers of disappointment stroked my breastbone at the thought.

Dr. Davis rubbed the heel of her hand over her forehead. "No, they *are* state funded, at least in part, they've been around for decades, and there has never been any scandal around them that I could find." She turned doe eyes on me. "But they've—they've taken people from us in the past, people we could have helped."

"Isn't getting us out of here the general idea?"

She shook her head, clearly frustrated. "What they offer isn't healing. They all—they live together; there's this intense secrecy. The whole operation looks like some sort of cult, but there has never been enough justification to investigate. I can't be more specific without breaking patient confidentiality, but they've interfered before, once with a little girl I had invested a great deal in. I care about you, too, Millie, and I feel you could make real progress here, given enough time."

"Speaking of time," I said, pointing to the clock on the wall. We'd gone ten minutes over, which meant she was keeping someone else waiting. She was paid to say she cared, so I never believed it, but clocks don't lie, and this one said she was holding on past the point she should have let go. That in and of itself made me feel that I ought to get as far away as possible.

Dr. Davis sighed and ran her fingers through her hair; it fell back to sleek perfection. "My job is not to tell you what to do," she said. "My job is to help you find the answers for yourself."

"I understand."

"Then understand what it costs me to say this: leave the Arcadia Project alone. Please, just leave it be."

3

At eighteen, I drove two thousand miles west toward the siren call of Hollywood, hoping it would drown out the cruel voice in my head that I thought was my father's. By the time I found out that the cruel voice in my head was my own, my father was two years dead and I'd already let the voice talk me off the roof of Hedrick Hall. Whoops.

That song had been silent ever since, silent until Caryl brought it back, and I bitterly regretted telling Dr. Davis about her. After a year spent following orders and eating institutional food, a dose of reality was exactly the *last* thing I needed.

Don't get me wrong; neither Davis, dead father, nor demons had the power to talk me out of meeting Caryl Vallo that Tuesday. But they did manage to leach some of the joy out of my first sight of Los Angeles in months.

"June gloom" was in full effect, draping the sky in silver mink, but it was early enough in the month that a few lacy blooms lingered on the jacaranda trees. After six months of the Leishman Center's relentless beige, the violet glow of the petals sang through my every nerve. I kept trying to frame them, to set up a shot in my mind, but I'd been too long without a camera, and the trees slipped by too quickly.

I felt like a tourist in my own city. The cabdriver took the Fourth Street exit off the 10, and I made a nose print on the window trying to see everything at once. Fourth Street ran parallel to the ocean; at every intersection the western horizon flashed by like chrome.

A little ways south we entered a residential district, where the streets were lined with pastel stucco apartments. The cab pulled in beside the tiny park where Caryl had arranged to meet me. The inviting patch of green sloped down toward Main Street and the sea.

I got carefully out of the cab, relying on my hands and my right knee to get me to a standing position, then grabbed my cane off the seat and used it to steady me as I went around the back of the cab. I hadn't tried using my prosthetic legs on anything but hospital tile, and I didn't trust my balance.

The driver pulled my suitcase out of the trunk as I wrangled the folded wheelchair onto the street with excruciating awkwardness and opened it back up. He helped me put the suitcase in the chair, I laid my crutches and cane across the arms behind it, and then I tipped the guy hugely before rolling all my earthly possessions in front of me into the park.

The sea-kissed breeze, the rustle of leaves over my head, the dappled dance of shadows on the grass: it was all enough to make me giddy. Holding on to the wheelchair made me feel more secure, even though I was supporting it and not the other way around.

Caryl Vallo sat with her back to me on a bench in the center of the park. She was nondescript to the point of invisibility;

she'd have made a fantastic background actor. She was dressed in neutral shades again, this time a lightweight summery pantsuit in dove gray and cream. She looked over her shoulder as I approached, then hesitated for just a moment before rising and coming around the bench to meet me halfway.

"Miss Roper," she said, holding out a hand. Gloved, again, to match her blouse. As she stepped into the shade, her hair appeared coffee black.

"Millie is fine." I gripped her hand firmly, then lifted it to our eye level. "Why do you wear these?"

"I am eccentric."

"Fair enough." I let go of her hand, watching her face. As always, she gave away nothing.

"Please sit," she said, gesturing back toward the benches.

I decided to be cooperative, even though I'd already been sitting for an hour and could have sworn I'd told Caryl I preferred standing. I wheeled my stuff over and sat on a different bench from her; something about her discouraged even the most basic of intimacies.

To repay her for my discomfort, I started the conversation by saying, "Dr. Davis warned me about you."

Dr. Davis had also encouraged me to continue dialectical behavior therapy on an outpatient basis, but I could tell by the doe eyes she'd given me on my way out that she wasn't holding her breath.

Caryl offered me a thin smile. "Amanda doesn't know what she is warning you about, and therein lies the source of her distress. She is not a woman who enjoys being left out of the loop."

"You know her that well?"

"I suspect she knows me better than I know her. I am a former patient."

That brought me up short. "She—didn't mention that." I looked Caryl over, reconsidering the gloves. Obsessive-compulsive?

"Of course she didn't mention it," Caryl said. "Whatever else Amanda may be, she is a consummate professional."

"And what else may she be?"

"Uninspired."

It's funny how your own thoughts sound meaner when they come out of someone else's mouth. "She's helped me a lot," I said.

"Sometimes after a trauma, mediocrity is exactly what we need. But I think you are past that now."

I leaned forward. "Look. I'm going to need some kind of reassurance that this is on the level. You obviously weren't authorized to recruit at the Center."

"No, I was not."

"It's all right, I get it. I was a film student. I've faked my way into plenty of parties and offices where I didn't belong. What I'd like to know is how you disappeared out of my room the second I turned my back—*while I was standing in the doorway*."

Caryl met my eyes evenly. Hers were—hazel? No, gray. Or were they reflecting the sky?

"Magic," she said.

I actually entertained the idea for a minute before concluding that this was her flaccid attempt at sarcasm. But that's a weird side effect of BPD; your perception of truth shifts so often in the normal course of daily life that crazy talk doesn't automatically trigger your bullshit reflex.

"Seriously," I said. "How did you do it?"

"The details of the technique are proprietary."

"Look," I said. "I know my employment options are basically this or McDonald's. But I'm going to need more to go on than some vague references to free housing and industry connections. What *is* the Arcadia Project? According to Google, it's either an anthology of postmodern pastoral poetry, a platform for the publication of illustrated environmental histories, or a phenomenology of attentional economics."

"A what?"

"I have no idea; I don't speak grad-student. But when I mentioned your name to Dr. Davis, she advised Extreme Caution."

One of Caryl's brows lifted about a quarter inch. "I had no idea I'd left such an impression," she said.

"Why the secrecy? Aren't we here to talk details? What exactly is it you'd be hiring me to do?"

Caryl leaned back, resting her elbows on the back of her bench. Not dirt-phobic then, or at least not concerned about her jacket.

"To begin with, there would be a trial period; you would stay as our guest and assist in some minor errands for the Project."

"What sort of errands?"

"They will vary from day to day. Deliveries, filing, finding things. If it works out, I can offer you a key set production assistant position that DreamWorks has earmarked for one of ours in September."

"Key set PA." My negotiation skills were rusty, but I tried to apply some grease. "You know I was in the running for Best New Director at the Seattle Film Festival, right? *The Stone Guest*? That was mine."

Caryl gave me a mild look, so long I felt my ears go hot. Even before she spoke, a dagger of shame centered itself above my gut, and her next words drove it home.

"The Arcadia Project is here to reopen a door that *you* closed," she said. "But we only open it. You will have to be the one to shoulder your way through it past the crowd of people in your way."

"I know how Hollywood works," I said, shifting my weight. "But let's not ignore the fact that you said 'creative positions' before I packed up everything I own and came out here. I worry what else you're going to shame me into accepting further down the road."

"If you are looking for guarantees," Caryl said in a bored tone, "you are in the wrong business and quite possibly in the wrong city." She turned her head to study a smudge on the heel of her glove. "I saw *The Stone Guest*," she added, seemingly as an afterthought.

A flush of a different kind stole over my face. "What did you think?"

"I trespassed on private property to recruit you."

My tongue felt thick, and I looked away, studying the abstract statue at the edge of the park. When I looked back at Caryl, I couldn't remember what we'd been saying. The human brain holds a grudge about being bounced around in the skull, even after thirteen months.

"So what's next?" I bluffed, lobbing the ball into her court.

She caught it smoothly. "If you are not averse to riding in my car, I will take you to the place where you would be staying, so you can see for yourself if it would be agreeable to you."

I considered. Though unsettling, Caryl didn't seem dangerous, and on a good day when I'm not "splitting" people into angels and demons, I'm actually a pretty excellent judge of character.

"All right," I said. "But I may need your help getting my stuff into your car."

For someone who apparently made her living placing the mentally ill into part-time jobs, Caryl had a really nice SUV. The smell of sun-warmed leather made me drunk and drowsy. As Caryl drove, I found myself picturing a close tracking shot: Caryl's gloved hand moving from the steering wheel to settle on my left knee. Since it was fantasy, I still had a left knee.

I forced myself to sit up straight and look out the passenger-side window. Dr. Davis and I had talked about my history of using sex as a painkiller. Combine that with the lack of attractive staff at the Leishman Center, and apparently now I would project sexuality onto a stack of cinder blocks.

It was eerily silent in the car: no radio, no chatter, no GPS. The farther east we drove on the 10, the more uneasy I became. "Where are we going exactly?"

"The North University Park district, near USC."

An instinctive sense of rivalry flared up before I remembered I no longer gave a damn about UCLA. They'd washed their hands of me the moment I'd bloodied up the pavement under Hedrick Hall, and I guess I'd washed my hands of them a few miserable weeks before that.

We exited the freeway at Hoover, and as someone who had always clung to the Westside, I found myself bemused by our surroundings. It looked as though a ghetto and a college town had been shaken together in a bag and dumped out in no particular order. North University Park itself served to further confuse my sense of atmosphere; a handful of residential streets were lined with Victorian-era houses in Easter egg shades, most of them lovingly restored.

Caryl hung a right just past Adams and drove by several picturesque residences before making another right into the shaded driveway of a sprawling Queen Anne. At the sight of it I had the sudden certainty that I'd just exchanged one loony bin for another.

4

Next to its neighbors, this house looked like a cat lady at a PTA meeting. It was painted a deep teal green and crowded by thuggish trees that seemed intent on intimidating if not outright crushing it. At the far right was an emphatic octagonal turret that looked likely to tip over the entire house.

I took only my cane with me, figuring I could get help with the rest later. We left the car and crunched our way through a mulch of leaves to the front porch, which was adorned with three mismatched rocking chairs and a wicker love seat with traces of mildew on the cushions. Caryl didn't help me on the porch steps, which were the first real-world stairs I'd encountered in more than a year.

"I'm completely fine here," I said to her back. "Don't mind me." Since my left knee was prosthetic, it was impossible to climb step-over-step; I had to lead with my right knee. Having carbon feet made it tricky to get a sense of where the steps began and ended, but I got to the top more easily than I'd expected and felt a little smug about it.

Caryl pulled out a key from an inside pocket of her jacket and gave it a few savage thrusts and twists in the lock.

I could smell garlic even before the door opened with a muffled moan into a cavernous living area. The hardwood floor was magnificent where it could be seen; rugs were thrown about with no obvious design. Placed with equal randomness were two couches that faced each other, a small trampoline, assorted bookcases, a hydroponic garden, a springy toy horse, and a black grand piano that looked like a cougar had used it as a scratching post. I heard sizzling sounds and muffled conversation from somewhere behind the wall that faced the front door.

"Holy shit," I said.

"Would you like to see what would be your room?" Caryl asked, continuing toward a wide, airy wooden staircase. The living room was two stories high; doors that might have been bedrooms or bathrooms were visible over an ostentatious balustrade on the second floor.

"Upstairs? Really?" I aimed for a scathing tone, but I was feeling a bit nauseated. After the orderly neutrality of the hospital, this place was a brutal assault on the senses.

"It's the only unoccupied room," Caryl said, not seeming apologetic in the slightest.

"Have you noticed this place is not particularly, ah—wheelchair accessible?"

Before Caryl could answer, a freckled topless woman with wavy hair and Asian eyes wandered in from the presumable direction of the kitchen. She was partially covered by a cloth sling that supported the black-haired baby she was suckling.

"Hey, Caryl," she said with a dreamy smile. "Teo's making gnocchi. Who's this?"

Caryl turned to me expectantly.

"Nobody," I blurted. "I'm nobody."

Caryl turned back to the young mother. "We'll be down in a moment, Song," she said gently, then started up the steps without looking to see if I was following. Using my cane and a light touch on the rail, I was able to make fairly good time.

"Was that one of the other . . . mentally ill people you're finding work for?" I whispered when I reached Caryl, who had been kind enough to pause at the top of the staircase.

"No. Song is the manager here at Residence Four."

"Residence Four? Out of how many?"

"Three."

My head was starting to hurt. The garlic smell was not helping.

Caryl headed along the balustrade to the right, past numbered doors that were set into the narrow hallway. Tantalizing hints of graffiti could be seen where the fleur-de-lis wallpaper had peeled away.

A door faced us at the dark dead end of the hall. Like the other doors, it had a brass number attached to it, presumably a six if you took the other numbers into account, but it was canted at a decidedly nine-like angle.

Just before it on the north side of the hall stood an unnumbered door; Caryl rapped on it lightly with her knuckles before easing it open to reveal a murky three-quarter bath with a dripping faucet. A one-eared tortoiseshell cat darted out like something from a horror movie and raced for the top of the stairs, where it crouched warily.

"You'll be sharing this bathroom with Stevie," said Caryl, not seeming to notice my distress. "She's in room five. I doubt you will hear from her."

"Caryl," I began as she produced another key and turned it

in the dead-end door. I wasn't sure what to say, how to tell her how very *wrong* this all was. I was trying to frame a protest that didn't contain the word "insane" when she opened the door and made me lose my train of thought.

Sunlight poured across the one-and-a-half-story octagonal room like honey, illuminating the emptiness of the freshly refinished floor. Five of the eight walls were mostly glass; the bamboo Roman shades had been rolled all the way up, flooding the room with afternoon sun.

I don't know how to describe the feeling that overtook me except to call it love. It had the same bouquet: electric top notes of want, smoky warmth at the heart, and a bitter base note of unworthiness. I glanced at Caryl and found her watching me closely. I have a lousy poker face.

"This is the nicest room in the house," Caryl said flatly.

"Then why is it empty?"

"It used to be an art studio, but it hasn't been used enough to justify the designation. My original plan was to offer the room to Song and give you hers, but she raised concerns about not being able to make the room dark enough during the day. For her baby," she added when I looked confused.

"Right, right," I said, walking farther into the room. My imagination ignited so powerfully that I felt nostalgic, as though I were remembering a past rather than planning a future. My inner set dresser placed phantom film posters on the two windowless walls, a bed with a folding screen at the foot, a hot plate and coffeemaker, a cluttered desk with a bra slung over the back of the chair. Months' if not years' worth of compressed longings unpacked themselves to fill the empty space.

Using my cane for security on the unfamiliar floor, I crossed to one of the windows and touched it with my fingertips. It had been a long time since I had been awakened by a sunrise, and I'm one of those rare people who adores it. I love a day I haven't screwed up yet.

"It's not furnished," said the last rational part of my brain before it stopped waving its arms and drowned.

"We have an air mattress and an extra chair or two you can use until you make other arrangements," said Caryl. "Would you like to see the kitchen?"

Suddenly I was ravenous. Caryl held the door open for my exit and then locked up behind us as the one-eared cat skittered back into the bathroom. I fought an irrational surge of possessiveness when Caryl slipped the key into her pocket.

She led me downstairs and took a right toward the grand piano, then another right through a framed opening into a quaint dining room complete with dark oak china cabinets. A third right through a narrow doorway brought us into a clay-tiled kitchen with an island in the center. There, Song and two others sat on bar stools, watching a young man cook.

The chef had the chiseled, dark-browed beauty of a tele-novela heartthrob, but his hair was dull as tar and cut to hide his face. I guessed him to be in his early twenties, despite the practiced, almost presentational way he handled the kitchen equipment. When he glanced my way, I noticed the shadows under his eyes. He smiled, quick and devastating.

"Six plates or five?" he said, his gaze lingering briefly on the more severely scarred side of my face. Until that moment, I had forgotten what I looked like now. My tongue stuck to the roof of my mouth.

"Will you be eating?" Caryl prompted me gently.

"At some point," I said. "It's kind of a regular thing with me."

"Another wiseass," said the dark-bearded white guy next to Song. "She and Teo will get along fine."

"That is my hope," said Caryl.

A soft *ohhhh* of understanding rose from everyone but Teo. Teo just turned and looked at me again, more penetrating this time and a lot less friendly. Finally he muttered a bitter "Fantastic," and turned back to his cooking.

"Mateo Salazar," said Caryl politely, "allow me to introduce Millicent Roper. Millie, this is Teo. You will be working together."

"Charmed," said Teo in a tone that meant the opposite.

"Don't mind Teo," said a cloying, high-pitched Southern voice. "He's a Grouchy Gus." The woman on the other side of Song leaned around mother and baby to look at me.

She was a blonde dressed in business casual. I was so disoriented by her accent—North Georgia, if I wasn't mistaken—that it took me a moment to process that she wasn't quite four feet tall. She was pretty despite an overlarge forehead; her bare feet dangled above the floor, where a delicate pair of beige pumps rested beneath her bar stool. "I'm Gloria," she said.

"I, uh." My brain felt like a bumper-to-bumper traffic jam.

"You've never met a little person before." She giggled, in that cute way Southern women do instead of punching you in the teeth.

Pretty blond Southern girls had tormented me all through high school, but I just nodded and smiled, knowing she'd mistake the reason for my instant revulsion.

Teo, bless him, chose that moment to start plunking down plates of gnocchi on the tiled island. He put down six, so I took one, but I elected to hunch over the counter instead of sitting. The first bite made my fork hand go limp with pleasure.

"Sweet Jesus," I said, earning a frown from Gloria.

"Good thing you like Italian," growled Nameless Bearded Guy. "It's all he ever makes, and the rest of us can't cook for shit. Sorry, Gloria," he added, though whether for the language or the slight on her cooking I couldn't tell.

"Sometimes I do Chinese," protested Teo, "or Jamaican. I'd do Indian more often if Phil didn't make a point of bringing back Wendy's every time I did."

"Would it kill you to make a burger?" grumbled Bearded Guy.

Mexican was my favorite, but there had to be some reason that particular elephant was shuffling unmolested around the room. So I just shut my mouth and ate my gnocchi, trying not to make pornographic sounds about the oily-smooth Gorgonzola cream sauce.

"Should Song start getting your room ready for you after lunch?" said Caryl as she settled down with her own plate.

Song gave me a smile. Now that her baby was finished drinking from her boob, it was dozing comfortably in the sling.

I looked back at Caryl. "Do you live here too?"

"I don't, though I often dine here." That got a grin from Teo.

I said nothing, just gave Caryl a look that said, *You're leaving me alone with this menagerie?*

My expression must have been transparent, because Caryl said in as close to a reassuring tone as she could manage, "Song will look after you."

5

Song had Teo bring up my stuff, as well as a folding chair, a card table, and a box containing an air mattress twice the size of anything I'd slept on in the past two years. While Song inflated the mattress with an electric pump, her offspring sat with his chubby legs sticking out of a round rubber chair, gnawing a slimy fist and trying to figure out what exactly I was. I found myself profoundly disinterested in him.

"Someone gave me a baby monitor I don't use," said Song, looking at my legs with concern. "Do you want me to set it up so that you can call for me if you have any problems?"

I swallowed down a sudden rush of indignation and managed to keep my tone polite. "I'll be fine," I said. She took the hint and left as soon as the mattress was inflated.

It hadn't occurred to me until the sun started going down that the same windows that let in light could let in a lot of darkness, too. It was a cloudy night without moon or stars, just a velvety blackness that seemed to press in at the windows. By the time I was finished rolling down all the shades, my back and hips were aching fiercely. I allowed myself the luxury of a single

Vicodin just to get to sleep. I took off my legs and went through the routine—checking the sockets for cracks and scratches, checking the stumps of my left thigh and right shin—and then went to bed.

Even drugged, I didn't sleep well. The old house was full of strange sounds, not the least of which was the susurration of leaves outside my windows. I imagined them whispering to one another: *That's her—that's the thoughtless girl who broke a dozen perfectly good branches on her way to the pavement.*

I didn't remember the fall; I didn't even remember the roof. The last thing I remembered was the smoky iodine smell of whiskey dripping down the wall of my room. I'd been trying to finish off the Laphroaig Professor Scott had given me, since I knew we'd never share it again. But I got too sick to finish. I shattered the bottle against the wall and stood there staring, wishing I could shatter all of it: the truths Scott had told me to reel me in, the lies he'd told the whole department to shut me out.

I couldn't think of it, not if I wanted to go forward. I tried the mindfulness exercise Dr. Davis had been teaching me, following my breath in and out. Eventually I slipped down into fitful dreams of snakes and broken glass, only to wake from a shockingly vivid nightmare that a vortex of null space had appeared where the ceiling used to be. Like an idiot, I woke calling for a nurse; it was a good thing I had refused the baby monitor.

Even awake, I found I couldn't shake my terror of the high ceiling; I was afraid to even look up at it, afraid of seeing a mind-numbing, gut-curdling nothingness. I did some more mindfulness work and reminded myself that if I couldn't handle this, I'd have to check back into the hospital.

At the rate I was burning through my dad's inheritance, I had maybe six months left of that fallback. Eventually I was going to have to enter the workforce again, unless I planned on living under a bridge or jumping off one. The latter wasn't really an option for me anymore now that I'd lived to see strangers coping with the aftermath of my last attempt. Suicide is not a way of ending pain; it's just a way of redistributing it.

By about two in the morning, I dropped off pretty solidly. Even with the shades rolled down, morning crept in the way I'd hoped: a soft rosy kiss to wake me. The house was silent now, the night wind having died down and those other layabouts still in bed.

I'd been too freaked out to take a shower the night before, and morning showers don't allow enough drying time to don my prosthetics. So I just put on my legs and my bathrobe, made my slow, careful way down to the kitchen, and bullied the vintage coffeemaker into doing my bidding. The tortoiseshell cat was there, but it kept its distance, lone ear flicking nervously back and forth. Under the kitchen lights I could see the graying of its fur and the crimp in its tail; it was a decrepit wreck, just like the rest of the house. I felt right at home.

"Well, look who sneaked down to the kitchen!" chirped Gloria as she came in fully dressed, pink foam rollers in her hair. At the sound of her voice, the cat darted away. I briefly considered doing the same.

"I, uh, didn't want to wake anyone," I said.

"Bless your heart. Minnie, right, like the mouse?"

"Millie, actually," I corrected her, feeling freakishly tall as she went by.

"And just where are you off to so early?"

"Nowhere, really; just couldn't sleep." I watched her rummage through the pantry for a box of cereal. Aside from the rollers and a lack of lipstick, she looked ready to green-light a three-picture deal. "How about you?" I ventured.

"Well, we can't all collect disability, now can we? I'm a script supervisor, and we're wrappin' up a shoot this morning."

Gloria filled a cereal bowl, then appraised me, eyes quick and bright as fireflies. Her gaze stopped on my scars, and her nose wrinkled as though I were covered in gravy. Before I could even respond, her face brightened.

"You know," she said, "you should try Pure Porcelain, by Fournier. That stuff could cover a pothole in the road. I hardly need foundation myself, so my bottle's yours if you want it. I think we've got just about the same skin tone."

I tried to make words. I really did.

"I just love Fournier," she pressed on in the face of my silence, taking her bowl to the fridge. "They don't sell it in *this* part of town; I have to order it special. But listen to me prattling on. You must have a ton of questions. After Caryl I'm the best one to ask, so go on, sugar, hit me."

I imagined landing a crisp little smack to her dimpled cheek. (I could exaggerate the sound later in Foley—*thwap!*) Then we'd close in on her shocked expression before cutting back to me. *Cover* that *with foundation,* I'd say. Then I'd saunter out in the casual, distracted way I used to saunter.

"You all right, hon?"

"I, uh—don't really know enough to have questions yet."

"Do you know what Arcadia means?" she asked, pouring milk on her cereal.

"It's . . . the name of the project?"

"Don't get smart, now."

"Um, it's a Greek province," I tried again, "but I imagine it's being used here more in the sense of a pastoral utopia."

"All right," she said ambiguously. "Did Song go over the house rules at least?"

"Not yet."

Gloria used a step stool to help herself sit at the kitchen counter with her cereal. "Most common rule broken is: don't ask personal questions of anyone who lives here, not even their names. Anything Caryl doesn't tell you, wait for them to bring it up. Everyone at the Residence gets to live their life how they want, and for some that means pretending the rest of us aren't here."

Gloria jabbed her spoon into her cereal and gave me a look that dared me to prove I wasn't one of *those* people. Her eyes were unsettlingly blue.

"You can ask me whatever you want," I heard myself say.

"Not by the house rules, I can't," she said, shaking a finger at me in a way that was just a bit too vehement to pass as playful.

"All right then," I said. "What other rules should I know?"

"No drugs, alcohol, or tobacco allowed on the premises, prescribed or otherwise."

My mind went to the Vicodin in my suitcase, and I wondered if the nice lady was about to ask me to pee in a cup. "What if I need antibiotics or something?"

"Then you talk to Caryl. Antibiotics are probably okay, but we can't keep anything around that some *addict* could kill themselves with." She said "addict" the way a hellfire preacher would say "sinner."

I found myself wondering, but contractually obligated not

to ask, what had gotten Miss Goody Two-Shoes tangled up with this crowd in the first place.

"The rest of the rules," she said, "should wait till Caryl shows you the contract."

"If no one's told me a rule, can I still get fired for breaking it?"

"I don't know, Minnie Mouse," said Gloria with a sweet smile. "Guess it depends on whether we figure it's worth it to keep you."

I stared back at her. Was I hearing this right? *Nice new job you've got here. Shame if something happened to it.*

Gloria giggled at my expression. "Look at you!" she said. "You are too precious."

I noticed she did not, however, say that she'd been joking.

6

I fled upstairs to put on a T-shirt and some baggy shorts, then feigned rapt interest in the dog-eared paperbacks in the living room to avoid further "chitchat" with Gloria. Reading was one of the slowest things to come back to me after my head injury; thirteen months later printed words still sometimes seemed to lose their moorings on the page. When Caryl arrived dressed smartly in a sage-green pantsuit, I was stretched out on a squishy couch, reading the fifth page of *Prisoner of Azkaban* for the third time. The decrepit cat lay curled up near my feet, despite my having displayed no signs of interest in the creature.

"Monty," Caryl snapped as she seated herself on the other couch. "Shoo." The cat leaped down from the couch and skittered off into the dining room. "Have you had breakfast?" Caryl asked me. I got a strange feeling on the back of my neck, as though a snake had draped itself across my shoulders.

"I had coffee and a bear claw," I answered. "I figured if it didn't have a name on it, it was up for grabs."

When she didn't reply, I turned my eyes to the book, flipping back to the last part I remembered clearly. Caryl sat there for what felt like hours with no apparent inclination to talk.

"Is that cat friendly?" I ventured. "I'm not sure if I should touch him."

"Don't."

"Roger that. Is there something I'm supposed to sign today?"

Caryl shook her head, studying me. "Our employment contract contains proprietary information, so you will be staying here as our guest until such time as you are formally initiated into the Project."

"Initiated." I set aside the book and cracked my knuckles one at a time. "Is there chanting involved? Will I be anointed with something?"

"No, but you will be given some additional information and equipment."

"Equipment? Sexy. I love all this mystery. Are we ghostbusters? Please say we're ghostbusters."

"I like the way you think," she said in her usual bored tone. "Ah, Teo. He is nothing if not punctual."

I glanced at the nearest clock, which read 9:09. Sarcasm then, probably. Following her gaze to the stairs, I saw that Teo was wearing a different black T-shirt and the same pair of jeans as yesterday. Either he hadn't washed his hair or he had spent a good deal of time making it look that way.

Teo flopped down on the couch next to Caryl and leaned over as though to kiss her cheek; she just as casually intercepted the gesture with a gloved hand and applied enough force to his jaw to nearly knock him off the couch.

"Morning, ladies," he said nonchalantly once he'd righted himself. "Time to break in my new partner?" He stretched his arms along the back of the sofa, his left hand resting behind Caryl for just a moment before he yanked it back sharply. Caryl wasn't even looking at him; she had turned her inscrutable gaze back to me.

"We're partners?" I asked Teo. "Like on the cop shows?"

"Kind of a cross between that and an AA sponsor," he replied. "We all need babysitters, and Caryl has us babysit each other."

I looked at Caryl, but she seemed content to let the two of us talk.

"Are you new too?" I asked Teo.

"Nope," he said. "Been here since I was twelve."

"What happened to your old partner?"

"Killed herself, just like the first one."

I stared at him. "This—seems a less than ideal job for me."

"It's not the job," he said, crossing his arms over his chest. "Caryl just gives me the craziest ones."

"And how sane are you?"

"I'm the one-eyed man in the land of the blind. Bipolar."

Caryl interjected quietly, "But he is more reliable than many of our members."

"So . . . he's okay?"

Teo gave me a *hey, I'm right here* sort of wave.

"He's had mild recent symptoms of mania," said Caryl. "He may be overconfident and hard to keep on task, so I will need you to watch out for that."

"Am I invisible?" said Teo. "Or is this a subtle joke about the fact that I don't exist?"

I blinked at Caryl.

"He's being melodramatic," she said. "He means he has no legal identification; his mother didn't register his birth."

"Or my existence, really, except for the occasional attempt at an exorcism. So! Is it my turn to talk about people like they can't hear me? What should I watch out for with her?" He jerked a thumb toward me.

"Sexual advances," Caryl said. "Paranoia under stress. Also, any criticism you offer, however mild, may be met with verbal abuse or even physical violence."

He eyed my legs. "I think I can take her."

I snatched up my cane; I'm not sure whether I intended to prove him wrong or just awkwardly flounce out of the room. Either way, I thought better of it and focused instead on the chill smoothness of the aluminum against my palms. As Dr. Davis had taught me, I filled my mind with the object's shape and temperature, color and texture. *Be one-mindful. Empty your thoughts of the asshole on the other couch.*

"This is perhaps not the ideal pairing," Caryl said as she watched me. "You are both prone to impulsive behavior, but I prefer not to break up any of the existing partnerships."

I dragged my eyes away from my cane, feeling calmer. "So what do we need to do?"

"There are some recent local difficulties that only I can address," Caryl said, "and because of them, I have not been micromanaging schedules and deadlines as well as I ought. I'll need the two of you to pay a visit to Viscount Rivenholt."

I glanced at Teo, who looked as bewildered as I felt. He ran a hand through his hair, making a worse mess of it as he eyed Caryl. "What's the viscount done that requires a visit from the Project?"

"His visa expired two weeks ago, and he has neglected to return home. A gentle reminder is in order."

"Immigration issues?" I said. "I thought we were an employment agency."

"It's complicated," said Teo. "You'll figure it out."

I thumped my cane emphatically on the hardwood floor. "Fuck that. I'm not going to tell some British lord or powerful space dude to pack his bags and go home, not without some idea who I'm speaking for."

"First off," said Teo, "'space dude'? Your second guess after England is outer space? Second off, I'll be doing the talking. It's all going to make a lot more sense if you shut up and pay attention."

I bristled. In the entertainment industry you have to be okay with kids treating you like dirt, but this wasn't a movie set, and quite frankly, even on set I was used to being top dog. My mounting anger interrupted the fragile connection between mind and mouth, and before I could articulate my feelings, Teo was already flapping his gums again. I breathed slowly and pulled my mouth into a slight smile I most definitely wasn't feeling.

"He's probably eating bonbons at the hotel," Teo mused to Caryl. "He's got no reason to fight us on leaving."

"Precisely," said Caryl. "And I think meeting him would be an excellent introduction for Millie."

"Where is he staying?" I asked.

"The SLS Beverly Hills," said Teo.

I let out a low whistle.

"Teo, you will drive."

I thought about my old Celica with an uneasy pang; Dad's last gift to me. I honestly had no idea what had become of it. I chased the thought away quickly. When you're Borderline and want to survive, you learn to shrink from guilt, because it can spiral out of control and leave you staring down a bottomless void. People throw around the term "self-loathing" without really knowing what it means. I wouldn't wish it on my worst enemy.

"Why don't you drive?" I said to Caryl. "I haven't seen Teo's car, but I'm willing to bet Disney money yours is nicer."

"As I said before," said Caryl, "I'm consumed with larger-scale problems at the moment. I won't be accompanying you."

"Ah." One syllable managed to leak my disappointment everywhere.

Caryl held my eyes for a moment without changing expression, but there was comfort in her silence. Or maybe I was just starting to fill in her blank expression with whatever I wanted.

I hadn't realized until that moment how desperate I was for a friend, and I was about to be stuck in a car with Teo. Fantastic.

I was right about Teo's car; it stank. Literally. It reeked of cigarette smoke, and I found out why about three and a half seconds after we got in. While I was trying to find a good place for my cane, he lunged for the pack of smokes in the glove compartment as though it were going to keep us from rolling into oncoming traffic.

Before he could even open the pack, my hand shot out as though of its own accord and clamped around his wrist. I hadn't realized until just that moment how strongly I associated the sight and smell of cigarettes with those god-awful patio breaks at the hospital. Teo looked equal parts startled and annoyed, but he didn't pull his arm away.

"Problem?" he said.

I let go of his wrist and couldn't help but notice the thick ridges of scar tissue that slid under my fingertips. Lumpy, ugly, the kind that came from years of cutting the same place over and over again. And this was the reliable guy.

He was obviously waiting for an answer, and I didn't want to get into it, so I spun some bullshit.

"My lungs had a bunch of ribs poked through them last year. They're still weak; the carbon monoxide in cigarette smoke could kill me in, like, five minutes."

For all I knew it was even true. I never listened to half the stuff my doctors told me.

"Fine," he said curtly.

After tossing the pack back in the glove compartment, he turned the radio to JACK-FM, so I got to hear an aggressive mix of classic rock, eighties synth-pop, and punk all the way to the hotel. Since we were headed to Beverly Hills, I'd changed into a pair of jeans to camouflage my prosthetics and classed things up a bit with a shimmery tank top. My hope was that the shimmer would distract from the particularly obnoxious patchwork of scar tissue on my left arm.

The exterior of the SLS is deceptively sober: it's a blocky white building with a metallic logo that looks a little like a chandelier. Once you reach the main entrance, all pretense of conservatism is promptly defenestrated. Horse statues with lampshade heads, geometric potted shrubbery, and paintings of dogs in Renaissance garb dare you to question them. It's as though whoever furnished Residence Four was given a vanload of money and turned loose in a hotel.

"Don't say anything, not one word, until we leave this building," Teo hissed direly at me as though I had some history of embarrassing him. "Just watch. Learning's optional but highly recommended."

"The hell?" I muttered, but he silenced me with a glare and a quick jerk of his head in the direction of the elevator lobby. I rolled my eyes and followed, carrying my cane but trying my balance without it. The lobby was a recursive crimson purgatory of mirrors; I kept my eyes firmly on the carpet. When the elevator arrived, we took it to the fifth floor, where Teo hung a right, seeming confident of where he was going.

"Who *is* this guy exactly?" I asked him under my breath, aware of the way voices carry in hallways.

"I'm hoping he'll be kind enough to tell you himself," Teo said, stopping in front of a room at the end of the hall. "Now hush." Despite the DO NOT DISTURB sign, he rapped his knuckles confidently against the door.

7

There was no answer.

"Hey," I whispered. "What if we find his body in there or something?"

"I think standard procedure is to make a bad pun and put on sunglasses." Teo knocked again—nothing.

"He's out," I said, tamping down my overactive imagination. "We should try back later."

"Nope. We park right here till he comes back."

"That could be hours."

"Have you got a hot date or something?"

"Eventually I have to eat lunch. Or pee. And I don't see you calmly sitting here until midnight either, Mr. Manic. For all we know he took a day trip to San Diego."

Teo seemed to chew on this. "All right, you stay here. I'm going to check the restaurant, since he knows me."

"Aren't we supposed to stay together? In case one of us goes crazy or something?"

"I promise not to cut myself if you promise not to"—here he eyed me speculatively—"step in front of a train. Deal?"

"Whatever. You're the boss."

That seemed to please him; there was a strut in his step as he headed back to the elevator. I leaned against the wall, ignored the dull ache in my lower back, and waited.

And waited.

I got more fidgety with every passing moment. This was my first assignment, a test of sorts, and so far I'd been worse than useless.

I wished I had a phone or a watch or something, so I could know when the wait started getting ridiculous rather than just *feeling* ridiculous. I was pretty sure it shouldn't take so long for Teo to find a restaurant, scan it for a familiar face, and come back.

My imagination ran haywire. What if Teo had tried to confront the viscount downstairs and a fight had broken out? What if one or both of them had been hauled off to jail, and I had no ride home? What if—

My thoughts were interrupted by a distant clinking sound. I glanced down the hall and saw a housekeeping cart. An elderly Latina was loading room service dishes onto it. I smiled and lifted a hand in a little wave.

"Yes?" she said. "How can I help you?"

I'd actually only waved to be friendly, but since she offered . . .

"Good morning," I said with a warm smile. "I don't suppose you know when the man staying in this room is likely to come back?"

She knew *something*; I could tell by the way she frowned when she saw where I was pointing. "If he is out, you can leave a message downstairs for him," she said.

"Right, I know," I said, feeling like an idiot but hoping she'd

assume my blush was attached to a scandalous story. Fancy
Los Angeles hotels are full of those stories, though admittedly
I didn't quite look the part.

"Why do you ask about him?" she said in a tone that suggested she was strongly considering notifying security.

"I left my phone in there," I improvised. "I have an audition
in an hour, and I don't know the address. God, I hope he comes
back soon."

The housekeeper approached me with a skeptical expression, and I could tell when she was able to see my scars. I call
it the "what-the-hell" distance. Strangers who approach me
always look harder for a split second, then quickly away. The
what-the-hell distance seemed to be less than twenty feet now.
Interesting.

"I think he is gone all during the day," she said a bit more
kindly. "'Do Not Disturb' was on his door every day this week."

"Damn it!" I sighed in what I hoped was an actressy fashion,
leaning on my cane and covering my eyes with my free hand
to hide how pleased I was to have turned up a scrap of information. "I'm sorry," I said tragically. "It's not your fault. Thank
you anyway." I looked up and gave her my best *please don't call
security* smile.

The housekeeper looked up and down the hall. "I'll open it
quickly. You can look for your phone. Hurry, please."

I stood for a moment in stunned disbelief. Jackpot! Teo
was going to kill me, but how could I pass up the opportunity?
I'd just pop in briefly and make sure the viscount wasn't rotting
in a bathtub in there or something.

"Thanks so much," I said as she opened the door.

The golden-brown leather seat in the window looked like

a waffle; it was next to a table like a dish of creamy butter and two sleek backless chairs that reminded me of coffee mugs. It would have been enough to make me hungry if the room hadn't been so relentlessly full of mirrors. It was hard to find somewhere to look that didn't nauseate me with the wreckage of my face.

A tiny orange light blinked on the phone next to an unmade bed. Since the housekeeper was watching, I opened drawers, moved the curtains around, bent carefully to look underneath the edges of the bed, but meanwhile I was noticing something else entirely: there was nothing in the room but some papers in the trash can. No clothes strewn about, no suitcase, no razor, no hair product. I tried to touch as little as possible in case this was a crime scene, but I did nudge open the mirrored closet door to find no clothes hanging. No shoes, no bags. I looked at the glassy surface of the computer desk, and the microscopic layer of accumulated dust was the final nail in my certainty: this viscount fellow had packed up several days ago, hung a DO NOT DISTURB sign, and never come back.

I turned my attention to the window for a moment, trying to get my damaged brain into gear and make some sense of this. The curtains were open, affording me a view of Los Angeles that might have been striking if I'd been in a different mood. At the moment it was just a bunch of palm trees and terra-cotta rooftops, and me failing at my first assignment.

"What are you doing?" Teo's voice was sharp from the doorway.

I turned around, trying not to let the *oh crap* show on my face.

The housekeeper said something to him in Spanish, and he waved her away irritably, pushing past her into the room.

"Teo, please be nice to the lady. She's helping me look for

my phone." I tried desperately not to emphasize my words, waggle my eyebrows, or do any other kind of *work with me* dance, because I can smell stupid a mile off, and this woman was not giving me the faintest whiff of it.

Teo visibly clenched his jaw, then turned to the house-keeper. "Can you give us a few minutes alone?" he asked her.

She said something else to him in Spanish.

Teo shook his head irritably again. "Do you not speak English?"

"I speak it fine," she said, her eyes cold.

"Okay then," he said. "I need to have a private conversation with my friend here." He pulled out a wad of bills and held them out to her.

She made a sound of disgust and walked away without taking his money. She muttered something in Spanish as she went, and I know Teo understood her, because his slouchy pos-ture went ramrod straight before he came in and shut the door behind him.

"I was getting along with her just fine," I snapped. "Would it have killed you to be polite? Now she'll report us."

"To who? Anyone important knows I do business with the viscount. Now relax. Since we're here, we may as well get some-thing out of it. Go through the trash."

"I beg your pardon?"

"You're the one who decided to trespass, so you get to be the one to touch his snotty tissues or whatever."

"Don't these sort of people use handkerchiefs?" I went to the bathroom and found a shower cap to put over my hand.

"Lady, you have no idea what sort of person you're talking about."

"A vampire?" I guessed. I picked up the trash can—which held a frankly absurd number of Reese's cup wrappers—and sat on the edge of the bed.

"Nope," said Teo, casually, like it had been a decent guess.

"I was kidding," I said, taking out the wrappers carefully, one at a time, using the shower cap as an ill-fitting glove.

"You weren't kidding," said Teo. "Not really. I bet you believe all kinds of crazy shit, or Caryl wouldn't have recruited you."

I found something near the top that wasn't a candy wrapper: a folded piece of white paper. I clumsily eased it open with my shower-capped hand, hoping to find a scribbled address or phone number like you always do in the movies, but instead it was just a little sketch made with a ballpoint on hotel stationery. I stared at it.

Teo chattered on, poking around the room. "So apparently instead of checking out, the viscount extended his stay by a whole month. Either he completely forgot when his visa expires, or—Millie, you okay?"

The sketch was of the view out the window, the one I had just dismissed, but somehow in a few spare lines the artist had captured L.A.'s restless energy. DREAMLAND was written at the bottom in a bold, masculine hand. I stared at the paper and remembered, on a primal level, the thrill I'd felt when I first saw the city from the freeway eight years ago: sun low and heavy in the sky, downtown's high-rises glittering in the vermilion light. I felt a stinging at the back of my eyes and let the drawing slip to the floor.

"What is that?" said Teo.

"Nothing. Just a sketch of the city."

He bent and picked it up as I continued sifting through

candy wrappers, and then he did something odd. He pulled a pair of nineties-retro mirror shades out of his pocket and put them on, peering at the paper through them. He hadn't worn them the whole ride over, even when we were driving into the sun, but now he put them on in a fashionably dim hotel room?

"He drew this," he said. "The viscount."

"Or maybe some lady friend who got bored waiting for him to come out of the shower."

"Nope," he said. "There's fey magic on this."

"What's fey magic?"

"You can look through my glasses," he said, "but give them back when you're done. At this rate you'll have your own pair before long."

I took the glasses from him and slipped them on, looking at the paper in his hand. My breath caught, and I felt every hair on my body lift away from my skin.

Everything else in the room looked normal through the shades, only darker. The drawing, on the other hand, lit up like the Fourth of July. Radiant curving strands like flowering vines danced and shimmered from its surface.

"What the *fuck* is that?" I breathed.

"Magic," said Teo. And this time, I was pretty sure it wasn't sarcasm.

8

I stared at the shimmering swirls on the paper; they moved as though they were *alive*. I'd misplaced the speech center of my brain again. When I found it, I said a little drunkenly, "What kind of glasses are these?"

"It's like an advanced version of the fairy ointment from the stories," he said. "One side of the lens shows you what kind of magic a thing has; the other side shows you things as they really are."

I waited for my rational mind to put up a fight, but it rolled over and showed its belly. I gave the glasses back to Teo, my hand shaking slightly. He slipped them into his coat pocket, along with the drawing itself.

"You need a minute?" he said, watching me closely.

I shook my head. "I'm fine. What was that? I mean, I get that you're saying it's a spell or something. But what does it do?"

"It's a type of charm. Basically he draws something and sort of . . . weaves his magic into the paper, so that whoever looks at it feels exactly what he was feeling when he drew it."

"And he threw it in the *trash*?"

Teo shrugged. "Nobles like Rivenholt—they call them *sidhe*

at World HQ in London—they're into heavy-duty magic. Wards, enchantments. Charms are low-class, like parlor tricks."

"If it's so beneath him, why make one?"

Teo considered. "I guess even low magic would be pretty valuable on this side of the border. Because it's tradeable. Maybe that's a draft of something; maybe a human offered Rivenholt something irresistible."

"Like a lifetime supply of Reese's cups?"

Teo glanced at the pile of wrappers that had accumulated on the bed and made a disdainful little sound. "Typical fey."

"If somebody wanted low magic, why would they ask a noble?"

"It's really just nobles who come here. I've only met two commoners ever, a dryad and a goblin. There's all types of fey in Arcadia I've never seen."

"By fey you mean fairies. This guy's a fairy."

Teo shrugged. "Maybe? The word is spelled F-E-Y—it just means weird or supernatural—but London HQ tends to see everything through a fairy filter anyway. Honestly, we don't know what the fuck these things are."

"Reassuring."

"When they're here, they enchant themselves to look human. I think 'facade' is the official HQ word. Do you know John Riven?" When he saw my confused expression, he clarified. "Actor; he was in *Accolade*."

"Which part?"

"Some white dude in a suit; I don't remember all their names. Anyway, John Riven is Viscount Rivenholt. He's way more involved on this side than most fey. I've got a photo back at the Residence; you'll know him when you see him."

Teo looked at me like he was waiting for me to argue with him, but I've never understood the pointless ritual of denial. I had a job to do, so I'd assume it wasn't bullshit until I found out otherwise.

"So what next?" I said.

"Still with me?" He looked dubious, but he at least stopped staring at me and went over to peer at the telephone, which continued flashing its tiny light.

"I think so," I said. "Where is Arcadia, exactly?"

"It's like a parallel world or whatever." He held up the phone receiver to his ear and punched in a few numbers on the cradle. "We call it Arcadia just to be calling it something."

"What do the fey call it?"

"Uh, 'the world,' I guess," he said distractedly as he punched in another number.

"What do they call our world?"

"Earth mostly, because we do. There's some weirdness with them and language."

"What do you mean?"

He held up a hand to shush me, listening intently to the phone, then scribbling something on the message pad. "Two messages from Inaya West."

"What?" I forgot Arcadia for a second. "The actress?"

Teo glanced skyward. "No, Millie, the postal clerk. Who do you think?"

"You're screwing with me."

"See for yourself," he said, pushing a couple of buttons and holding the handset out to me. I grabbed it from him.

"Johnny, it's 'Naya," said the first message, dated a week earlier. It did sound like her. *"Call me back when you get this, gorgeous."*

The next one had yesterday's date. Same voice, completely different tone.

"*Inaya again. I know something's up, Johnny, and I know this isn't your cell number. And now all of a sudden David won't return my calls either? I don't get it. Whatever's going on, I'm reasonable; you don't have to hide from me. Just talk to me. Please.*" And this time she left a number.

I tried to commit it to memory, since Teo had already torn off the paper he'd scribbled it on and stuffed it into his pocket. You never know when the phone number of an A-list actress might come in handy.

"What do you think that's about?" I said to Teo.

"No clue. Maybe Rivenholt was having a fling with Inaya and broke it off. Still doesn't explain why he extended his hotel stay and then left the room. It's like he's running from something. I didn't want to bother Berenbaum with this, but it looks like we're going to have to."

My stomach dropped to my knees. "Berenbaum? David Berenbaum?"

"No. Oprah Berenbaum."

"I went to school for directing," I said numbly. "He—I—my dad took me to see *Blue Yonder* when I was ten. David *Berenbaum*." The name tore open some hermetically sealed pocket of naïveté I had forgotten I had.

"Oh Jesus. You're not going to piddle on the floor of his office, are you? If so, I'll just crack a window and leave you in the car."

"David Berenbaum. We're going to see David Berenbaum." I couldn't stop saying it.

"He funds, like, half the Project. Rivenholt's his Echo. Uh, partner, you might say. Not in a gay way, that I know of; Rivenholt's like his muse. That's what the Project's for, to regulate travel between here and there. So we can get inspiration from fey and vice versa. Anybody who's anybody has an Echo."

"All of them? You're saying Martin Scorsese hangs out with fairies?"

"Yup. Not all fey are sunshine and rainbows."

"Kubrick, Eastwood, Coppola?"

"Kubrick's before my time, but probably. Eastwood and Coppola, yeah."

"Spielberg?"

"He doesn't need one; he's a wizard."

The wave of vertigo that swept over me suggested that this was a good time to stop asking questions.

"Let's get you back to the house and feed you some lunch before we go see Berenbaum," Teo said. "Half the reason we get to hang out with these people is that we stay cool about it, and you are not looking cool right now."

When we got back to the car, which was badly parallel parked under a palm tree, Teo reached into his jacket for the drawing and studied it again in the sunlight. I peered around his arm at it curiously; it gave me the same icy-bright rush of exhilaration as before. No matter how many times I looked away and back, the feeling was the same, like traveling eight years into the past.

But the drawing was showing me what *Rivenholt* had felt when he looked out his window, a fact both intimate and puzzling.

"Do you remember when Los Angeles made you feel like that?" I said to Teo.

"Nope," he said, folding the paper and tucking it away. "Unlike ninety percent of this town, I was born here."

• • •

We arrived back at the house to find a crisis in the living room. We heard it as soon as we opened the car doors, actually, but had to see it to believe it. When we walked in, a very tall black man was kneeling behind Gloria, holding her by the arms. Gloria was shrieking, red faced, at the bearded white guy I'd met briefly the day before. The bearded man—whose name I'd already forgotten—was slumped at one end of the couch, face buried in the crook of his elbow, sobbing.

"Look at me, you coward!" Gloria shrieked at him. "Have the decency to say it to my *face!*"

"Quit it," said the man holding her, barely audible over her screams. "Settle down."

When it comes to drama, I am both amplifier and sponge. You want to keep drama as far away from me as possible. Faced with this spectacle, I planted my sneaker-clad carbon feet on the hardwood floor as though I were staring down headlights.

"Where is Song?" Teo asked briskly of the only other calm person in the room.

"She went to the store," said the man holding Gloria. For just a moment I saw the strain on his high-cheekboned face, the coiled control. When he spoke again, he sounded almost bored. "Gloria, you know they need you back on set in twenty. You need to stop it now."

Teo touched my elbow, startling me. "Let's go up to my room," he murmured. I was too disconcerted to make any smart-ass remarks; I just nodded and tried to follow as Teo gave a wide berth to the tableau and practically vaulted up the stairs. I stumbled on the steps myself, dropping my cane as I grabbed for the rail with both hands. Teo doubled back, picking up my cane and helping me up the stairs none too gently.

"Unless the rent is dirt cheap here," I said breathlessly once we'd reached the top, "I think I'll take my chances on some other living arrangements."

"Three things," he said crisply, handing me back my cane. "One, Gloria's normally very sweet, and when she's not, it's always Phil who gets it. Two, rent is free here. Three, employees at our level have to live in a Project Residence."

"Why?"

"There are wards on the property and stuff; it's a little complicated for your pay grade."

"I'm not being paid."

"My point is, there are reasons we all live together. Working for the Project isn't dangerous, but only because we follow the rules to the letter. It's extra important that new people don't do stuff on their own, but the perks get better as you work your way up. You should see Caryl's place."

I wanted to, once I stepped into Teo's room. There was barely enough space for his loft bed and the computer desk he'd shoehorned under it. His Avengers bedspread hung off the footboard in a lumpy tangle, and I could smell the dirty laundry that had piled up all the way to the windowsill. His closet was partially blocked by a chest of drawers that was missing the bottom drawer. The only available floor space was dominated by a suspiciously streaked beanbag chair.

"Ugh," I said. "Doesn't it seem like a terrible idea to you, hiring a bunch of crazy people and penning them up together?"

"I like it here," said Teo. "It's nice not to be judged all the time. So maybe don't start, okay?"

"Seriously, what's the deal? Does mental illness give people some kind of sensitivity to magic?"

"I dunno; Caryl's cagey about it. But I get the feeling it's just—we're all creative people who might not get a shot anywhere else, you know? And I guess we're open-minded 'cause we've got no illusions that life makes any sense." He gestured toward his "chair" as he rifled through the file drawer in his desk. "Sit if you want."

"Even if I had a prayer of getting back out of that thing, I wouldn't sit in it for a hundred dollars."

"How about a thousand?" he said absently as he flipped through folder after folder at near-light speed.

"Nope." I was only half listening to him; I could still hear Gloria's raised voice from downstairs, and it twisted my stomach into a knot. I wanted to get away from it, but where was there to go?

"Everybody has a price," he said without looking at me.

"Yeah?" I forced my attention away from the confrontation downstairs. "What's yours?"

"That depends. For what?"

"Oh, I dunno. An hour in a cheap motel."

He shot me a look. "With you? Not enough money in the world."

He said something after that, but I didn't hear it. It was as though a glass capsule of boiling acid broke inside my head. Before I knew what I was doing, my cane swung in a swift arc and struck the side of Teo's head.

9

My swing wasn't hard enough to seriously hurt Teo, but it was more than enough to throw me off balance and send me toppling to the floor by way of the beanbag chair. Even with all those little plastic beans to absorb the shock, it felt like every pin and nail and plate that held my shattered bones together suddenly jarred loose and sent me back to pieces.

"Shit, you okay?" I heard Teo say somewhere over me.

A few moments went by before I could speak. I lay half propped up on my side, staring down. I'd twisted my ankle hard enough to break the suction suspension on my BK prosthetic.

"My leg came off," I said, staring at it.

"I see that. Do you need—"

"And my elbow's bleeding."

He knelt next to me, smelling of hair product and stale cigarette smoke, sitting me up with careful hands. It had been a year since I had a hug, so I sort of turned it into one.

"You dumb shit," he said. "Why did you hit me? Now I have to report you."

"Please don't."

"Don't move; I'll be right back." He tried to pull away. "Let go, you nut job; I'm not reporting you this minute, I'm getting something for your elbow." He eased me onto the beanbag chair and hurried out, returning with a wet washcloth.

I grabbed his arm. "Please don't report me."

He pulled free, then handed me the cloth. "I have to; it's the rules."

"I don't want to go back to the hospital. I've got nowhere else to go. Please."

"I'll tell her I provoked you. And I'm sorry about that, I only meant—"

"I know what you meant, just shut up now please." I adjusted the silicone sheath on my shin and slid it back into the suspension, but the seal was sloppy.

"No, you shut up," Teo said. "Even if you were Inaya West, I wouldn't touch you. Among other things, if I molested a newbie, Caryl would have Elliott rip out my entrails."

"Who's Elliott? The black guy?"

"Wow." He blinked at me. "Racist much?"

"How was that racist?"

"If you have to ask . . . But no, Elliott is Caryl's, uh—" He looked at me and seemed to think better of it. "I dunno if she wants me talking about that yet. You'll meet him later."

I held the washcloth against my elbow, watching Teo irritably rub his head where I'd hit him. My brain sort of flatlined; I lost track of what we were talking about.

"You okay?" he said, his hand still in his hair. "I was about to show you the viscount's file."

"What's the point, if I'm fired?"

"You're not fired," he snapped, leaning down to rummage

through his desk. His hair stuck straight out where he'd been rubbing it. "I'll tell her I like you."

"You'll *tell her* you do?"

He ignored me. "Look at this." He handed me a folder neatly labeled RIVENHOLT. It hardly seemed to belong in the mess of his room. Inside the folder were some sort of forms, filled out in careful block print with information that mostly made no sense to me. I wasn't really looking at the words any-way, because the photograph clipped to them was the kind of thing that captures attention.

I remembered him now, though like Teo, I couldn't remem-ber his character's name in *Accolade*. He looked to be in his early thirties, with aristocratic cheekbones and a generous mouth. His hair was nearly as pale as his skin and fell in waves just to his collar. It was his eyes that I couldn't stop star-ing at, though: almond shaped, fog gray, their chill softened by tawny lashes.

"God," I heard myself say.

"I know, right?" said Teo scathingly. "Must be nice to be able to design your own face."

It was hard to reconcile Rivenholt's distant expression with the feelings he had poured into his drawings. "What's he like?" I asked. "Have you met him?"

"Once or twice. Your basic aristocrat stereotype. Thinks he's better than everyone, vain about his appearance, doesn't like humans touching him."

"There are reasons besides snobbery that someone might not like to be touched."

"Either way, when we find him, my boot is going to touch his ass." He hesitated, then turned to fix me with a grave look.

"You know that's a joke, right? I play by the rules, even if Mr. Pretty Boy thinks he's above them."

"May I remind you," I said, "that I know approximately jack about the rules?"

"This is important, She-Hulk, so listen up. No violence against fey, ever. Not one drop of blood spilled. Not a scratch."

"What if one attacks me?"

"Then you take the beating. Smiling optional."

"That's bullshit."

"There are really good reasons for that rule—like, *epic* reasons—but those details are way above your clearance level. But this is all you need to know: we do not want to piss the fey off, and not just because if it came to war they'd wipe us out like a termite infestation. They're behind every great—well, anything, really. Our whole society depends on them."

"Do they depend on us, too?"

"Yeah. To them, our way of reasoning and organizing is the most amazing thing ever. Like their whole ranking system, with viscounts and barons and whatever? They got that from the Brits, ages ago, and it's practically religion to them now. Even simple stuff like counting time, it's totally foreign to them and they love it. Fey without human Echoes just sort of . . . drift around like they're in a dream. Don't even really have memories."

"Huh."

"I'll let Caryl do the rest of the lecturing. I need to make some lunch."

While Teo went downstairs to rummage in the kitchen, I set up camp in the bathroom. After a quick shower and a cleaning of my prosthetics, I debated with myself: using the wheelchair would be a pain in the ass, but if I wasn't dry enough when I put my prosthetics back on, I could cause skin problems that would put me back in the chair for days. Finally I decided to risk it: I used a hair dryer on both my stumps and the prosthetic sockets, praying that would be enough. I put them on, along with a nice skirt and a short-sleeved button-down.

Then came the hard part.

I wiped a clear patch from the foggy bathroom mirror and rubbed some styling wax between my palms, trying to tame the worst of my cowlicks without really looking. I didn't like being reminded that I no longer matched the image in my head, that I never would again. But there was no getting around it; I was going to need to put on some makeup.

The ritual of application was like riding a bike, even after a year. Foundation blended out the slight pinkness of my scar tissue but couldn't hide its cobbled texture. I could cheat with lip liner, redraw the left corner of my mouth, but I couldn't erase the deep vertical slash through both lips where they'd split to the teeth against concrete.

Putting on eyeliner took a kind of scrutiny I'd come nowhere near since my fall; I noticed for the first time how the scarring had pulled the corner of my left eyelid out of shape. I tried to wipe the liner off and reapply, but then I had to stop because my eyes were too wet. I grabbed tissues and tried some of the imagery Dr. Davis and I had worked on: a snowy cabin in the woods with a crackling fire. Once I was calmer I took a deep breath, deftly created the illusion of symmetry with my eye pencil, brushed on some mascara, and called it done.

Down in the kitchen there was a sandwich waiting for me.

Teo had already finished eating his and was poking around the fridge, muttering something about marinades and leftovers while Monty the cat wound figure eights around his feet.

I'd never have expected to like a sandwich with no meat, but the way Teo made mine, I didn't miss it. Sweet cucumber, onion, buttery-fresh avocado, some kind of tart cheese, tomato, and crisp lettuce with just the right amount of freshly ground pepper. An ecstatic profanity escaped me; Teo snorted and told me to wash out my mouth.

"I am never washing my mouth," I said. "I may keep the last bite of this sandwich in my cheek like a hamster."

"Gross, and not necessary." Teo picked up the insistent cat, who seemed to be made of elastic covered in rusty steel wool. "I can make you lunch anytime, if you stop hitting people. I love cooking."

"That's hot," I said.

He responded with awkward silence, filled only by the cat's loud purring. A bite of my sandwich went down sideways.

"So," Teo said when the moment had passed. "Ever been on the Warner Bros. lot?"

"Not since I worked as an extra." It had been an easy way to watch other directors work, requiring no résumé or references.

"I called ahead to let Berenbaum know we're coming. If you need to do anything else to get ready, be quick."

Mr. Yesterday's Jeans was insinuating that I wasn't presentable enough? "What about you?" I said. "When's the last time you had a shower?"

Teo put the cat down irritably. "This isn't a date, Roper. Get in the car."

"No. If can manage a shower, so can you. This is a big deal

to me; I don't want you walking in there smelling like sweat and cigarettes."

"For fuck's sake," said Teo. But he slouched upstairs, picking off cat hair as he went.

The Warner Bros. lot, like all major studio lots, is a massive complex of buildings that dwarfs certain small towns. Every building has the same warm butterscotch-taffy exterior, accented with lush landscaping that gives the place a homey, welcoming feeling. It's an illusion, but a nice one.

During my days as an extra, I had always parked in the garage across the road and waited for the WALK light to wheel my suitcase of clothing changes and supplies over to the main gate. This time, we got to drive the car right onto the lot. Teo gave the guy at the security booth his ID and got a pass for the dashboard of his crap car. The security guy didn't look nearly as judgmental of us as I thought he should.

Berenbaum had his own little bungalow on a shady back corner of the lot, a cozy stucco outbuilding with a dozen parking spaces out front. Teo pulled right in like he owned the place, and despite the pass we'd been given, I couldn't help feeling like an intruder. Even tourists were given a warmer welcome here than extras; the sight and smell of the place brought back sense-memories of debasement and exhaustion.

As we got out of the car, I winced at the loud, grinding creak of the passenger-side door and glanced around for Berenbaum's trademark red Valiant. Of course it wasn't there; you don't drive an icon to work every day. Teo as usual was not slowing down for me, so I hurried to catch up, making heavy use of my cane.

Just inside the door of the bungalow was a cozy reception

area with barely enough room for the sexy assistant's desk and a few soft chairs. As if I weren't dazzled enough, the walls were hung with illustrious photographs from Berenbaum's career. In the oldest of them he had shaggy dark hair and bell-bottoms, but by the time we got to his first Oscar acceptance his hair was already zebra-striped white. Most of the photos showed him as I had always known him: a craggy, snow-capped man with intense dark eyes.

And then there he was, standing in the doorway behind the reception desk. He had to be pushing seventy by now, but aside from a comfortable sag in the middle and some deep crevices around his mouth and eyes, he looked ready to live another half century.

"Teo," he said warmly.

He reached out to shake the kid's hand while I forgot how to stand up. I used my cane to steady my wobble and put out my own hand just in time for it to receive the same quick, decisive shake.

"Another new partner?" Berenbaum said with a wry smile as he gestured for us to precede him into his office.

"Just mixing things up," Teo said.

Berenbaum's office was roomy, congenial, and strikingly absent the kind of self-congratulation that was so prevalent in the reception area. The walls, shelves, and floor were graced with the work of local artists; the only nod to his career at all was a set of framed posters from the Cotton trilogy, each covered in signatures. Even those were nearly obscured by a pair of potted ficus trees. I noticed two pictures of the red Valiant and three pictures of his copper-haired wife, each placed to be visible from his L-shaped work space.

He gestured to a dark leather couch and perched lightly on the edge of his desk.

"I didn't get your name," he said to me, his eye contact almost unnervingly steady. If he'd checked out my prosthetic legs, he'd been clever enough to do it while I was ogling his office.

"Oh. Yes, thank you," I said.

Only when Teo looked at me as though I'd grown a nipple on my forehead did I realize what I'd said. Or rather, hadn't said.

"That's Millie," Teo cut in. "She's in training. She doesn't talk much." The look he gave me suggested that I had damned well better not.

"So what can I do for the Arcadia Project?" said Berenbaum, the corners of his eyes crinkling a bit.

"We're trying to track down Rivenholt," said Teo.

Berenbaum waited for more, then glanced at me to see if I'd be any help. I just shook my head slightly.

"You're looking for him here?" Berenbaum asked, scratching his chin with a benignly puzzled look. "*Black Powder* wrapped almost two weeks ago. He'd be settled in back at home by now."

"He never returned to Arcadia," said Teo flatly.

Berenbaum's hand dropped to his lap. "What? Are you sure?"

"There are only three Gates inside the Southern California perimeter," said Teo. "They're all watched by people and double-watched by magic. If he had crossed over, Caryl would know."

Berenbaum pushed off from the edge of the desk, moving behind it. "That's just crazy. Let me try his hotel."

"We were there this morning. Apparently he extended his

stay for a month, but also packed up everything and left. It looks like he hasn't been there in days."

Berenbaum stood very straight, looking at Teo with a face so blank I suspected he was starting to panic. "Teo," he said carefully, "what does that mean?"

"If we knew, sir, we wouldn't be bothering you in the middle of your workday. Do you know if he was in any kind of trouble? Did he do or say anything to make you think he might be trying to hide, or get away from someone?"

Berenbaum let out a frustrated puff of breath, raking a hand through his hair. "No, everything was just the same as— Wait." He stopped then, giving Teo a penetrating look. Then, just as suddenly, the iconic man seemed to wilt, covering his eyes with his hand. "I'm an idiot."

"What's wrong?" I said despite myself.

Berenbaum didn't look up. "This is my fault," he said.

10

My heart went out to the old man, but Teo seemed unmoved. "How is Rivenholt's disappearance your fault?" he asked.

Berenbaum straightened slowly, meeting Teo's eyes. "At the wrap party, he was acting a little off. I was all caught up in my own stuff and didn't really register what he was saying."

"Which was?"

"He kept going on about how we should just get out of L.A., take Linda and go somewhere, just the three of us—forget about everything and have fun together like we did when we were young. I figured he was just being fey, you know? Forgetting I had all this work to do in post. So I was kind of short with him."

"And this is a big deal?"

"Johnny isn't other fey. He doesn't just take off on a whim. I should have realized something was wrong. If I'd listened to him, he would have trusted me enough to tell me what was going on."

"I hardly think that makes it your fault," I cut in, earning myself a sharp look from Teo. I leaned back into the couch with a sigh.

"So you think he went on some sort of a . . . vacation?" said Teo dubiously. "On his own?"

"It sounded like he needed an escape," said Berenbaum. "But I didn't bother to stop and ask myself what someone like Johnny would want to escape from."

"That's not our business," said Teo. "Our business is getting him back to Arcadia. You know him better than anyone; where would he go?"

Berenbaum steepled his hands in front of his mouth, tapping his fingertips together as his eyes took on a distant expression. The silence stretched out long enough that I shot Teo a nervous look. Teo gave a staccato shrug, seeming generally impatient with the whole business.

"A spa resort," Berenbaum said. "Winningham Grove or Regazo de Lujo maybe. Something inside the Project perimeter, with orange trees. Somewhere we've been before. Maybe Elysienne. Check for him at places like that. Under all his old names, too."

Teo nodded, scribbling on a memo pad, then glanced at me. "He can't make up new aliases," he said in a teachery voice, "because fey can't lie. Not with words anyway. Our languages are foreign to them on a really deep arcane level, so they can't use them to create anything. We have to invent their human names. Rivenholt's been coming here so long the Project has to keep giving him new names and faces every decade or so to hide the fact that he doesn't age."

"Huh," I said stupidly.

Teo turned back to Berenbaum. "Do you know any reason why Inaya West would be trying to get in touch with him?"

Berenbaum frowned. "They worked together on *Accolade* a

few years back, but they don't really socialize. I try to minimize Johnny's contact with people who aren't hip to the Arcadia thing."

"We intercepted a couple of messages from her meant for him. She seemed to want to talk to him about something, and she said you weren't returning her calls either."

Berenbaum gave an odd little snort. "She hasn't called me in days," he said. "Or maybe Araceli has been aggressively screening my calls since I'm behind schedule."

My eyes drifted over to the signed poster for *Red Cotton*. I wondered if seven-year-old Inaya's scrawl was somewhere under the glass. She had never so much as been in a school Christmas pageant when Berenbaum found her chatting up a snow goose in New Orleans City Park and directed her straight to her first Oscar nomination.

"Don't worry about 'Naya," he said. "I'll give her a call later on today and find out what's going on from her end."

"All right," said Teo, rising. "Call us right away if you get any new information."

"You do the same," said Berenbaum, moving forward to give Teo's hand a brisk shake. "I'll tell Araceli to put you guys through no matter what."

Teo was already halfway out the door by the time I managed to get off the insidiously pliant couch and back to my feet. Berenbaum reached for my hand more gently than he had Teo's, and his eyes did a quick circuit over my face that made me feel as though he had just scanned the deepest contents of my psyche. He spoke quietly, still holding my eyes.

"It gets better," he said.

The words blew into me like I'd left a window open. My

brain was a white noise of the thousand things I wanted to say, and then I realized I was still holding on to his hand. I blushed to the roots of my hair, managing only an awkward smile and a half bow before hurrying after Teo.

"Did he say something to you?" Teo asked after we got back into the car.

"To me, not to you."

"As long as we're partners, anything said to you on the job is to both of us."

"It was personal."

"How can it be personal? He just met you." Suddenly he swiveled in his seat, looking aghast. "Did he *hit* on you?"

"No! It wasn't like that! God, why do you have to spoil *everything*?"

"Oh man, don't cry; that's not fair."

"I'm not!" But I was.

"Fine, you don't have to tell me." He started the car, looking irked, as though I had started crying on purpose. Men seem to think that women do this on a regular basis, which is bullshit. Just because you don't feel something, it doesn't mean the other person is faking it. You know who thinks like that? Sociopaths.

I sat in silence for most of the way back, trying to figure out what Berenbaum had meant by his parting words. Maybe it was a reference to working with the Project. Maybe he was referring to the physical healing process. But I had received the comment at a much deeper place.

I love people randomly and suddenly, and it's a curse most of the time. When it isn't, it's a lifesaver. I wasn't sure if I wanted to work with Teo, and I wasn't sure I wanted to live at Residence Four, and I wasn't sure if I gave a crap about Viscount Rivenholt or expired visas or Arcadia. But I would have walked across the 405 for David Berenbaum right then, and that was enough.

Teo chose that moment to say, "If something bad happened to Rivenholt, I'll bet Berenbaum's behind it."

"Don't be a dick," I countered. "You have no reason to believe that, other than to be contrary."

"Don't you watch TV? It's always the husband, or the boyfriend, or the business partner. Someone close. And there's no one closer to Rivenholt than Berenbaum."

"Can you succinctly sum up the nature of their relationship?"

"As far as we can tell, all artists, inventors, people like that, they have a kind of soul mate in Arcadia. It's like each has a radio tuned to the frequency of the other one. You can communicate a little without knowing it, across the border, but if you make physical contact, it's like putting a puzzle together. You get these incredible leaps of genius."

"So why would Berenbaum want to harm his own muse?"

"I dunno. Maybe he's ready to retire and Rivenholt's making a thing of it. Berenbaum is the Project's biggest donor; maybe that ties in somehow. Or maybe it has something to do with Rivenholt fading."

"Fading?"

"When you spend too much time in the wrong world, your body starts to change. The stuff in fey blood that makes them fey—norium, London calls it—it gets replaced with iron and their magic quits working, or humans who spend too long over there get norium in their blood and either go insane or turn into wizards or both. Either way we call it fading."

"So what happens when Rivenholt can't do magic anymore?"

"It's already starting," said Teo. "Did you see *Accolade*?"

I didn't like to admit it, but I knew what he meant. Berenbaum's recent work was all right, but "all right" was pretty disappointing from Berenbaum. *Black Powder* was supposed to be an unofficial fourth part of the Cotton trilogy, but people in the business were already doubtful that it was going to be worthy of comparison.

I shook my head, unconvinced. "Let's not slap a black hat on Berenbaum until we know for sure that Rivenholt's not shacking up somewhere with a supermodel or getting a seaweed wrap at Elysienne. Or both."

It wasn't time for dinner yet when we got back to the residence, so Teo excused himself to make some phone calls. At my request he directed me to Song's room, which was off to the east of the living room, around a corner on the first floor. The door, marked with an *A*, was partly open, but I knocked anyway.

"You can come in," said Song.

The room had no window, but was well lit and decorated in a homey fashion with undyed fabrics and natural woods. Song had her eyes closed, bending her knees and waving her arms in what I could only assume was some sort of hippie ritual, baby seated comfortably in the wrap that was crisscrossed over her chest. Her serene expression and the freckles across her nose made her look too young to have a child.

"Abbada," said the baby when it saw me, and peed. I could tell, because a wet stain appeared at the bottom of the wrap.

Song, smiling, made a gentle *sssssssssss* sound at the baby as she opened her small, dark eyes and began to lift it out of the wrap. I said a prayer to whoever was listening that I would never become the kind of person who was happy being peed on.

"Hi, Millie," she said as she moved to hold the undiapered baby over a small bowl to catch the last of his dribbles. I could now add the fact that the baby was uncircumcised to the list of things I didn't need to know.

"Hey," I said, trying to unwrinkle my nose. "Is everything okay with Gloria and um . . . the guy with the beard?"

"Phil?" she said with a smile. "Oh, everything's fine now. Sorry if you caught their little lovers' quarrel."

"Lovers'—okay. Uh, also, I was wondering, where is the house phone?"

"There is no house phone," Song said, dabbing the baby's doodad dry with a towel and then setting him on the changing pad as she began to unwind her wet wrap. And here I'd thought I would make it an entire day without seeing my landlord's breasts.

"No phone?" I echoed stupidly.

"Once Caryl gives the go-ahead, you'll get added to our mobile plan. But this house doesn't have a landline."

"Because of the wards?" I still had no idea what "wards" meant, but sometimes you can get people to tell you a lot if you pretend you know most of it already.

Song just gave me an odd look. "No," she said. "A landline just makes it harder to keep track of who's calling who. This way it's all nice and separate, and if anyone starts abusing phone privileges, it's easier to deal with."

"Phone . . . privileges." I could feel myself climbing the rungs of anger. "I've just spent six months in a psychiatric hospital, and I was really looking forward to being done with that kind of crap."

Song smiled gently, tickling her son's feet as he tried to

stuff them in his mouth. "I know it's hard. But sometimes the Project works with people who are very ill, and it seems cruel to treat them a certain way based on a diagnosis. So Caryl doesn't tell me the diagnosis. I just start everyone at nothing and then give privileges based on behavior."

It sounded fair, to what Dr. Davis would call my Reason Mind, but my Emotion Mind was digging my nails into my palms. Borderlines are not good at patiently earning things; we tend to take any "no" as a personal insult and feel driven to turn it into a "yes" on the spot.

"Was there someone you needed to call?" she asked me.

I thought of Dr. Davis—I was allowed to use her for phone coaching any day other than Sunday—but I shook my head. "Not really."

Song's baby made a weird face, and she quickly held him over the bowl again as he ejected an alarming quantity of yellowish-brown goo from his bowels. This was clearly my punishment for staying to argue about the phone.

"Do you need anything else for your room?" Song asked.

I considered asking for a bowl to poop in, but restrained myself. "I'm all right for now," I said, already backing out of the room, "but phone coaching is part of my therapy. If you could at least let Caryl know next time you talk to her, I'd appreciate it."

Out in the living room, Gloria's alleged lover was sitting at the grand piano. Not playing, just sitting, staring at the keys. I pretended not to see him and hurried up the stairs toward Teo's room.

When I knocked, I heard Teo saying, "Uh-huh, uh-huh," to somebody as he approached the door. He opened it and stepped away to allow me inside without even looking at me. From downstairs I heard the gentle opening chords of something familiar—Chopin?

The one-eared cat was perched alertly on Teo's loft bed, watching him pace. I noticed Rivenholt's drawing on Teo's desk and eyed the cat warily as I picked up the paper. It was still a spare, skillful piece of work, but this time it didn't give me the same rush of feeling.

"The magic's gone from the drawing," I told Teo once he had hung up and stuffed his phone back in his pocket. Even that slight weight seemed to endanger his jeans' purchase on his skinny hips.

"Nuh-uh," he said. "Charms last for months, years even." He snatched the paper from me and stared at it. "Huh. I guess he really sucks at it." Carelessly he set it back on the desk.

"Isn't that a clue or something?"

"Why would a faded charm be a clue?"

"Well I don't know. It could mean he died or something."

"That's not how charms work," Teo said. "They're like paintings. They don't care about the painter once he walks away, they just . . . are. Until they're not. Anyway, Regazo de Lujo put me through to a room when I asked for Forrest Cloven, which was Rivenholt's first alias with us. I hung up as soon as they transferred; I'd rather he not know we're coming."

"Nice work," I said. I meant it, but it came out sarcastic somehow.

The cat made a sound like a rusty door hinge, and Teo grabbed him to set him down on the desk. "We'll have to get Caryl's approval to go up there," he said as he scratched behind the cat's missing ear. "She's not answering right now, but I'll keep trying."

"Where is this place?"

"Santa Barbara, just inside the Project's perimeter. Couple hours' drive."

Fantastic. A four-hour round trip in the tobacco-mobile with Mr. Grouchy.

"What's the deal with the cat?" I asked. "Caryl told me not to touch him, but he seems nice enough."

"Monty belonged to our last boss, and that . . . bugs Caryl. Long story. But he likes me. He's attracted to angst."

I guess I was angsty enough for Monty too, because he let me run a hand down his back. His fur was softer than it looked, but I could feel his ribs under it.

Downstairs, I heard a cascade of spiraling eighth notes from the piano. I thought of my father for a moment, his straight back at the baby grand in our foyer. The pain wasn't as fresh as it ought to have been; we'd been distant for years before his suicide.

"You know," I said, "since we have time to kill anyway while you keep trying Caryl, why don't we look into why Rivenholt ran off? If we know what made him run, we might have better luck getting him to come back."

Teo looked annoyed, but he did seem to think it over. "We could snoop around some of his hangouts, see if anyone heard anything. Maybe the Seelie bar."

"The what now?"

"Oh. Um, so to go along with the fairy theme, London HQ calls the rival fey kingdoms the Seelie and Unseelie Courts. It breaks down to 'pretty' versus 'scary.' Mostly it's the pretty

Seelie that come to this part of the country looking for their Echoes, and they have their own little watering hole out in West Hollywood."

I opened my mouth.

"Don't even think of making a fairy joke; it wasn't funny the first dozen times somebody said it."

"I wouldn't dream of it, boss."

11

There's a saying that somebody tilted this country on its end, and everything that wasn't securely attached fell into California. I think it's the main reason I feel at home here. But when Teo and I started hoofing it through the very gayest part of West Hollywood late that afternoon, I discovered that even in Los Angeles it is possible to feel like a freak.

I think some of the more hostile stares were rooted in jealousy. Teo was a nice piece of ass, and the fading light suited him, making him look brooding and mysterious.

"Are you gay?" I asked him.

"I dunno," he said.

"What do you mean, you don't know? Do you like guys or not?"

"Shut up a second," said Teo, slipping on his mirror shades. He looked ridiculous; there was barely a blush of sunset left in the western sky. "There it is." He stopped at an intersection and pointed across the street.

"The sushi place next to the bookstore?" I blinked. What was a Christian bookstore doing half a block from a drag show anyway? The thought had barely entered my head before it fluttered away and I found myself looking at the sushi place again. I don't even like sushi. I looked back at the bookstore, only to find my attention wandering across the street to a coffee shop.

"Look at my glasses."

I turned and looked at him. "Very nineties, Neo."

"Not what I meant."

"You want me to look through them?"

"No, look *at* them. Look at what they're reflecting."

Teo leaned down a bit. I reached to turn his face to the proper angle, and when I saw what he was talking about, I got goose bumps. I could just barely make out the reflection of what was really next to the sushi place: a pink stucco building with a neon martini glass in one window and a winged neon female in the other.

"Holy shit," I said, looking back and forth from the glasses to the street over and over. Seeing isn't always a straight shot to believing.

I yanked the glasses off Teo's face and put them on, looking back across the street. Now I could still see the fake bookstore, but it was covered in shadowy mesh and snaky gold figures that reminded me of Arabic writing.

"Why don't they make it so that the glasses look through the illusion when you're wearing them?" I said.

Teo wrapped an arm around me, pulling me close and nuzzling my ear. What the hell?

"*Cállate,*" he murmured as people gathered behind us waiting for the WALK sign. "Look, if I'm wearing these and don't even know that bar is supposed to be hidden, I might say something to give it away."

"And this is all a big secret." I slipped an arm around him too, because why not?

"There's a Code of Silence written into the Accord," he whispered, his breath giving me goose bumps. "The Accord's like a treaty; it keeps the Unseelie from invading and fucking up the planet for kicks." Then he nabbed the shades off my face the way I'd done to him and pulled away, slipping them back on.

I adjusted the valve on my prosthetic knee so I could move at a better speed for street crossing. When the light changed, Teo grabbed my hand and pulled me toward the hidden bar. I trundled awkwardly along, cane thumping in the street.

"Your hair smells girly," I said.

"Your opinion means so much to me."

The closer we got to the bookstore, the less worthy it seemed of my attention. It gave off a faint odor suggesting moths and mildew. As Teo stepped toward the doorway, I grabbed his arm.

"Wait," I said. "We need to double back; I dropped my—" I stopped. I hadn't brought anything besides my clothes and my cane, and the latter was still clutched firmly in my hand.

Teo just grinned at me. "It's so cute watching the noobs get glamoured."

"That's creepy," I said, staring at the bookstore. "I mean, it's creepy because it doesn't even feel like magic."

"Uh-huh. Keep moving."

"Sorry," I said, and obliged him.

"Millie."

"Yeah?"

"You're moving *away* from the bookstore."

"Damn it!" This time I let Teo take my arm and escort me. Stupid fairies.

The moment we passed through the doorway, the spell dropped like a sheet from a birdcage, and the world burst into song.

Not just song, but deep, pulsing rhythm and color, so much color. Fuchsia and lime and orange and forest green and robin's-egg blue, splashes and streaks and spatters and stars. There was no rhyme or reason to it; the colors seemed to have blossomed spontaneously from the walls. I don't know why it was beautiful, but it was. Unlike most nightclubs, it was as bright as a movie set. Great feathered ceiling fans rotated slowly, sending iridescent bubbles drifting through the space.

The little venue wasn't highly populated, but everyone in it looked as though they'd just stepped off a fashion shoot.

"Wow," I said. "Who *are* these guys?"

"*Sidhe*. Nobility of the Seelie Court, like Rivenholt. If you think they look good now, check the reflection in the glasses." He took them off and handed them to me.

I tilted the shades toward the woman behind the bar. Even distorted by the shape of the lens, what I saw in the reflection made my one good knee turn to Jell-O. Huge, luminous lavender eyes, hair gleaming and writhing as though in its own private wind. Her skin shimmered like liquid opal.

I handed the glasses back to Teo. When looked at directly, the bartender was just an ordinary supermodel: strawberry blond and lightly tanned, with glitter-dusted eyes and a rack to die for.

"Baroness Foxfeather," said Teo as he approached her. She flashed him a smile, then looked at me. Her expression changed immediately to an equally bewitching pout.

"What is that," she said, pointing at me, "and why did you bring it in here?"

Teo stopped short, looking as surprised as I felt. "This is my new partner," he said. "Millie."

"Lisa is still dead?" the fey said sadly.

"Yes."

She stabbed a manicured finger at me. "It's half metal."

"I'm just a regular person," I reassured her awkwardly. "I got hurt really badly, and they had to, uh, repair me with metal bits."

"Like, surgery?" said Foxfeather, her suspicion turning to fascination as quickly as the lamp over the bar shifted from pink to periwinkle.

"Yeah," I said, nodding like a bobblehead doll. "Lots and lots of surgery. Well, the legs weren't surgically attached; they can come off. But some of my bones needed to be held together with—"

"What do you need, Teo?" Foxfeather had already lost interest in me. "Is it another inspection?" She tossed her hair over her shoulder; even the mundane facade was enough to make me rotten with jealousy.

"No, nothing like that." Teo didn't seem in the least distracted by the lightly freckled cleavage on display. Yup, definitely gay. "We were just wondering if you'd seen Viscount Rivenholt recently."

"Yeah," said Foxfeather. She then wandered off to the other end of the bar and pulled a slim knife from her pocket, absently digging its point into the wood.

"Milady," said Teo in the patient tone people use with small children. He moved around to the end of the bar so he was facing her again. "How recently, would you say?"

I followed and saw that Foxfeather was adding details to an

impressive rendition of a goat-legged man. It was captivating—
something I might have expected to see in a museum—and
she was just carving it right into the bar. "I don't know," she
said, intent on her work.

Teo gave me an *I hate fairies* look.

"I love that," I said, pointing to her art. "Is that a satyr?"

"I don't know what it's called," she said with a vague smile.
"I can't keep all the commoners straight. They're not allowed in
here. But they have such interesting faces, don't they?"

"What about Rivenholt?" I ventured. "Does he have an
interesting face?"

For a moment Foxfeather looked scandalized, and I was
afraid I'd made some unforgivable fey faux pas. But then she
giggled. "I'm only a baroness," she said. "He's a *viscount*."

"I didn't ask if you were dating him; I just wondered if you
thought he was handsome. He seems very handsome to me."

She giggled again nervously. "I like his facade better than
his real face," she said. "But I think I'm just starting to like the
way humans look."

"You look really pretty both ways," I said.

"Thanks!" she said. "Hey, why don't you have a facade? You
don't have to look like that."

Teo opened his mouth as though to intervene, but I put
up a hand. Gloria had said damn near the same that morning,
and with less excuse. "I don't know much about facades," I said.
"You're actually the first fey I've talked to."

"Ohmigod!" she squealed.

Several of the other patrons turned to see what had her so
excited. They all seemed to find me offensive at first sight, as
she had.

"We have a dry-eye in the bar!" Foxfeather shouted.

Whatever a dry-eye was, it seemed exciting enough to over-come the patrons' disgust. Some of them rose from their seats and approached; the rest went back to their drinks. I glanced at Teo; he looked uneasy but not panicked, so I tried to calm my suddenly racing heart as the curious fey closed in.

One of the interested patrons, a tanned hunk of beefcake, flexed a bicep at me and then turned abruptly into a lemon tree. I started, nearly knocking over the bar stool I'd been leaning on and setting off a chorus of giddy laughter.

"Now you've done it," said Teo. "They'll never leave you alone."

"Rivenholt," I stammered at them. "Do any of you know Rivenholt?"

"Rivenholt," said a slender brown man in a three-piece suit, using my exact voice and inflection. "Do any of you know Rivenholt?"

"You smell horrible," said a brunette who had sidled up next to me. "You stink of death." She reached out to do something to me, change my scent perhaps, but the moment her hand touched me, her facade dropped.

It was only for a second—a flash of autumn wings and blowtorch hair. The moment she let go of me she looked like a leggy brunette again.

"What the hell?" she and I said simultaneously.

"She has iron inside of her," Foxfeather supplied helpfully, leaning forward on the bar behind us.

Teo blinked at me. "What is she talking about? The leg?"

"I have a steel plate in my head," I said slowly. "Also various nails and pins and things holding my bones together."

"Holy shit," said Teo. "Steel. That's what happened with the drawing. All that iron . . . You kill magic."

The fey, with the exception of Foxfeather, were now backing away from me. I felt a slow sinking inside. So Caryl hadn't picked me for my leadership skills, or for my creativity. She'd probably lied about seeing my stupid films. She wanted me on her team because I was walking fairy kryptonite.

12

It seemed to take a minute for Teo to grasp the repercussions of this, but when he did, he gave the assembled fey a feral grin. "All right, kids," he said jauntily. "Unless you want me to sic Ironbones on you, I suggest you start racking your flighty little brains for some details about when and where you last saw Viscount Rivenholt."

My anger shifted from cold and dark to bright and hot. I didn't appreciate Teo's using me as a threat. I groped for my emotional reins, tried to remember some of my distress tolerance skills, but the calm mediocrity of Dr. Davis's office seemed like a fading dream in this chaotic atmosphere.

"We ate fish!" blurted the man who had turned into a tree earlier. He cringed when I looked his way. "Next door," he said. "He was going to eat raw fish, and I was curious, so I went too. It was terrible. I don't remember when it happened. Not very long ago. Please don't touch me."

My anger fled at those last words, leaving nothing but a chill void. I barely felt Teo's hand on my back as he guided me out the door of the bar, and I didn't hear a word he said, although there were a lot of them.

Don't touch me.

The image of John Scott, my UCLA screenwriting professor, tumbled out of my memory like a Polaroid out of a drawer. The sag of the skin under his ribs as he'd rolled away from me, suddenly tired and old, was photograph sharp. I'd reached for him, trying to rewrite what had just happened. He'd flinched away as though I'd wounded him.

Had I? I no longer even knew what was real. I tried to wrench my mind into the present; looking backward was intensely dangerous.

When you're Borderline, by the time you get a diagnosis you've done so many vicious things and blamed so many other people for them that the guilt of facing even one truth sets off a mental landslide. You start to wonder which of the evils done to you were real, and which were just reflections of the evil in you.

I felt sick and sweaty as I followed Teo into the sushi bar, but he wasn't paying attention to me. My stride turned lopsided and ugly even with the help of the cane; walking normally with prosthetic legs takes conscious, front-of-the-brain thought. The reek of fish and vinegar brought me partially out of my downward spiral—*Distract with strong sensations*, said Dr. Davis in my mind—and I tried to focus on what Teo was saying.

He showed the viscount's picture to several employees, and a waitress recognized "John Riven" and remembered seeing the actor there. Her words weren't really coalescing in my brain, so instead of listening, I reached into Teo's pocket for his sunglasses and slipped them on.

"Don't lose those," he growled at me before turning back to the waitress.

I wasn't expecting to see anything weird, which was why the faint glimmer of golden light on the bulletin board surprised me enough to pull me out of my funk. It was just a tiny flicker, mostly covered by ads for acting lessons and used furniture: cheap ink-jet printouts with phone number tear-strips at the bottom.

I made a beeline for the board, then realized I shouldn't touch the paper myself, not unless I wanted to suck all the magic out of it. I limped back over to Teo, still too preoccupied to pay attention to my stride.

"You didn't hear anything interesting in their conversation?" Teo was asking the waitress. I handed him his glasses and politely waited my turn to speak.

"Not really," she said. She looked Japanese, but her accent was pure Valley Girl. *California roll*, my brain unkindly supplied. "Mostly John was explaining sushi to the other guy."

"Did you get any idea of their relationship?"

"Friends, I guess? Acquaintances?"

A redheaded man stepped out from behind the prep area. "Are you guys talking about John Riven?"

"Yeah," said Teo. "Did you talk to him?"

"You guys cops?"

"No, just friends," Teo said. "Why, do we look like cops?"

"Jeff said the police were in here looking for John Riven the other day."

"Shit," said the waitress, making a washing-her-hands kind of gesture and getting back to work.

Teo just stood there for a minute, looking as floored as I felt. "What kind of cops?" he asked the redhead when his brain cells reassembled.

"I dunno. Jeff didn't give loads of detail."

"Can you give Jeff my number?" said Teo, handing him a card. "I want to know what's going on."

"Uh, sure," said the redhead, and took the card with a skeptical expression before disappearing into the back again.

"Teo," I said quietly, "I think there's another drawing on the bulletin board."

Teo crossed back toward the entrance, slipping on his shades as he went, and had no trouble spotting the page in question. He gave it a tug, detaching it.

It was a sketch of two young men I didn't recognize, one leaning his head on the other's shoulder in a booth just like the one in the back corner. The pose was casual, intimate, and as I looked at the nested figures, my surge of affection for them was bittersweet. The two were so young. I was glad they had each other and dared to hope that one day I, too, would no longer be alone.

Written at the bottom were the words *Hold on*.

"Weird," said Teo blandly. "I wonder if he and Berenbaum have had some kind of falling-out."

It took me a moment to realize what Teo was talking about. As with the other drawing, the viscount's emotions felt so native to me that I hadn't realized I was subject to an empathy charm.

I pondered for a moment. "You can be in a relationship and still feel alone, you know."

"Having an Echo isn't like having a boyfriend," Teo said with a puzzling level of condescension for one who apparently had neither. "It's like finding the other half of your soul. You never really know another human the way you know your Echo."

"Well, obviously Berenbaum and Rivenholt are anything but intimate right now. Berenbaum doesn't even know why he ran off. So your perfect-soul-mate theory isn't really holding water."

"Or it means that something has happened to Rivenholt that's so bad he doesn't want Berenbaum involved. In other words, this is *definitely* above my pay grade. Let's just report to Caryl and let her handle it."

I stared at the drawing a moment longer, a little unnerved by the strong compulsion I had to grab it, hold it, inhale the scent of the paper. Even knowing that my touch would destroy it, it was hard to resist. I put both my hands on top of my cane and gripped it tightly as Teo put the paper away.

When we returned to Residence Four, Caryl was already sitting on a couch in the living room. For a moment I was surprised to see her in the same pantsuit she'd worn at our last meeting, but then I remembered it had only been this morning. Wow.

"There is a pizza in the kitchen," Caryl said by way of greeting.

"You didn't tell me I could cancel magic by touching it," I replied.

Teo made an *ouch* face and tiptoed melodramatically past the two of us toward the kitchen. Food was the last thing on my mind.

"Can you?" said Caryl.

"Don't act like you don't know. Fifty bucks says it's the whole reason you recruited me."

"I have no reason to deceive you," she said. "But then, I suppose you have no reason to trust me, either." Her expression strongly suggested that she didn't give a damn either way. "I had considered that the abnormally high iron content of your body might afford you more protection than most, but if I had known you could actively disrupt spellwork, I'd have been more careful where I sent you."

"Whatever," I said. "Teo wants us to hand this assignment back to you anyway. It looks as though it's way more complicated than you thought."

"How so?"

"The cops are asking about Rivenholt in West Hollywood, and he seems to have fled to a resort in Santa Barbara. Berenbaum is completely out of the loop."

"I'll find something else for Teo to work on," she said. "You, on the other hand, are suspended from all duties for twenty-four hours."

"*What?*"

"You may continue to stay here at the Residence during your probation if you refrain from further violence."

"Violence?" Shit. Teo had ratted me out. I didn't bother defending myself; I suspected it was pointless. "What am I supposed to *do*?"

"Something that doesn't involve assaulting people, I should hope. You are very lucky I didn't reject your application outright. If it happens again, I will."

I waited to get angry, but I just felt defeated and miserable. I sank down onto the other couch, staring at the floor.

Teo returned from the kitchen with a mouthful of pizza, the remaining half of the slice still in his hand. "I hope I didn't miss a good catfight," he said, flopping down on the couch near Caryl. He immediately tensed, and then laughed. "Dammit, Elliott, not the ear."

I stared suspiciously at Teo. "What the hell are you talking about?"

Teo tossed me his sunglasses. I fumbled the catch, and the glasses bounced off my knee onto the rug. With a muffled groan, I bent my stiff back to retrieve them.

"Teo," said Caryl firmly. "If you break those, you are not getting another pair."

Righting myself, I slipped the glasses on and immediately blurted out an obscenity, recoiling back against the couch.

Perched on Teo's shoulder, as seen through the glasses, was a small dragon. Or at least that's what my brain decided to call it. It was a black creature about the size of a falcon, with bat wings and an iguana face and a scorpion tail. It looked as though it couldn't decide whether to nuzzle Teo or tear out his jugular. I sympathized.

"What . . . is that thing?" I said.

"My familiar," said Caryl.

13

The little dragon, Caryl's familiar, turned its head to look at me. Its beady gaze was friendly.

"You're a witch or something?" I asked.

"A warlock," said Caryl.

I took off the glasses and turned them so I could look at Teo's reflection in them. Nothing sat on his shoulder in the reflection.

"If you strip away the magic," said Caryl, "there is nothing to see. Elliott is itself a spell, albeit a very complicated one."

"So I can't touch him."

"You have, numerous times."

Even as she spoke, I got a crawling feeling on my right shoulder. I put the glasses back on to find Elliott sitting there. My yelp made Teo laugh, and even Elliott seemed to grin as I tried futilely to swat him away. My fingers sank right through him, tingling as they did.

"Why doesn't he vanish when I touch him?" I said. When I turned to look at Caryl, I saw a weird, smoky aura around her, so I took the glasses off again.

"Human magic is not identical to the fey's," she said. "Human spell casters have certain limitations that fey do not, but on the plus side, since iron is native to human physiology, the spells humans cast have no weakness to it. Your touch would only disrupt fey magic."

"Do humans cast the fey's facades?"

"We have to design them, since fey seem unable to grasp the rules of what humans can and can't look like. But the spell-work is their own. Why do you ask?"

"When I let go of the fey at the bar, her facade came back. I didn't destroy it."

"That's 'cause it's an enchantment," said Teo.

"The fey," said Caryl, "can bind magical energy into a place, person, or thing."

Teo ticked off three fingers. "Ward, enchantment, charm."

"Think of magic as paint," Caryl said. "For a charm, the paint is applied and left there. It can stay a long time because it's on an inert substance, such as paper. But flesh is alive and constantly changing, shedding cells; you must keep reapplying the paint. So enchantments, or spells on people, draw continuously on the caster's essence."

"They're plugged into the fey who cast them," clarified Teo.

"Because of that connection, enchantments can only be dispelled by the caster, or by the caster's death. Thus the mythology around curses, which are actually a type of Unseelie enchantment."

"So when I touched the fey, I just sort of, uh, interrupted the circuit?"

"If that helps you understand."

"What about the other one? Wards?"

"Wards are the most complex; humans cannot cast them. They are bound to the earth, or to structures that are themselves bound to the earth, such as trees or buildings."

I thought of the Seelie bar. "Would I destroy wards if I touched them? Or just interrupt them?"

"Some wards are . . . 'plugged in' and some are not, depending on their purpose. Just try not to touch any wards unless told otherwise."

I felt a weird tingling on my left ear and didn't dare look through the glasses. "Which of those things is Elliott?"

"None of the above. Elliott is a construct: a recursive arcanolinguistic lie bound to itself by pure logic. Only wizards and warlocks create them; nothing could be more foreign to a fey than a construct."

"And I can't hurt a construct."

"That's correct."

Teo shifted restlessly. "Speaking of Millie's phenomenal powers of destruction," he said, "we found another of the viscount's drawings."

Teo handed it to her, and she scanned it briefly, not visibly affected by its magic. "I'd like the other one, too, for comparison, when you have a chance."

I hardly noticed as Teo took his glasses back and started upstairs. I felt a slight pang as I stared at the back of the drawing. "You'll need to be gentle with him," I said.

"With Teo?" said Caryl, arching a brow.

"No, with Rivenholt. He seems very . . . vulnerable, right now, to judge by his drawings."

Caryl studied me. "You're concerned about him?"

"The drawings really affected me for some reason."

"Apparently the iron doesn't stop the psychic elements of fey magic from reaching you. A pity."

"What are you going to do now? About Rivenholt?"

"I am going to drive to the resort and confront him."

"By yourself?"

"I want to handle this personally; it's crucial that we keep Berenbaum happy, as he's our primary donor. I don't require a partner; Elliott serves a similar function for me."

"But I'm guessing Elliott can't give you information you don't already know. Maybe you should take me with you. I was there for the conversation with Berenbaum; I might spot a clue you can't."

"This would defeat the punitive purpose of your suspension."

"Negative reinforcement doesn't really work with Borderlines."

"Then how do you suggest we improve your functioning?"

I sighed and tried to remember what Dr. Davis had explained to me. "Dr. Davis says BPD has something to do with sensitive people being raised in 'invalidating environments.' Whatever that means. So I guess, you know, don't invalidate me."

Caryl looked at me for a long time. I would have given anything to know what she was thinking. Sometimes the first thing laypeople learn about Borderlines is that they can't be trusted, and after that, further learning isn't too likely.

"Be ready at four a.m.," she finally said. "If you are not dressed and waiting when I come by, I will leave without you."

Even for a morning person, being ready for a road trip at four a.m. was a little harsh. And since we were planning to run into the viscount, I didn't want to just slouch in there with my hair sticking up every which way.

I started to put on the same outfit I'd worn to meet with

Berenbaum, as it was my nicest and still fairly clean, but then I thought of the slim possibility that Berenbaum himself might show up at some point and decided not to risk the embarrassment. I chose my only other skirt and a matching knit top, then girded myself to face down the mirror.

I went through yesterday's makeup ritual, trying to convince myself that it was a little easier this time. I used styling wax to make it look like my hair was messy on purpose, and even tried on a pair of earrings before I started feeling a little too much like crying. I sponged a bit more makeup on my left arm and decided that was as much whitewash as this mud fence could handle. I went to the living room to wait.

Caryl arrived at one minute till four, looking as put-together as always. After a brusque greeting, she handed me a pair of glasses like Teo's. "I am lending you these," she said. "If you behave yourself, you can keep them."

I took them in the hand that wasn't holding my cane and slipped them on, noting once again the odd purplish-green haze that surrounded Caryl. "I'd rather have a phone," I said. At this hour I sounded almost as hoarse as she did.

Elliott attached himself to my shoulder, and Caryl pressed a fat file folder into my hand. "Familiarize yourself with that during the drive," she said, and headed for the door, giving me little choice but to follow.

"Does this mean I'm back on the case?"

"For the moment."

"This file . . . I actually get kind of queasy if I try to read in a moving car."

"Then bring a bag if you like," she said, "just so long as you bring the file."

I got into the car, belted myself in, pushed the glasses to the top of my head, and settled the folder into my lap, watching Caryl as she backed out of the driveway. "What kind of a name is Vallo?" I said. "Italian?"

"My father is Czech-Indian and my mother is of Moroccan Berber descent, if that satisfies your need for ethnic categorization."

It didn't, really, and then Caryl turned on some baroque harpsichord music at a punishing volume to discourage further small talk. Reading was hard enough for my rattled brain at the best of times; now I was squinting in the narrow glare of a reading light, trying to block out complicated melodies and keep down a bargain-brand bear claw.

To keep myself from ruining Caryl's leather seats, I mostly looked at the pictures. Some were stills from a recent film I had apparently missed due to either being in an anesthetic coma or locked up in the loony bin. There were reviews tucked into the file, too; they mostly praised John Riven's ability to look stunning in various kinds of light.

From what I could pick up between long, restorative bouts of staring out the window, Rivenholt had been visiting our world regularly for forty-seven years, and every decade or so he changed his human identity. He always favored pale hair and skin and always appeared to be in his late twenties to early thirties.

"Hey, Caryl," I said over the music. "Is it possible that Rivenholt could have changed his face since you saw him last?"

"Not without returning to Arcadia to replenish his essence, and not without a human's help."

"Because they don't really get what we're supposed to look like."

Caryl nodded, then turned up the music a bit more. I took the hint and dived back into the file.

The viscount's latest persona, John Riven, was the only one who had dabbled in acting; the rest had stayed out of the limelight aside from being occasionally photographed as a "close family friend" of the Berenbaums. His earliest alias, Forrest Cloven, had almost no paper trail at all and only one photograph, taken by the Project itself in 1971. None of his four faces really resonated with me the way the drawings had. They weren't *him*.

I was overcome by an urge to look at the drawings again, to study them, as though somehow I could solve the mystery of this man by following the strokes of his pen.

"Did Teo give you both the drawings?" I half shouted at Caryl. "I want to see them."

She turned the music down: a small victory. "You'll destroy them," she said.

"Then give me the one I already destroyed."

"Why?"

"I don't know," I said irritably. "For the file."

She kept trying to give me one of her long, searching looks, but it was hard to do while driving in the dark. Finally she gave up. "Open my purse for me, but do not touch its contents."

It was an odd little bag, held together with leather straps and wooden rings. I managed to wrestle it open and presented it to her. Slipping my glasses back over my eyes, I saw the faint glow of magical objects inside the bag. I also noticed that Elliott was curled up in my lap as though dozing.

Caryl, surrounded by that odd dark haze, felt around for the drawings without taking her eyes off the road, then handed me the one that had been crumpled and folded and drained of its magic. I snatched it from her with a little thrill.

"Why did you hit Teo?" Caryl asked me before I had even unfolded the paper.

I tensed, glad the glasses hid my eyes. "I thought he already talked to you about it."

"I want to hear your version."

I proceeded carefully, not sure what he'd told her and not wanting to contradict. "I was rattled," I said. "Dr. Davis would call them 'vulnerability factors.' I had just walked in on Gloria screaming at what's-his-name, and then I went up to Teo's room, which was all cramped and dirty, and I was feeling kind of . . . trapped. I overreacted, and I'm sorry. If I had access to a phone, I could keep up my coaching with Dr. Davis; it's very helpful."

"Overreacted to what exactly?"

"Just something he said. Something I interpreted as . . . an insult about my appearance."

"Is your appearance important to you?"

I snorted. "This is Los Angeles."

"That isn't an answer."

"And you're not my therapist. Give me a phone and I'll call her."

Elliott fluttered from my lap to Caryl's side of the car. I came within a hairbreadth of apologizing to the creature, then stopped myself.

"Does Elliott have feelings?" I said.

"In a manner of speaking, I suppose it does. The emotions of a child: unschooled and volatile."

"I'm sorry," I cooed gently at the creature. "You're a sweet thing. I didn't mean to scare you."

Elliott crawled back across the car to me, wings limp. He lay back down in my lap, then rolled over, exposing a fine-scaled belly.

"Aw, I want to pet him," I said. I stroked my fingers through the air where his belly was, but I had no way of knowing if he could feel it.

"Showing affection to the construct serves no purpose," Caryl said.

"What the hell is wrong with you?" I blurted, sending Elliott skittering away again. "Do you have no feelings at all?"

"Not when I am at work."

"Wow. Must be nice to be able to just switch them off."

"It is."

I ground my teeth and opened up the paper to look at the drawing, pushing my glasses back to the top of my head. The confident, evocative lines of the sketch soothed me, even without the magic. Idly I traced a fingertip over the angular Ds on either end of DREAMLAND.

"I am concerned by the way you are fondling that drawing," Caryl observed languidly. "I know how easily someone with your disorder can become infatuated."

I stiffened, folding the drawing back up. "You know just enough about BPD to be really unhelpful."

"I know how bored and restless you must feel when you have no one on whom to focus your passion. It's why Teo's dismissal enraged you; he was your best candidate."

"Stop it," I said.

"I need you to understand that you would find no happiness with Rivenholt either. He would always put you second. No romance can approach the bond between a fey and his Echo."

"I guess it sucks that you don't have one," I said acidly.

"My dear Millicent," she said lazily, "if that were the greatest tragedy of my life, I would be a lucky woman."

I felt a twisted stab of contrition, mixed with concern and curiosity, but when I opened my mouth, what came out was, "Poor you with your magic powers and your nice clothes and your SUV."

Most Borderlines are virtually incapable of a sincere apology. Tell a Borderline she has hurt you and she responds with a list of ways you've hurt her worse. Why? Because in a "split" world, someone has to wear the black hat, and for a person with suicidal tendencies, avoiding guilt is quite literally a matter of life and death.

"The difference," Caryl said to me, "is that virtually everything that has gone wrong in your life, you have done to yourself."

"Fuck you," I said, because nothing pisses off a Borderline quite like the truth.

14

The Regazo de Lujo Spa and Retreat was spread over fifty acres of green, sea-kissed land in Santa Barbara, but when we arrived, the sun had yet to rise to paint it in all its splendor. Even in the dark, the sprawling grounds and distant stucco villas looked inviting—but the REGISTERED GUESTS ONLY sign and dour-looking security guard at the end of the long, narrow driveway were decidedly less so. Caryl drove past the entrance as though planning to circle back around, but this place took the word "retreat" seriously; I hadn't seen any sign of public parking for miles.

"Where are we supposed to put the car?" I said. "Are you expecting us to park five miles away and walk?"

Caryl turned off her headlights and began to slow down, easing her car over to the side of the road. She checked her mirrors, then drove over the curb onto the grass, coming to a lurching stop.

"Get out of the car, quickly," she said in a crisp tone that brooked no hesitation.

"You're going to get us towed." I heaved myself awkwardly out of the passenger-side door, still queasy from my attempts at making sense of Rivenholt's file. My nausea was not abated in the slightest when Caryl, now standing next to the hood on the driver's side, rolled her eyes back and began to murmur under her breath in a foreign tongue.

When I say foreign, I don't mean foreign in the sense of "from another country" but in the sense of "invading virus." The harsh, wet consonants and dripping diphthongs made the hairs on my arms and neck lift away from my skin. I slipped the fey lenses down over my eyes and saw that the shadows around Caryl's form had thickened; Elliott had gone as still as a gargoyle on her shoulder.

A sickly webbing the color of an old bruise began to spread across the windshield, then the windows, then the entire SUV. My hair stirred in a breath of wind that stank like an abattoir; I shuddered and pushed my sunglasses back up into my hair.

The car was gone.

No, of course it wasn't. I stepped forward and touched the window, just to prove myself sane. I could still feel and almost see the cold gleam of glass under my fingers, but all my baser instincts were stubbornly telling me there was nothing there at all.

"Glamoured," I said, remembering the bookstore. I cleared my throat when I heard how hoarse I sounded.

Caryl sagged against the hood for a moment, seeming supported by thin air. Her eyes started to roll back again, but she fought it, easing herself onto the grass to keep from outright falling. There was now a car between us, but to my stupid hoodwinked brain it looked as though she had simply vanished.

"Caryl," I said in alarm, hobbling around the invisible SUV to look down at her. She was sitting on the grass with her head between her knees. I felt a familiar tingling on my shoulder, and lowered my glasses, pointlessly putting a hand up to steady Elliott. He buried his face in the curve of my neck, and I tried to kneel next to Caryl. I half expected to smell or feel the smoky darkness that surrounded her, but I couldn't.

"I'm fine," she said without lifting her head. "I really shouldn't cast spells of that magnitude while I have Elliott out."

"Why did you?"

"You'd rather park five miles away and walk?" she said dryly.

Impulsively I laid a hand on her shoulder through the haze. Elliott fluttered away from me and curled into a ball on the grass.

"Please do not touch me," Caryl said. "Ever."

I yanked my hand away and stared out into the dark road, focusing on my breath. Elliott, fickle child that he was, came back to my shoulder and nuzzled me.

"I am aware of the intent of your gesture," Caryl said behind me. It sounded as though she was slowly getting to her feet. "And your concern is appreciated."

I didn't look at her. "Are you sure it's not Elliott who's real, and you're the construct?" I said. Elliott cringed on my shoulder, but this time Caryl didn't deign to reply.

"Come along," was all she said.

The sun was starting to color the eastern sky, but the grounds of the resort were still dim enough that lamps glowed all over. I kept my sunglasses on nonetheless, not wanting to lose sight of Elliott or miss signs of magic. Caryl didn't wear glasses herself; maybe being a warlock gave her all the otherworldly sight she needed. One of these days I intended to find out exactly what the hell a warlock was.

Since we'd slipped in at the edge of the grounds, the man guarding the driveway never saw us, and there was no one to stop us from walking across the grand spread of green lawn right into the main lobby. Apparently unauthorized pedestrians weren't a big problem.

Caryl paused for a moment on the lawn, pulling out her phone and dialing. "Forrest Cloven's room, please," she said. After a few moments she said, "Hello?" in as warm a tone as I had ever heard her use, though her facial expression didn't change to match. "Are you there? It's Caryl Vallo from the Project."

She listened for a moment, then ended the call and slipped the phone back into her pocket.

"You kind of just ruined the element of surprise," I said.

"He did not know where I am calling from."

"What did he say?"

"Nothing at all. He picked up the phone without a greeting, then hung up when I identified myself."

"So what now?"

"I believe you would call it a 'stakeout.'"

The spacious lobby had slick hardwood floors the color of tea and scones, flanked by archways that let in just a hint of a sea breeze. Caryl ignored the drowsy woman working third shift at the front desk and seated herself in a comfortable chair out of the woman's eye line, as casually as though she belonged there. I followed her lead.

There was a bar just off the lobby, currently abandoned. I thought about the last bar I'd been in, the clink of Scott's glass against mine, and shuddered.

Elliott fluttered over to land in my lap, where he appeared to go to sleep. While I had doubted Teo's ability to manage a stakeout the day before, Caryl seemed like just the sort of person to sit patiently for hours if not weeks at a time. I suddenly wished I'd brought a book.

"This was your cunning plan?" I whispered. "I woke up at three in the morning so we could hurry up here and wait?"

"I needed to catch the viscount sleeping, in order to confuse him into answering the phone and possibly flush him out. I also needed darkness and privacy to hide the car."

"What do we do if he comes down here?" My stomach did a weird little flip at the thought.

"We'll have a pleasant conversation. He needs to remember that whatever sort of trouble he is in, we are here to help him. He may have forgotten that he does not have to answer to local law enforcement. All he needs to do is go home."

"There's some kind of doorway for that, right?"

"There is an Arcadian Gate at each Residence."

I stared at her. I had spent two nights in a house with some kind of magical portal and had completely failed to notice? "It has a glamour on it," I guessed.

"Glamour is a sloppy term, but yes, it does have a psychic ward protecting it, as does the locked door that leads to it. Even I would not be able to locate it if I did not have the key and know exactly where it was."

"Is the Gate an actual door?"

"It is a semicircular archway constructed of graphite and diamond. Well, technically, it is two identical archways that exist at the same coordinates in either realm. They must be built in those rare spots where a corresponding structure can be built in Arcadia, and where means can be used to protect the Gates on both sides. The space described by the semicircle exists in both realms at once, so when you pass under the arch you start in one world and end up in the other."

"Weird. Does it hurt or anything?"

"Only if you touch the archway itself. Even then it is not so much pain as intense discomfort."

"What does it feel like?"

Caryl seemed to give it some thought. Elliott stirred restlessly in my lap. "Some describe it as similar to the feeling you get when you first begin a free fall."

"That awful thing in your stomach, like on a roller coaster?"

Caryl gave me a very long look, then shrugged. "Possibly."

"Have you not used one?"

"A Gate, yes. A roller coaster, no."

"Of course you haven't." I rolled my eyes.

"Millie?"

"What."

"I find it strange that a roller coaster was the first free fall that came to your mind."

My mouth fell open, then shut again. I stared at her. "I don't remember the fall you're referring to," I said as evenly as I could manage. "I don't even remember being on the roof. They had to tell me about it later." I turned away from her, stared into the empty lobby, and didn't say, *asshole*.

It was quite a while before anyone at all made an appearance. They mostly seemed to be guests checking out of their rooms, and none of them were people Caryl seemed to know. I thought I recognized at least one woman myself; someone from TV, maybe, but I couldn't place the name.

"Do celebrities come here?" I asked Caryl. "I'm not familiar with Santa Barbara."

"Most of our human clientele prefer more expensive resorts," she said. "But fey enjoy this retreat because of the orange grove on the grounds. Fey are obsessed with fruit. Citrus fruits in general are probably the most common smuggling problem we have."

"Candy, too, to judge by Rivenholt. Fey are weird."

"The word 'weird' descends from the Old English *wyrd*, by way of the Old Norse *urðr*, meaning fate. So, yes."

"Have you noticed that you're impossible to have a normal conversation with?"

"I am not inclined to elect you arbiter of normal."

Since talking was futile, we sat around some more. Eventually the woman at the front desk was relieved by a man. Elliott got restless and started doing aerial acrobatics. When his attempt to dive-bomb a departing family made me laugh out loud, Caryl recalled him to her side.

"I think I will take a brief stroll about the grounds," she said. "Stay here, and if Rivenholt appears, find some way to detain him."

With those vague instructions, Caryl left. Now that Elliott wasn't around to amuse me, I pushed my fey lenses up onto my head and settled in to people-watch. Having sunglasses that weren't dirt cheap made me a little nervous; I had already gone longer without losing these than any other pair I'd owned.

I spotted only one other familiar face, a curly-haired Latina from a canceled police procedural. Time began to drag, and my AK prosthetic began to dig uncomfortably into my butt cheek. Trying not to attract too much attention, I rose and stretched, keeping myself out of the eye line of the man at the front desk. I practiced walking, letting my cane dangle in my left hand and seeing if I could smooth out my stride without its help. It was beginning to seem as though Rivenholt would not be spooked enough to check out, so this could be a long siege, and I had nothing better to do.

As I moved, I saw another vaguely familiar man seated at the bar. Messy hair the color of coffee grounds, rough features, a pretentious goatee. I amused myself for a moment by trying to remember what show he was on, and then he turned his head to look directly at me.

From the expression on his face, it seemed he recognized me, too.

15

Shit. My mind raced. Someone from UCLA? Someone who'd worked on one of my films? I looked away, feigning disinterest even as my stomach began to churn. My memory was a little unreliable thanks to my brain injury, but there weren't many people from my old life who would remember me fondly. I hadn't just burned my bridges; I'd nuked them from orbit.

After a moment I dared another look at him. He was still staring at me. He stroked his goatee for a moment, then slid off his bar stool and started toward me. He was tall, and I had a sudden feeling he was going to come over and give me a big Hollywood hug. At the thought of being crushed against his rumpled button-down shirt, my palms went damp.

Without thinking, I turned and headed for one of the archways, fleeing the lobby without even trying to be subtle about it. I heard the man working at the front desk say, "Miss?" politely, but I pretended not to hear him.

When my eyes slammed up against morning sunlight and glittering sidewalk, I slid the shades down again, but I didn't slow until I'd rounded the corner of the nearest villa. I took a few deep breaths and then peeked around the corner back toward the lobby.

He hadn't followed me.

I wasn't sure what to do now, though. I didn't know where Caryl was, but I didn't want to go back to the lobby again either. So I ducked back around the corner and stood there admiring the landscaping and taking deep breaths of the sea air.

Before much longer I caught movement out of the corner of my eye: a figure wreathed in shadow was headed toward me. Recognizing Caryl's magical haze, I pushed my glasses back up onto my head so I could see her.

Only it wasn't Caryl.

The woman looked around forty or so, but a Beverly Hills forty. Her lustrous chocolate-syrup dye job had little gleams of raspberry where the sun caught it. I'd have called her handsome rather than beautiful; even her plump garnet-glossed lips did nothing to soften the severity of her features. Frankly, she looked like the kind of person who might cheerfully break my neck and toss me in a closet.

She didn't notice me until she was about to stride directly by me, and then she only gave me a vague smile before continuing past me toward the lobby. I shuddered involuntarily as she passed.

I'm not sure how long I stood there trying to make sense of this before I felt a familiar tingling on my shoulder and lowered my glasses to find Elliott sitting there.

"Where's Caryl?" I asked him. He responded by launching himself into the air and doing a little twirl to see if I was following.

Elliott headed straight over the lobby, but I decided to walk around it rather than risk running into Goatee Guy or Ms. Scary again. Once I made it to the other side of the building, I spotted

Elliott bobbing impatiently. I followed him until I found Caryl. Her haze wasn't as thick as the other woman's; I could easily recognize her through it.

"I just returned to the lobby looking for you," she said. "Why did you leave?"

I evaded the question by describing the woman I'd seen. Elliott collapsed on my shoulder, hiding his eyes in my neck.

"I know who that was," Caryl said. "If she is here, something is deeply wrong. She was not in the lobby just now, but if she is still on the grounds, I can track her."

She hesitated.

"What?" I said.

"It requires me to support another construct, and as badly as I drained myself hiding the car, I cannot do it unless I reappropriate the energy I used to make Elliott."

"You mean unmake him?"

"Temporarily."

"It's nice of you to warn me, but I think I can stomach it. He's just a spell, right?"

Another hesitation. "I apologize in advance."

From her warnings I expected Elliott to be torn limb from limb, but he just winked out like the beam of a flashlight. The incoming rush of magical energy seemed to disorient Caryl, though; she wobbled like a newborn foal. I reached to steady her, then remembered and retracted my hand. Caryl flushed, clearing her throat.

"I use Unseelie magic," she said, her voice unsteady. "So does she. I can cast a construct that will be drawn toward the nearest source of the same. The disadvantage is that our target will feel the spell too and will know we are coming. It can't be helped, though; I refuse to believe this woman's presence is coincidence. It's likely she is the source of the trouble Rivenholt is in, and if so—" She broke off ominously.

"Caryl. Do you need to rest from the . . . Elliott thing? Your hands are shaking."

She looked up at me, and her eyes were so nakedly terrified I actually took a half step back. "I'm fine," she said.

She moved to brace her back against a wall and murmured more of those disturbing Unseelie words. Even prepared for it, I couldn't stop the primal wave of unease that made my skin go clammy. When she finished, a vaguely spherical blob hovered in the air, visible only through my glasses. It was paradoxically dark and glowing, like the afterimage from a camera flash. After a moment it began to drift away.

"Now we follow it," Caryl said.

At first the shadowy sphere floated across the lawn with all the urgency of a bit of dandelion fluff, but then it slowly began to gather speed and direction. Caryl had no trouble keeping up, but by the time it had reached the villas on the other side of the pool, I was starting to feel twinges of pain in my lower back and my gait was faltering.

As the spell disappeared around the back of a four-story villa, Caryl glanced back at me, looking torn.

"You don't have to wait for me," I said.

"It will be fine," she said. "We'll find it."

It took a bit of searching, but we finally looked up and spotted the construct on the third floor, bumping gently against an exterior door. You'd think that people trying to relax would want elevators, but apparently not. I leaned on the stair railing with the hand not already gripping my cane, and Caryl hovered next to me looking fretful during the entire climb.

When we arrived at the door, Caryl knocked gently. She was pale, and the palm of her glove was dark with sweat. No one answered.

"Fantastic," I said. "That was worth the effort."

"She's in there," said Caryl. She dispelled the construct and laid her gloved hand on the crack of the door, right where the latch would be.

"You know a spell to unlock it?"

"Not exactly," she said. She left her hand there and muttered something under her breath. A stink like a septic tank wafted toward me, and through the fey lenses I could see a web of brownish cracks appearing around her hand. Curious, I pushed my glasses to the top of my head; the wood of the doorframe looked normal for a moment but then slowly darkened, warped, and split as though it had undergone decades of decay. The latch slipped free of its slimy purchase as she pushed, taking splinters of rotten wood with it.

"Charming," I said.

She turned to me, and without the faint haze from the lenses veiling her face, her fear was even more apparent. "I have known this woman for years. I have exacted certain promises from her that should keep me safe. But you must do exactly as I tell you at all times, and if I ask you to leave, do so without questioning me."

"Yes, ma'am."

I'm not sure what I was expecting to see inside the room, but it certainly wasn't our quarry relaxing in a lounge chair with a plate of strawberries in her hand and her stiletto-clad feet up on the edge of the bed. There was an open bottle of champagne and an empty glass on a table nearby.

"Caryl, you brought company!" she said in a breezy Hollywood voice that didn't match her severe looks in the slightest. "Champagne?"

"Don't tell her your name," Caryl said to me quietly. "Don't touch her, don't look directly into her eyes, and don't take anything she offers you."

"Is that what passes for a greeting these days?" the woman said lightly.

Caryl reached into her pocket and pulled out her phone, dialing without taking her eyes off the woman. "Forrest Cloven's room, please," she said into it.

"I'm Vivian Chandler," the woman said, smiling at me. "And you are?"

My polite Southern upbringing chose that moment to kick in, and I almost answered her. The only reason I hesitated was that her name sounded vaguely familiar, and I was trying to place it before I decided how to introduce myself.

Luckily, the ringing of the phone on the bedside table startled me out of my train of thought. I was confused until Caryl ended her call and the ringing on the table stopped.

"Why are you in Rivenholt's room?" Caryl said. "And where is Rivenholt?"

16

"Oh, Caryl," said Vivian, plucking a strawberry from the plate, "I do hate to disappoint you, because I know how *desperately* you want to catch me being naughty, but I haven't harmed the boy. I haven't even seen him in weeks." She sank her teeth into the strawberry and gave me a little wink.

"Then why are you in this room under his name?" said Caryl.

"You would have to ask him for the full story. He sent me an e-mail offering me a spa package he couldn't use, so I decided to take a few days off. Work has been so *stressful* lately. Far be it from me to say no to a deep-tissue massage and a facial."

"This doesn't make sense," Caryl said to me. "Vivian is exiled Unseelie nobility; there is absolutely no reason why a Seelie viscount would—"

"I'm sitting right here, darling," said Vivian, a hard edge creeping into her voice. "And you know I can't lie."

"No," said Caryl, "but you have a history of presenting the facts in a way that suits your purposes."

"Oh, and what *are* my purposes, aside from a bit of relaxation, which you have rudely interrupted with your breaking and entering? I would absolutely love to hear your theory." She carefully selected another strawberry.

My brain finally clicked the name Vivian Chandler into place. She was an actors' agent. A good one, with a sharkish reputation and an A-list roster. I tried to remember whether she represented Inaya West, hoping for at least two pieces in this puzzle to fit together. But last I'd heard, Inaya was with ICM.

"I am currently without a theory," Caryl admitted. "But if you haven't done something to Rivenholt, then I am sure you would not object to helping us locate him before the Los Angeles Police Department does."

At this, Vivian straightened, a strawberry poised in her fingertips. Slowly it browned and shriveled in her grasp. "I don't understand," she said, her tone as brittle as glass. "What's he done? Am I an accessory to something?"

Caryl looked childishly pleased by Vivian's discomfort. "We don't know," she said. "But local law enforcement was looking for him in West Hollywood near the Seelie bar, and he has broken contact with his Echo."

Vivian set aside the spoiled strawberry and rubbed at her chin, her expression guarded. "Interesting," she said. I tried to see behind her mask, but whatever she had once been, she was now Hollywood to the core, glossy and impenetrable.

"Do you think Rivenholt is trying to set you up for something?" I asked her.

"It *talks*!" she squealed, making Caryl wince. "And what an *interesting* look you have, sweetheart. I don't suppose you're looking for representation?"

"Leave her alone," said Caryl.

Vivian looked delighted. "Awwwww, little Caryl has found a new mommy. I do hope this one's better to you."

To my utter shock, tears filled Caryl's eyes. Before I could say anything, Vivian turned her savage smile on me. "It's so nice meeting you," she said. "Let's play a game, shall we? You be the fox, and resort security will be the hounds." With that, she plucked a mobile phone from the table and tapped it to her lips, eyeing me up and down. "You don't look very agile, sweetheart, so I'll be sporting and give you a head start."

Security did catch up to us—it wasn't hard—but since we looked harmless and were on our way out anyhow, they sent us off with a warning.

Removing the charm from Caryl's car was a complicated matter, though, now that there was traffic. First we had to get inside the vehicle, which is harder than it sounds when your every neuron is thoroughly convinced that there is nothing there at all. Then we had to wait for what felt like hours for a lull in traffic so that no one would see an SUV materialize out of thin air. Even as rapidly as Caryl worked, we still got honked at furiously when we were caught driving over the curb back onto the road.

As soon as we found a legal place to pull over, Caryl put on the parking brake without turning off the engine and started into a long incantation that made me taste bile at the back of my throat. When she was finished, she released the brake and pulled back into traffic. Before I could ask what that was all about, I felt Elliott land on my shoulder.

"What happened back there?" I said.

"A great many things," she replied. "Which of them do you mean?"

"That woman made you a complete wreck."

"It wasn't entirely her fault."

I thought about the way Caryl had flushed when Elliott's construct dissolved. "Did you take on some of Elliott's emotions when you reabsorbed his spell?"

"Elliott doesn't have emotions."

"You said he had the feelings of a child."

"I didn't say which child."

"Ah." Finally I got it. "Yours."

Caryl nodded as though we were discussing the way she preferred her coffee. "Elliott is a sort of storage device."

"For psychological trauma?"

"It serves as a repository for certain parts of my thought process when I am in a professional situation. My emotions are underdeveloped and . . . damaged, and that makes a bad mix with the amount of power I command."

I studied her face. Once again I realized I had no idea of her age. No older than her mid-thirties, certainly, no matter how much she sounded like someone's grandmother. But then again, I didn't know the first thing about warlocks. She could have been two hundred years old, or two thousand. "What happened to you? What did Vivian mean about your mother?"

"That isn't relevant."

"If my boss has crippling mommy issues, I feel like it's pretty damned relevant."

"The auteur of *The Stone Guest* has no call to throw stones about mother issues."

"That was fiction," I said. "But I saw the real you back there."

"Why is some accident of uncontrolled neurochemistry the 'real me,' and a carefully reasoned system of priorities somehow false? I have lived more of my life without emotions than with them. If you have to choose a me to be 'real,' this is it."

I had a sudden desperate urge to talk to Dr. Davis. This woman, her former patient no less, had torn her mind in half. Her Emotion Mind was perched on my shoulder while her Reason Mind drove the car and told me it didn't matter. It was fascinating and horrible, and I was deeply, sickeningly envious. I looked out the window.

Caryl glanced over at me, then back at the road. I felt Elliott nuzzle my cheek, and I realized that was as close as I would ever get to an apology from my boss.

"So who is Vivian exactly?" I said when I'd pulled myself together. "I mean, I know who she is in Hollywood, but who is she in Arcadia?"

"She *was* Countess Feverwax of the Unseelie Court, but she was exiled at the end of the nineteenth century when she unleashed a plague on her own people for reasons she has yet to explain—if she even has reasons. She talked the Unseelie King out of executing her, and so she's this world's problem now."

"What did she do before she was a talent agent?"

"She's most often an entrepreneur, favoring businesses with a touch of the macabre: slaughterhouses, funeral homes, that sort of thing. In the olden days she would invest through a husband who would then mysteriously die. She founded Cera Pest Control in 1970 and still holds a controlling interest. Over the years we suspect her to have committed any number of baffling, sadistic crimes, including murdering my predecessor, Martin, but we have never managed to pin her to anything."

"I thought fey lost their magic if they stayed here too long."

"Your attention to detail is one of your finer qualities,

Millie." I couldn't tell if she was being sarcastic. "Normally yes, but certain Unseelie exiles use . . . legal but unsavory means to preserve their youth and power. We believe it may be these exiles who are the origin of the vampire legends."

"What!" I couldn't help grinning stupidly. "Are you telling me I just had an interview with a vampire?"

Caryl pretended she hadn't heard me, and I couldn't really blame her.

When we arrived back at the Residence, Caryl pulled into the driveway and stopped the car, releasing the locks on the doors without a word.

"Aren't you coming inside?"

"No," she said.

"Are you angry at me about something?"

By way of answer, Caryl gestured to my lap; I slipped down my fey lenses and saw Elliott curled up there contentedly. "If you hurry, you may still be in time to give Teo your requests for dinner," Caryl said.

"I—I just thought—I mean, usually people say good-bye or whatever."

"Shall I walk you to the porch and kiss you good night?"

The fact that I found the idea vaguely appealing was evidence of the severity of my social famine. "That's quite all right," I said. "Uh, see you, I guess." I began gathering myself to get out of the car.

"I'll call Song when I get home and tell her to give you Lisa's phone."

The name rang a faint bell. "Who's Lisa?"

"Teo's last partner."

I sat there for a moment, letting the weight of that settle on me.

"Millie?"

"Yeah?"

"Are you going to get out of the car?"

I did, and I slammed the car door just slightly harder than necessary, which hurt me more than it hurt the car.

I found Teo in the kitchen. Apparently I was too late to influence his choice of dinner, because he was already manically slicing long, thin strips of zucchini.

"Hey," I said. "What are you making?"

"Lasagna," he said without turning to look at me.

"Need any help?"

"Nope, I'm good."

"I don't mean to interfere with your cooking or anything, of course, just . . . You know, if you need something stirred or peeled or whatever."

"Nope."

"Just trying to be friendly," I said. "I know you don't like people, but I've learned the hard way what happens when you push everyone away."

This time he didn't bother to respond.

"Are those pumpkin seeds?" I tried again. "What are they for?"

"Seriously, Millie, just let me cook."

I stood there for a moment, fighting what I knew was an irrational amount of hurt. I knew I should probably just walk away and respect his space, but part of me couldn't accept the rejection and the other part was genuinely worried about him. I tried to think of something to say that wouldn't irritate him further; I wasn't quite ready to surrender.

"I found it!" piped up a cheery Southern accent as Gloria materialized from behind the island with a fine-mesh sieve.

I almost fell over. "Gloria, I didn't see you there!"

I wanted to take it back the second it came out of my mouth. Judging by the chilly look she gave me, there was no chance in hell I could convince her I hadn't meant any insult. As Teo started to turn toward her, she quickly replaced the glare with a pretty smile.

"Oh, good," said Teo to Gloria as though I'd already left. "The quinoa's there on the counter."

She'd heard my whole little speech. And apparently it wasn't *company* Teo couldn't stand, just me. My face heated all the way to my ears. Since neither of them was even looking at me, I didn't bother saying anything else before I turned and left the kitchen.

17

I could tell my face was still red when I got to Song's room, but I didn't care; I just wanted my phone. My landlord sat on the floor supervising her son's attempts to devour himself toes first. Song exuded the kind of bland serenity that's usually accompanied by a stench of stale marijuana, but all I smelled were diapers.

"Caryl wants me to have Lisa's phone," I said.

Song looked up at me in surprise. "She didn't mention it to me."

"She's going to call you as soon as she gets home, she said."

Song rose, moving to what looked like a lost-and-found box. "If you're sure," she said mildly as she rummaged through it.

Her implied doubt skimmed across my nerves. "Do you figure I'm just making this up?" I said. "How would I even know who Lisa is? Do you think Teo and I have just had some intense little heart-to-heart, and now I'm using his dead partner's name so I can steal a phone? Am I wearing some kind of sign that says 'Beware of Lying Bitch'?"

Song flinched but kept rummaging; my only answer came in the form of a high-pitched keening from the floor. I looked down and saw the baby's face scrunched up, his arms and legs pulled in toward his body as he drew in breath for an even louder wail.

Song hurriedly pressed a phone into my hand, then rushed to kneel down and take the baby into her arms. It occurred to me that in all the time I had spent in that echoing old house, day and night, I had never once heard the baby cry. From the stricken look on Song's face, she apparently didn't hear it often either.

Song clasped the baby to her chest as though trying to reattach a severed limb. With a half-assed apology still caught in my throat, I made an awkward exit.

I felt bad, but not as bad as I should have felt, which only made me feel worse. I had never understood the fuss over babies. My own window of cuteness had been wasted on a man too eyeballs-deep in grief to notice, and I'd managed to survive.

My new phone was saying "Connecting . . ." before I even realized I'd dialed it. It was a cheap relic with a tiny screen and no Internet capability, but at the moment it felt like a life preserver. I heard the receptionist at the Leishman Center answer as I unlocked the door to my room. A blast of heat greeted me; I'd forgotten to roll down the shades before I left that morning.

"If Dr. Davis is there, I'd like to speak with her. It's Millicent Roper. I need phone coaching, but I don't know her direct number."

It was like an oven in there. To distract myself from how hard it was to breathe, I sang along with the hold music and struggled out of my clothes and prosthetics. Sitting naked on the air mattress, I stared at my ungroomed hands. Hangnails everywhere.

BPD whispered to me that Dr. Davis was never going to answer the phone. She was avoiding me, just like everyone else. Why wouldn't she? What had I ever done to deserve anyone's patience?

They've all given up on you. Dr. Davis, Dr. Scott, your own father. They can't all be wrong, can they? There's something wrong with you, deep down. Everyone can tell.

Stop it. Stop thinking. Fix something you can fix, like those hangnails.

Breath coming fast, eyes burning, I found a pair of cuticle scissors in the suitcase next to the mattress. One of my hangnails was stubborn, so I tore it off with my teeth. The stinging little notch it left in my skin filled in slowly with red. The pain was like a lighthouse, sweeping away the dark.

By the time Dr. Davis answered the phone, it was too late, and all I could do was cry.

"What's the matter, Millie?"

Her voice didn't belong to any reality that made sense anymore. I had washed out of dialectical behavior therapy. I was never going to see the beige walls of her office again. So I just cried, and she sat silent on the other end of the line. Except there wasn't even a line. Not even the barest thread of physical connection linked me to anyone on this planet.

"You know I have to ask you, Millie. Are you having suicidal thoughts?"

I stopped crying, finding annoyance. "No. Never again. I've told you."

"Have you engaged in any self-harm behaviors?"

I looked down at the cuticle scissors in my hand, the wetly welling slashes of red on my bare thighs.

"You could say that."

"You know how this works," she said calmly. "Once you've engaged in a target behavior, it's too late to call me for coaching. I have to end the call now."

I started crying again, the ugly kind of crying that's like your eyes are throwing up.

"I want to go home," I said.

"Where's home, Millie?" When I didn't answer, she asked it again. "Where's home?"

I didn't have an answer. I ended the call so I wouldn't have to hear her hang up.

I woke to a rap on my door. It was still dark outside. I groped by the air mattress for my bathrobe and pulled it on. As I hefted myself clumsily up into my wheelchair, there was another knock at the door, louder. "Just a minute!" I snapped. "For God's sake, I'm a cripple."

I took the brake off the chair and wheeled my way to the door, throwing it open to find a groggy and pissed-off Teo. "Let me in," he said forcefully. I was so startled that I backed off the chair and did as he asked; he shut the door behind us. "Show me your arms," he said.

I wasn't quite awake enough to process what he was saying. He grabbed my hand and yanked it up toward him, pushing back the sleeve of my robe. There was nothing there, but now I knew where he was going with this. I twisted my fingers out of his grip and started to back the chair away again.

"Don't you try to hide," he said. "Take that off."

"*Excuse* me?"

He went for the ties of my robe, and a smoky phantom of

whiskey teased at the back of my throat. I shoved the heels of my hands hard into his chest; he grabbed my wrists. My gut liquefied with terror. Even as we struggled, some half-rational part of my brain knew that he was trying to help in his twisted idiot way. "Don't, Teo, *don't*, what are you *doing*? Get your hands off my body!"

I have never seen a man let go of anything so fast. He turned and walked away and leaned his forehead against a window. I stared at the back of his head, feeling the pulse pounding in my ears.

"I didn't mean it like that," he said.

"Yeah, well, in general, don't ever fucking *do* that to a woman. Or a man. Or a *dog*."

"I'm sorry, okay?"

I took a minute to catch my breath, slow my heart. Then I said, "If you're looking for something in particular, try using your words like a big boy." Carefully I inched my robe up to expose as little of my skinny, fuzzy, cut-up thighs as I could while still showing the damage. "How did you know?" I said.

He knelt by my chair and peered at the carnage with a clinical eye. Monty's claws could have done worse; the puckered flesh around my thigh amputation was a far more dramatic sight than anything I'd just done.

"Is this all?" he said, sitting back on his heels.

"Yeah." I was glad, at least, not to have to explain why I'd done it. Not to this guy.

"Davis called Caryl, and Caryl called me. So now you don't get to sleep either."

"I'm sorry."

He leaned forward on the arm of my wheelchair, staring

me down. "If Caryl ever calls me in the middle of the night again because of something stupid you've done, there won't be enough sorry in the world."

"I called Dr. Davis, not Caryl! It was supposed to be confidential! How does she even know Caryl's number anyway?"

"They're like, arch-nemeses. Davis calls Caryl all the time to grill her about the Project and beg her to come back to therapy. For all they both knew, you could be bleeding out in here. Caryl thought it was her fault, Millie; she was raving some crap about a fight you two had. She was *crying*."

"Bullshit."

"She's like a ten-year-old inside, and she worships you, thanks to that stupid movie."

"What movie?"

"Yours."

"*The Stone Guest*? How would you even know?"

"Because I pay attention to shit besides myself. Try it sometime. For all your little lecture about needing other people, you spend a lot of time wallowing in your own misery. You've got to find something to care about besides yourself, or you will literally die of the pain."

"Like Lisa?"

For a second he looked like I'd hit him in the chest, but he rolled right over it. "Like Lisa. Hanged herself in Residence Five. It's why I don't live there anymore. P.S. I'd moved *there* because I found my first partner, Amir, with his head in the oven in Residence One. And I'd moved *there* because my mom thought I was possessed by Satan and begged the Project to take me away."

Without even meaning to, I catapulted headfirst into one

of the distress tolerance skills Dr. Davis had taught me, namely, comparing your problems to someone else's larger ones. It pisses you off if it's forced on you, but if you do it on your own, it's like a hit of refined sanity straight to the veins.

"Teo, I'm sorry," I said. And I meant it. Not just the usual frantic Borderline apology that means *I'll lie and say I was wrong; just don't leave me.* For a moment I genuinely wanted to undo the hurt I'd done him, and any other hurts he might have collected in his lifetime. Just feeling that kind of sorry gave me a weird hope for myself. I put my hand over his where it rested on the arm of my chair.

He looked at his hand as though a bird had landed on it.

"Let me guess," I said. "Don't touch you, right? I get that a lot."

"Naw, touching's okay, I guess." He turned his hand over and closed it around mine for a minute before standing up and turning toward the door. "I draw the line at making out, though."

"Yeah, I'm way too hideous for that to be any fun."

He turned back to me, annoyed. "Look," he said, "I need you to know that it's not going to happen with us. But it's not personal, okay? And it's not your scars. Caryl said you were all freaked out that I rejected you or something."

"I am never telling *anyone* anything again."

"You don't get to have it both ways, Millie. You don't get to have people care about you but no one poke around in your business."

"Are you saying you care about me?"

"Go back to sleep, Roper," he said, heading for the door. He paused in the doorway. "Should I get Monty for you? He's very comforting."

"Not a great idea with open wounds on my lap."

"Good point." He started to leave, then stuck his head back in. "By the way, Caryl will be collecting all the sharp objects from your room later today. So if you want to slit your wrists, I suggest you do it in the next couple of hours."

Caryl did not, in fact, come to Residence Four in the morning but sent Song to do her dirty work instead. Song avoided my eyes as she took my cuticle scissors, my nail clippers, even my stupid electric razor. So much for grooming.

I was worried that when Caryl showed up she would send me back to the hospital despite the steel in my bones unless I did something to prove I was an asset. I wheeled myself down the hall to Teo's room, looking for information. He refused to give me Caryl's number—that was Against the Rules—but he gave me enough other people's contact info to get some work done.

First on my to-do list was David Berenbaum.

I was frankly shocked to hear the effusive warmth in Berenbaum's voice when I identified myself. I had to give myself a firm reminder that Hollywood people always sound like you're just the person they've been dying to see.

"Did you find something out about Johnny?" Berenbaum asked. "Things have been so nuts in post that I haven't had the chance to do any real digging. Part of me still expects it to be him every time the phone rings."

"We do know he was alive and well very recently. He arranged for Vivian Chandler to stay at Regazo de Lujo under his name. We ran into her there, but she doesn't seem to know what's going on either."

There was a long silence on the other end of the line.

"Mr. Berenbaum?"

"This is bad."

"You know what she is?" I said tentatively.

When he spoke again, it was quiet and a little muffled. "Look, can you meet with me somewhere? I can't talk about this with the post crew breathing down my neck."

"I'd love to," I said, then slapped a hand over my mouth. Could I sound any more like a fan? Hastily I tried to smooth it over. "The sooner we can get this figured out, the better. Where would you like to meet?"

"My office. It's one of the few places we can talk safely about this kind of stuff. Teo can tell you the basics about Vivian on the way."

A lie fell out of my mouth before I had time to examine it. "Ahh, no, Teo's tied up with another thing. It's just me today. But it's all right, Caryl gave me the nutshell version."

"You wouldn't rather wait for him?"

"Nah."

"Okay." He paused. "You know, that's all right, really. Maybe it's my age, but I find Teo a little hard to talk to."

"It's not your age. I'll be there in an hour."

18

Reason Mind told me I should give the shallow cuts on my thigh more time to air out before I put my AK prosthetic back on, especially since I hadn't showered the night before, but Emotion Mind didn't want David Berenbaum to see me in a wheelchair. Cleverly masquerading as Reason Mind, it argued that I wouldn't be wearing the AK for very long and that time was of the essence. I took it as an encouraging sign that the cuts didn't hurt too badly once my thigh was nestled firmly in the socket.

I put on my third-nicest outfit and some fresh deodorant and decided that would have to do. I considered telling Teo that I was going out for a while, but after last night I was afraid he'd get too nosy about it, so I just left.

I had enough cash for a cab there and back, but after that I was going to need to visit an ATM. Little details like this drove me nuts; life seemed too full of speed bumps when I just wanted to Get Things Done. This was why I made a better director than a production assistant.

The trouble with taking a taxi to the Warner lot was that because I wasn't driving through a security booth, I had to limp my way down the sidewalk to the place where people from the parking garage checked in. That normally meant extras or tourists, so when I told the freckled white guy at the turnstile that I was here to see Berenbaum, he looked at me like he was fitting me for a tinfoil hat.

"He knows I'm coming," I said, but my voice sounded uncertain even to me. "Can someone contact him?"

"Ma'am, you'll want to get a pass for your dashboard and drive through the main entrance."

"I don't have a car," I said, feeling my cheeks go hot. In L.A., that's like admitting you don't have a place to sleep.

"How did you get here?"

"Taxi."

"What's your name?"

"Millie."

"Millie what?"

"He doesn't know my last name. Millie from the Arcadia Project."

"I don't know what that is."

"Mr. Berenbaum will know, if someone can get hold of him."

"Can you stand over there a minute?"

I got out of the way of the tourists and "background talent" and stood against a hedge, feeling the sun beat down on my hair. I suppose my lack of outrage wasn't helping my case for being Someone Important, but I had too many humiliating memories associated with the Warner lot to cop an attitude.

Anyone who does background work more than twice is either a starry-eyed wannabe, an out-of-work actor slumming to keep his SAG card, or someone unemployable at any other job besides taking up space. Generally speaking, extras are an unruly mob with a variety of unpleasant attitude problems, and sometimes in desperation they try crazy stuff like, oh I don't know, claiming they have an appointment to see the most famous person on the lot.

I stood there long enough that it was beginning to seem like the guy was hoping I'd get bored and go away. Finally I approached him again. "Hi," I began, but he cut me off.

"I can't get through to Mr. Berenbaum right now," he said. "When that changes, you'll be the first to know."

"He invited me here," I said. But even as I spoke, I could feel a Borderline paradigm shift. Without a stable sense of identity—something most people have mastered by the age of four—it becomes very easy for other people to tell you who you are just by the way they treat you. As I stood there, in my own mind I was becoming what he saw: a crazy and slightly scary woman with delusions of importance.

I frantically did a mental replay of the conversation I'd had with Berenbaum earlier, trying to reinterpret. I wasn't really supposed to have his number in the first place; I shouldn't have called him. His delight in hearing from me could easily have been faked. But he had specifically said that I should come to his office. I was right and the security guy was wrong. Right?

I pulled out my phone—painfully aware of how cheap and obsolete it looked—and dialed Berenbaum's number myself. His assistant answered.

"Hi, Araceli," I said, feeling a moment's delight that my slippery brain had held on to her name. In Hollywood, knowing the assistant's name is crucial. "This is Millie with the Arcadia Project again."

"One moment please," she said politely.

I turned to give the security guard a glare, but he wasn't paying me the least attention.

After a few moments, Araceli came back on the line. "He doesn't seem to be available right now. Can I give him a message?"

I stood there, disoriented, starting to dissociate a little. Dissociative episodes are a Borderline thing that happens under maximum stress; you just kind of check out, leave yourself. My brain damage didn't help matters. In that moment if she had asked me my name, I couldn't have given it. I didn't understand what was happening, why I had taken a taxi to the Warner Bros. lot, why I was now going to have to take a taxi right back home. I chewed my bottom lip, furious at myself for losing it now of all moments.

"Do you have a message for him?" she prompted again.

"I . . ." I struggled to assemble words. "I'm outside. At security. They won't let me in. He said for me to come."

"Can you put me on with the security guard, please? Tell him Araceli wants to talk to him."

I approached the guard again and held the phone out to him. "It's Araceli," I said.

The beginnings of an *I'm in trouble* look came into his eyes and gave me a flutter of hope. He looked at the phone as though it were a rotary-dial antique, then took it from me and grunted a few monosyllables into it. Glancing at my prosthetics, he said, "Yes," in a tone of deep chagrin. Then, crisply, "I'm on it." He hung up the phone and handed it back to me.

"Well?" I said, still too shaken to be smug.

"Go on through," he said.

I was so relieved that I forgot how very far away Berenbaum's office was, and that I didn't quite remember the way there, until

I was all the way at the intersection of four enormous sound-stages. I knew the general area of the lot where his office was located, so I kept hobbling along in the right direction until I spotted another security guard, a black guy with a sprinkling of white hair. Once he spotted me approaching, he moved to meet me halfway.

"I'm supposed to meet David Berenbaum," I told him, "but I can't remember exactly where I'm going."

"Let's see if we can get you a lift," he said. He called in his location on the radio. "Got a young lady here with a cane, en route to DSB on foot."

I couldn't hear the response, but he laughed out loud and said, "I'll bet!" He put his radio back on his belt. "Just sit tight a minute," he said to me.

"I could kiss you," I said.

"That won't be necessary."

"What's your name?" I asked him. "I want to tell Mr. Berenbaum how helpful you were."

"I think he can see for himself," he said with a smile. He pointed over my shoulder, and I turned; a golf cart was approaching. Its driver had an unmistakable head of white hair. The sight of him was like daylight pouring through clouds.

"Millie!" said Berenbaum as he stopped the cart by the curb and got out. "I'm so sorry. Minor crisis in editing. Please tell me you didn't have to walk far." He took my hand and held it solemnly for a moment. His grip was firm, his hand soft in that old-man kind of way.

"It's fine," I said. "Exercise is good for me." I didn't mention the cuts under my silicone prosthetic socket, which were starting to smart a little.

He moved to help me into the cart, then stopped, suddenly boyish. "You want to drive?"

"Is it . . . I mean, do you think I can, with my . . ."

"It's just a gas pedal and a brake, nothing fancy. A kid could drive it. Go on."

He seemed so delighted by the idea, I couldn't refuse him. I limped around to the driver's side and eased my way into the seat. I hesitated, looking for somewhere to put my cane, but Berenbaum just took it and laid it across his lap as though he were always holding women's canes for them, no big deal. I grabbed the wheel, and after Berenbaum released the parking brake, I used the muscles of my right thigh and knee to push my BK prosthetic against the accelerator. The cart puttered forward.

"Straight on, then make a left at soundstage twenty. Also, feel free to go faster than this."

I pressed down harder. It felt odd without direct contact between me and the accelerator. Also I hadn't been behind the wheel of anything in over a year, and now here I was, driving David Berenbaum around in a golf cart.

"We're headed to the editing suite," he said. "We're behind schedule, so I want to stay nearby. Is that all right with you?"

"That's fine," I said. "As long as it's safe to talk freely there."

"I'll kick everyone out of the room for a few. You know, you can really floor it if you want, it's okay."

I looked dubiously down at the golf cart, which was starting to vibrate and whine like a frightened dog. "Honestly, I'm afraid this thing is going to fall apart under me."

"Don't talk about Bessie that way," said Berenbaum. "She's a good soldier. Pedal to the metal, come on."

"I—"

Without further ado, Berenbaum simply bumped my right leg with his left, knocking my prosthetic foot off the accelerator and stomping down on the pedal himself. The high-pitched shriek of alarm I made as I clung to the steering wheel made him laugh out loud. I'm sure the average grandmother could still have outrun the thing on foot, but to me it was exhilarating, steering while he accelerated, trusting him to brake in time to keep us from hitting anyone.

"Remind me to never get behind you on the freeway," he said.

Soon we came to the northeastern edge of the lot, to a larger bungalow than the one where his office was located. I guided the golf cart into a parking space; he put on the brake and helped me out of the driver's seat. He also held open the door to the building for me, and while that sort of thing would have driven me nuts a year ago, I had recently stopped resenting people for making my life easier.

The editing suite itself looked more like a living room than an office. A large flat-screen TV hung on a wall opposite a comfy-looking caramel couch, and a skinny college-aged kid sat at a computer desk with an older man leaning over his shoulder, staring at the screen. Nearby a young woman was writing on a spiral pad, looking stressed out and sleep deprived. Three of the four walls were decorated with framed movie posters and photographs of people shaking hands; the fourth was almost entirely covered in stills from *Black Powder*.

"Can we have the room for a few?" said Berenbaum to the other three. They were gone almost before he finished his sentence, and Berenbaum looked back at me, gesturing to the couch.

I sat at one end, he sat at the other, and he glanced to make sure the door was shut before letting out a long exhale and turning to the subject at hand. All his boyish good humor vanished.

"Vivian Chandler is probably planning to kill you," he said. "In fact, I'm worried that she may have killed you already."

19

"What do you mean, she might have killed me already?" I couldn't decide whether to laugh or have a panic attack.

"Did she ever touch you, even briefly?"

"No. Caryl warned me about that the minute we went into her room."

"Oh, Caryl was with you?" He gave a deep sigh. "Thank God. If Vivian had cursed you, Caryl would have known right away and would probably have executed her on the spot. Vivian's on thin ice with the Project as it is."

"Why would she want to curse me?"

"Why do cats chase birds? If someone is no use to her, it's just . . . a thing she does."

"And she's never been caught?"

"There's never anything to investigate. She shakes a guy's hand and a week later his aorta ruptures, or he has a stroke, or something else perfectly plausible. It's her specialty. Did you know Martin?"

"Who?"

"The guy who used to be in charge over at the Project. He was a real sweetheart. Drowned in his own blood because he was dumb enough to grab Vivian's arm one day to keep her from tripping over a split in the sidewalk."

"My God."

"Generally she tries not to curse people who are obvious obstacles; she's too smart for that."

"Do you ever worry she'll do something to you?"

"The studio would tank without me, and she knows it."

I figured it might be rude to ask him how Warner Bros. had managed to make *The Jazz Singer* and *Casablanca* without him, so instead I asked, "Why would Vivian care?"

"Hell if I know. But she does, enough to give me her word. Someone like you, though? Teo? Perfectly safe to do whatever she likes with."

"Actually, I'm not sure she *could* kill me that way," I realized aloud. "Because of the nails and screws and stuff holding me together, I cancel out fey magic when I touch it."

"Seriously?" Berenbaum looked floored. "Millie. This could help us. A lot." He got up from the couch and began to pace; I could almost hear his mental gears turning.

"Why do you think the viscount gave *her* a free spa room, of all people?" I asked him.

"Those two are definitely not friendly," Berenbaum said. "He knows exactly what she is, better than any human would."

"Maybe that was the point," I said, trying to use my storyteller's brain to unravel cause and effect. "He was obviously trying to lead someone astray, someone unfriendly who would be looking for him pretty hard. So why *wouldn't* he set the equivalent of a bear trap in the room?"

Berenbaum turned to me abruptly, his eyes sparkling. "You clever girl!" he said in surprise.

I felt my cheeks warm. "Uh, thanks?"

"That makes total sense," he said. "Let's run with it." Then just as quickly, he looked stricken again. "You don't think he set that trap for the two of *you*, surely. He and I have been huge supporters of the Arcadia Project from way back. We owe you guys everything."

"I know how much you've given to the Project," I said. "That's why this is a huge priority for us. Who *would* Johnny want to set a trap for? And," I continued on a sudden inspiration, "who would he do something so bad to that the cops might get involved?"

Berenbaum began to pace again. I would have liked to do the same; that kind of casual, spontaneous movement was something I missed, a lot.

"I can't imagine," he said. "Johnny keeps a low profile, so he doesn't have any enemies."

"Do you?"

A light seemed to go on over his head; he snapped his fingers and pointed at me. "Susman," he said.

"What?"

"Aaron Susman."

"The Aaron Susman who's produced everything of yours since *Red Cotton*? He's your enemy now?"

Berenbaum gave a mirthless laugh. "Well, he's livid about the studio, of course, but I didn't think he'd go this far."

"What about the studio?"

Berenbaum hesitated, then flexed his hands and grimaced. "Look. If you want the facts, you might be better off hearing his side. I don't want him yelling to the tabloids that I've slandered him. *Again*."

"Well, I'd be happy to talk to him."

"I don't mind giving you his number, but be careful. He doesn't know about fey or the Project. Think you can manage that minefield?"

"I'm sure of it."

Berenbaum moved to the computer desk and scribbled on a sticky note, then handed it to me.

I felt a private satisfaction at having ferreted out a new lead on my own (not to mention scored the phone number of a major movie producer), but I wasn't about to let it rest there. "Have you been in touch with Inaya yet?"

"I haven't; I'm sorry."

"Has Vivian said anything to you that might give you the slightest clue what Johnny's up to?"

Berenbaum shook his head slowly, looking thoughtful. "He has to be staying *somewhere*, though. I wish I had time to call around."

"I'm not sure anyone has time to call every hotel in Southern California." I thought for a moment. "You and Johnny are close, right? Do you share any bank accounts or anything?"

Berenbaum did his little snap-and-point gesture again. "At home, I have all his passwords written somewhere. Online banking, credit cards, everything. Linda will know where. Can I call you later tonight?"

"Sure."

"It might be really late."

"Anytime, I mean it. Three a.m., that's fine." Assuming I wasn't fired by then.

I gave him my new number, and I felt absurdly gleeful as he programmed it into his phone.

"Hey," he said as he punched it in, "what do you think about keeping all this just between us for a while?"

"You mean the investigation?"

"Just until we know more. Vivian and your boss have history I'm not privy to, and it makes me uneasy. Not sure what I'm walking into there."

As much as I loved the idea of having a secret with David Berenbaum, I had good reason to be suspicious of the words "Just Between Us." Professor Scott had used them, a lot.

I gave him an apologetic grimace. "I have to tell Teo and Caryl about anything I work on. Especially since I'm sort of on a trial period right now."

"Of course," Berenbaum said immediately, looking abashed. "I keep forgetting you're a newbie. I'll trust you to know who to trust. Let's talk tonight, all right? And we'll see what we can patch together from his transactions."

I carefully rose from the couch, ignoring the disturbing crescendo of pain in the skin of my left thigh, and held my hand out for him to shake. He reached for my shoulders, catching me off guard. Just as I was about to freak out, he turned me toward the wall, so that I was facing the collection of *Black Powder* stills.

"Speaking of confidential information," he said, "what do you think?"

I looked at the images. *Black Powder* appeared to be a Western with a tight color palette and a lot of wide shots. A quick scan showed me four instances of the exact same composition in different settings. Was it a motif, or had he simply not noticed the redundancy? It bothered me that I wasn't sure. Was I not as sharp as I'd been before my injuries, or was he the one who was losing his touch?

I knew I should be impressing him with my knowledge of cinematography. If I wanted to hitch a ride on his coattails, he had just given me a gold-embossed invitation. But something about the idea felt tasteless. We'd managed to connect on some level without me mentioning my aspirations, and I didn't want to trade that in for something every other director wannabe in the city would be trying.

"Looks great!" I said, and left it at that.

As he walked me back to the golf cart, I saw him eyeing my prosthetics, which he'd never done before.

"What?" I said.

"You're walking funny today," he said. "Something hurt?"

"Oh, I uh . . . just a skin irritation."

"Is there something you need to do for it?"

I hesitated, but he seemed genuinely curious. "If it's bad," I said, "I have to use the wheelchair for a bit, air it out. So in other words, I'm going to ignore it."

"Hey," he said firmly. "I'd rather have you on wheels than getting gangrene or something."

"Jesus," I said with a laugh, "your imagination is worse than mine." I approached the cart and turned back to him with a grin. "Who's driving?"

During the cab ride home I tried to get through to Aaron Susman by giving my name and saying it was personal, but all that got me was voice mail, so I hung up and decided to call back when I had a better idea. After paying the driver, I had exactly fourteen dollars and eighteen cents left in cash.

A couple of blocks from Residence Four was a small cluster of shops providing such urgent necessities as brow waxing, ice cream, and dry cleaning. It also boasted a staggeringly surcharged ATM, so after pausing to open the windows, close the shades, and otherwise try to make my room less like a sauna, I changed into some baggy knit shorts and took off my AK prosthetic to see if my wounds were going to allow me to walk.

I didn't like what I saw. The cuts were shallow, but the deepest of the bunch had gone red and puffy around the edges. I had been trained too well in the signs of a nascent infection, and the sight of it made me flash back to that first hospital: chills, fever, misery. It had taken three tries to find an antibiotic that my infection wasn't resistant to, and at one point I had been sure that I was just going to finally get my wish and die.

Now, dying was not on the menu. I grabbed supplies and some crutches so I could make my one-legged way down the hall to the bathroom. I washed the cuts carefully, applied Neosporin, covered the area lightly with gauze, and then headed toward Teo's room for help getting my wheelchair down the stairs.

His door was shut and locked, and no one answered my knock, so I got to experience the fun of descending stairs on crutches without any feeling in my prosthetic right foot to tell me where the edges of the steps were. Falling off another roof would have been less scary. Halfway down, I noticed the man I'd seen restraining Gloria Wednesday afternoon. He was sitting on the couch, petting Monty and reading a battered paperback, utterly unmoved by my plight.

When I got to the bottom of the stairs, I noticed the smell of curry and heard some muffled cursing from the kitchen. Not a good time to ask Teo for help. But I couldn't get the wheelchair on my own, and I wasn't comfortable rolling around by myself in South L.A. looking vulnerable anyway.

I looked back at the man on the sofa. He was dressed in a faded, mustard-yellow T-shirt and threadbare jeans. I felt intimidated, then guilty about being intimidated, torn between the white liberal fantasy of color-blindness and the stereotypes I'd been fed my whole sheltered life. *For God's sake, Millie. He's reading a book and petting a cat. How much less scary can a person be?*

"Hi," I said. "Do you think you could help me get my wheelchair down the stairs?"

He lowered the book and fixed me with a flat look. "What did you take it up the stairs for?"

I found myself momentarily floored by the question. "Well—that's where my room is," I said lamely. "But I need to go to that ATM over by the ice cream place, and one of my legs is too messed up for a prosthetic today."

He sighed, set aside the book, and headed for the stairs with an air of resignation. I wasn't sure of his age, but there was a world-weary quality to his annoyance. Monty moved to sit in the warm spot he'd left, and I tilted my head to read the title of the discarded book: *Which Lie Did I Tell?* by William Goldman.

Aspiring screenwriter, then. Now there was a stereotype I was comfortable with. They say in L.A. you can ask anyone on the street, "What's your screenplay about?" and get a polished sales pitch.

I called up the stairs after him. "I'm in the room that used to be—"

"I know where you are," he called back. In a few minutes he came back down carrying the chair and even helped me unfold it.

"I don't suppose you'd walk with me to the ATM," I said.

"In case you run into some black people?"

My mouth went dry. "No."

He looked me over, one brow lifting. "Nobody's gonna bother you. Dressed like that, with that castoff-looking wheel-chair, all you're missing is a cardboard sign."

"I might look a little less like a bag lady when they see me taking fistfuls of twenties out of the ATM. Will you please come with me? I'm Millie."

"Tjuan," he said, pronouncing it like the last half of Antoine. "I'll go if you get me some ice cream."

"Uh, okay."

"I'm just fucking with you. I'll go."

"Okay then."

Although his long legs could have eaten up the distance between the house and the shopping center in about two bites, he kept pace with me as I wheeled myself along. The silence started to get to me; I remembered I wasn't supposed to ask him anything about himself, which meant he couldn't ask me any of the usual small talk stuff either.

"So!" I volunteered. "This is my third day. So far everyone seems pretty nice. But I get the feeling Gloria doesn't like me very much."

"You are not wrong."

I didn't know what to say to that, not without asking a question, so I floundered for a bit. When we got to the inter-section across from the shopping center, he hit the button and we waited for the light.

"You were reading a book on screenwriting," I said. I figured a declarative statement was within the letter of the law.

"Yeah."

"I'm a director. I've done a few features. One of them, *The Stone Guest*, was screened at the Seattle Film Festival. It's about a retired porn star who abandoned her daughter as a baby, and then the girl shows up—"

"I know. I've seen it."

Christ. Had they had a special screening or what?

I shifted my weight. Somewhere in the distance, a car horn blared out the opening notes of "La Cucaracha."

"I'm curious about you," I said, "but I'm not supposed to ask anything."

"That's right." I waited for more, but he just turned in a slow, casual circle, as though taking in the scenery.

"If you're wondering about my legs, I fell off a seven-story building. They say a tree partly broke my fall and I dropped from it feetfirst. I guess I hit at just the right angle for my legs to act as a crumple zone and save the rest of me."

He didn't say anything. The light changed, and I shoved the chair across the street as fast as I could while a column of drivers glared at me, waiting to turn left. When we got to the parking lot of the shopping center, Tjuan scanned the area, that same slow circle, and something in his wary expression paradoxically made me feel safe.

"Did you really want ice cream?" I said as I wheeled over to the ATM. "I'll get you some if you want."

"Nah."

I glanced at him before entering my PIN, but he had his back to me. There was a tension in his stance that I couldn't interpret until I'd taken a couple hundred out of the machine, stuffed the bills into my shorts pocket, and wheeled back close enough to hear him murmur under his breath.

"Look right at me," he said. "Just keep looking at me and keep smiling when I say this."

My gut knotted up. "When you say what?"

"Somebody followed us."

20

I had never been further from a smile in my life, but I managed to locate one after an exhaustive search. "Who is it?" I said under my breath.

"Young white guy, late twenties, maybe thirty. He was standing around on the sidewalk near the house and followed us across the street. He's coming right over here now, so go ahead and look."

I turned, feeling cold all over, but when I spotted the guy he was talking about, my fear turned into something more like vertigo. It was the same goateed guy I'd seen at the resort, in the bar at Regazo de Lujo.

"What the hell," I said, loud enough for the approaching man to hear.

He stopped a respectful conversational distance away and hooked his thumbs into the pockets of his jeans. He was dressed in a short-sleeved blue button-down, open over a gray T-shirt. I caught a hint of aftershave, something woody and macho.

"Hi," he said. "We keep running into each other."

"Maybe because you're following me."

He showed us a badge: LAPD. "Do you mind if I ask you a couple questions?"

Hello, paradigm shift.

"You do not have to talk to him," Tjuan said.

"Actually," I said slowly, "I suspect we're looking for the same person."

The cop squinted at me as though my wheelchair were parked in front of the sun. "Would you be looking for an actor by the name of John Riven?"

"That's right. What's he done to get the law after him?"

"I can't go into the details," he said. "How well do you know him?"

"We've never met."

"May I ask why you've been looking for him?"

"A friend of mine is concerned about him."

He frowned. "Is your friend David Berenbaum?"

"Why?"

"Because I think Berenbaum knows where he is."

"I think you're wrong about that, but I don't have much information to give you except that Johnny's not at Regazo de Lujo. That much you know."

"It's very important I find him," the cop said firmly.

"I need more than that," I said.

He seemed to think for a moment, then said flatly, "A young woman has disappeared, and there's evidence he may have abducted her."

He couldn't have surprised me more if he had clubbed me over the head.

"Who is it that's missing?"

"I can't go into that."

I searched the officer's eyes. They were dark as motor oil, old in his boyish face. He seemed earnest, but there was something else there too: anger. Not my brand of fast-rising flame that exhausts itself within the hour, but something that burned slow and cool. I suddenly really wanted him to be on my side.

"You want me to contact you if I hear anything?"

"That would be great," he said. He pulled out a business card and handed it to Tjuan, who was closer. Tjuan handed the card immediately to me as though it had peed on him.

I glanced at the card—it simply said BRIAN CLAY and gave a number—then tucked it into the pocket of my shorts. When I looked up again, Clay was giving me that *where do I know you from* look. Now that I knew he was a cop, I could narrow it down. I didn't exactly have a rap sheet.

"I remember you," I said. "At least I think I do. I'm Millicent Roper."

He shook his head slowly, searching my face.

"The film student who tried to kill herself by jumping off a building at UCLA last year. Big news for a couple of minutes."

His expression went tight and blank like I'd sucker punched him. "Oh," he said.

"Did I . . . ?" I trailed off, ready with a stab of guilt without needing to know quite why. "What is it? Is there something I don't remember?"

He looked as out of sorts as I felt; I almost felt sorry for him. He combed a hand back through his hair, then mussed it again. "Are you all right now?" he said.

I looked down at my wheelchair.

He flinched a little. "I mean besides—I'm sorry, that was—"

"No, I know what you meant. I'm fine. It's okay. I think some cops spoke to me early on, in the hospital, when I first woke up. You were one of them?"

He shifted his weight, shook his head. "I was the guy who showed up too late to save you."

You think you've given yourself forty lashes for everyone you hurt, and then you realize you'll never know the numbers.

"I'm so sorry," I said. The improbability of it all hadn't hit me yet; I was too busy looking into those too-old eyes and realizing I was just one more reason for the shadows in them.

"It's okay," he said. "A lot worse has happened to me since."

"That's supposed to make me feel better?"

"Does it?"

"Kind of."

To my surprise he laughed, a weird short burst like a dog lunging for an open door. "Well . . . Well, good," he drawled. He jammed his hands in his pockets and nodded to me, and to Tjuan, who had apparently turned his back on the two of us some time ago. "Give me a call if you find out anything," said Officer Clay, and then he took off down the sidewalk like it was pouring rain.

As soon as Clay was out of earshot, Tjuan spoke in a dire tone. "Never let a cop *near* a fey," he said.

"What?" I said distractedly, still staring after Clay.

"Put steel handcuffs on a fey, you've got a problem. Give one a nosebleed and you've got an even worse problem."

That blood thing again. But I was barely listening, because it had just hit me. I turned to Tjuan and gaped at him.

"What are the odds?" I said. "I mean, what are the fucking odds? *That* cop and me, both after Rivenholt?"

Tjuan stared off where the man had disappeared around the corner of the ice cream shop, slowly shaking his head. "Odds have got nothing to do with it," he said.

"What do you mean?"

"Do this job long enough, you stop believing in coincidence. Somebody's always pulling the strings."

It was close to two a.m. when Berenbaum finally called. I'd figured I'd be tossing and turning all night waiting, but somehow the phone caught me in the deepest part of my sleep cycle and by the time I woke up I had already been talking to him for a second or two. The first thing I was completely aware of was his laughter.

"Are you high?" he said.

"I was asleep," I said. "What did I say?"

"Something about handcuffs. I'm not sure I want to know."

"I'm awake now," I said. "Let me get to the computer and call you right back."

At dinner, Teo had been impressed enough with my progress to give me permission to use his computer during the night. So I threw on my robe over the tank top and shorts I'd been sleeping in, wheeled my way down the hall, and knocked on Teo's door. He answered drowsy and shirtless—ye gods— before turning without a word, climbing back up the ladder to his loft bed, and flopping back onto the mattress.

"There's no way you're sleeping through this," I said. "I'm going to be talking the whole time."

"I'm not sleeping anyway," Teo grunted.

With a sigh, I wheeled myself over to the desk underneath

him, shoving his chair out of the way and opening up a web browser before dialing the phone.

"You ready to do a little snooping?" I said to Berenbaum when he answered.

"I've got his usernames and passwords and secret questions and all that. For a checking account and two different credit cards."

"How does a fairy get a credit card?"

"Most of them don't, but Johnny's got a whole fake identity set up, complete with job history and credit rating."

"Why?"

"Even before all this went down, he was pretty sure he was going to retire here. He's spent too much time on this side. Are you at the computer?"

"What am I looking for?"

"Go to the B of A site and put in the username Rivenholt."

"So what happens to you if he starts, uh, fading?"

"You've seen my last couple of films, right?"

I decided not to answer that one. "If he spends more time in Arcadia, would it cure him?"

"Would take a long, long time. I'm sixty-seven years old, Millie. Maybe I'll be around twenty years, maybe twenty minutes. Whatever time I have left, I'd like to have Johnny around."

"We'll find him," I said. But as I entered Rivenholt's info into the sign-in screens, I felt a twinge of guilt over the cop and the missing girl.

I wasn't sure how much I should share with Berenbaum. Caryl, Berenbaum, and now this cop were all looking for the same man for different reasons. I honestly wasn't sure I trusted any of them. My loyalty should have been to Caryl, but she had been the least forthcoming of all. She admitted she was damaged, she didn't trust me with her phone number, and I'd seen wood rot when she looked at it funny.

"Here we go," I said, looking at Rivenholt's transaction record. I blinked at a charge from Amtrak. "Looks like someone skipped town."

"I see that." Berenbaum's voice on the other end of the line was quiet; I'd have given anything to know what he was thinking.

"I wish it said where he was going," I said.

"For that, check out credit card number two," said Berenbaum. "Place d'Armes, that's a hotel in New Orleans. Big fey hot spot. We stayed there when we were shooting *Red Cotton*."

"Why would he take a train? That'll take days. Plus, Union Station is creepy."

"It's his facade. Works like one of those ankle bracelets. If he goes outside the perimeter, some kind of alarm goes off and he becomes trackable. But Caryl says train tracks act like a signal scrambler or whatever; something about parallel lines of iron between him and the earth. Anyway, the good news is that an airplane could easily get there before he does."

"Imagine his surprise when the Project greets him at the New Orleans station and offers to take his bags." I was already on the Amtrak site, clicking and searching. "Wait, wait, hold up a second," I said.

"What is it?"

"Would he be trackable on a bus?"

"If he was outside the perimeter, yeah."

"There are only three times a week he can take a train straight to New Orleans," I said. "Soonest one after his ticket purchase is three o'clock tomorrow. We can still catch him!"

There was a short silence on the end of the line. "Millie," he said quietly, "I don't think you ought to be working for the Arcadia Project."

I blinked in the darkness. "Why not?"

"Because you ought to be working for me."

21

My face flamed so hot I was afraid I would fry the circuits of my phone. It was a joke, right? I bit my tongue.

"You want to direct, right?" he said.

"What makes you think that?"

"Millie. I'm a UCLA alum, and I'm on the selection committee for the Seattle festival. When these words pop up in the news, I look at the pictures."

"That was more than a year ago."

"I'm good with faces, and yours rang a bell, so I did a little research."

"I feel like an idiot."

"You are an idiot. You've got more rage than brains, and it showed in *The Stone Guest*."

Was there anyone alive who hadn't seen my stupid film?

"If you ever learn to leash that, you could be good. Maybe great if you track down your Echo, and I know somebody who could help with that."

I dug my thumbnail into the edge of Teo's desk. "I don't know what to say."

"Just say you haven't given up. If you can make sure nothing bad happens to my Johnny, I will owe you one. A really big one."

I wanted to be more exhilarated. But all I could hear was the condition he'd placed on the offer and recognize it for what it was. Payment for a favor, not a validation of my talent.

Then again, this was Hollywood. When a door opens, you don't make a fuss over who's holding it and why. On the other hand, after everything that had happened, wouldn't I be better off keeping a low profile?

"Thank you, Mr. Berenbaum," I said. "You have no idea what this means to me." How could he? I wasn't sure myself.

Teo pounded on my door at eight a.m., sounding like he'd already had nine cups of coffee. "It's omelet day!" he yelled through the door. "What do you want on yours?"

"Um."

"Make up your mind and get your ass downstairs! No one sleeps in on Saturdays!" And then he was gone.

He wasn't kidding. When I finally pulled on my BK, some shorts, and a tank top and carefully made my way downstairs on crutches, I saw that the dining room and kitchen were alive with cheerful chaos. Everyone else was already there, half-dressed, drinking juice and coffee and mingling like actors at a producers' party.

I managed to awkwardly hobble my way between Tjuan and the doorway into the kitchen, where a bewildering array of possible omelet ingredients were on display on the kitchen island. Teo was already hard at work at the stove; the bearded man whose name I always forgot hovered just behind him like a nervous father waiting to cut the cord. I smiled a little as I watched Teo intent on his work.

"So," Gloria's voice rose above the din, "Tjuan opens up Lilydrop's jacket, and I give you my word, no less than a dozen oranges come falling out onto the floor. We had to give her a three-year ban; I feel so bad for poor Jenny. I told her this might be a good time to get pregnant." Amid the scattered laughter that followed, Gloria noticed me and gave me a cheery wave. "Have y'all met Minnie yet? This is the new gal, everyone."

I didn't bother correcting her about my name; I hadn't given up hope that I could get on her good side. My house-mates greeted me with varying degrees of enthusiasm, except for Teo and a petite greasy-haired brunette I didn't know. Teo was occupied with his latest creation, and the young woman seemed wrapped up in her own little world.

"Have you met everyone?" Gloria asked me.

"Not officially," I said. "It's okay, though, if—"

"I know you've met my partner, Tjuan; and my boyfriend, Phil; and Song, who's out in the dining room with Miss Caryl."

"Caryl is here? I didn't—"

"Song keeps things running like clockwork, and her baby boy is something special. Over there, that's Phil's partner, Stevie—don't be rude now, Stevie!—and you know Teo, of course."

"Thanks. It's nice meeting everyone. Would you excuse me a second?" I tried to do a one-eighty in the crowded kitchen, and ended up planting one of my crutches on Tjuan's foot. The look he gave me was frosty.

In the dining room, I didn't spot Caryl right away. It must have been a subtler version of her car-hiding magic, because when I specifically focused on finding her, there she was next to Song, working her way through a plain omelet that had been cut into dozens of tiny pieces. Her gloves were lying next to her on the table. Curiously, I looked at her hands but didn't spot anything odd. I'd been half hoping for acid scars or something.

"Hey, Caryl," I said, working my way over to her side of the table. "Where've you been?"

"Arcadia," she said, without lifting her eyes from her omelet.

"What for?"

"Replenishing my magic."

I wished I hadn't left my fey glasses in my room; I couldn't gauge her mood without seeing Elliott. Song looked between the two of us and immediately took her plate to the kitchen, baby snoozing on her back in a sling.

"I'm sorry about the other night," I said.

"You're not in any trouble," she said, finally meeting my eyes. "I am aware that you must be feeling especially vulnerable in a new situation, which is likely to exacerbate your symptoms. I have asked Song and Teo to make themselves available for anything you might need, and I take full responsibility for the lack of support you have received during your first few days. I've been trying to track down the source of an anomaly in the perimeter ward, and I assumed that this Rivenholt situation would be a simple introduction for you. Obviously I misjudged the situation on a number of levels, and you have my sincerest apologies."

"Wow," I said, when Caryl had stopped. "You're really upset, aren't you?"

For a moment her eyes wandered. "So it would appear," she said, apparently watching Elliott.

"Is there anything I can do?"

"Nothing comes to mind, but I could probably draw up a

list of things I would like for you *not* to do, at least until I can resolve some of the other issues that are currently on my plate."

"Gotcha," I said. "I'll try not to be an extra slice of crazy. You'll be happy to know, with Berenbaum's help I got some great new info on the viscount's movements. He's got a ticket for a train to New Orleans that leaves this afternoon. I thought maybe Teo and I could go intercept him at the station."

"New Orleans?" Caryl tapped a finger against her lips. Lack of sun exposure made her hands childishly smooth. "That's where our national headquarters is located. I wonder if that is significant, or if it was just his way of trying to get from one perimeter to another without triggering the alarm. You see, train tracks—"

"Berenbaum told me."

"Good. Either way, I'm afraid that leaving his Gate city without authorization is a very serious offense."

"How many cities is the Project in?"

"Worldwide, I couldn't begin to count. Here we have at least one office in every state, but Gates exist in only three US cities."

"Here, New Orleans, and . . . ?"

"New York. Each traveler is assigned to a specific Gate, and fey are not allowed to leave the respective perimeter without an escort. On top of everything else Rivenholt has put us through, this attempt to flee may be enough to earn him permanent expulsion."

I felt a pang for Berenbaum at the thought. "He may be running from the cops," I said. "A plainclothes detective staked out the Residence and followed me across the street, asking me about 'John Riven' and some missing girl."

Caryl made a severe shooing motion at what I could only

assume was an overexcited Elliott. "Law enforcement knows to associate this address with him? That is bad."

"I saw the same cop in Santa Barbara, too."

"Most likely Vivian set him on the scent to make our lives more difficult."

"Berenbaum thinks Vivian was a trap Rivenholt set for the cop, or possibly for Aaron Susman. Best theory I have right now is that Rivenholt got involved in a feud between Susman and Berenbaum and did something that's gotten him into deep trouble. Does Susman have a daughter, or a young girlfriend?"

"Not that I know of."

"I've tried calling him a couple of times, but I can't get through, and Berenbaum was vague about what they were fighting about."

"Aaron Susman?" came a cheery voice from the direction of the kitchen. Apparently Gloria had decided to eavesdrop. "You don't know why he's mad at Berenbaum? I thought you were involved in the industry."

"I was in film school a year ago," I said, turning to her with as pleasant an expression as I could manage. "But I'm not caught up on the latest. What do you know?"

"Oh, honey," said Gloria. "I thought *everybody* knew. Berenbaum's giving Warner Bros. the old heave-ho and starting his own studio."

I gaped at her. "After working with Warner for thirty-odd years, and pushing seventy now, he's starting a new *studio*?"

"Sure is. He and his partners started construction on the main office complex a couple of weeks ago, down where they bought all those soundstages in Manhattan Beach."

Caryl's brow furrowed. "But this must have been in the works for months, if not years."

"They were trying to keep it under wraps till *Black Powder* was in the can, since that's one of Susman's, but apparently word leaked out sometime last month." She put a hand to her mouth in an exaggerated *oops!*

"I still don't understand," said Caryl. "I assume Susman was left out of the project, but why? Whom did Berenbaum choose?"

Gloria looked at Caryl with bald astonishment. "Do you two girls honestly mean to tell me you hadn't heard? Minnie I can understand, bless her heart, but Miss Caryl, as much as you dog Vivian Chandler's every move, I thought sure *you* would know."

"*Vivian?*" I blurted. "The damn vampire we've been talking about for two days is his *business partner*?"

"Uh-huh. Her and Inaya West."

22

Breakfast was officially the last thing on my mind now, but in the interest of improving my relations with my partner, I waited patiently for my turn. As I headed toward the dining room with my omelet, I heard Tjuan in mid-conversation with an agitated Phil.

"Your name's not on it?" Phil said. "You rewrote the damn thing from scratch!"

"That's how it works," said Tjuan, feeding a scrap of bacon to Monty, who was perched nearby on the table. "I get the money, they get the credit."

Phil snorted. "I wouldn't ghostwrite *one note* of a song; I don't care how much they offered."

"I don't want the damn credit. My name does a script more harm than good anymore."

I must have been gaping at Tjuan like a fish as I sat down; I left an empty chair between us for the sake of politeness. "You're a for-real screenwriter?" I said.

"Nope." He slammed shut like a vault. Monty's ear flicked backward, and he jumped down off the table, bacon notwithstanding.

"Sure you are!" said Phil. "Just because you don't get any—"

"We're done talking now," said Tjuan, and Phil sighed. I took the hint and gulped down the rest of my omelet in silence.

Was that why Tjuan was so hostile to me? Did he see me as competition? If so, he'd be thrilled to hear that Caryl's grand plans for my career involved me fetching lattes and picking up dry cleaning. When I was finished eating, I went to pay Teo my compliments before excusing myself to call my more tempting career option.

"Berenbaum," he answered, packing about as much stress as a man could cram into three syllables. I felt a stab of guilt but powered past it.

"It's Millie," I said.

"I know, kiddo, I've got caller ID. What's up?" Short, clipped. I knew not to take it personally; Dr. Davis and I had worked on this. *What is the goal of this interaction?* My goal was to get information, not to stroke my ego.

"I found out what you and Susman were arguing about."

He didn't respond right away. I hated not knowing if it was distraction, guilt, annoyance, confusion, or something else entirely.

"And?" he finally said.

"I just wondered why you didn't bring it up before."

"Didn't I?" He sounded so confused it was contagious. Had he?

"I'm pretty sure you didn't."

"I don't know what to tell you. Are you still planning to go to the train station today?"

The change of subject set off alarm bells. "Absolutely. But don't you find it odd that one of your business partners was leaving Johnny insistent voice mails and the other one was invited to his resort room?"

"You're saying you think this has to do with the studio?"

"That didn't occur to you when Teo brought up Inaya the first day?"

"He said she was having drama with Johnny. Johnny's not a partner in the studio, so why would she call him about it instead of, I don't know, *me*?"

"A good question."

"Ask her if you want, so long as you don't mention fairies, but I'm serious about staying off Vivian's radar."

"If she's so dangerous, why are you even working with her?"

"She promised not to cause me harm."

"And you believe her?"

"Fey," he reminded me.

"Right, fey can't lie. Sorry, I'm used to doubting everything people say."

"With fey you only have to doubt what you see. Look, sorry I can't be any more help, but I'm putting out fires right and left today."

A rule I had made for myself when trying to bluff my way through Hollywood was always to be the first to start wrapping up a conversation. I seemed to be repeatedly failing at this with Berenbaum, and it irked me.

You deserve an answer. Stand up for yourself.

"Mr. Berenbaum—"

"David."

"David, just tell me straight up. Why didn't you mention that this might have to do with the studio? You've had a dozen opportunities, and the fact that it never came up is really bothering me."

Another brief silence. I was starting to hate the phone.

"Millie, I honestly don't know what to tell you. I could swear I brought it up when we were talking about Susman. I'm just so scattered right now. I'm obsessed with getting this film out and—to be honest—not knowing anymore if it's going to save or tank my career. My head is not in a good place for this."

"I'm sorry," I said, "but if you want to see Johnny again, you might need to shift your focus a little."

"Duly scolded. I'll call you tomorrow, early, while my head's still clear. Promise."

After hanging up I felt a rush of anxiety. Had he blown me off? Was this flash powder? Even if not, the conversation hadn't gone well. I knew he was already over it, but I couldn't stop tormenting myself with the idea that his last thought of me was that I'd interrupted his already stressful workday with an accusation.

I had to resist the urge to think of something brilliant to say and call him right back. Only Dr. Davis's voice, almost a part of my own consciousness by now, kept me from behaving like an idiot.

Push it away. He already has.

Caryl was sitting on her favorite couch in the living room, so I took myself and my crutches over to her.

"Whatever is going on," I said, "I'm ninety percent sure it's about the new studio. At least this gives us something to research. Berenbaum doesn't want me talking to Vivian—"

"Neither do I."

"—so I thought I would try Inaya West."

"Just be certain that you do not—"

"—mention fairies or magic. I know, I know."

My crutches were starting to bruise my armpits, so I decided to have a seat in my wheelchair, which now had a permanent parking spot in the living room. I idly turned myself in circles with my free hand while I waited for Inaya's voice mail. Her outgoing message was an automated one that just spit back the number I'd dialed, so I couldn't be certain I had the number right.

"My name's Millie," I said to her machine, keeping my tone warm and friendly. "I understand you've been trying to track down John Riven. I think you and I should talk." I gave my number and left it at that. The simpler the better when dealing with people who are, as Teo would have put it, way above your pay grade.

As I relaxed in my chair to plan my next move, Gloria's boyfriend, whose name I'd forgotten *again*, wandered in and sat down at the grand piano. After a moment's hesitation, he started into a somber Rachmaninoff prelude.

As I listened I found my mind wandering back to the LAPD officer, feeling retroactively puzzled by the way he'd looked at me. Not because there was anything all that special about it, but because there *wasn't*.

As wrong as it is, people in wheelchairs don't get treated normally by strangers. People see the chair first and wrestle with their discomfort, then their guilt over their discomfort. Sometimes they cover for it with extra-friendly smiles; sometimes they look sympathetic; mostly they just avert their eyes for fear of being rude. Brian Clay hadn't done any of those things, and it made me wonder why. Did he have a disabled friend or family member? Or was it just seen-it-all syndrome from years at a tough job?

I got back on my crutches and carefully levered myself up

the stairs to my room, my phone tucked into my pocket. There was no point in holding my breath waiting for a celebrity to return my call, and I wanted to do something useful between now and the train station, so I found Clay's card, and I gave him a ring.

"Yeah?" he answered more quickly than I'd expected.

"It's Millie. Millie Roper, the girl you were following."

"Do you have something for me?"

"I might," I said. "Do you think we could meet somewhere? Coffee or something?"

There was a long pause, and I started to feel stupid, but then he said, "Where?"

I picked the closest coffee shop to the Residence to save on cab fare, and he said he'd meet me there.

Before leaving, I invaded Teo's room to use the computer. I double-checked the time and departure track of Rivenholt's train, then sent an e-mail to Berenbaum with the details in case he wanted to show up and catch me being heroic. I printed a copy for myself and stuck it in my backpack along with some cash, my ID, ChapStick, a roll of Certs: the usual sort of things you take with you when you are going to meet an attractive police officer.

The coffee shop was a corporate clone, utterly lacking in personality, and Clay was an odd match for it. He sat at a table against the wall, and as I hobbled over on my crutches, I was struck once again by the long, coarse lines of his face. He evaded handsomeness by a narrow margin, and his macho blue-collar vibe was heavily mitigated both by his goatee and by the metric ton of sugar he was dumping into his caffè mocha.

"Careful," I greeted him. "I think there might still be some coffee in there."

"Millie. Sit."

"I hope you haven't been waiting for me too long."

"All my life," he said, about as suave as a sack of bricks. I burst into startled snorts of laughter. "Sorry," he said immediately, one corner of his mouth turning up. "I watch too much TV."

I sat down, plopping my backpack onto the table and leaning it against the window. "I'll try not to keep you from work too long," I said, trying to hide the massive rush I felt at being flirted with. By a *cop*. What the hell?

"This could be work," he said with a shrug. "You have information?"

"Yeah, but I don't know if I should give it to you. This whole situation is just beyond weird. Is there anything you can share with me about the abduction you mentioned? When it happened? Johnny's relationship to the girl? Anything?"

"No," he said.

"Well, this was a huge waste of time for both of us, then," I said, sitting back.

"Unless we find something else to talk about."

My pulse kicked up a notch, and I sat up straight. "Like what?"

"Like why you jumped off a building."

"Ah." I sat back again. "Not to be rude, but why does it matter?"

"It . . . was a bad day for me," he said. "I'd always—ugh, I don't know, it'll sound cocky."

"I like cocky."

"Well I'd always been kind of a prodigy. Everyone thought I could do no wrong. So after that I kind of—well, I lost my grip for a while. Lost my job for a bit; had to fight to get it back."

"I'm so sorry."

"You don't have to apologize. I just want to know why you jumped."

"It was a rough year. I'll leave it at that."

"You don't have to leave it. I actually want to hear. Do you think I'm going to judge you or something?"

For some reason, I really didn't. I probably should have felt weirder talking about this stuff to a complete stranger, but it had been a long time since I'd had anyone but a stranger to talk to, and this particular stranger had a wry, haunted vibe that was kind of working for me.

"I slept with one of my professors," I said, looking at my hands. "It didn't end well."

He slurped at his drink and didn't say anything for a while. Finally he said, "You're not going to do anything like that again, right?"

"Sleep with an authority figure? No promises."

"I meant, try to end your life."

"No," I said more soberly. "I won't be doing that again."

"You understand why I ask, right? I mean, if life looked hard to you back then . . ." He gestured unashamedly to my legs.

I could have been offended, but in truth I was surprised no one else had said that to my face. I traced figure eights on the table with my fingertip, then sighed. "Here's the thing, Brian. From across the room, I'll admit death looks like a real babe. But I've been close enough to see what's under her makeup, and no thanks. Really."

"All right," he said.

"Will that help you sleep better?"

"I'm a long way from sleeping well. But it's good to hear."

"What would it take to help you sleep?"

He didn't respond, just lifted his gaze from his drink. I instantly regretted my innuendo; his eyes were empty pits of misery. Even without a direct rebuke, I got the message that whatever was keeping him up nights was something that I should have treated with more respect.

An apology rushed into my throat, but as always, my Borderline allergy to contrition made it stick there. So I just looked back at him, hoping I was as easy to read as he was.

"I wish I could tell you," he finally said.

"Why can't you?"

"You've said you're a friend of Berenbaum's, and I can't—"

He broke off as my phone rang. I fumbled in my backpack, hurrying to answer. "This is Millie."

"Millie," said Inaya West. "Who the hell are you?"

23

"Hold on just one second," I said to the movie star, "and I'll explain everything." I mouthed, "Be right back!" to Clay and tried to get back up on my crutches, which was awkward with the phone in my hand. Clay did a little half lurch forward before changing his mind and leaning back again. I appreciated the vote of confidence, and sure enough, I managed to get up and out to the sidewalk without face-planting on the tile.

"I'm so sorry," I said once I was out of Clay's earshot. "I was in a coffee shop, and I wanted to make sure I could hear you. I'm Millie Roper; I've been working with David Berenbaum." Best to keep things as generic as possible and let her lead the conversation. The fewer lies I had to remember, the better. "There seems to be some weirdness going on with John Riven lately, and I'm trying to sort it all out."

"Do you know how I can get in touch with him?" she asked. "He hasn't been returning my calls, and now David won't either."

"I know David's been wrapped up with problems in post-production and hasn't had—"

"Bullshit. Pardon my French. But that's a load of shit. Either he's slinging it at you or you're slinging it at me. Which is it?"

This was not the kind of conversation I'd hoped to be having. "If he's been dodging your calls," I said, leaning back against the wall of the coffee shop, "I honestly have no idea why. I just know that you've been trying to contact Johnny, and Johnny is being a pain in my ass too, and I thought we could help each other."

"What would help me," said Inaya with tightly controlled fury, "would be if people would stop pumping twenty gallons of sunshine up my ass every time I try to find out what's going on with a project I sold my house to help finance."

"So this *is* about the studio."

"I'm not answering any more questions until you answer some of mine. I'm not surprised Johnny's blowing me off, but David I expected better from. This is bullshit."

A motorcycle roared by, giving me a moment to think. In my years of dealing with touchy actors and underpaid crew, I had learned that trying to soothe an angry person is like pouring gasoline on a fire. There are only two good ways to deal with someone's anger: give it what it wants, or failing that, agree with it.

"You're right," I said as soon as the motorcycle had passed. "It's bullshit."

I was rewarded with a few seconds of silence. "What?" she finally managed.

"Screw him," I said. "He gets what he wants and then kicks you to the curb. It'll be me next, just watch. I don't blame you for wanting to punch him in the mouth."

"Well, it's not right." I could hear her relax a little.

"Damn right it's not. And since when is John Riven anything but a hot piece of ass? Why does the world seem to revolve around him all of a sudden?"

"What *is* he up to?" Another pause as she reengaged her Reason Mind. "What exactly is your relationship with David?"

"He prefers I don't talk about the specifics."

"Oh my God," she said. "You're a PI, aren't you?"

Sure, why not? "Well, at least I can honestly say I didn't tell you that. David hired me to look into Johnny."

"Wait, wait, wait. Just hold up a minute here. David hired a PI to check out his best friend? What the hell?"

"I don't ask my clients a lot of unnecessary questions in this economy." I loved dropping "in this economy" into conversation; it was like a get-out-of-logic-free card, especially if you were talking to people who couldn't remember the last time they had to pick up their own dry cleaning.

Inaya started to laugh. "Sweet Jesus, this is a clusterfuck. You know Ellis Barnes?"

"Rings a bell." It didn't.

"I hired him to follow Berenbaum around."

"Unbelievable," I said. "People never just *talk* to each other."

"If they did, you'd be out of a job."

"You know I'm going to have to tell Berenbaum you're investigating him, right?"

"Good!" she said. "Maybe that will get him to answer my damned calls. I never get ugly on voice mail, because I don't want to see it on YouTube cut to paparazzi shots of me picking my nose. So you can be the one to tell him, I know about all those late-night trips to the construction site with Johnny and Vivian."

"You do?" I said, trying not to sound thrown as I groped my memory for details. "Down in Manhattan Beach?"

"Mm-hmm."

But I couldn't ask what trips, or when, without casting severe doubt on my credibility.

"Tell you what," I said. "I will tell Berenbaum you know about the Manhattan Beach meetings. I'll tell him he'd better call you if he doesn't want a PR disaster. In return, I would love to hear any juicy tidbits you have about Johnny's life these days. The more illicit the better."

"You have no idea how much I'd love that," Inaya said. "But Johnny has always been the perfect gentleman. Almost suspiciously so."

"I need more than that," I said. "Like why the police would be looking for him."

"The police? Shit, I had no idea." But she was grinning; I could hear it.

"I just made your day, didn't I."

"Hell yes."

"Do you have any reason to suspect Johnny did anything to Aaron Susman or anyone in his family?"

"Not that I've heard. But I'm going to put Ellis on this; he's brilliant. I promise, whatever he finds out, after me you'll be the very next person to know."

My new pal and I said our good-byes, and I hobbled my way back into the coffee shop to find the table empty except for my backpack. My disappointment was intense until I saw the napkin that had been pushed over to my side of the table. I gave my damaged brain a moment to process the words on it.

WORK CALLS, URGENT. LET'S DO THIS AGAIN. And then his number, which I already had, but it lent sincerity to what might otherwise have seemed like a blow-off. I grinned as I folded the napkin and tucked it into my pocket.

Thanks to a reckless cabdriver, I returned to the Residence in plenty of time to head upstairs and check out my thigh wounds in the privacy of my room. They were looking better after some fresh air and attention, so I took a chance and carefully donned my AK prosthesis again. Then, grabbing my cane, I walked down the hall to pester Teo.

His door was ajar, and he was at his computer, surfing a recipe site at light speed while muttering something about butternut squash.

"Hey," I said. "Do you post your recipes online?"

"Are you kidding?" he scoffed. "Would da Vinci make a YouTube tutorial on how to paint the Sistine Chapel?"

"Get up, Leonardo; the cripple needs your chair."

To his credit, he did get up, pulling the chair out for me. I sat down with a muffled groan, and he started kneading my shoulders.

"What's up?" he said. "You disappeared, and now you look like the cat who ate the canary."

I didn't answer right away; I was too busy trying not to fall over from how damned amazing it felt to have his fingers digging into the knotted muscles of my back. It would do no good to let him know this, because then he would stop.

"I have a *suitor*," I finally said.

He didn't respond, just kept massaging.

"Jealous?" I teased.

"Mostly just confused."

"Well, I don't know if it's a suitor. But I'm going to pretend it's one, because it makes me happy, and happy is hard to come by."

"Is he cuter than me?"

"Not really."

"Smarter, I bet."

"He wants to date me, so I'm guessing no. But he's older." I let out a dazed grunt as Teo did something complicated with his knuckles under my shoulder blades. Rivenholt's folder was sitting open on Teo's desk, and as I leaned forward, I fiddled with the paper clip holding the photo to it.

"He doesn't sound too awesome," Teo said.

"It's the cop who's been looking for Rivenholt, okay? So I have an ulterior motive." Did I? I couldn't even keep track anymore.

"Is everything about work for you?"

"What else have I got?" I said, trying not to sound too drunk. "But it's interesting. Berenbaum thinks Inaya and Vivian are plotting against him, and Inaya thinks Vivian and Berenbaum are plotting against her. By my math, that suggests that Vivian is plotting against both of them. How Rivenholt and an abduction are involved, I still don't know."

"I just want to boot him back to Arcadia. I don't need to know all the drama."

"Want to drive me to the train station at three so we can nab him?"

Teo's hands stilled. "Wait, what?"

"Weren't you there when I was talking to Berenbaum?" I slipped the paper clip off Rivenholt's folder and picked up the photo, staring at those breathtaking eyes.

"Listening to your phone call would've required more of a shit than I actually give about any of this," he said, starting up the massage again. "Are you sure he's going to be there?"

"Tell you what," I said, admiring Rivenholt's cheekbones and trying to ignore the way Teo's hands were encroaching on side-boob. "If we go and he's not there, I'll do your laundry for a month."

"You just want to rifle through my underwear."

"Says the guy copping a feel."

Teo retracted his hands, but it was worth it to score the point. "Fine," he said. "I'll drive you."

I slipped Rivenholt's photo into my pocket. "Don't get me wrong," I said. "I'm all for fooling around, but I think we skipped first base."

"Excuse me for not knowing the rules."

"What are you, a virgin?"

His spine stiffened, and he headed for the door. "You're not even allowed to ask me that."

"Oh my God, you *are*."

He stood there holding the door open and not looking at me.

"Aw, hey," I said. "Don't feel weird. It's kind of awesome, actually. Good on you. I just—well, now I get the mixed-signals thing. I thought you were just being a dick."

"Can't I be a virgin *and* a dick?"

"If you ever have any questions about anything—"

"You know what would be awesome? If we talked about something that wasn't this."

"Fine. To the train station."

24

By the time we got on the road, traffic had mysteriously qua-drupled in the way that it often does in L.A. I glanced at the clock—2:13—and tried to take calming breaths. Teo, on the other hand, was not even trying for calm and was driving like an asshole.

"Teo, if we get pulled over, we are going to miss the train. The Mythbusters proved that weaving in and out of lanes doesn't get you there any faster."

"You're welcome to walk."

"Right. Sorry, I keep thinking I'm talking to an adult."

To minimize suffering, according to Dr. Davis, you must apply something called "radical acceptance." Basically, this means ceasing to fight things that are beyond your control. As both Teo and Los Angeles traffic fell firmly into that category, I did my breathing exercises and pulled my face into an imitation of a serene smile. Strangely, it helped. It was possible, my Wise Mind reasoned, that I had guessed wrong about the three o'clock train, in which case all this stress and hurry would be for nothing.

We pulled up to Union Station at 2:43. "Get out and I'll find a place to park," said Teo.

There were about eight things wrong with that plan, but I had no time to argue. I got out of the car as fast as I could and shut the shrieking passenger door behind me.

Union Station is the sort of place that looks like it ought to have ghosts. And it does, if you count the dead-eyed people shuffling through the cavernous main terminal or perched in uncomfortable chairs, watching rows of demonic red numbers. I checked the boards to remind myself which track the viscount's train was leaving from and then started down the fluorescent-lit tunnel of doom.

Picture one of those endless corridors in an airport, but take out any windows, moving sidewalks, ads, artwork, or other relief. Make it all concrete and aging tile instead of carpet and plaster. Now add in creepy dungeonlike stairways every twenty feet or so that lead tantalizingly upward, teasing promises of sunlight and air that only make the endless slog to your platform all the more unbearable.

The tired-looking kid trying to sell me candy was probably the least depressing thing in the place, and that's saying something. I would have stopped and bought some off-brand peanut butter cups for Rivenholt if it hadn't already been 2:49. I climbed the stairs to track twelve, ignoring aches and pains and a stitch in my side that made me wonder if I hadn't torn a brand-new hole in something.

Passengers were boarding. Shit, I could have already missed him. I scanned the crowd frantically for blonds, then addressed a friendly looking conductor lady with overprocessed hair. "I'm looking for my friend. He might be on this train."

"Do you have a ticket?"

"I don't."

"I'm sorry, I can't let you on board."

"Could you at least check around, see if you see him? It's important."

"What's his name?"

I pulled the photo from my pocket and showed her.

One of her brows lifted. "He's an actor, right? You looking for an autograph?"

"No! There's kind of a family emergency."

She looked at me skeptically. "If he were on the train," she said, "I'd have noticed him."

"Can you please just check? And if you find him, tell him Aaron put David in the hospital." Even if that didn't make sense, it seemed a fair bet he'd want to know what the hell had gotten lost in translation.

She gave me a once-over, and her face softened. "Okay, hon. Calm down, and I'll try and find him for you."

From 2:51 to 2:56, I repeatedly wiped clammy palms on my jeans and rehearsed a dozen different things to say. I tried to figure out how to work "don't touch me" into my greeting without seeming unfriendly. But then the conductor came back out, shouting at people to hurry and board. She spotted me and gave a sad little shrug.

"I don't think your man is on this train," she said.

I swallowed a bitter lump of disappointment. How was it that nobody ever managed to see him at any of the places he was expected to be? Was he going to a lot of trouble to lead people astray? Or was he somehow here all along, invisible, pressing his hands against a barrier that only his drawings could cross?

I thanked the lady and made my way carefully back down

the stairs to the Corridor of Broken Dreams. Now that my adrenaline was easing off, I could feel every ache and pain in my patchwork body.

Teo came jogging up, looking out of breath and displeased. "I take it we missed him," he said.

"I got there in time to ask a conductor to search the train, but she said he wasn't on it. I have no way of knowing for sure if that's true."

"No biggie," said Teo. "If he came through here, I'm sure someone noticed him. And if he got on that train, we can still beat him to the next stop."

"Right," I said, feeling both relieved and foolish.

It didn't take long flashing Rivenholt's picture around before we found an old man with a charming Slavic accent who remembered him. "I think this is the man who is arrested here in the terminal," he said.

"*Arrested?*" said Teo.

A sudden dread seized me, and I tore open my bag, rifling through it. The e-mail I'd printed out, the one telling Berenbaum what train Rivenholt was boarding, was gone.

"Work emergency, huh?" I muttered bitterly as Teo continued questioning the old man. I pulled out my phone and the napkin from the coffee shop and dialed Clay's number. No one answered. He could forget about a date.

The old man stroked a thumb thoughtfully over his moustache as he regarded Teo. "The blond man is standing over there, looking around," he was saying. "Then the policeman, darker, comes to him and shows a badge," he was saying. "They have serious conversation which I do not hear. Then they walk together to track two. As they pass me, I try to tell them that train has left already, but I get a little afraid. Policeman has his hand on the back of the other's neck, tight, like holding a dog."

Before I could even respond, Teo had bolted toward the stairway in question. I thanked the old guy, slipped him a twenty, and went after Teo with a sigh.

When I finally limped my way to the top of the platform, I found Teo standing with his hands buried in his hair, looking down at the deserted train tracks. His sunglasses served to partially hide his expression, but the way he'd squished his mouth into a tiny line strongly suggested he was freaking out. I moved closer to his side and looked down.

"What is that?" I said, looking at the dark splash marks and streaks on the tracks.

"Blood," said Teo. "Fey blood."

I did a double take. The stains and the track were both too dark for me to be sure, and any telltale scent was covered by other metallic odors.

"That's bad, right?"

"You have no idea."

"Because no one will tell me. Are you sure it's blood?"

"Put on your glasses."

Feeling a qualm, I did as he asked—and made a strangled sound. The faint stains shimmered with golden light. It was brightest on the track where the liquid looked to have pooled; then the stains made a wide, smeary trail from the tracks to the platform.

"Oh, shit," I said. I remembered the coldly simmering anger in Brian Clay's eyes and shuddered.

Teo nodded grimly. "The cop must have held him down on the tracks and—I don't know, shot him? Bashed his head in?

Then I guess dragged him over there—" Teo looked blankly at where the blood trail disappeared. "Picked him up, maybe?"

"How did no one see this?" I hated how high-pitched my voice suddenly sounded. "I get that the platform was empty, but Clay had to take him somewhere after he— How is this place not swarming with cops and EMTs right now?"

"I don't know," said Teo, hands in his hair again. "I don't know. This is *fucked*."

While Teo panicked, I kept my glasses on and tried to see if there was more blood anywhere. I noticed a few drips near the top of the stairs.

"Teo, is it possible that Rivenholt is still alive?"

"Could be. Fey anatomy is different from ours, so blood loss doesn't stop them. Fey essence isn't even really blood, it's . . . more a kind of liquid energy, like fuel, for their spells."

"So maybe he just walked out?"

Teo considered it, then shook his head grimly. "Here's the thing," he said. "Being held against iron like that, plus having essence literally pouring out of him, it would drain his fuel tank, right? He can't refill without going back to Arcadia. He wouldn't be able to hold his facade anymore. That means there's no way he's just walking out of here."

"So why is there more blood at the bottom of the steps?" I pointed to a faint glimmer, barely visible from where I was standing. Teo moved past me jackrabbit quick, bounding down the stairs in a way that made me green with envy. He knelt to look.

"This isn't blood," he said. He bent down, picking up a piece of paper and unfolding it. He stood there for a long moment, then slowly took off his glasses. He turned his head and looked up at me with the kind of look people give you when the burning house on the news is yours.

"What?" I said, when he didn't speak. "Is it another of Rivenholt's drawings?" I pushed my own glasses up to the top of my head and made my way down the stairs.

Teo nodded and turned the paper around toward me. When I was close enough, I laced my hands together behind my back and looked. The air collapsed out of me with a *whoosh*.

The woman in the drawing wasn't beautiful in the way Hollywood stars are beautiful. More like a rock face worn away by wind and water. Her short hair left every scarred line of her face exposed, a lean face dominated by intelligent eyes. She stood with the careful straightness of someone who took pain for granted. Her cane gleamed like wet ice, as did the sleek mechanical construction that stood in for her left leg.

She had flesh, somewhere, past the metal and the loosely draped clothes that had once flattered a less gaunt frame. I wondered if her skin was warm, if by reaching it, by fitting the curve of a naked hip into the hollow of my palm, I could change the grim expression in her eyes. But she was as off limits as though she were surrounded by barbed wire. Written at the bottom of the paper were two words: COLD IRON.

Rivenholt had drawn *me*.

After a moment Teo folded up the drawing, leaving me staring blankly at his T-shirt, and tucked the paper into his back pocket. I didn't notice there were tears on my cheeks until he wiped them away with the back of his hand.

And then he was holding me and murmuring in my ear— *no llores, mija*—and I wanted to explain that I wasn't sad, I was happy. But then I couldn't explain because he was kissing me.

He was terrible at it and tasted like cigarettes (the bastard had sneaked a smoke while parking the car, maybe while Rivenholt was bleeding out on a railroad track), but I kissed him back anyway because I couldn't kiss the man who had drawn me. We stood clinging to each other like a soldier and his wife at the bottom of the stairs, and I shook like a cheap washing machine and he shhh-shhhh-ed me between kisses. His hands were careful, but mine were reckless; they found soft cotton T-shirt and rough jeans and then—paper, because while I was groping him I accidentally touched the drawing, goddamn it.

25

Teo didn't talk in the car; he just lit a cigarette. I opened my window but didn't say anything. I let him finish his smoke and stab it out in the ashtray between us before I broke the silence.

"It's not a big deal," I said.

"It was the drawing."

"I know." I did know. I'd been there.

He fumbled with his pack of cigarettes but didn't light another one, setting it aside. "I feel like I cheated on her."

"Who?"

"My Echo."

I twisted around to look at him, ignoring the protest from my spine. "That's who you're saving yourself for? It's a she?"

"I don't know. I think it is. I don't care. It isn't always like that with Echoes, but it is with us. I don't even know who it is, I just know I don't want anybody else. And I know that she—or he, or whatever—feels the same way. I don't know how I know; I just know."

"That's the dumbest and sweetest thing I've ever heard." I looked down at the drawing in my hands. Now that I'd destroyed it, I was allowed to keep it.

What preoccupied me most about this particular piece was a nagging, inchoate sense of familiarity. Even more than his others, this particular sketch gave me an urgent sense that there was a clue in it I should be able to place, an element that I should recognize—besides myself, of course.

I should have been disturbed to know that Rivenholt had somehow managed to observe me without my seeing him, but I wasn't. I had no room to question his motives; I'd *felt* them. He respected and cared about me on a level that didn't make any sense, given that I had no memory of meeting him. I put the drawing away and stared at Rivenholt's photo instead. It was starting to seem familiar too, but was that just because I'd seen *Accolade*? Or did I have some preexisting relationship with the man that was now lost to my head injury?

"Is it possible Rivenholt isn't really Berenbaum's Echo?" I asked Teo.

"You're thinking he's yours? He doesn't have to be your Echo to have feelings for you."

"But we've never met."

"I dunno. Maybe his connection to Berenbaum gives him some way of observing you. Hell, maybe he's been hiding nearby every time you and Berenbaum talked."

I frowned. "Clay said something like that. That he thought Berenbaum knew where Rivenholt was. I just don't want to think Berenbaum would lie to me."

"Who is Clay again?"

"The cop who just arrested him, I'm pretty sure." On that note, I dialed Clay's number for the eighth time. Still nothing. Finally I gave up and dialed ASK-LAPD, choosing dispatch from the menu options.

"Hey," I said to the woman who answered the phone. "I've been working with Brian Clay on a missing persons thing, and he's not answering his phone. I wondered if you have some way to get in touch with him? It's urgent."

"Can you give me the name again?" Her tone was crisp and competent, and there was a trace of Mexico in her accent.

"Brian Clay." I spelled it for her.

For a moment I heard nothing but background chatter. Then, "We have no officer by that name. Did this person specifically claim to be with the LAPD?"

The bottom dropped out of my stomach. "He did." Too many paradigm shifts in one hour; I was getting queasy.

"Was he in uniform?"

"No, but his badge looked legit."

"Did he stop your vehicle or act as a police officer in any capacity?"

"All he did was ask me some questions about a friend of mine, but I'm pretty sure he just, ah, arrested someone at Union Station and hurt the man pretty badly in the process."

"We'll send someone to investigate. If he contacts you again, please call us right away. You can even use 911 for this. Authentic-looking badges are not hard to come by, so in future if you have doubts, it's always okay to call us and confirm identity before giving an officer any information."

But I hadn't had doubts. That was the part that bothered me most. I'd been so distracted with magic and fairies that it hadn't even occurred to me to apply a healthy dose of skepticism to the mundane stuff.

I described Clay in as much detail as I could and gave the nice lady my contact information in a kind of shame-haze. I'd sent this guy after Rivenholt; I might as well have spilled the blood on the tracks with my own hand.

"Was that what I think it was?" Teo said when I hung up.

"If you think I found out Brian Clay is a lying, thieving piece of shit with a fake badge, then yes."

I called Berenbaum's mobile, but he wasn't answering. I tried his office number, but Araceli didn't answer either, and with so much up in the air, leaving a message seemed pointless.

"Teo, give me Caryl's number," I said.

"Only Caryl is authorized to do that."

"For God's sake, Teo, this is a disaster of epic proportions. Exceptions can be made."

"No. She can't have just anyone calling her when she might not have Elliott out. But more importantly, it's the rules. Once you sign the contract, you don't ever break the Project rules, Millie. Instant termination."

"I hope you mean firing."

"Usually."

I let that one slide. "Fine, then, you call her and hand me the phone."

"I'm driving, Millie. We'll be at the Residence in, like, ten minutes."

"Do it, Teo, or I'll tell her you kissed me. That's against the rules, right?"

"No, dumbass," he said. "Remember Phil and Gloria?"

"I keep trying to forget."

He was already groping in his pocket for his phone, eyes still on the road as he tilted his hips up off the seat. I idly painted a mental picture of myself straddling him—my old self, of course; I doubted I was nimble enough to do that anymore.

He held the phone up in his line of sight, flicking his eyes over to it as he drove. "If a cop drives by and pulls me over right now, you are paying the fucking fine."

"Just make sure it's a real cop first."

He held the phone to his ear and listened. I studied his face, trying to feel something other than embarrassed amusement at what had happened between us at the station. He was sexy in theory, but not really in practice. It wouldn't take much tweaking to make him dangerously crush-worthy, but I'd been in the dating pool long enough to know that what you see is what you get.

"Caryl," Teo said, "call Lisa." A pause as Teo lost a shade of color. "What? I didn't—did I not say Millie? Sorry. Just call her, all right? Same damn phone."

I watched the unintentionally erotic display he made trying to put his phone back in his pocket. "Were you and Lisa close?" I said.

"Not really. Learned my lesson after Amir. But she was all right. She and I were both *pochos*, so there was stuff I didn't have to explain."

"What's a *pocho*?"

He winced a little, then laughed. "You don't get to say that. It means spoiled, overripe. A term Mexicans have for people like me who are more American than Mexican, you know? They say it like it's a bad thing." He snorted another laugh, but his body was drawn and tense.

"I . . . obviously can't relate. I never had any culture to begin with."

"Of course you do," he snapped. "We're swimming in your culture every minute. Meanwhile, my culture thinks bipolar disorder's my fault for not going to church. My culture can go fuck itself."

"Teo, your mom was an asshole. You can't judge a culture by its assholes."

He fumbled for the cigarette pack again, shaky. I laid a hand on his arm, and it seemed to calm him, or at least change his mind about smoking.

"I hope you realize," I said, " that I'm not going anywhere. Everything I've seen about the aftermath of what I did—" But now my phone was ringing. Of course.

"Hello?"

"What has Teo so upset?" said Caryl's voice.

"It's Rivenholt," I said. "It seems he was abducted from the train station, most likely by this guy who's been posing as a cop and trying to track him down."

"I don't like 'seems' and 'most likely.' What are the facts?"

"The facts are, it turns out the cop I'd been talking to about Rivenholt is not really a cop, and the train departure info went missing from my bag when I left it with him. Afterward someone flashed a badge at Rivenholt at the station and took him to an isolated area. When we went there, we found a bucketload of spilled fairy blood and nothing else."

There was a long silence on the other end of the line.

"Spilled fairy blood is bad, right?" I said. "Epically bad, Teo said. What's the deal with that, anyway?"

"I may need to share that information, despite your tenuous status, but this is not the moment. I am . . . overwhelmed."

"That prick just got us in deep trouble with Arcadia, didn't he?"

"Without knowing the full situation, I cannot say if we have a convincing argument against our apparent criminal negligence."

"If we don't?"

"Let's not talk about that just yet. Was there any sign of where they went?"

"They seemed to just vanish into thin air. Could Rivenholt have cast some kind of invisibility spell?"

"No, but an Unseelie fey could have done so."

"An Unseelie such as Vivian Chandler?"

"For example, yes. There are only four Unseelie fey in Los Angeles at present, and the other three have no connection to Rivenholt whatsoever that I'm aware of."

"How do you know there are only four?"

"The perimeter ward counts and displays the fey population at any time within its boundaries. Seelie and Unseelie are counted separately."

"Isn't that the thing you said was on the fritz or something, though?"

There was a brief silence. "Again, I am impressed by your attention to detail. There have been some odd readings lately, yes."

"Do you think the odd readings have anything to do with this business with Rivenholt?"

"Correlation does not imply causation, but we should not entirely ignore the fact that Rivenholt's uncharacteristically lawless behavior is occurring at the same time as the anomaly."

"Can you explain what the anomaly is?"

"I'm not sure you'd understand. I will show you later."

"This is the thing you've been preoccupied with, though?"

"Yes. It's why I brought you on when I did. Once I began to spend time on this, it became apparent that we had too few people with leadership experience to keep things in order while I was distracted. You were a director; you have experience with executive-level decision making. But then Rivenholt's disappearance complicated things, and your training has suffered accordingly."

"I'm doing everything I can to help," I said. "But mostly I'm stumbling around in the dark. No one tells me the rules until I break them, which seems like a horrible way to run an organization."

"I'm sorry," she said. "But now we have multiple crises on our hands. A fey abducted by a human is a serious matter for the Code of Silence, but we can contain the problem if we find the abductor. The spilled blood, on the other hand—well, no matter, it is done."

"I'll keep trying to contact the fake cop," I said. "For now I'll pretend I still think he's legit."

"Meet me back at the Residence," Caryl said, "and let's start combing through files. Perhaps we'll find some connections that will help."

By the time I got there, Caryl had turned the living room into a war room. Everyone I'd seen at breakfast was sitting on a couch or a piano bench or a chair dragged in from the dining room, looking through folders and entire drawers that had simply been yanked out of their cabinets and brought to the room in their entirety. Monty was having a field day with unattended stacks of paper. There were at least three different arguments going on, but the only one I could hear was Gloria's with Caryl on the sofa, and only Gloria's side of it.

"I'm just concerned, that's all," Gloria was saying. "She hasn't been through the whole training; she doesn't know what all they can and can't do."

Caryl said something calmly that I couldn't hear, and at the same time I felt Elliott settle onto my shoulder. When Caryl spotted me, she grabbed some photographs and rose from the couch, moving to me without even formally breaking off her discussion with Gloria. As if Gloria really needed another reason to be annoyed with me.

"Do you recognize any of these people, aside from Vivian?" Caryl asked me.

I glanced over the photos and shook my head. "Not in the least." I pointed at a lumpy-nosed old woman. "That's a weird facade for a fey to choose."

"Thus far you've only seen the *sidhe*; they share our standards of beauty, for the most part. Commoners, especially Unseelie commoners, have a different aesthetic."

"Who are these people?"

"These are the only four Unseelie fey who are currently in Los Angeles. Seelie magic is designed to attract attention, not divert it, so these four and myself are the only beings in the city who might have cast spells to assist in removing Rivenholt from the train station."

"Is it safe to assume that our fake cop knows about Arcadia?"

"Not necessarily. For example, he could be conspiring with Vivian in some mundane criminal capacity and unaware of exactly how she managed to get them all safely out of the station. A spell caster of Vivian's skill can be subtle."

"But given the amount of blood loss, Teo said Rivenholt's facade would have dropped."

Caryl nodded. "It does seem likely that if the man was unaware of the existence of fey before, he has just had a very shocking introduction to the concept."

For a moment I almost felt bad for Clay, but then I remembered that he was a lying sack of crap who was probably in cahoots with the queen of the damned.

"Is there any reason that Vivian would want to harm her business partner's Echo?" I asked Caryl, perplexed.

"Leverage, possibly?" she mused. "You say she promised not to hurt Berenbaum, but if she didn't extend that promise to Rivenholt, she could still use him to ensure Berenbaum's cooperation with something."

"That means Rivenholt is almost certainly still alive, then, because if she killed him, she'd lose the leverage."

Caryl gave me a long look. "If he is in Vivian's custody, you had best hope she has already killed him."

"Caryl!" scolded Gloria, approaching the two of us. "Look at her face. This is exactly the sort of thing I'm talkin' about."

I eyed Gloria, suspicious of this sudden defense of me.

"I appreciate your concerns," Caryl said, "and I share them to some extent. But Millie and Teo have done a tremendous job of getting information thus far."

I made an incoherent sound of disbelief. "She wants to take the assignment from us, doesn't she."

"Aw, don't take it personal, honey," said Gloria, and gave me a sugary smile.

26

I looked down at Gloria's smug, pretty face and felt equal parts panic and fury. She wore sweetness like armor; I could fight, too little too late, and it would only make me look petty and threatened. I'd done this dance a thousand times with a thousand saccharine Southern girls, and I always ended up getting danced right out the door.

"What's in this for you?" I asked Gloria, making no apology for towering over her.

"It's not about me, hon," she said with an expression of tender concern. "It's just, you haven't been here a week, and already Caryl's got you interviewing Unseelie bloodsuckers and mopping up at crime scenes?"

She actually sort of had a point, which made me more furious. "You didn't answer my question," I said. "Is there money in it for you or something?"

Gloria looked like someone had dropped a worm down the back of her shirt. I looked at Caryl, who only gave a weary sigh.

"Because fey blood was shed," Caryl explained, "I had to alert my contact at the Department of Homeland Security to the possibility of Arcadian retribution."

"Wait, the *government* knows about fairies?"

"Not most of the government, no. But we have people at the DHS, and they will be paying us a substantial cash reward if we can keep the Accord intact."

"To whom would this reward go, exactly?"

"To the Los Angeles Arcadia Project. Generally, when we are paid for resolving a conflict, I give most of the proceeds to the employees involved in the resolution."

I gave Gloria a hard look. "Oh, is that so."

"Don't make it sound like that," Gloria chided, giving me a disappointed-mom look.

"I don't have to make it sound like anything," I said. "This is my assignment. There is no one, not even Teo, who could do it without me at this point. In the few days I've been, here not only have I become best buddies with David Berenbaum, but apparently Viscount Rivenholt has fallen in love with me."

"*What?*" said a few people at once. Then the room got very quiet.

I pulled the drawing out of my pants pocket and showed it to Caryl. "I already touched this," I said sheepishly, "but Teo can attest to the feeling that used to be in it."

"Yup," said Teo. "He seriously wants to hit that."

Caryl looked at the drawing for a moment. "I'll confess this development surprises me," she said evenly, "but between the viscount's inexplicable infatuation and your magic-canceling abilites, I will admit you have become valuable. The best solution would be for the four of you to work together."

"Are you fucking kidding me?!" someone blurted.

Oh. It was me.

"I think that sounds like a fine idea," said Gloria, the very picture of humility.

I forced myself to take slow, deep breaths. "Fine," I said. "But this is a complicated enough situation without everyone just going off and doing their own thing. If you want my help dealing with Berenbaum and Rivenholt, then I want to be in charge."

"Now you're just being a silly goose," said Gloria. "You don't even work for us yet. Caryl can't put you in charge of a major crisis response."

"So hire me," I said. "Give me a pen and I'll sign the damned agreement right now. Don't act like there is any chance you lot could fire me at this point. I could blow your Code of Silence to bits."

Gloria put a hand to her mouth, a cute little *oh my!* gesture. "Oh, honey," she said in tones of deepest pity. "You haven't figured it out?"

"That's enough," said Caryl. Two calm words, but it was as though someone had cut Gloria's strings. She drooped submissively on the couch, hands in her lap.

"I haven't figured what out?" I said.

"That is quite enough bickering," Caryl said. "I am taking all four of you to Residence One so we can find out if Rivenholt is still alive and plan what to do next."

"Let me just freshen up first," said Gloria, sliding down off the couch and hurrying to the downstairs bathroom.

I watched her go, ashamed of myself for focusing my loathing on her short-legged gait instead of her scheming mind. Once she was gone, I muttered between clenched teeth, "I thought everyone came here straight out of the loony bin. Does passive-aggressive qualify as a personality disorder these days? What's her story?"

The room was very quiet. Uncomfortably so.

"Right," I said. "I'm not supposed to ask. If someone will give me one of those agreements to sign, I'll follow the rules and shut up about it. But since no one seems to find me worthy of such a document, I wouldn't mind a damn answer, since I'm stuck working with her."

To my surprise, it was Tjuan who spoke. "She stabbed two men to death with a steak knife," he said. "Says she doesn't remember it, got off on insanity."

Everyone was looking at me in a way that suggested that they already knew about this. I tried to stop the color from draining out of my face, but emotions are slippery things, so everyone got to enjoy my moment of bald horror.

"Maybe think on that," said Tjuan, "next time you feel like giving her attitude."

"All right, I get it," I snapped.

I didn't like the slow way he smiled. I didn't like any of this. I didn't like that I was lower down in the social pecking order than Blondie just because I hadn't killed a guy. The rewards for kindness and sane behavior seemed to be pretty sparse at Residence Four.

Gloria emerged from the bathroom so glowingly smug that I was almost sure she'd heard Tjuan schooling me.

"I call shotgun," I said quickly. Gloria stopped in confusion, then frowned. Sometimes you have to savor the small victories.

The ride to Residence One was awkward and Bach-filled. As always, Caryl had turned the music up to a conversation-killing volume, and her gloved fingertips kept precise time on the steering wheel. I flipped down my sun visor and opened the mirror, angling it so I could check on Teo in the backseat. The seat was made for two adults and a child, but Teo and Tjuan were both such beanpoles that Gloria fit comfortably in between. Teo saw me and made a face. I laughed, and caught my own eyes in the mirror as I did so.

For the first time since my tumble off the roof, I didn't have to look away. Because I was the girl in the drawing.

There had to be some way Rivenholt could *feel* me if I just thought at him hard enough. He had to know I was looking for him, that I was on my way, that I was going to make it all right.

We headed west on the 10 to Santa Monica and got off on Lincoln, heading south toward Ocean Park. We took a little zig-zag path through some residential streets and ultimately pulled into the driveway of a tiny yellow house on a postage-stamp lot. The tall wooden fence around it overflowed with scarlet bougainvillea.

BEWARE OF DOG, read the sign on the gate.

"What kind of dog lives here?" I said nervously when Caryl had turned off the car.

"No dog," said Caryl as we got out. "But I thought 'Beware of Interdimensional Portal' might be a bit confusing to the average home invasion specialist. The sign serves the same purpose: it encourages any interested parties to rob the house next door."

"Why doesn't Residence Four have a sign? Isn't there a Gate there too?"

"Residence Four was the first property we built specifically to protect its Gate. The Gate here had to be built inside a pre-existing house, so it is placed . . . more awkwardly."

"Why is this called Residence One? Was it the first?"

"The sixth, technically. The original LA1 Gate was demolished along with the Hotel Arcadia in 1909, and we were unable to replace it until we could acquire a suitable property two years later. This was the best we could manage."

"Do you live here?"

She shook her head, unlocking the wooden gate. "Management lives in independent housing; agents live in Residences and deal with the fey that have been assigned to their Gate. Rivenholt uses LA4, and that is why you and Teo were assigned to him." Caryl waved us all through into the yard. "Residence One is more of an office than a residence, in truth; it houses the majority of our arcane equipment. Travel through the Gate is limited to our oldest and highest-ranking visitors—the reactionary sort who take offense at being assigned a lower number."

The tiny front yard of Residence One boasted a lemon tree and several carefully staked tomato plants. A disheveled old woman with stark wide eyes stopped her weeding to stare at us as we walked by and up the front steps.

"Sick sick stinking ugly fuckpiss!" the woman gargled.

"Hello, Abigail," replied Caryl. No one but me seemed to find this odd, and I was not in the mood for any more public demonstrations of my ignorance.

The inside of the house looked like the inside of every other house in Southern California; there wasn't even anything worth stealing. Overwhelmed by ennui, I turned to leave, running headlong into a snickering Teo.

"That just never gets old," he said, taking me by the shoulders and turning me back around to face the interior. "Don't know why you bother with the dog sign, Caryl."

"The fey did not put up that ward for sport, Teo. It is a last resort."

Teo gave me a push out of the tiny foyer into the living room, and as he did so, the ward released its hold on my psyche. The shimmering black archway in the center of the living room suddenly struck me as decidedly *not* normal, and I made a small sound to that effect.

Gloria was at least polite enough to put her hand over her mouth to hide her smile. Tjuan, as always, was tombstone-serious.

The archway looked like a massive ring half-buried in the floor, its inner radius around seven feet. Its foot-wide rim was a metallic gray so dark as to be almost black, and it threw off light like glass. Inside the arch was the part that fried my brain: the space described by the semicircle simply wasn't *there*. When I tried to look at it, my visual cortex got some kind of horrible feedback, a cross between a low-grade electric shock and a free fall. My mind filled in the space with a variety of interesting stuff: analog TV fuzz, a gaping black hole, swirls of color like sun on oil on water.

"Stop looking at it," said Caryl, and I felt the silk of her glove over my eyes. "You will never make sense of it, and you can have a stroke or a seizure if you keep trying."

I turned to her, aghast, as she took her hand away. "Why would you even put that there!"

"As I've mentioned, ours is not the only world under consideration. Gates must be built in the exact same spot in both worlds, which is extraordinarily difficult to balance."

"Arcadia is on the other side of that?"

"Not if you walk around it," said Caryl. "But come; that is not what we are here to see."

27

Caryl led us down a short hallway to what would have been the master bedroom, if this had been a normal house. There was one other bedroom, but the door was shut and there was Latin pop music playing inside.

"Someone lives twenty feet from that thing?" I said. *"How?"*

"Two people. Luis is blind, and Abigail lives in a separate apartment beneath. Most of our agents live in Residences Four and Five; by the time we built them, we had learned from our earlier mistakes."

All at once I started shivering and couldn't stop.

"Someone hold her hand," said Caryl.

The men both just stared at me, but Gloria slipped her hand into mine, and my body stopped shaking before my brain could remind me that I hated her guts.

"You get used to it," Gloria said. Her voice grated on my nerves, but the feel of her palm against mine was a comfort that was hardwired into my humanity, all the more powerful because I so rarely felt anything like it anymore.

Gloria let go of my hand when we reached the back bedroom and wiped her palm on her thigh. So much for warm fuzzies.

The room was furnished like an office, with a computer station and cherrywood desk and credenza, filing cabinets and corkboards, office chairs and a couple of armchairs for reading. The only object that seemed unusual was a small device lying flat on the credenza: a tablet computer, perhaps, but designed in the improbable size and shape of a bread plate.

Only as we got closer did I realize it was not an electronic device at all. Its frame was made of a pale silvery wood, and as we approached it, the "screen" trembled ever so slightly, a liquid response that obscured the display. We gathered around close enough to see it, and then Caryl held up an ivory-gloved hand. *Hold still,* the gesture said, and we obeyed.

As the "screen" settled and became glassy once again, it revealed an image: an open flower with blue-white petals against a burgundy backdrop. The colors were too lush, too raw and textured to have been created by any means I understood. They looked, for lack of a better word, *real.*

"Show the census," Caryl said. The petals folded in on themselves, and then a series of golden dots began to appear slowly on the screen, one at a time in random locations, like the beginning of rainfall. I thought I spotted a couple of darker dots as well, but the overwhelming majority were golden, varying slightly in size. They appeared more rapidly for a moment, then began to slow and finally stopped.

Two numbers appeared: 88 and 5. The first figure was silver-gold, the second a dark purplish green. Seelie and Unseelie.

But even as we watched, the Seelie number flickered. Another number fitfully tried to replace the 88, but it came and went subliminally fast, making it impossible for me to read.

"In the past," said Caryl quietly, "the display has only done this at the moment when a fey was in transit via one of the Gates. It would show, for example, both eighty-eight and eighty-seven during a fey's exit, but would settle at eighty-seven afterward."

I glanced at Caryl's face, forgetting for a moment that I would read nothing there to tell me the relative seriousness of the matter.

Gloria craned her neck to see. "And it's been doing this for days and days?"

"Not precisely this," Caryl said. "The numbers have changed as fey have come and gone, but the difference between them has been constant, and the base number has always exactly matched the number of expected Seelie in the area. Until now."

"What should it read?" I said.

"Eighty-nine. One Seelie fey who should be in Los Angeles is not being counted."

I stared at the eighty-eight, chewing my bottom lip.

Teo was the one to say what I was afraid to speak out loud. "Does that mean Rivenholt is dead?"

Caryl shook her head slowly. "Normally that would be my first assumption. When the number drops without record of an exit through the Gate or perimeter, it signifies a death."

"You say that as though fey have been killed here before," I said. "Wouldn't that have broken the whatsit? The treaty thing?"

"The Accord? No. There are ways a fey can die bloodlessly. There are consequences, of course, if a human does the killing, but it's the shedding of blood in particular that is the Accord breaker."

"That seems like a fairly stupid technicality."

"It is not. Spilled fey essence is of more concern to Arcadia than any particular citizen. The short explanation is that when norium touches the earth—"

"—or a train platform," Teo cut in.

"—or a train platform, it exerts an arcane pull on the corresponding spot in Arcadia. Norium is what designates a thing 'of Arcadia' rather than 'of Earth.' So when our ground is tainted with norium, it acquires . . . strange properties, and we have to seal that area off from the public. Worse yet, the corresponding location in Arcadia essentially . . . falls through into the space between worlds. Leaves a hole."

"Holy shit." I ran a hand through my hair. "So I'm assuming the Arcadians already know about the bloodshed this afternoon."

"It will take a while for the rupture to occur, but no more than a few days. I would prefer that we had some sort of explanation, at the very least, by the time that happens. The iron in the tracks may help mitigate the effects, especially on our side, but there is no telling what the extent of the destruction in Arcadia will be."

I stared at the screen again as though it would help. It didn't. "You said you don't think Rivenholt is dead? Why?"

"Look." Caryl pointed to the Seelie number as it flickered. I squinted at it but still couldn't make out the other number.

"Ninety-four," said Tjuan.

"Does that number have some significance?" I asked.

Caryl nodded. "When the anomaly began, the difference was always five. For example, if the base number was eighty, it would flash eighty-five. If the base number dropped to seventy-nine, it would flash eighty-four. This is the first time the two numbers have had a difference of six."

"Which means—?"

"That somehow there were five 'half-present' fey before, and now there are six. Given that the change took place sometime after I checked the census this morning, logic suggests that the new half-present fey is Rivenholt."

"What does half-present mean? Maybe fading, becoming human?"

Caryl shook her head. "A life-form that organically contains even a trace of norium is counted by the census, which is why the Unseelie number reads five instead of four. It is counting me."

"The, uh, norium—it's in their blood, right? So, what if Rivenholt's last bit spilled out onto those railroad tracks?"

"Then he would not be counted at all, the same as if he had died."

"So, what then? There are six fairies just standing in a Gate somewhere?"

Caryl shook her head. "You cannot *stand* in a Gate; the body's reaction to being between worlds is a violent repulsion to one side or the other. Also, there are only three Gates in this perimeter, and I have inspected all of them daily."

"I give up then. What exactly is going on?"

"I have been preoccupied with that question for over two weeks now."

Gloria spoke up softly. "This is why y'all need more experienced help," she said.

Teo snorted. "I've been with the project longer than you have, and so has Caryl."

"That hardly counts, sweetheart. Y'all two spent the first few years playin' dolls and buildin' pillow forts."

I blinked and looked at Caryl. "How old *are* you?"

"Hon, you're not supposed to—"

"Nineteen," Caryl said.

Yet another moment of everyone watching me react to something they already knew. I looked at Caryl's impassive face. She had no visible lines around her eyes or mouth, but in L.A. you can't read by that sort of thing. She dressed old. *Sounded* old.

"Nineteen?" I said skeptically. "You sound like a forty-year-old smoker."

"Vocal cord damage."

"From what?"

"From screaming," she said. "A great deal of screaming."

You'd think after a week with these people I would have learned to stop asking questions.

I ate dinner at the table with everyone at the Residence that night, but I decided to take a lesson from Stevie and sit around brooding while the others talked.

Teo's exquisite nectarine jerk chicken salad might as well have been McNuggets for all I could taste it. But I sat through dinner because Caryl was there, and I didn't want to let her out of my sight. Judging by the constant tingling sensation on my neck and shoulders, Elliott had been all over me like a prom date since we left Residence One, and I knew that meant Caryl wanted something from me, even if she herself was eating one-handed while reading through Rivenholt's file for the eighty-fifth time with the other. I just had to wait until her Reason Mind came up with a justification to ask for what her Emotion Mind wanted.

I could see it now, past the dark liner around her eyes, the expertly applied shading under her cheekbones. How could I have missed the veinless smoothness of her skin? She didn't exactly exude good health, but there were no signs of age, either, aside from her voice and manner.

When she had finished eating and began pulling her gloves back on, she finally spoke up. "Millie, I need to see you in your room."

Gloria eyed us both as we left; I could feel her stare boring into my back. My mind half formed a cliché about fitting me for a knife; then I remembered I wouldn't be her first victim. I followed Caryl up the stairs and let her into the dark warmth of my room, where I turned on the overhead light and shut the door behind us.

28

"You've only one chair," Caryl said, looking around my room.

"You're young," I said. "Sit on the floor."

She did, folding her legs carefully and resting her gloved hands on her knees. "There's something you probably ought to know," she said.

"Just one thing?" I pulled my folding chair closer to her and sat in it, then slipped on my fey glasses. Elliott was settling himself comfortably on my knee. "Does this have anything to do with your mother, or your gloves, or why you've done forty years' worth of screaming?"

Elliott blinked at me, his wings drooping.

"No," Caryl said.

"Well, those are the things I want to know about, before you start in on any more terrifying revelations about parallel universes."

"Is my history important?" said Caryl. Elliott was making himself very small on my lap.

"I don't know," I said, "because I don't know your history. Take off your gloves."

"I don't think that is a good idea," she said dryly.

"It's just us," I said.

Caryl shrugged and began to pull off her gloves one finger at a time. "It doesn't really matter what I feel, much less why. There is no rhyme or reason; it's nothing more than a chemical bath in the brain. Could we discuss instead what I came up here to talk about?"

"Come over here. Give me your hand."

Elliott rustled his wings in apparent frustration. "I cannot do that," said Caryl blandly. "That is the entire point of the gloves."

"I'm starting to get that. Why are you so weird about touching?"

"Skin-to-skin contact creates so much conflicting neuro-chemical input that it overloads the Elliott construct. Shatters it. If I am not the one to deconstruct the spell, I cannot reabsorb the lost energy, and I must take a trip to Arcadia to replenish myself."

I sighed, looking at her Buddha-like posture and then at Elliott, who was attempting to hide his eyes in my shirt. "I don't know what to do with you," I said.

"You could start by letting me return to relevant matters."

"Damn it, Caryl," I said. "I guess you don't have to tell me what made you this way. But it's going to keep bothering me, and I'm going to keep asking."

Elliott wrapped both wings around his head, looking miserable. Caryl studied me a moment before speaking again.

"They took me when I was a baby," she said, starting to put her gloves back on. "The Unseelie Court. I don't remember my life before that—I was too young—and I will not talk about what it was like there."

"Okay," I said, drumming my fingers on my knee. "How did you get back here?"

"Eventually the Unseelie King discovered me and reported me to the Project. The Project returned me to my parents. I was seven years old."

"Did they even recognize you?"

"No, nor I them. To be frank, I was hardly human. They'd had two more children, built another life. I was institutionalized. After two years my predecessor, Martin, took an interest in me, taught me how to make Elliott. Once my behavior improved, I was released. My parents gave me into Martin's custody, and I began to work for the Arcadia Project as his assistant until he passed away four years ago."

"Was horribly murdered by Vivian, you mean."

"Yes." Caryl gave the wrist of each of her gloves a tug to settle them on more snugly. "I was the only wizard or warlock not already entrenched in a more important position, and so National allowed me to take over for him."

By my math, that made her fifteen when she was put in charge. "Was Martin good to you?"

"Martin was a wizard, not a warlock, and he found most of my powers disturbing. But he understood what it was to be a changeling and helped me come to terms with that. He also admired my intelligence, which I come by honestly. I understand my sister and brother are clever as well."

"You don't know your siblings?"

She shook her head. "We aren't family; even our blood is not the same. If I consider anyone family, I suppose it's Teo. He came to the Project a few months before I did, under similar circumstances."

I wondered all the more, now, what she'd thought of *The Stone Guest*, of the young heroin addict trying desperately to connect with her estranged mother after her father's death. I reached out to pat the air where Elliott appeared to be, absorbing all this before speaking again. "So what was it that you wanted to talk about?"

Caryl rose from the floor and moved to the window, looking out into the night. "Gate LA4 is right above you," she said. "The stairs leading to the tower are right outside your room."

"What the hell?" I looked up at the ceiling like an idiot.

"Do you want to see it?"

"Is it like the other one?"

"Almost exactly."

"Then no."

Caryl turned to look at me, leaning back against the window. "There is a ward on the door to the tower stairs, hiding it from sight."

"Can it hurt me, being so close to a Gate while I sleep?"

"Not in the way you mean. Its power is contained entirely within the archway. That is why the Gates are precisely semi-circular. Magical energy cannot escape a circle."

"Even half of one?"

"If it were a full circle, magic could travel perpendicular to the plane of the circle, within its boundaries, like a tunnel. An incomplete circle disrupts the tunnel effect, but if the missing portion is not bound to earth, magic can escape from the incomplete side as well."

I pointed above my head. "That's not earth."

"It is a solid surface perpendicular to the force of gravity, moving with the earth's rotation. For the purposes of magic, any floor is earth."

"So basically what you're saying is, don't punch a hole in the ceiling."

"The Gate is not dangerous in and of itself," Caryl said. "If you damage it in any way, it simply stops working, unless the one on the Arcadian side happens to be damaged in exactly the same way. Gate LA3 had to be dismantled in 1938, because damage was done to it so small it could not be located for repair."

"And you didn't build a new one? Like LA1?"

"We lost our only builders in 1913. So when we lost our lease on the LA2 property in the twenties we couldn't replace that one either. By the time everyday overseas travel made it practical to import builders from elsewhere, we'd become accustomed to operating with only three gates."

"If the Gate isn't dangerous, why even tell me about it?"

"You need to know," said Caryl, "because there is a possibility that Arcadia will declare war. And if they do, you are sleeping directly under a possible invasion point."

I sat up straighter, skin prickling. "Can't we close the Gate? I could go touch it with my Hands of Metal Death."

"Your touch would not disable it," Caryl said, "as it is not strictly speaking a magical object."

"Okay, but if you break it, that closes it, right?"

"To what end? There are others, and it would take only one to admit an Unseelie horde that could end human civilization in a fortnight. Furthermore, the closure of a Gate would provoke immediate inquiry and rob us of the time advantage we currently have."

"Probably not a fair trade for a good night's sleep. All right, so if the Unseelie horde does come through Gate LA4, what exactly am I supposed to do?"

"Die horribly. But swiftly, I'd think. They'll be eager to get on with their world conquest."

"Okeydokey then. Thanks for the heads-up."

"If you want to go back to the hospital, I understand. The safest place would be a church or temple, though; Unseelie fey can't enter sacred ground."

"Why not?"

"Fey's perception of reality is based on consensus rather than fact. A symbol imbued with power by the sincere belief of millions can manifest that power in a very real sense to a fey."

"But I couldn't stay in a church forever. So I'd still die horribly, right? Just later."

"Almost certainly."

"Then there's no way I'm not staying and at least trying to stop things from coming to that."

Caryl moved back toward me, reaching a gloved hand into the inside pocket of her jacket for a business card. It had only a number, no name. "Call me if you need to," she said. I felt a whisper of silk and card stock against my palm, and she left.

I showered, removed my prosthetics, and lay in bed with a racing heart, leaving the door open to ease my trapped feeling. I understood the magnitude of Caryl's gesture of trust in giving me her number, but I didn't call her. Nor did I take the Project-forbidden Vicodin that was so temptingly concealed in my suitcase, even though it would have helped.

I woke up every fifteen minutes or so all night long, and what little sleep I snatched from the jaws of dread was sullied with dreams of gorgeous angry things with sharp teeth. Halfway through the night Monty wandered in and settled on the air mattress next to me, giving me something to focus on so I could use my mindfulness exercises.

More than once I lulled myself to sleep by focusing on deep breathing and warm fur, only to have the same dreams wake me again on a half-strangled scream.

When the darkness weakened enough that I could justifiably declare it morning, I donned my prosthetics, put on my least stained clothes, and went down to the kitchen. I still hadn't bought any food of my own, so I was left picking through the unlabeled stuff. There was no way I was eating another bear claw after tasting one at the back of my throat for two hours on the way to Santa Barbara, so I settled on a slightly overripe banana, some saltines, and a cup of weak coffee.

Halfway through the coffee I became so suddenly, crushingly sleepy that I couldn't even make it back up the stairs. There is no sedative that works quite so well as the aftermath of adrenaline. I face-planted on a couch in the living room and blacked out, waking only when my phone rang at a quarter to seven.

I was careful this time and gave myself a few sound slaps across the face before picking up. "Hello?"

"Millie." It was Berenbaum. At the sound of his voice I remembered Rivenholt's blood all over the platform. My throat closed, and my eyes filled up. "Millie?" he said again.

If I said anything, he'd know I was crying. But the silence was getting awkward, so I squeezed out a "Yeah."

"I'm sorry," he said. "I know it's the ass-crack of dawn, but I wanted talk to you before I got to work. What happened at the train station?"

"I tried to call you," I said.

"I'm so sorry; I was up to my ass in alligators. Sweetheart—are you crying?" The softness, the lack of fear in his voice, meant he hadn't put things together yet.

"I screwed up," I said. "We didn't get there in time. I think Johnny's been hurt. I'm so sorry." I quit pretending I wasn't upset and just let go. He couldn't yell at me if I was already sobbing, right?

"Millie," he said. Firmly, bravely. As though he were about to explain to me why it was okay. But there were no facts to support that, so he just said, "Fuck work. Where are you?"

"I'm at Residence Four," I said. If he didn't know where that was, I was pretty sure I was not allowed to tell him.

"Don't go anywhere," he said. "I am going to come get you, and we're going to drive up the PCH, and you are going to stop crying, all right?"

I love you, I almost said.

I don't think that the instant desperate attachment Borderlines feel really counts as love, but I had never felt any other kind of love, so I didn't know. I knew that David Berenbaum was eventually going to break my heart, either by turning out to be a scumbag or deciding I was, but my crush on Brian Clay had been stillborn on the railroad tracks, and I was like Tarzan reaching for another vine. So I grabbed.

29

At five till eight in the morning, David Berenbaum pulled up to Residence Four in one of the most recognizable automobiles in the United States and maybe the world. When I glanced out the window and saw a flash of red in the morning sun, some eight-year-old inside of me said *oh my gosh*, because you don't say *holy shit* when you are eight years old.

A cherry-red 1967 Plymouth Valiant convertible—*the* cherry-red 1967 Plymouth Valiant convertible that David Berenbaum had been driving since, well, 1967—gleamed like imminent sin at the curb. It had been the hero car in six films, two of which Berenbaum didn't even direct. He was really pulling out all the stops to cheer me up, and I couldn't begin to wrap my brain around why.

I opened the front door and walked carefully down the steps, leaning on my cane. By the time I stepped onto the front lawn he was out of the car, keys jingling, door slamming. He ate up the ground between us like he was the twenty something and I was the senior citizen. He swept me up in a big hug, and I laughed even through the sharp pain in my ribs.

He looked at me as he set me down; his eyes were a little misty. "You okay?"

"Weirdly great at the moment," I said.

He put an arm around me and helped me across the lawn into the passenger's seat. The inside was red and white as a strawberry sundae, with black analog gauges. It was inefficient and sprawling; it screamed of hubris and excess and obsolescence; it was America on wheels.

As he started up the car, the insane anachronistic engine he'd put in there rumbled like the wrath of God. And off we went.

"There's a scarf in the glove compartment if you need it for your hair," he said.

"You take out a lot of women in this thing?" I said playfully.

"Well, my wife," he said. We'd just stopped at an intersection, so he turned and gave me a pointed look.

"I wouldn't touch anything that belonged to such a classy lady," I said, equally pointedly. "My hair will be fine."

"You are fantastic," he said, and the light turned green.

The traffic was not good at this hour, but who could possibly have cared? I had the whole blue California sky above me and one of the most famous men in the world sitting to my left. People were pulling out their phones to snap pictures. Twenty-four hours earlier I would have slumped down, used that scarf to hide my face, but now I just leaned my head back against the seat and enjoyed my fifteen minutes of fame.

Berenbaum respected my need to bask; he waited until we got onto the scenic portion of the Pacific Coast Highway to start talking business.

"I don't want you to worry about Johnny," he said. "If anything serious had happened to him, I would know. I still believe everything is going to be okay, and I need you to believe that with me, all right?"

"I do, I do, I do believe in fairies," I said. If he'd asked me to set his car on fire by a police station, I'd have said yes.

To our left, blue ocean shredded itself on golden rocks, and to our right the same rocks rose up to make a high wall, broken up with desert scrub and the occasional improbable patch of wildflowers. The highway writhed like a snake scaled with too many cars, hiding another gorgeous view around the next curve.

"Mr. Berenbaum!" called a young male voice a couple of lanes over and behind us. I turned and saw another convertible with a young guy leaning over the passenger's side.

At the look on the guy's face, I felt something dark and petty twist in my gut. I'd dreamed of being looked at that way, once. I'd imagined having fans, going to glitzy parties, winning Oscars. It hurt, remembering optimism that now looked like idiocy.

My self-pity didn't last long; David Berenbaum's presence was like a fire hose of sunshine.

"Read my script!" the guy shouted at him.

"I will if you can get it into my car," David called back over his shoulder.

The guy seemed to be doing some calculations and seriously thinking about throwing the thing. I felt bad for him; he had clearly never passed a physics class. But this was a Hollywood Moment. This could change his life. I didn't want to watch him make an ass of himself, but I also couldn't look away.

The screenwriter leaned over in an urgent conference with the driver, and I saw the turn signal go on.

"He's changing lanes," I said, now alarmed. "He's coming over here."

"Good for him!" Berenbaum said.

So much for my idyllic little date with David. "What if he has a gun or something?" I said.

"I hope you're not saying that because the driver is black."

"He is?" He was. I hadn't noticed. Or had I? Goddamn it. "It's not the driver I'm worried about," I said. "He has both hands on the wheel."

"Use your eyes, Millie," said David. "Be a director. What story are the visuals telling?"

I tried to relax, even as the other car tailgated the one next to us, trying to close the space. "It's a BMW. The writer's younger than the driver, maybe early twenties. Driver and passenger are both wearing designer stuff, but understated. I'm guessing old money."

"Rich kids are brought up with the idea that violence is beneath them," Berenbaum observed.

"Well, it is," I said as the BMW flashed its lights, honked, and otherwise made itself a nuisance to the car ahead of it.

"Grew up rich, eh?" He laughed. "It's easier to dehumanize someone than to try to understand the context of a violent act."

"Johnny's blood is splattered all over Union Station," I said recklessly. "Does the context of that violence matter to you?"

"Of course it does," he said without hesitation, making me wonder if he'd heard the extent of the carnage already. "Johnny may look like a pampered pretty boy, but he's also a savage motherfucker when he's cornered. I'm guessing he threw the first punch."

I had no time to consider this, because the guys in the BMW had finally caught up to us. I could see more telling details now: the Urth Caffé travel tumbler, the smugness, the slightly bored expression on the driver's face as he forced a panicked woman into the other lane. The dude in the passenger's seat looked excited, but the way you do when your home team is about to score. This was a kid who had never been denied anything.

He pulled up alongside and held the script out to Berenbaum, a stack of pages fluttering in the wind, sun glinting off the two brads holding it together. He knew proper industry format at least.

"Hold the wheel a second, will you?" said Berenbaum. Before I could tell him he was out of his mind, he let go and took the script.

"What is the *matter* with you?" I said, laughing from hysteria as I leaned against him to hold the wheel steady. Berenbaum barely slowed the car as he skimmed the first page, a page in the middle, and the last page.

He turned, then, and held the script back out to the kid in the BMW. "Sorry!" he said over the road noise. "Not for me!"

Either Berenbaum let go too soon or the kid's grip was as bad as his writing; the script fluttered free and bumped against the side of the BMW on the way to the pavement. Three cars had already run over it by the time I turned back around to stare incredulously at Berenbaum.

"Why did you do that?" I said when there was enough space between us and the now-crestfallen rich kid. "You knew the odds were strongly in favor of that script being a piece of shit."

"But what if it wasn't?" he said, giving me a big grin, his white hair dancing madly. "What a story that would have made."

That silenced me, and I just sat staring at this icon of a man, realizing how very far I was from understanding him. "Are we going anywhere in particular?" I said.

"Nope. I just like this drive. Been a long time since I've done it in this car, though. Not my smartest idea this time of day. But my gut told me that getting some blood pumping through your veins was the most important thing I could do this morning."

"Why?"

"I'm going to level with you, Roper. You're a mess, but you're my kind of mess. You're wasted in the Arcadia Project; it's nothing but a lot of hard-luck cases trying to scrape by."

"You're serious? You want me to leave the Project for good, work for you full-time?"

"I think we'd work well together. We could start you small, see how it goes. So much of this business is just who do you like spending time with? Who gets you? I'm sure you know what I mean."

"Not really. When I made films, I never worked with the same people twice. We always ended up hating each other."

"That's the kind of thing I could teach you. Give me two or three years and I could have people willing to take a bullet for you." He looked away from the road to pin me with those sharp eyes. "Do you think I'm a nice guy, Millie? Really?"

"You've been nice to me. Is that an act?"

"No. I'm crazy about you. But I'm saying that sometimes it *is* an act, when it needs to be. You have to protect your heart, or you have to kill it. And if you kill it, well, what happens if you come across someone who needs it?"

"Nobody needs mine," I said. "I think you have a hard time understanding the idea of complete insignificance."

"What about your family?"

"Don't have any."

"Everybody has family."

"I have redneck grandparents on my mom's side; last talked to them on the phone when I was twelve. Never knew my dad's parents. He and my mom were both only children, and they're dead."

"What happened to them?"

"Nothing happened to *them* as a couple. My mom got some weird cancer that killed her in about two weeks when I was a baby. My father was a suicide, about three years ago now. A four-story building, I might add. I don't know why I'm still here after seven."

"Destiny," said Berenbaum, with enthusiasm. I couldn't help but smile through my annoyance. If I was looking for commiseration, I was in the wrong car.

"Okay," I said, "so what do I have to do to come work for you? I haven't signed an agreement with the Arcadia Project yet; ideally we should set this up before they ask me to."

"Well, I'd love for you to meet with Inaya, and I think now it's safe for you to meet with Vivian as well."

"Ooh," I said, and sucked air between my teeth. "This is a couple kinds of awkward."

"Why?"

As I was considering how much to tell him about my conversation with Inaya, my phone rang. I glanced at the number. It was blocked. Inaya? Caryl? I gave Berenbaum the universal gotta-take-this finger and put the phone to my ear. "This is Millie."

"I need you at Residence One," said Caryl's voice, barely audible over the road noise. "Can you get there? Do you remember the address?"

"I do. What's up?"

"An emissary from the Queen is waiting for us."

"From the Queen?" I said stupidly.

"Of the Seelie Court."

Berenbaum, ever alert to nuance, was already changing lanes to make his way to the nearest exit.

"I'll be right there," I said to Caryl, and hung up.

"Where to?" said Berenbaum.

"Santa Monica."

30

When Berenbaum's Valiant rounded the corner of Pier Avenue, four heads turned. Caryl was leaning casually against the BEWARE OF DOG sign while my coworkers orbited her with varying degrees of nervousness. Teo appeared to have actually combed his hair, and Tjuan was squatting down on the sidewalk, letting Gloria pick lint off his button-down. They all stared as we pulled up to the curb.

"Hey, guys!" called Berenbaum, waving from the driver's seat like the grand marshal of a parade. "Sorry it took so long. Traffic was a bitch!"

I got out of the passenger's side and used my cane and the hood to steady myself as I walked around the car. The devil made me lean over and give Berenbaum an airy good-bye kiss on the cheek. His eyes twinkled with repressed laughter.

"Later, darling," I said. "I'll call you."

My moment of glory didn't last. The minute Berenbaum drove away, the stares all moved to me, one blank and three decidedly unfriendly.

"We thought you were back at the hospital, or hiding out in a church," said Teo. "All that time you're just out for a joyride."

"You shouldn't have called her," said Tjuan.

"I was working!" I said as Caryl unlocked the gate. "I can't help it if I make it look fabulous."

Tjuan gave me a look of such withering contempt that it smothered the last gasp of my good humor. What was his deal with me? Teo and Gloria had good reason to dislike me, but I'd never been anything but civil to Tjuan. I tried not to dwell on it; it was far from the first time a clique had reacted to me as though they shared a brain.

"Berenbaum assures me Rivenholt is still alive," I said more seriously, "and he's going to arrange for me to meet with Vivian Chandler and Inaya West." Those things were both true. If they chose to connect them in a way that sounded Project-related, all the better.

"It might be too late," said Teo, offering me his arm as we headed for the sloping sidewalk. I ignored it but made a mental note under the heading Reasons Not to Strangle Teo. "In the ten years I've been with the Project," he said, "the Queen has never sent an emissary here. I think the shit's already hit the fan."

Caryl gave Teo a bland look. "Let us postpone hysteria until we have spoken to the man."

Caryl's use of "man" notwithstanding, the creature sitting in the leather armchair in the back bedroom had not even bothered with a facade. I suppose he looked vaguely human, aside from being beautiful enough to burn trails of fire down my optic nerves. The green raccoonlike markings around his eyes might have passed for a mask in dim light, but the eyes themselves shone like pools of mercury, and on closer examination he had only four fingers on each hand.

"Greetings, allies mine," he half sang, rising to reveal a height in excess of seven feet. "My name is called Duke Skyhollow, Right Hand of Her Majesty, Queen Dawnrowan of the Seelie Court." He put his emphasis on all the wrong syllables. Not someone who spent a lot of time on this side of the Gate, apparently.

"We are honored by your presence, Your Grace," said Caryl. "I am Marchioness Caryl Vallo, and my companions are Viscount Tjuan Miller, Viscountess Gloria Day, Baron Mateo Salazar, and Lady Millicent Roper."

What the hell?

"I thank thee of thy welcome gracious, my lady," Skyhollow said with a theatrical bow.

"And I thank you for your patience. How may we serve Her Majesty?"

"The Queen is under large distress," the duke said. "We wish to know why Her Majesty's agent reports not."

"Her Majesty's agent?" Caryl echoed. "You must mean our errant viscount. I was not aware that he was representing Her Majesty in any capacity."

"Nay," said the duke. "Not a viscount, the agent of whom I speak. It is a commoner."

Caryl was speechless for a full four seconds, though no sign of shock or distress appeared on her face. "I see. So you mean to say another fey *besides* Viscount Rivenholt has failed to return to Arcadia as scheduled?"

"At this time, the return of the commoner was not to expect. It was to report at dawn and dusk on its progress. However, twice it hath failed to report, and thus demandeth Her Majesty its ASAP return to Arcadia. Thou art ordered in this matter to assist."

"Because we're so great at rounding up rogue fey this week," muttered Teo behind me. He seemed to be having an easier time than I was untangling the duke's syntax.

"Give me the commoner's name," said Caryl with the alacrity of someone given a stay of execution. "I shall locate the corresponding file and begin the search immediately."

"Of the hircine persuasion is this commoner, and its name is called Claybriar."

"I know him," said Caryl. "A regular through LA5. There was nothing on his latest entry form about a mission for the Queen. You are certain the Queen said Claybriar?"

Fuck, I thought. Out loud, apparently, to judge by the way every head swiveled around to look at me. *Claybriar.* Brian Clay. He was fey, he was fey, he was fey. What the double *hell.*

The duke turned his masked silver eyes on me. "Wherefore doth the lady ejaculate?" Teo attempted to stifle a sudden coughing fit.

"It's Brian Clay," I said to Caryl.

"That is Claybriar's registered alias. What of it?"

"Brian Clay is the fake cop I've been talking about."

She stared at me a moment. "If you had told me the man's name," she said crisply, "it would have saved me a great deal of confusion."

The duke made an irritated sound. "Speak please to *me.*"

I turned to him. "Tjuan and I, uh . . . Viscount Miller and I ran into this 'agent' in another part of town," I said.

"Provide more detail," demanded the fey.

This was an awkward position for me for a number of reasons. "I . . . I defer to Viscount Miller."

Tjuan studied me for a moment, his expression shifting

subtly; then he turned to the duke. "This was a couple of days ago," he said. "He was looking for Viscount Rivenholt. He said something about a missing woman."

The duke sniffed. "I see."

Caryl spoke up gently. "Claybriar is one of the few commoners who visits here regularly. He has never posed as a police officer before, however. May we ask the exact nature of his mission?"

"You may not," said the duke. "In this matter, the Queen and I alone are authorized." He gave "authorized" the same tone a new bride uses with the word "husband," half-sincere and half as though it were all a crazy joke.

"Forgive me, Your Grace," I said, "but don't you think it would be easier for us to find Claybriar if we know his purpose here?"

"Mayhap," said the duke, his silver eyes giving off such an intense radiance that I saw spots when I looked away. "But of less concern to me is your ease than my imperative to following Her Majesty's commands."

"Of course," said Caryl. "When shall we report back on our progress?"

"Dawn and dusk, until the commoner is returned," said the duke. "Advised are you to more seriously adhere on this matter than has done the commoner agent."

Caryl escorted the duke back to the Gate, and everyone avoided looking at the Gaping Maw of Nothingness as he stepped through. Even so, there was a strange shudder in the air, and my stomach turned a flip. I was pleased to see that even Tjuan looked a bit queasy, and Gloria sat down on the floor and put her head in her hands.

Fascinated, I approached the Gate, averting my eyes from the void in the middle and focusing on the dark glassy arch that surrounded it. "Is it safe to touch?"

"It will do you no lasting harm," said Caryl, "but it will make you feel very uncomfortable."

"Can I try it?"

"Why?"

"I don't know. I'm just curious. I tend to try anything once if it can't kill me."

Teo snorted. "What can?"

I ignored him and reached out to the edge of the Gate, slowly, not quite finding the courage to make contact.

"So how should we go about finding this commoner?" said Gloria, still sitting on the living room carpet at Tjuan's feet.

"He has a name," growled Tjuan.

"Sorry, sweetheart," said Gloria, and patted his shin. How he managed not to kick her across the living room, I can't imagine.

"I'll try calling Clay again when I—AUGH!" I didn't mean to scream when I touched it. But try not screaming when someone cuts your elevator cable. That's what it felt like: a horrible rickety noisy rushing and falling that left no room in my brain for anything but *aaaaaaaaugh*.

Even Tjuan laughed this time. I guess it was pretty funny, in the way it's funny when a cat gets a luggage tag stuck to its tail and runs around the house like the devil is chasing it. In other words, funny to everyone but the cat.

I staggered back from the Gate and wondered why my ribs suddenly hurt. Oh, because Teo had slung his arm around them to keep me from toppling to the floor. Everything sounded muffled, and people looked like those old-fashioned sepia-toned photos with the edges darkened out. It passed quickly, and when my head cleared I was seated semi-comfortably on the floor. People were still laughing, except for Caryl, of course.

"Poor thing," said Gloria. "Someone really shoulda warned her not to do that."

"Nah," said Tjuan, wiping his eyes. He looked like he had really needed that laugh. "That's how it's done. You do it when we're all just messing around, so you know not to do it when you're trying to push some wriggly-ass goblin through."

There must have been a story to go with that, because Teo made a taunting *oooooh* sound, and Gloria reddened. Another point for Tjuan, because Gloria was quiet after that.

I dialed Brian Clay, listened to ringing, and hung up. "Surprise surprise," I said to everyone. "He's not answering."

"So what kind of a thing is this Claybriar?" said Teo. "Green Lantern forgot to mention that, so we don't know if he has any weird powers."

"He did mention it," said Caryl. "You just don't know what hircine means."

Teo shrugged. "Got me there."

"Hairy?" I guessed.

"That's hirsute," Caryl corrected me. "Hircine means goat-like or pertaining to goats. So, a faun."

"Ah," I said. Then in another tone entirely, *"Aaaaaah!"* I looked at Teo, but he just stared blankly back at me.

"Caryl," I said, "how common are fauns?"

"Claybriar is the only one I have ever seen."

"In that case, I need to talk to Baroness Foxfeather again."

• • •

Baroness Foxfeather, Seelie noble and bartender, was renting a posh little one-bedroom apartment during what was apparently an extended stay in our world to search for her Echo. Since Caryl felt that five people was a bit much for an interrogation, she managed to talk Gloria and Tjuan into staying home with her to look through files.

When Teo and I arrived at the painstakingly restored Hollywood apartment building, Foxfeather buzzed us in and answered the door naked.

"It's Ironbones!" she said in delighted surprise, as though I had not identified myself at the buzzer. "What a terrifying honor! Would you like to come in for sex and oranges?"

I'll confess I missed a beat. "I'm honored by the invitation," I said solemnly, "but we're just here to chat."

"Okay," she said, letting us in. She gestured to a closed door off to our left. "Three of my friends are sexing in there, but I told them to be quiet since the Authorities were coming. How can I help the Authorities?"

I tried not to stare at the closed door. "You carved a faun into the bar in West Hollywood."

"Mmm," she said. "Now everyone has started carving things. I'm wonderful that way." She turned and padded off to the right toward the small kitchenette, separated from the living room only by a long stretch of countertop. Her long braid was a strawberry-blond arrow pointing right at her magnificent ass.

"Should I ask her to put some clothes on?" I said to Teo quietly.

"I promise she's safe from my evil groping man-hands."

"What? That's not what I— You know what, never mind. I'm just going to let people keep thinking I'm an asshole. It's so much less trouble."

Foxfeather grabbed an orange from a basket on the counter and dug into the peel with her fingers, her eyes hot. "You sure you don't want some?" she said, as the sharp citrus smell began to waft over to us.

"Orange?" I said. "It's just a regular orange?"

"No," she said with wide, serious eyes. "It's *Valencia*."

I glanced at Teo. He slipped on his shades for a moment. "It's clean," he said, and slipped them off again.

"Uh, okay," I said, turning back to her. "So, this guy you carved, was that someone you know?"

Foxfeather tore a long spiral strip of peel from the orange, shivering with anticipation. Her eyes never left the fruit as she answered me in a dreamy tone. "I don't know the faun *personally*," she said. "But yes, it did come into my bar one day, and I had to throw it out."

"Why?"

Foxfeather looked up at me and gave her thumb a long, slow lick. "It was a bad faun," she said. "Very, *very* bad."

31

"In what way was this faun bad, exactly?" I asked Baroness Foxfeather, watching her peel long white fibers away from the pulp of her orange.

"Mmm, it put on such an interesting human face, I didn't think to look underneath until we were already talking. And then I had to throw it out of the bar. Filthy thing."

"So his crime was—being a commoner, basically. Got it. Was his name Claybriar?"

"Probably. That sounds like the sorts of names those things have." Her fingers savagely tore loose a slippery wedge of orange and pushed the end of it into her mouth. As she bit it in half, her eyes grew fixed and bright with joy. She beckoned me closer with one finger.

I glanced at Teo, who gave me a *go on* gesture. He himself looked like his feet had grown roots in the floor.

Leaning heavily on my cane, I made my way toward her. The countertop was between us; she leaned her elbows on it and continued to beckon me as though intending to whisper. I leaned over the counter helpfully, but instead of speaking she held out the other half of the orange wedge. When I reached for it, she laughed and moved it behind her back.

I sighed. "Do you remember what Claybriar talked to you about?"

"Not really," Foxfeather said, holding out the orange wedge again. I didn't reach for it this time. "It had three drinks very fast and asked me a lot of very boring questions." She was still holding out the orange and beginning to look both impatient and hurt, so I reached for it, only to have her snatch it away again.

I gritted my teeth and took a deep breath. "Did the faun ask you about Viscount Rivenholt, or mention the Queen?"

"May Her Majesty, Queen Dawnrowan, reign for eternity. Hold still and open your mouth."

I leaned my elbow on the counter and did as she asked. Foxfeather leaned forward in all her spectacular nakedness. Either she had put on some of that body lotion with glitter in it, or else a bit of fey was bleeding through her human skin. She slipped the orange wedge into my mouth, making no effort to avoid touching my lips with her fingers. At the contact, her facade dissolved like sugar, leaving me struck dumb by her starlight-and-opal beauty. When she withdrew her fingers, the facade snapped back like a rubber band.

"It hurts a little to touch you," she said. "It feels like ice water pouring under my skin, and now I'm sleepy."

I had a mouthful of orange and a head full of fairy and could only say "Mm." I looked over at Teo. He was watching us intently, but more like he wanted to take notes than join in.

I swallowed and turned back to Foxfeather. "It's very important that you tell us what you remember about Claybriar, and what he said to you."

"Remembering is hard; I haven't found my Echo yet. Why is this important?"

"Because Claybriar is missing and so is Viscount Rivenholt."

"The viscount is missing?"

"Yes, we told you that before."

"I don't think you said that. I would have been worried."

I could feel a headache starting just behind my left eye. "Well, he is missing, and we think Claybriar may have hurt him, so we need to know everything we can about him."

"I don't know anything about the viscount."

"No, I meant Claybriar. I need to know about Claybriar."

"I'm sorry, I get confused because you keep saying 'him' like it's a person."

"He seemed like a person when I talked to him."

"It's a *facade*," she said as though I were the stupidest thing ever to crawl out from under a log.

"Just tell me what Claybriar wanted with you. Why he was in the bar."

"It had misplaced some commoners or something. That was how I smelled something rotten. Why would anyone care if a few commoners went missing?"

Missing persons again, just like "Officer Clay" had mentioned. This had to relate to his mission for the Queen.

"Apparently the Queen cares about at least one of them."

"She has to pretend she does, or they band together and loot and murder and it gets so *ugly*. Orange?"

I held up my hand in a sharp *no thank you* gesture, fighting the surge of fury that clenched my jaw. When dealing with the unknown, it's important not to assume that it parallels the known. I was 80 percent sure Foxfeather was full of shit about commoners, but 80 percent wasn't enough to justify choking the magic out of her right there in her kitchen.

"Anything else you remember?"

"It used your language well," she said, "so it obviously comes here a lot."

I watch too much TV, I suddenly remembered him saying at the coffee shop. I felt a weird twist in my gut. I should have known he was fey by the ridiculous amount of sugar in his drink.

"Did he say anything about when these commoners went missing? Was it all at once, or one at a time? How many are missing? Anything you can remember will be a huge help to the Arcadia Project, and to your Queen."

To her credit, she really did seem to be trying hard to remember. She frowned, and her eyes crossed slightly. "It came in, looking not very pretty, but nice dark hair. It ordered cherry-pomegranate juice. Talking, talking, talking, missing commoners, it held up its paw like this"— here she splayed her hand out in my face, sticky with orange juice—"then it said bad things about the viscount, so I peeked at its real face. Then I kicked it out. I was mad. I carved it into the bar, but then I forgot to set the bar on fire. It's still a very nice carving."

I turned to Teo, splaying my hand in the same gesture Foxfeather had made. "The hand might mean five missing. He only mentioned one girl when he was pretending to be a cop, but I don't think it's a coincidence that five is the same number of fey that have been half counted on the census for weeks. I think the Queen's trying to figure out where they've gone."

Teo studied Foxfeather for a moment. "My lady," he said, "do you know of any way, or any place, where a fey could be both here and in Arcadia at the same time? Like, stuck in transit?"

Foxfeather laughed. "No, silly. That would be like falling halfway down a hole. Sideways." She tilted her body charmingly at a near right angle and smiled. "One time, I held on to the edge of the Gate just for fun, but it stopped being fun very fast."

"No arguments here," I mumbled.

Teo caught my eye and gestured with his head toward the door, then looked back at Foxfeather. "If you hear or remember anything else, do you know how to contact our office?" he asked her.

"Yes," she said. "Are you leaving?"

"For now," said Teo.

"Come back if you want sex later."

I looked at Teo.

"Not a word from you," he said, and left.

I followed. "How do you know Foxfeather isn't your Echo?"

"I shook her hand the first time we met; I'd have felt it."

"What does it feel like?"

"I don't know, because it wasn't her. Come on, let's stop by the bar while we're on this side of town."

The Seelie bar wasn't quite open for business yet, but neither was it locked. I supposed the ward removed worries about people wandering in and looting the place.

Even without all the lights on, the colors of the paint and fabric and glass were breathtaking. The wooden bar, as Foxfeather had suggested, was embellished with new carvings, all of them masterpieces. I'm not sure what Teo expected to find there, though. Foxfeather's homage to the Very Bad Faun was an impressive work of art, but there were no clues to be found in it. The figure was carved from memory by a woman who admitted to a bad memory, and who had only glimpsed Claybriar's true face for a moment.

The portrait reminded me of Mr. Tumnus in my childhood copy of *The Lion, the Witch, and the Wardrobe*, minus the umbrella and parcels. Hadn't Tumnus been a traitor too? Despite an elongated jaw, the face in the carving could have passed for human. Foxfeather had carved him with a vapid expression, but I didn't read much into that. Was he awkward? Yes. Stupid? Not that I could tell.

I snapped a photo of the carving with my phone, for what it was worth, and then we stopped by the sushi place. Jeff, the guy who'd supposedly spoken to the "cop" about John Riven, wasn't working that day, but I left my number for him and stressed that it was very important. I wasn't holding my breath for a call back, though. I was not the kind of girl whose number guys wanted.

When I arrived back at the Residence, Tjuan was pacing the living room. "Did you see him?" he greeted us.

"See who?" said Teo.

"Black guy sitting in a car about half a block down," said Tjuan. "Been there an hour at least."

"You think he's staking us out or something?" said Teo dubiously.

"He doesn't live around here. I went for a run an hour ago, heard his door locks click when I went by. He's still there."

"What kind of car?" Teo asked.

"Old Taurus. But I looked in when I heard the locks, and he was dressed like some Beverly Hills bullshit."

I didn't get why a nicely dressed black man sitting in a car was a big deal, honestly, but I wasn't about to tell Mr. Hostility that he was being paranoid, especially since that might be part of his actual diagnosis. I went into the kitchen for a snack while he and Teo hashed it out. I was on my way back to the living room, banana in hand, when a knock sounded on the front door. Tjuan and Teo and I all looked at one another, me with a mouthful of banana.

Tjuan eased his way to the front door and very carefully peeked through the curtain. He turned back to us as though he'd seen a ghost.

"It's him," he said. "He's here."

"Well," said Teo, "should we answer it?"

"Fuck that," said Tjuan. "Locking his doors when I go by. Cheap car, nice clothes. This smells bad. Don't open the door." He looked genuinely panicked, more so than I felt the situation warranted.

Teo held his palms out. "Settle down, Tjuan. I think you're having one of your 'moments.' Let me have a look."

While Teo peeked out the curtain, Tjuan paced and took slow breaths. I felt an unexpected surge of sympathy for him.

"From the clothes," said Teo, "he's either selling something or preaching, and either way he can fuck off."

"Oh, for God's sake, you two," I blurted, and made my way to the door, cane thumping on the hardwood, banana still in hand. "Let's at least find out what he wants. I'm perfectly capable of slamming the door in his face if he tries to sell me a Bible."

I stuck the banana in my mouth to free a hand, opened the door, and sighed. There comes a point where surprises start to get tedious. It was the driver of the BMW from the PCH.

I popped the banana out of my mouth. "Relax, guys," I said over my shoulder. "It's just the paparazzi."

"Paparazzi do not ring the doorbell," said the man on the porch. His voice had an effeminate Ivy League snobbery to it that set my teeth instantly on edge. "I'm Ellis Barnes," he said. "I expect that name is familiar to you?"

It really wasn't. "I've had a rough morning," I said, still standing in a small wedge of open door between him and the interior of the house. "I'd appreciate a memory jog."

"I was so sure you'd know me," he said. "A fellow private eye, working for A-list Hollywood clients, you really should be more familiar with your competition." His tone was mocking, his words too on-the-nose. He knew I wasn't a private eye.

"You're the guy working for Inaya," I said. "What do you want?"

32

"May I come in?" said Ellis Barnes, PI.

"This isn't my house," I said, not budging from the doorway. "I don't have the right to let you in, and I don't think my friends are too keen on meeting you. State your business and let's keep this brief."

"I want to know why you called my client and why you lied to her about who you are."

"It's true I'm not a licensed PI," I admitted, "but I never explicitly said that I was. I am working for Berenbaum and trying to track down John Riven, and that's really more than you have any need to know."

"I'm investigating Riven too," said Ellis slowly, an odd expression on his face. "It seems as though we could help each other."

"Things aren't always what they seem. Anyway, I thought you were tailing Berenbaum, not Riven. What was that about this morning, with the screenplay?"

Ellis sighed. "My brother-in-law. He's obsessed with Berenbaum and likes to tag along when I do surveillance of him. I finally let him make contact because I wanted to get a better read on the relationship between the two of you. I'll confess

I'm intrigued. If Berenbaum were having an affair, he'd hardly flaunt it. So what's going on there?"

"I've already told you more than I need to."

"What if I had something to tell you in exchange, about John Riven?"

"I have the feeling that between the two of us, I'm probably the one with better dirt on Riven."

I heard a hissing noise from behind me and turned to see Teo making a slicing motion across his throat. I made a face at him and turned back to Ellis.

Ellis said, "Does your 'dirt' include his whereabouts last night?"

I blinked. "No, and neither does yours."

"Doesn't it?" Ellis said with a smile. "All right then. I'll leave you to your day. Here's my card if you decide you want to talk." He held it out, and I just glared at him, leaning on my cane. Unfazed, he smiled wider and left the card on the arm of the moldering love seat on the front porch. "Stay in touch," he said.

I waited until he had driven away, then took the card, went back inside, and bolted the door behind me.

Tjuan had apparently left during my conversation, but Teo was half sitting on the arm of the nearest couch, his eyes narrowed. "What did that dude mean, asking you if you knew where Rivenholt was last night?"

I shrugged. "He needs info about Berenbaum, so he's trying to get me to slip some. First he weakens me with guilt, then tempts me with dirt. If I weren't such a stubborn cuss, I'd probably be eating out of his hand."

"What if it's for real?"

I rolled my eyes. "He left his card. Take it if you want to call him." I held it out, but he didn't take it, so I stuck it in my pocket.

"You know, maybe you and I should straighten out who's Good Cop and who's Bad Cop."

Teo made a sound that wasn't quite a laugh. "Until now, I would have said there was no one in the world who would be worse at Good Cop than me. Whatever. I'm gonna go have a smoke."

"Isn't that against house rules?"

"I'm not going to smoke in the house, and I don't keep 'em in the house. If Caryl wants to make a thing out of it, she can change the wording in the contract."

"Hey, Teo, before you go . . ."

"Yeah?"

"It's probably against the rules to ask, but . . ."

"Spit it out."

"Why does Tjuan hate me so much?"

Teo stared at me for a second, then laughed. "You're kidding, right? The dude's got massive trust issues. When I first moved here, it took him three months to even answer when I said hi." He shook his head, walking away. "Not everything's about you, *mija*. Really gotta get that into your head."

After Teo left, I allowed myself a few moments to enjoy the peace and quiet and have a few crackers from the kitchen. The place was a little spooky when not populated, even in the daytime. The cracks in the bathroom tiles, the water stains on the dining room ceiling, the sun discoloration on the carpet by the sliding glass door: all symptoms of a house that wasn't cared for by its owner. I felt a little sorry for it.

I had just stuffed a handful of crackers in my mouth when I turned and saw Gloria in the kitchen doorway, staring at me with a look of naked contempt.

I coughed, spraying crumbs. "Uh, hi there," I said.

She smiled, sweet as antifreeze. "Does Caryl know you have plans to become a celebrity?" she said.

"Beg pardon?" I yanked a paper towel off the roll and attended to the mess I'd made.

"You're all over the paparazzi sites," she said. "Cuddling with David Berenbaum in his convertible. What's that all about, hon?"

I froze, feeling my hands go cold. As always, my first reaction to anyone talking to me in that tone was shame, as though I, and not the paparazzi, were guilty of something. I took a moment to talk myself down so I didn't go into a full-on panic attack. All I was guilty of, as far as I could see, was being interesting enough to be photographed. So just exactly what was Gloria's problem?

"I don't know what to tell you," I said. "He and I hit it off. It's perfectly innocent."

If anything her smile got frostier. "Shall we expect you to be starring in your own reality show soon?" she drawled. "Or do you think you've maybe attracted enough attention to the Arcadia Project for now?"

"I'm sorry about that," I said. "I didn't really think it through."

"And just what good is 'sorry' going to do if the paparazzi start camping on our doorstep? Is there anything else you haven't thought through that we should maybe know about before it shows up all over the Internet?"

My pulse accelerated. By the grace of Dr. Davis I managed to keep it together, though I couldn't stop my hands from shaking or think of anything clever to say. In my directing days I could have won a shouting match with a howler monkey, and now I was trembling at a few sugarcoated rhetorical questions.

"What exactly is it you'd like me to do?" I said as calmly as I could.

"There's nothing you can do," she said. "I e-mailed some of the worst links to Caryl. I normally keep out of this kind of stuff, but ever since I heard about what you did to Teo, I've been keeping my eye on you. I don't take kindly to people who mistreat that boy, so you'd better step real carefully from here on out, hon."

"I—*what*?" Mistreating Teo? She must have meant the time I hit him, but who had told her? And she was full of shit anyway; she'd been trying to cut me down to size from minute one. But before I could retort in any coherent manner, she'd already made her exit.

I used my good knee to deliver a weak kick to the kitchen cabinet, leaning both hands on the counter. Venting anger is a hard thing to do when you have no one to yell at and very little kicking power. I fumbled through Dr. Davis's exercises in my mind, but it was hard because I was dealing with anger and panic at the same time. Through my Borderline filter, everyone in the house had turned against me and was plotting to bring me down. All it takes is a fragment or two of evidence, and my mind leaps to join dots that aren't there, constructing a picture of conspiracy that is almost impossible to unsee.

My attempts at calming myself with DBT skills were not working, at least not fast enough to satisfy me. So I answered that frantic little voice saying *do something, fix it, fix it*, and called Berenbaum. Another bad move straight out of the What-Not-to-Do Handbook. Never, ever call someone important when you're having a spell of "intense episodic dysphoria," as the DSM-V calls it.

Araceli put me through to Berenbaum without a lot of fuss, but he didn't sound as warm as I wanted—no, needed—him to sound. It was probably because of work, my Reason Mind should have prompted, but my paranoid Emotion Mind was making everything about me.

"What can I do for you?" he said.

"I don't want to work for the Arcadia Project anymore," I said. It was by far the least crazy thing I could have said under the circumstances. Perhaps Dr. Davis's lessons in self-control were buried somewhere in my subconscious after all.

"You'll want to set up a meeting with Vivian," he said.

Not what I wanted to hear. Very much not.

"I've met her before. We didn't get along."

"She doesn't get along with anyone. But she will play ball on this, I guarantee. She's been desperate for someone who can mediate between the studio and the Project."

"Can you call her and set something up?"

"I would, but I'm up to my ass in a new pile of alligators. Crocodiles, too, and I think there's a Komodo dragon in there somewhere. Are those things poisonous? Besides, you need to make the call, because you have to get her to promise not to cause you harm."

"Oh, I always do that when I set up job interviews."

He laughed, thank God. I could feel all the tension draining out of me like he'd stuck me with a pin. "Just be sure you say it like that, 'cause me harm,' not 'hurt me.'"

"Why?"

"Well, if she somehow causes an anvil to fall on your head, technically it's the anvil, not her, that hurts you."

"Jesus. Okay. Can I have her mobile number?"

I programmed it into my phone, then called it while I was still on a high from talking to Berenbaum; otherwise I would have chickened out.

"Hi there," I said when she answered. "It's Millie. David told me to call you."

"Millie who?"

Oh right. She'd never gotten my name in Santa Barbara. Then I remembered why, and panicked. Could she do scary hoodoo with just a first name? I hoped not. It also occurred to me that connecting myself with the resort incident might not be to my advantage anyway.

"I'm a protégée of David's," I said instead. "He told me there was some stuff about the studio he wanted you to explain to me, and that we should meet to talk about it."

"I can't imagine what he was thinking."

"You can ask him if you like," I said. "He just told me he wants me involved and that I have to meet with you."

Vivian let out a delicate snort. "If he thinks I'm going to bark on command like everyone else in his life, he can think again. I'm not interested in bringing in anyone else." I could tell she was winding up to a curt good-bye, so I pulled out the stops.

"I'm with the Arcadia Project. We've met, actually."

I held my breath, wondering if the silence on the end of the line indicated that she was taken aback, that she didn't remember me, or that she'd hung up before I had the chance to blow her mind.

"You were the one with Caryl at Regazo de Lujo," she finally said.

"Yes, ma'am."

"You're right. David did mention you. I'm sorry; I've been a bit distracted lately."

An uncanny number of people in my life were saying that right now, and I was beginning to suspect that they were all distracted by the same thing.

"So you'll meet with me, then?"

"How about tonight? Latish."

"First, promise you won't cause me harm."

"David's been coaching you, I see. I promise I won't cause you harm *tonight*, but that's all the commitment I'm ready for. Does nine o'clock work for you?"

"So long as you promise you won't keep me past midnight."

"Ugh! Fine. I promise I will end the meeting before midnight. Two promises in one phone call! I'm going soft. Meet me at nine o'clock at Gotham Hall."

"Goth— That weird bar on the Promenade? Didn't it close ages ago?"

"Did it?" she said with a smile I could hear through the phone. "You may want to check again. Really look hard, and think of me when you do, darling."

33

When I told Caryl that I intended to meet with Vivian, Elliott turned a flip and fluttered blindly into the wall of Teo's bedroom.

Caryl had found me there snooping around on the computer, but I was pretty sure she hadn't seen exactly what I was doing, which was for the best. You'd think that "Gloria Day murders" would have turned up something on Google even without adding in "dwarf" or "midget," but no matter what combination of keywords I tried, I couldn't dig up a speck of information on the alleged crime. How was this not plastered all over the Net?

"No," Caryl said calmly. "You are not going to meet with Vivian Chandler."

"David pretty much ordered me to," I said, adjusting my fey glasses farther up the bridge of my nose. They weren't a great fit.

Caryl folded her arms and leaned back against the wall. "Why would he do that?"

Oh. Right. Probably not a good idea to tell her that part.

"Well, we're pretty sure she was involved in getting Rivenholt out of the train station, right?"

"Even if she was, it remains ambiguous whether she was helping him or whether she was part of the attack."

"That's exactly what I'd like to find out."

"I will go with you," she said as Elliott fluttered back to her shoulder.

In my experience, it's generally a bad idea to take your current boss along on a job interview, so I groped for an objection. "Vivian doesn't like you."

"True, but you'll be defenseless without my magic."

I started to tell her about Vivian's promise but hesitated. She might wonder why Vivian would take the meeting seriously enough to offer that promise. "Why would she bother hurting me?" I said instead.

"She owns a pest control company, Millie; she had a large fortune and chose to invest it in wholesale extermination."

"Killing me would harm Berenbaum, wouldn't it?"

"Negative emotions do not fall under the fey's understanding of 'harm,' since humans frequently and demonstrably seek them out."

"Vivian can't lay a hand on me without destroying her own facade. What harm could she do?"

"She doesn't need to lay a hand on you. She can create metaspells."

"What the hell does that mean?"

"Her wards can cast their own enchantments. Say Vivian is in Paris and you try to break into her warded house in Los Angeles. The ward casts an enchantment on you when you pass over the windowsill, and the enchantment causes your heart to explode. She has a perfect alibi."

"Wouldn't my touch disable the ward, though?"

"Not if she was still powering it."

"But it couldn't work *while* I was touching it. Anyway, I'm not sure a curse on me would even stick."

Elliott spread his wings halfway out and bared his teeth, shifting from foot to foot. "She could cast a charm on an object," Caryl said, "a charm that psychically compelled you to kill yourself. You've seen that you're not immune to psychic spells."

I exhaled, defeated. "Look. I made her promise not to cause me harm."

"I find it hard to believe she would consent to that."

"Well, she promised not to cause me harm *tonight*, or to keep me past midnight."

"That sounds slightly more plausible." She considered. "But I didn't hear the conversation; there may be a loophole."

"This is like Russian roulette with six thousand chambers. I'm okay with that level of risk."

"If you find yourself on the end of the wrong chamber, it does not matter what your odds were."

"If I die, you can say 'I told you so' at my grave, and that would probably be more fun than working with me."

Caryl gave me one of her long, blank stares as Elliott tucked his head and closed up his wings. "Very well," she said, "do as you like." She turned for the door as Elliott gave me a tragic look over her shoulder.

"Caryl . . . ," I began. But she was already gone.

Gotham Hall, as best I remembered from my dance-club days, had been near the Broadway end of the Third Street Promenade in Santa Monica. It was a quarter till nine when I got there, so the Westside's pedestrian shopping paradise was aglow with strings of lights and loud with the music of street performers. I paused by the vomiting-stegosaurus fountain to slip on my fey glasses.

I still couldn't see the entrance to Gotham Hall, but I could now see a suspicious dark webbing stretched across the narrow space between the clothing store and the mortgage broker on the corner. It reminded me of the glamour on the Seelie bar, but it was infinitely more intricate, a thing of mesmerizing fractal beauty.

I wasn't sure how literal Vivian had been when she said, *Think of me*, but I gave it a shot, holding her image in my mind. As I did so, the strands of the dark web began to snap, parting dramatically like a theater curtain to reveal the red maw of Gotham Hall. The doorway was narrow, oppressed by the two buildings on either side of it, and just inside the dimly glowing passage stood two gorgeous, bored-looking bouncers.

"Ten dollars, please," said the ebony idol on the left as I approached.

"Vivian told me to meet her here."

"Do you have an invitation?" said the bronze idol on the right. They were both human, according to my sunglasses, but *damn*.

"If you mean a written invitation, then no."

"Ten dollars, please," said the ebony idol.

I grumbled and fished for my wallet.

Inside, the narrow hallway was a dim Looking Glass nightmare of venous red walls, purple curtains, and chessboard tile. Just the sort of place a homesick vampire might find comforting. Soulless dance music pulsed in my ears as I tried vainly to adjust my eyes. Weirdly, the patrons seemed to be human. If any of them found it odd that I was wearing sunglasses in the dark, they neglected to say so.

As I recalled, the downstairs consisted only of a dance floor and a billiards room, so I painstakingly climbed the surreal stairs—almost too narrow for two people to pass each other— up to the bar and eating area. The second story was elegant, though still moody: cinnamon wood floor, honey-gold wallpaper with the texture of crushed velvet, cloudy violet ceiling. There were a dozen or so people wandering about in various states of substance abuse.

Vivian sat with her back to me at the bar, posed with casual grace, dark hair shining. She wore Elvira heels and sheer black stockings with a seam up the back. Despite her come-hither attire, three bar stools on either side of her were clear. Perhaps the patrons could sense what I saw through my glasses: the aura of bruised misery that hung over her like San Fernando smog.

The sound of my cane caught her attention as I approached. She swiveled and held out her hand without getting up, speaking with that bubbly L.A. lilt that mismatched her appearance so disturbingly. "Millie. A pleasure to finally have a name to go with that unforgettable face."

"Forgive me if I don't shake your hand," I said, stopping just out of arm's reach and taking off my sunglasses.

"Oh my, my," she said with a Cheshire smile. "What has little Caryl been telling you about me?"

"More to the point, what has she told you about me?"

"Not a thing."

"Then first, you need to know I have so much steel holding

my bones together I get hit on by robots. Second, I'm pretty sure you don't want the good people here to see you without your makeup on." It was the best I could do to warn her without mentioning the word "magic" around a bunch of human eavesdroppers I didn't know.

"I see," said Vivian slowly, retracting her hand. "I *see*. Please have a seat. So Caryl has Ironbones on call now. Charming."

"People keep calling me that," I said, leaving a stool between us so our legs didn't accidentally touch. "Is that a thing?"

She laughed. "Not really. It's like, oh, what do parents say around here? The boogeyman."

"A monster with iron bones, I take it?"

"Also claws. The comic book character Wolverine is loosely based on him, in fact, or so the rumors go. Len Wein's Echo must have been very naughty as a child."

"I'm the fairy boogeyman," I said dryly. "No wonder everyone in the Seelie bar panicked."

Vivian let out a musical laugh, even as she touched a finger to her lips to silence me. She leaned in a bit, lowering her voice to an almost seductive murmur. "I'd love to have been there to see that," she said. "Seelie are so adorable when they're frightened."

"So all these people," I said quietly, "they're just regular people? Not . . . in the know?"

"That's right."

"How did they even get in?"

"They have invitations," she said. "If you have an invitation, it's a perfectly normal club. If not, it doesn't appear. That makes the bouncers' jobs boring, but it gives me *exquisite* control over my social life."

"Well, if we can't talk business here at the bar, could we move somewhere else?"

"Am I keeping you from a date? By all means then, let's hurry things along."

She moved us to a small corner table in the next room that was removed from the general flow of traffic, but unfortunately, it was still not secluded enough to allow us to talk with perfect privacy. The chairs were spidery and misshapen in a way I couldn't quite place.

I declined a stoned-looking waitress's offer of something to eat, but Vivian ordered a slice of chocolate cake before leaning back in her chair at ease. "Before we talk about the studio," she said, "let's talk about you a little."

"All right," I said warily. "What would you like to know?"

"What exactly happened between the time you slept with your screenwriting professor and the time you jumped from the roof of Hedrick Hall?"

If I'd had a drink, I would have choked on it. I had a feeling she was dying for me to ask how she knew, so I didn't.

"It's complicated," I said, running my fingertips over the wood of the table. Its gleaming, raspberry-chocolate finish echoed Vivian's hair. "And it's really not relevant to our business here."

Vivian did nothing more than shift her gaze directly to mine, but I felt as though she had grabbed me by the collar and yanked me across the table. "I asked you," she said in a tone that made my arm hair stand up. "That makes it relevant."

For maybe the length of two frames of film I *saw* her. I don't know if she dropped her facade, or if I disrupted it in some way, or if I simply saw through it. But for that subliminal

flash of a moment I was sitting across from a bat-winged creature of horrible grandeur, with spiderweb hair and mantis jaws
and eyes like bleeding wounds. And then it was Vivian again,
smiling sweetly.

"I'm going to ask you one more time," she said. "What
exactly happened at UCLA?"

34

When I was able to locate some saliva and peel my tongue off the roof of my mouth, I did my best to answer Vivian's question. "Like you said, I slept with my screenwriting professor," I said. Treading this old ground turned my stomach into a lump of lead. "We'd gotten pretty close outside of class by then, but he was . . . cold to me afterward. I was confused, and I confided in a couple of people I considered friends. After that, somehow the whole campus knew."

I paused as the waitress approached the table with Vivian's cake, setting it down in front of her. Both waitress and cake may as well have been invisible for all Vivian noticed them; her eyes were fixed on me. "So what happened next?" she prompted.

I waited until the waitress was out of earshot. "He told everyone that I had made the whole thing up. He was highly thought of, and I'd shown just enough signs of crazy by then that people believed him. Rooms got quiet when I walked in. I was miserable, started flunking classes, so I confronted him about it. He accused me of sexual harassment and said that if I ever tried to talk to him alone again or continued with my 'accusations,' he would involve the authorities."

"Fascinating," Vivian said, leaning forward slightly. "He lied even in private? How did you end up sleeping with him in the first place?"

"I wish I knew. I went over to his place, and was trying to get him to talk to me about what was bothering him, and then suddenly we were—" I stopped and shook my head.

"You were what?"

My hands went cold. "Please don't make me talk about this."

"I am not *making* you," she said. "Though I can. Would you like me to?"

I leaned over the table; the words spilled from my mouth like bile. "I was in his room, trying to get him to open up and— we kissed and he pushed me down on the bed and—we had sex." I wouldn't give her the satisfaction of the details: his strange, bleak urgency, the scratchy afghan against my cheek.

"Why were you alone with him at his place to begin with?" she asked, with the precision of someone locating a paralyzing nerve cluster.

Dr. Davis's voice said, *Your guilt is disproportionate. You were both consenting adults. He initiated sex; you were only there out of concern for him.*

Another voice answered: the same inner voice I'd tried to drown with expensive scotch. *Then why did you shave your legs and put on lacy underwear? Why did you wear his favorite perfume to class? Why did you spend weeks finding all the cracks in his armor so that you could painstakingly pry it open?* Even a year later the guilt was noxious, strangling.

"It was just—" I faltered. "It was the end of a long process of— It was like the frog in the boiling water."

Vivian looked at me blankly.

"I mean, our relationship escalated slowly. Got more and more inappropriate without our quite realizing it. He had some emotional problems too, though he was better at hiding them. I thought I could help him. I thought we were—" And then I couldn't talk anymore.

"Friends?" Vivian finished for me, with a slow smile.

I nodded. This was not what I'd hoped for in a job interview.

"Losing him made you want to end your life?"

"It wasn't the first time I'd thought of suicide. I guess it was just the first time I'd been drunk enough to do it."

"Fabulous," she said brightly, and finally picked up a fork to address her slice of chocolate cake. "Next topic."

I felt light-headed. I wished I had ordered a drink, even a soda, so I'd have something to do besides stare at the table, feeling my hands going numb. "The next topic is?"

"Why David wants to hire you."

I tried to find my footing in the conversation again. "He, uh, he seems to think I show—"

"It wasn't a question."

I sat back boneless in my chair while Vivian took a bite of cake. It was just like with Gloria. I should have fought. I would have, a year ago, or at least showed some spine. But I wasn't that girl anymore. Nor did I have that exact spine, not to put too fine a point on it.

Vivian slid the fork from her mouth, then studied the gory smear of red lipstick she'd left on it. "David's a horrible romantic," she said. "He can't resist the lure of a broken-winged bird. I'm not sure if it's about his immortal soul or about PR, but either way, you're like a steak dinner to him. A talented director with a tragic past who just needs a bit of inspiration. . . ."

"You think I'm talented?" *Millie. Sadistic vampire interrogating you. Focus.*

"I could care less," she said, attacking the cake again. "It's David who wants an apprentice, not me. I just want someone to lie to the Arcadia Project when they come calling."

I stared at her in disbelief. "And why is it you think I'd do that for you?"

Vivian laid down her fork and lowered her voice until it was almost inaudible. "You know what I do, right?" she said. "What I am."

I leaned forward to hear her, despite myself. "A bloodsucking vampire," I said.

She laughed. "There are no such things as vampires."

"But you drink blood."

"Listen, darling. I live here, but I maintain . . . connections in Arcadia. I use those connections to match actors with their Echoes and turn them into stars. In exchange, I request regular donations of the fey partner's essence."

"So . . . you drink blood."

Vivian rolled her eyes. "Anyone could do it. You could. If you were to have a little sip from a fey's wrist, you could hop right up and make the next *Reservoir Dogs* in a week. But something tells me they don't put this in the Arcadia Project employee manual."

"I wouldn't know," I said, not without bitterness.

"Anyhow, *I* don't drink the stuff to make art, I drink it to stay *me*, to stay fey. Humans are adorable, but their lifespans depress me. Without my Plan B, I'd have been rotting in the dirt for nearly a century now."

"Tragic."

"But listen. I'm at the point where I have more essence coming in than I need. Now, what if *everyone* who worked at Valiant Studios had access to it? Diluted, of course, just a little taste— but can you imagine the films that would come out of a studio like that?"

"Can you imagine the massive shattering of the Code of Silence?" I said. "Are you looking for war with Arcadia?"

"Arcadia aside, darling, I don't want war with every teenager who thinks she's Buffy the Vampire Slayer. Which is why none of our employees will have the faintest idea why they find our office environment so inspiring."

"How do you plan to get fey essence into an entire company without them knowing?"

"I buy businesses, a little side hobby of mine. My most recent acquisition is a water delivery service."

"You're going to drug everyone who works with you."

"Oh, please, 'drug' them? This is not like those ridiculous poisons you humans are so fond of. It's the actual arcane source of all human inspiration, and it has no side effects whatsoever. You call it norium; it's native to Arcadia and finds your laws of physics amusing. But until now, its effects have only been available to people the Arcadian nobles and their Project lackeys deem worthy."

"I don't think it's about worthiness," I said. "It's about bringing partners together, soul mates. This thing you're doing . . . you'd be enslaving a few fey to inspire a bunch of strangers, all for your own profit."

"My donors are willing. There's nothing in the Accord that says fey can't give or trade away their own essence. You see, fey have this idea, very strange to your people, that we may do with our own bodies what we please."

"I thought spilled blood was a huge no-no."

"There's no 'spilling' involved here; there's nothing accidental or violent about it. It's all consensual and hospital clean."

"Like what you did at Union Station? That kind of clean?"

Oh, the glory of that moment. Her face went blank with shock.

"Yeah," I drawled a little smugly. "I probably should have mentioned earlier that I know you smuggled Rivenholt out of there. So where is he now?"

I watched her slowly adjust to the fact that I'd taken the reins of the conversation. "I can't give him to Caryl," she said. "My project doesn't work without him."

"Because you need him as leverage over Berenbaum."

"Where are you getting this from?" She couldn't hide her tension. It was exhilarating; she was terrified I knew something, knew *everything*.

"Is the Seelie Queen one of your 'connections' in Arcadia?" I asked. "Is she in on this with you?"

Vivian's expression relaxed into one of baffled annoyance. "Of course not. I don't even know her name; they change queens like underpants."

"So it's just coincidence that her agent showed up at the train station exactly when you did?"

She made a scornful sound. "No, it's *your* fault the damned agent showed up. Who prints out an e-mail?"

Someone with an obsolete phone and memory problems. But I didn't answer her; I was too busy trying to untangle mental knots.

Vivian let out a sharp laugh. "You don't even know why I was there, do you?" She smiled as she took back the reins.

I don't care how long she'd been living among us; there was nothing human about her smile.

"Trying to catch Johnny?" I guessed.

"Darling, I'm the hero of this story. I know I don't look the part. But I was *helping* him. You were meant to spot him heading for the train. Then, at just the right moment, I was to make him disappear. Then we'd wrap things up here while Caryl wasted her time flying to New Orleans."

"Wouldn't she just call New Orleans and have them handle it?"

Vivian pretended to hold a phone to her ear, speaking in a fake raspy voice. "Hello, National Headquarters, this is Caryl, that teenager you put in charge of Los Angeles. I'm afraid I've lost a viscount." She laughed. "No, no, you don't know Caryl very well, do you? Anyhow, that damned faun stopped him before we could even set up the red herring."

"So you weren't working with Claybriar."

"Darling, my allies are rare enough that I'm not likely to stand and watch one get beaten unconscious on a railroad track."

That feeling again, like watching a duck turn into a rabbit. "That—that was Claybriar's blood, then."

Her smile vanished. "I thought—" She gave me a long look. "Oh God. You had no idea what happened at the station."

"Not until you just told me."

"A bluff!" She laughed nervously and ran a hand back through her hair. "Oh, we do need you, darling."

"I'm supposed to believe Johnny beat the snot out of an agent of the Queen?"

"Don't go making Johnny the villain either. He had no choice."

"There's always a choice."

"No, darling, literally, he was under a compulsion. But I'm not going to explain that part. Suffice it to say he could not return to Arcadia, and Claybriar was going to force the issue."

"Because Johnny abducted someone."

"Ugh, no! Johnny hadn't abducted anyone! And he told Claybriar as much. But he *had* broken the Accord, so Claybriar didn't care. He went all Tommy Lee Jones about the whole thing."

"How did Johnny break the Accord?"

"I'm not going to tell you that, either. But the penalty for Accord violations is death. Even trivial violations. Rivenholt had no choice but to get Claybriar out of the picture."

"You mean kill him."

"No, no, I'd never let someone die who could still be useful. You might want to keep that in mind as you're considering my job offer."

"Vivian," I said, hearing a pleading note creep into my voice, "I won't force Johnny to go back to Arcadia, especially not without knowing the whole story. But I do need to see him. Just tell me where he is."

"At the moment? I don't know. Ask David."

"But David doesn't—"

Of course David knew. Everyone knew he knew. Everyone except me.

"David sent me to Regazo de Lujo," I said, feeling suddenly tired. "David sent me to the train station."

"Yes, well, we're all just doing our best to keep that brat Caryl from destroying everything we've built."

"I'm supposed to work for a man who looked me in the eye and lied to me?"

"If you're on our side, he won't need to lie to you anymore."

"What's to stop me from walking out right now and telling Caryl everything?"

"Be my guest," said Vivian. "By the time Caryl shows up, we'll have circled the wagons, and she'll find nothing. And you'll have a long, happy career fetching doughnuts. David will be so disappointed; he's awfully fond of you. But go ahead, betray our trust. I lose nothing. You lose a job, and a friend, and most importantly, you lose *my goodwill*. I would think long and hard before you decide to do that."

"None of this matters anyway," I said. "We're all dead. What happened at Union Station will start a war with Arcadia."

"Not at all. The Accord specifies that a *human* spilling fey blood is cause for war. Fey merely get executed, and since Johnny had already earned that, he didn't have anything left to lose. Tell Caryl whatever you like, but if you really want to help Johnny, the last thing you'll do is let anyone find him."

35

Vivian gave me twenty-four hours to make up my mind, and as much as she personally sickened me, she had also successfully confused and therefore tempted me. Doesn't the devil always?

Poor Inaya. No wonder she'd been feeling out of the loop. But my sympathy for her only lasted until eight the next morning, when she sent her latte-swilling envoy to Residence Four again, this time with a manila envelope in one hand and a couple of breakfast burritos in the other.

"Mild or spicy?" he said, holding out the two wrapped bundles. They smelled tantalizingly of egg and salsa.

"Is 'get the hell off my porch' an option?" I glanced back over my shoulder at Gloria, who had been the one to come knocking on my bedroom door to inform me that there was "an African-American gentleman" at the door for me. When Gloria caught my eye, she immediately began fluffing couch pillows in a thin attempt to pretend she wasn't eavesdropping.

"Come," said Ellis. "Let's have a bite of breakfast and look at these photos. I took them just for you."

"If they're of your junk, let me save you some trouble."

"You're funny," he said with the precise enunciation that

people use when they're trying not to strangle you. "Even if I had the remotest interest in you, I can't see my husband agreeing to a ménage à trois. Your friend David, on the other hand . . ." He waved the envelope gently. I reached for it, but he held it away with a smile.

"Show me the pictures."

"Can I come in?" he asked.

"You can show me on the porch."

The look on his face as he contemplated the mildew-spotted love seat made this whole annoying encounter worthwhile. Finally he sat down as though the thing were covered in wet paint.

He handed me the burritos; they were warm, and I considered quickly snarfing both. But when he pulled three pictures out of the envelope, ink-jet printed on photo paper, I forgot about breakfast. They showed the front door of a salmon stucco house with a trio of people gathered at the doorway. It was either twilight or just before dawn, more likely the latter, to judge by the bathrobes.

In the first picture, a smartly dressed Berenbaum was giving a hug to a blond man in a white robe who could have been anyone, but in the next photo Berenbaum was kissing his robed wife, and the blond man's head was turned toward the camera.

It was, of course, Viscount Rivenholt. His hair was longer than in the file photo, and even just rolled out of bed, he was so beautiful I wanted to punch him.

"When did you take these?" I asked.

"About three hours ago." Ellis furrowed his brow at me, a surprisingly cute expression on him. "You don't seem all that shocked," he said.

"I'm afraid someone else beat you to the shock factor," I said. "I found out last night that Berenbaum's been protecting him, though I'll confess I didn't know he was giving him room and board. God, the brass balls on that man. Looked me right in the face and spun all kinds of bullshit. I don't suppose you could tell me his address?"

He slid the photos possessively back into the envelope. "I will if you'll tell me why David, John, and Vivian keep meeting in secret at the studio."

"They're not plotting against Inaya," I said, handing him the burrito marked SPICY and then starting to unwrap mine. "I promise you that much."

"Then why is she being cut out of the discussions?"

"It's personal stuff between the three of them that it wouldn't be right to talk about. But I know exactly what's going on, and it has nothing to do with Inaya, cross my heart. It's all Johnny drama."

"And I'm supposed to just take your word for this?"

For a moment I didn't have an answer for him, but after a bite of burrito to jump-start my blood sugar, my brain kicked back into gear.

"I have a better idea, actually. Give me David's address."

"What do I get in return?"

"I have an advantage that you don't. Johnny actually *wants* to see me. If I can talk to him, maybe he and I can figure out how to put Inaya at ease. It doesn't help anyone if she's so paranoid she's got people spying on him."

Ellis exhaled. "Fine," he said, standing and dusting off his trousers. "But if I don't hear from you by tomorrow morning, I'll be back, and this time I won't be bringing you breakfast."

• • •

The drive up into the Hollywood Hills in the back of a cab was both breathtaking and nauseating. Nice view, but I could have done without the speed at which the cabdriver decided it was safe to take the curves.

A gate closed off David's neighborhood from random traffic. The gal working there asked for my name ("Millicent Roper"), identification (useless driver's license), and reason for visiting ("friend of the Berenbaums"), then disappeared into her booth for a moment doing God knows what. Tense, I found myself wondering what exactly Ellis had told this lady, or if he had found a way to sneak past her that I hadn't thought of. Finally she emerged, handed me back my driver's license, and to my surprise waved the cab through.

Berenbaum's house was situated along a narrow lane with houses on one side and a steep dropoff on the other. There was nothing to mark the house as his other than the street number Ellis had given me and the blush-peach stucco I recognized from the photograph. It wasn't a palace; there were no peacocks or fountains, but anything in that location with any sort of yard was evidence enough of spectacular wealth. In lieu of a manicured lawn, the entire property was xeriscaped with native ground-cover plants, broken up by delicate splashes of California wildflowers and organic arrangements of rocks.

I knew Berenbaum was probably at work on a Monday morning, but it wasn't him I was here to see. I made my way down the walk to the front door and rapped on it, taking a deep breath.

The baying of dogs approached like a roll of thunder, and then a young man with artfully disheveled hair answered my knock. He looked like he was waiting for one small reason to give a kill command to the pair of ginger Dobermans behind him.

Since he wasn't glowing, I took off my sunglasses and conjured up a mental image of Rivenholt's latest drawing.

"Hi!" I said, using the rush of pleasure it gave me to power up my smile. "It's Millie. I'm here to see Johnny." Dilated pupils are what make eyes seem to sparkle. People respond to this sign of joy on an unconscious level, warming to you without really knowing why. An old sales trick.

He seemed to relax a little. "Nobody named Johnny lives here. Are you sure you have the right house?"

"Pretty sure," I said. "Johnny's staying with David right now, I thought."

"Uh . . . Can you wait here just a moment?"

"Sure!" I said, trying to project confidence.

I waited, and the dogs barked a few more times. When the door opened again, it was Mrs. Berenbaum.

I stood up straighter. David's wife had silver-streaked red hair, a creased forehead, and the kind of thick-waisted figure that most people in Los Angeles would find revolting. She could have afforded any kind of work she wanted done, but she'd apparently abstained even though women half her age probably hit on her husband every day. For a moment I was tongue-tied by a paralyzing wave of respect.

"Hello," she said with a wan smile. "You've caught me a little off guard; I'm not really set up for company. I'm Linda." At further barking, she called over her shoulder, "Stefan, take Rick and Ilsa out back." She turned to me. "Sorry, that's our housekeeper, Stefan, and those are David's dogs. Harmless, but loud. Kind of like David that way."

"It's good to meet you," I said. "I'm Millie, your husband's guinea pig. I was coming by to see Johnny, since I heard he was staying here."

Linda hesitated, but then her good manners overcame her good sense. "Please, come in," she said. "I'm sorry you came all this way for nothing, but I can at least make you a cup of tea or something. David's talked about you quite a bit."

There might have been tension in that last sentence, so I made a note to myself to tread carefully. Rule number one when befriending men: *do not* piss off the wife.

Linda opened the door, and I stepped inside.

36

I knew Linda Berenbaum worked as an interior designer, and so I expected her home to be well decorated, but its lived-in, homey quality surprised me. Everything was artfully cluttered and welcoming in a way that strummed some perversely unpleasant chords.

"Are you from the South?" I asked her.

"Alabama," she said with a faint smile. "Don't tell me I haven't lost the accent."

"No, it's the house; it reminds me of the ones I saw growing up."

"How long have you been out here?" she said, leading me into the small, sunlit kitchen. The window was full of potted herbs, some trailing from hanging baskets.

"Eight years," I said.

"Please have a seat. I have Earl Grey, chamomile, or jasmine; I'm afraid we're not coffee drinkers."

"I'd love some Earl Grey, thank you." I took a seat and leaned my cane against the kitchen table; the chairs had cushions tied onto them with dainty fabric bows.

Silence settled as she filled the teapot and set it on the burner. At last she spoke, her brows drawn together. "Why did you expect to find Johnny here?"

Nice people are easy to read; she was reluctant to lie to someone her husband cared about. I suspected that Rivenholt was in the house somewhere at this very moment, and the thought made me tense with anticipation.

"Vivian told me," I said.

Linda made a soft sound of dismay as she fumbled and dropped a tea bag on the floor. She bent to pick it up, then placed it in one of the cups. "Don't worry, that one's mine," she said with a wry smile when she saw me watching.

"You can afford to throw it away," I teased.

She laughed uncomfortably, running a hand through her hair. "You sound like David."

Fantastic, Millie. Wives love it when the Mysterious Younger Woman takes their husband's side.

"So Johnny isn't here right now?" I said.

"I'll let David field that one," said Linda. "He should be on his way back from work; I called him as soon as the lady at the gate announced you."

I sat up straight in my chair. "You didn't need to do that. If I'm not welcome, I'll just leave."

"I don't want to treat you rudely," she said. "But I'm not going to bail David out, either. This is his mess, and he can sort it out like a big boy."

"I really didn't mean to interrupt David's work," I said, rising carefully. "I'll go."

"Sit," said Linda sharply. My butt was back in the chair before I even knew I'd sat. For someone with no children, she certainly had the tone right. Then again, she'd been married to David Berenbaum for twenty-five years.

Awkward silence reigned as Linda poured steaming water

into the two cups and brought them to the table on saucers. She sat down next to me and idly bobbed her tea bag up and down with her spoon, staring into the cup.

"So, you're with the Arcadia Project," she said finally.

"For now."

"Do you have an Echo?"

"Not that I know of."

She was quiet and wouldn't look at me.

I studied her for a moment. "Having Johnny around, do you ever feel . . ." I tried to think of a word that wasn't insulting or melodramatic, but before I could find one, she shook her head.

"No," she said. "Their relationship isn't sexual, and it's also not exactly practical. Johnny has done wonders for David, since before I met either of them, but he doesn't *maintain* him. Do you know what I mean?" She lifted her eyes from her cup to meet mine. "A man like that needs an anchor," she said. "Someone to tell him it's time to get some sleep or take his vitamins."

"And what does David do for you?" I asked.

Her eyes softened then, and she looked out the window with a comfortable sort of joy that made me feel more of an intruder than any direct challenge could have done. "If I'm the anchor," she said, "he's the sail."

"You're lucky," I said, trying not to sound bitter.

"Just be careful," she said in a disturbingly compassion-ate tone. I didn't have time to ask what she meant before she changed the subject. "Have you ever been to Arcadia?"

"No, have you?"

"I'm not authorized. David goes sometimes."

I thought about it for a moment. "I probably can't. I've got steel pins and screws and plates everywhere; I can suck the magic out of something just by touching it."

Linda looked at me with intense interest. "Really?"

"It's true. It's happened twice already."

She stood up. "Will you do something for me, then, before David gets back?"

"What is it?" I rose from my chair and grabbed my cane, eager for any chance to get on her good side.

"Better to show you."

She grabbed a key from a hanging plant by the window and headed out of the kitchen. I followed her to a home office, where she unlocked a decorative box containing another key. She took the second key and led me upstairs, where she stopped in front of a door at the end of the hallway.

"Would you like to see Arcadia?" she said coquettishly as she turned around.

I was surprised into a laugh. "What?"

"It's not really Arcadia," she said, smiling back at me. "It's murals of Arcadia on four walls of a spare room, but Johnny's done something to them. Honestly, they give me the creeps, and when David's being reasonable, he admits that having magic things around will just make it harder for Johnny to—" She hesitated.

"It's okay," I said. "We've worked out that Johnny wants to stay here."

"David keeps saying it will hurt Johnny to undo the spell, but I think he's just putting it off, trying to keep some last souvenir of Johnny's magic. But now here you are, and I think David would appreciate the hand of destiny in that."

She turned the key in the door and then slowly pushed it open.

"Holy shit," I whispered.

"I know," she whispered back.

I was looking into a rain forest, on the second floor of a house in the Hollywood Hills.

Linda hung back, but I stepped inside. The air was thick and shadowy and warm, fragrant with nectar and rot. Frogs moaned a constant song, and somewhere a bird let out a shrill whoop that echoed through what sounded like miles of sky. I could hear the spatter of raindrops falling through the canopy of leaves over my head, even feel them strike my skin, but when I looked at my arms, they were still dry.

A pale flower, struck by a fat drop of water, trembled on a vine near my elbow. Without thinking, I brushed the petals with my fingertips. Quickly I pulled back, but the flower was undamaged. "I don't understand," I said. "Are parts of this real?" I bent down, scooped up a handful of soggy loam, watched it fall through my fingers. I could feel its gritty richness in my hand, but no grains clung to my fingertips or lodged beneath my nails.

"Your mind is telling you what you should feel," she said, still lingering in the doorway behind me as though she couldn't bear to enter. "All of this is just painted on the walls; Johnny glamoured it so you think you're standing in it. If he were here, he'd hear Arcadian birds; it would smell different to him. You're hearing and smelling and feeling what you expect from a place that looks like the painting."

"Walt Disney would be peeing right now," I said. Of course, now that I thought of it, old Walt had almost certainly been to Arcadia himself.

"I know you can't see the wall," she said, "but the glamour is on the actual painting, so you have to touch that. Just put your hand here next to mine."

I looked around and felt a little pang. "I'm sorry," I said. "I don't have the heart to spoil this. Let Johnny do it, if you think it's the right thing to do." I turned to look at her and saw something change in her face. Damn it, I'd taken David's side again.

"Well then," she said. "Is there anything else you'd like to see while you're here?" Meaning, *before I kick you out on your ass and tell the woman at the gate never to let you back in?*

She stepped back from the doorway, turning away to look down the hall. She seemed to be disappearing into a corridor of light surrounded by endless miles of tangled twilit wilderness. If she shut the door, I might be lost in there forever. I hurried toward her, feet squelching and crunching in the illusory undergrowth, and impulsively I slapped my hand against the tree that stood closest to the door frame.

Just as with the fey in the Seelie bar I felt nothing at all, no surge of power, no tingle on my skin. But the sounds stopped, and suddenly I was standing in an empty room. I looked around with an entirely different sort of amazement. Although the paintings were flat compared to the dream my mind had conjured from them, their colors were rich and bright, their detail spectacular. Even the ceiling had been painted to resemble a forest canopy with fading daylight streaming erratically through.

Linda turned to me with a surprised smile.

"Even without the magic," I told her, "this is an amazing room. Johnny could make a living doing this kind of thing."

Her forehead creased for a moment, and then she shook

her head. "No, Johnny just did the spell on it; the painting is David's. He did another one in the garage. Here, come look." She broke out in a sudden bright smile: still girlishly in love after twenty-five years.

I followed her back down the stairs to the sitting room just off the foyer; at the side of the room was a door that led to a roomy two-car garage. The Valiant was parked on the far side, but my eye lingered on it only for a moment before sweeping over the murals. Berenbaum had painted the whole place to look like a drive-in burger joint, complete with busty waitress on roller skates waiting expectantly by the Valiant's driver's-side door.

Carefully I made my way around Linda's silver BMW and the long, angular nose of the Valiant to get a closer look at the waitress. She had red hair and a very short skirt. I glanced back at Linda, noting the resemblance, and she gave an embarrassed laugh. "Yeah," was all she said.

"This stuff is great!"

"He does it when he's high, usually. You know, off of fairy dust or whatever. He's impossible to live with when he's under the influence, so we started these projects to keep him busy when he didn't have a film to obsess over." Leaving the door to the house open, she moved absently to the shelving on the wall nearest the door. Various props from David's films were inter-mingled modestly there with ordinary garden gloves, bicycle pumps, and other garage trivia.

"This is amazing," I said. "Thank you for showing me." I leaned against the wall by waitress-Linda, studying real Linda as she absently tidied things up and looked inside boxes. "I'd really like to see Johnny," I said.

Her shoulders stiffened. "Can we wait to talk about that until David gets here?"

"I'm not here to send him back to Arcadia. I promise. I just need to talk to him. I need to know he's okay. I'm kind of— fond of him, to be honest."

Linda frowned as she continued to open boxes as though looking for something. "I wasn't aware that the two of you had met."

"We haven't exactly. It's complicated. Sort of a *Sleepless in Seattle* thing."

She raised a brow dubiously. "Johnny's never shown any sign of being interested in humans that way."

"I'm not your average human."

"Do you mind if I ask you something personal?" she said, still rummaging gently through the objects on the shelves.

My phone chose that moment to ring. It was an unknown number, but I hadn't set up voice mail, and I didn't want to lose someone important. "Hang on," I said. "It could be David." I answered the phone in my best casual, not-trespassing sort of voice.

"Oh, hey," said the voice on the other end of the line. Young, male, not Teo. "Is this Millie?"

"It is," I said. "What can I do for you?"

"I dunno. You left your number at my work. This is Jeff."

"Ah! From the sushi place!" The guy Claybriar had apparently interrogated about Rivenholt. I mouthed "Sorry" at Linda and held up a finger. Her frown deepened. I was aware that I was already walking on thin ice, but I wasn't sure I'd ever catch this guy again, and I really wanted to know exactly what Claybriar thought Rivenholt had done.

"So what's up?" Jeff said.

"You remember that cop who came in asking about John Riven?" I said, making no effort to keep Linda from hearing. Her irritation quickly turned to intense interest, and I met her eyes, giving her a slow nod.

"Yeah," said Jeff.

"Is there anything else you can tell me about him, about what he asked you or what he was accusing Mr. Riven of?"

"Nah, sorry. I just remember he had a goatee, asked a bunch of questions about the guy, then ordered an orange soda and sat there taking notes in this big notepad thing for a while."

"Taking notes on what?" I said.

"I dunno. The two guys making out in the corner, from the look of it."

The floor under me seemed to tilt a half degree to the left. "Drawing them?"

"Could have been, I guess."

Claybriar was the artist. God *damn*.

Johnny had never seen me. Johnny hadn't painted the walls. Johnny was a nobleman, and noblemen didn't go around making cheap paper charms.

My hands went cold and sweaty. I remembered the napkin Claybriar had written on at the coffee shop, and the nagging sense of familiarity the COLD IRON drawing had given me. Was it the handwriting? Had he used the same pen?

"Thank you, Jeff," I said. "You've been . . . very helpful." I ended the call and stuck the phone back in my pocket.

"What's the matter?" said Linda sharply.

I just looked at her. What was I supposed to say? *I came here expecting to meet my soul mate, but instead of the handsome movie star, it's a surly, thieving, goat-legged agent of the Seelie Queen who got his head bashed to pieces on a railroad track and might be dead now.*

"Millie?" said Linda. "Is everything all right?"

"It . . . it really isn't," I said. "I need to make another phone call."

"Don't," she said, reaching into the box nearest her to pull out a handgun. She pointed it at me. "I'm sorry," she said.

37

I dropped my cane in shock and pressed my palms back against the wall where Linda's younger self smiled brightly with her cleavage hanging out. "Linda," I said breathlessly. "What the hell."

"If they kill Johnny," she said, "I'll be a widow within a week. And I swear to God I will hunt down every last person responsible and murder you with my own hands."

"I am not Johnny's enemy," I said in my most soothing tone. "Just tell me where he took Claybriar, the faun who was after him. If you do, I promise I will leave Johnny alone, and I'm almost positive I can get Claybriar to do the same. No one from the Project knows that Johnny's staying here, and I won't tell anyone, I swear on my life."

"Your life?" She gave a strange laugh. "Just how much does that mean to you, anyway?"

"Here I am, panicking at the sight of a gun."

Linda shook her head. "I can't tell you where he is."

"Why not?"

She clamped her mouth shut.

"Linda," I pleaded, "I think Claybriar might be my Echo. If something happens to him, I'll never know."

The gun in her hand dropped slightly, then steadied on me again. "Johnny and David have been together almost fifty years. You can't know what that means."

"I want the chance to find out," I said. "Please, Linda. If I have an Echo, I need him." I felt tears start to my eyes. "I *need* him; I'm a mess."

Linda's gun wavered again. "I know," she said, and exhaled. "Christ, David and his little projects."

We both jumped as, through the open door behind Linda, we heard someone slam through the house's front entrance.

"Linda?" came David's voice from the same direction.

"We're in the garage," Linda called over her shoulder.

Berenbaum appeared in the doorway and hurried toward her, effortlessly taking the gun. "Linda, what the hell is going on here?" He added with a quick glance to me, "It's a prop, not even loaded."

I felt like a first-class dolt. David turned back to Linda, hands gently closing on her shoulders. "What did she do?"

"What did *I* do?" I said incredulously. "I answered the phone, and when I hung up she was pointing a gun at me!"

"She knows about the prisoners," Linda told him.

The what now?

Berenbaum cringed. "They're not prisoners. Anyway, you thought pointing a fake gun at her was going to give her amnesia? What the hell, Linda."

They had to be talking about the missing commoners. Why did Linda think they were prisoners? Why did David disagree?

"I don't know anything, I swear," I protested. "No one said anything to me about—"

He kept grilling Linda as though I weren't there. "What

were you planning to do with her next? Hog-tie her and toss her in a closet and call Vivian here to wipe her memory?"

"That's actually not a half-bad idea."

"What?" I blurted.

Berenbaum still didn't look at me. "Forget it," he said to Linda. "Her mind's got enough problems without Vivian messing around in there."

Another slow shift in perspective. This time, I did not go gently, but held on fast. David couldn't be dismissing me. He couldn't have just reduced my mental illness to a punch line. I felt a need for support and bent to pick up my cane. The movement didn't catch their eye; I probably could have walked past them and out of the house without their noticing. I wish I had.

"You certainly can pick them," Linda said bitterly.

Give me two or three years, he had said to me, *and I could have people willing to take a bullet for you.* I would have taken a bullet for him after the first time he shook my hand. David, David, say it isn't so.

"What's that supposed to mean?" he snapped at his wife.

"I mean of all the people you could have cheated with all these years, you pick *that* one?"

"Linda! For God's sake! I would never *touch* her!"

The sheer horror on his face made my hands go cold. I leaned on my cane to keep from falling, but then I felt the break, like glass shattering inside me: that swift protective alchemy that turns hurt to white-hot rage.

"You can't be serious," Berenbaum said. "She's not even—"

"Not even a person?" I snarled between gritted teeth. "Like those 'prisoners' of yours? *I am a person, goddamn it, and I AM STANDING! RIGHT! HERE!"*

I heard the sound of splintering safety glass, saw the spider-web of cracks. I hadn't realized I'd started swinging the cane, but then it felt so good I couldn't stop; I slammed it against that cherry-red finish, against the vinyl top, tearing it, against the side mirror, knocking it askew.

I would have fallen then, if not for the wall behind me. David vaulted across the hoods of both cars in rapid succession and grabbed me, pinned my arms back against the wall, his face as stricken as though I'd tossed a baby down a flight of stairs.

"Linda," he said quietly. "Hit the garage door and call security."

She touched the switch on the wall, then disappeared into the house. With a soft clattering and humming, the garage door lifted into its track, letting in a slab of yellow sunlight. David picked me up and half carried, half dragged me toward the opening.

"Let go of me!" I said in a panic, still clutching my cane with both hands. "You're hurting me!"

"*I'm* hurting you?" he said, his voice ragged.

"It's a goddamned *car*!" I screamed at him. "I'm a person! I'm a *person*!"

But I wasn't, a familiar voice whispered to me. Not to him. Not to anyone.

He said nothing, just set me down ass-first on the driveway and turned to walk stiffly back into the garage. "Pull yourself together and get out of here," he said as he went, still not looking at me. "We're done."

"David," I called after his back as he walked under the door. I wondered for a moment if I should get up and follow him, do something, but then the door began to rattle back down, and I realized that everything hurt too much for me to stand.

There didn't seem to be much point in moving, anyway. Even if I called a cab, security would get here first, and I certainly couldn't outrun anyone on foot. I thought about calling Caryl, but given that I was already on probation, I didn't want to explain why I was sprawled on my ass in her number one donor's front yard.

A Prius pulled up to the curb before long, repainted in officious black and white with HILLSTAR SECURITY on the side. A uniformed rent-a-cop got out and approached me with a stormy expression. He was heavyset with suede-colored skin and a broad nose. He did not look like the kind of person prone to sympathy, and contrary to what you see in the movies, giving attitude to law enforcement types never ends in hilarity.

"You're going to need to come with me," he said.

I tried to get to my feet, but it was complicated. I seemed to have wrenched something pretty badly during my explosion of violence, though I hadn't noticed when I was still flooded with adrenaline.

Rent-a-Cop stared at me suspiciously. "If you do not cooperate, I will have to encourage Mr. Berenbaum to press charges. You are guilty of malicious mischief, which means up to a year in jail and a fifty-thousand-dollar fine. Do you want to spend a year in jail, or do you want to move things along?"

"I'm injured," I said. "And as you can see, I am also an amputee. I am trying to get up, but I'm in a lot of pain."

"Do not try to play the victim, lady. You might as well take a blowtorch to the Liberty Bell. If you think you're going to file a lawsuit, by the way, you had better think again."

"I would never—"

"I don't care how many limbs you're missing; this is *David Berenbaum* you're fucking with. Do you know how much money he and his wife gave to battered women's shelters last year? He didn't touch you, and no lawyer in the world could convince anyone otherwise."

This is the problem with security guards sometimes. Some of them have frustrated ideals and a tendency to editorialize when they have a bad guy in their sights. Thing is, though, he was right. Berenbaum hadn't assaulted me. But the guard's diatribe sounded so much like some of the stuff I was told about Professor Scott that my brain short-circuited. Suddenly I felt as though Berenbaum *were* responsible for my injuries. I gave up on standing and just started to sob.

"Stop that," said the guard. "That doesn't work on me. Get up. Now."

I forced myself to my feet and bit my tongue. Rent-a-Cop was looking for a reason to throw me on the mercy of the LAPD, and I was close enough to a complete mental breakdown without having a slumber party behind bars in Lynwood.

I painfully lurched my way over to the Prius and crawled into the backseat, still crying. I didn't have a tissue, and so I took great pleasure in wiping the snotty back of my hand against the seat when he wasn't looking.

"Where is your vehicle?" he asked me.

I resisted the urge to reply, *Probably in an impound lot in Westwood somewhere*, and instead just said, "I don't have one."

"Where do you live?"

"Near USC," I said.

"Do you have enough for bus fare?"

I did not say, *I have enough for a cab, jerk-off; I am not a bag lady.* I just said, "Yes."

He dropped me off at the nearest bus stop, and a heavily outnumbered faction of my brain cells noticed that this was more courtesy than he really owed me. The rest of my mind was fully occupied with imagining humiliating ways for him to die.

I called a cab, generating paranoid fantasies about the various people who were there waiting for the bus. I didn't breathe quite normally until I was safe in the backseat of a private vehicular bubble. A fresh wave of sobs caught up to me, but I had plenty of time to dry my eyes before the cab pulled up at Residence Four. I looked up to the turret and could see my windows at the base of it. I had never been happier to see the shabby old place.

When I limped wearily through the front door, I was greeted with the sight of my suitcase, zipped and standing in the entranceway. Song and Gloria were both sitting in the living room, giving me the same sad look, but I was pretty sure Gloria's was an upended grin.

"Caryl called me," Song said, her sorrow mixed with the look women get when they know they're about to get a beating. "I'm sorry, but she said that she's decided you and the Arcadia Project are not a good fit for each other."

38

I really should have been reporting news about prisoners and fey-on-fey violence, but when I found out I'd been fired, everything in my damaged brain scrambled like a credit card on a junkyard magnet.

"No," I finally managed to say.

"I'll need your fey glasses," Song continued gently, "and I'll need your phone back as well."

"I can't leave here without calling a cab," I said stiffly, even as I took the glasses and phone out of my pockets and handed them to Song.

"I'll call you a cab," Song said.

"Oh, honey," said Gloria, shaking her head. "Why did you have to go and bust up Mr. Berenbaum's car?"

I turned to Gloria, my guts hollow. "Don't pretend you're sorry," I said, "and don't pretend you've never lost control. At least I didn't stab anyone."

"Millie!" Gloria scolded. At least she finally got my name right.

I saw Tjuan and Phil appear from the dining room, looming, watching. But my anger felt good; I clung to it like a shotgun in a room full of zombies.

"I'm so sorry," I said acidly. "Is it unseemly for me to bring up the fact that Gloria stabbed two people to death? That she was elbow-deep in some guy's blood, watched the light go out of his eyes, and still felt mad enough to do it again?" I turned to Gloria, who had gone pale and still. "Who was the second person? Someone else who pissed you off? Or just someone unfortunate enough to catch you holding the knife?"

Now Teo and Stevie were leaning on the upstairs balustrade. I must have been loud. I couldn't even tell.

"I don't remember it," Gloria said, her voice pitched lower than usual. "And that isn't—"

"Bullshit," I said. "I'll bet you and your lawyers rehearsed the hell out of that. You sleep easy because you think those bastards deserved to die. And maybe they did, but tell that to some seven-year-old who loved one of them, or some father who never got to apologize. *It was not your right* to take those people out of the world. *You do not get to decide.*"

Gloria's eyes filled with tears. She didn't move.

Teo was coming down the stairs now, slowly. "Millie—"

"Fuck you, virgin," I said, halting him in his tracks. "If you ever meet your Echo, I hope she likes drinking dog slobber from ashtrays, because that's what kissing you is like, you fucking self-hating *pocho.*"

Teo slowly retreated back up the stairs. I was too far gone to read or care about the expression on his face.

I turned back to Gloria then. "I used to think I knew who deserved to die, and I took it on myself to wipe her off the face of the earth. But even the nastiest bitch means something to someone. Fuck, even *you* have a boyfriend."

Phil made a hurt animal sound, and I waited for him to say

something that I could turn inside out and throw back at him. But he didn't.

"Call a cab, Song," I said, "and also, fuck you. Your baby's ugly. Fuck you, too, Tjuan, while I'm at it, you paranoid, hostile dick, and fuck you, Stevie, for never saying hi or shutting off the goddamned faucet all the way, and fuck you, Gloria, for counting on your height to keep people from telling you what a two-faced, cloying little cunt you are. The whole crazy-ass lot of you have made my time here a seven-day cruise through all nine rings of hell."

I stormed out and was halfway down the sidewalk before I realized I'd left my suitcase. Damned if I was going to walk back in there to get it.

In case it isn't clear, this was not a victory.

I'll admit, there are few highs quite like using words to turn your enemies into a stack of bloody cubes. But then you cool off, and that stack of minced flesh doesn't just hop back together into a whole person. Long after you quit feeling that glorious rage, your words linger.

Memory is a sketch artist, not a camera. People add and subtract whatever detail they need to. They say they forgive you, but they don't.

Don't believe me? Just wait and see what your pal lobs back at you years later during an unrelated argument. There's your diatribe, like a fly in amber.

Even if what you said was true, that only makes it worse. Truth should be left in wrapped boxes for people to open when they're ready. When it's used as a blade, they vacuum-seal the pain somewhere deep inside, sealing the truth in with it, until it's time to turn it inside out and cut someone else.

I tried to forget the way Teo backed up the stairs, and how young Gloria looked, the end of her nose pink from tears. But I couldn't, and when it comes down to it, I shouldn't.

Kids, please don't try this at home.

With no phone, no other belongings, and no place to spend the night, I told the cabdriver to take me back to the Leishman Center. I was paid up through the end of the month, and so I guessed (correctly) that I'd be allowed back into my still-empty room without excessive bureaucracy. I had no things to unpack, so I just flopped onto the bed and stared at the ceiling. Dr. Davis showed up just before dinner, hovering gravely in the doorway. She looked older than I remembered, her sleek angled bob tucked behind her ears.

"I'm a little disappointed to see you back here," she said.

"That makes two of us," I said. I'd missed that bland voice.

"Do you want to talk about what happened?"

"Not even a little bit."

Dr. Davis hesitated, running her fingers through her hair. "You'll need to start arranging another place to stay," she said.

I sat up. "Why? I can pay for a few more months."

"You checked yourself out a week ago, Millie, and someone had his father on a waiting list for a private room. He'll be moving in at the first of the month."

Something squeezed at my insides, but I was too exhausted for full-fledged panic. "Where the hell am I supposed to go?"

"I still have your grandparents' phone number on file, if you'd like to call them."

"I don't have a phone."

"You can use one of ours."

"To call Mississippi?"

"Under the circumstances, yes."

I had only met my grandparents once as a child and hadn't spoken to them in more than a decade. But there comes a point at which familial awkwardness seems like a fart in a storm.

In a dead-end backwater like Graston, Mississippi, the money I had left could last me a hell of a long time. Sure, I'd never taste another fresh avocado, or watch another decent film. But I shoved that to the back of my mind, because when you've lived in L.A. for eight years, the word "homeless" is no longer abstract; it comes with vivid sense-memories of people you've passed that day on the street.

It wasn't eight p.m. yet in Mississippi, so I figured even old folks would still be awake. When someone picked up the phone, I was surprised at how instantly I recognized that dirt-and-worms voice.

"Hi, Grandpa," I said. "It's Millie."

"I'll be damned," he said. I waited for more, but that was it.

I knew Grandpa wasn't one for small talk, so I cut to the chase. "California isn't working out too well for me, so I wondered if I could stay with you and Granny for a bit while I figure out what to do next."

"You know your grandmother's dead, right?"

"I—I didn't. I'm sorry."

There was another long silence, but I knew he hadn't hung up, because I could hear a clock ticking loudly in the background. I remembered that damned clock, the way it had scared me as a kid.

"Would be nice to have somebody in the house again," he said. He coughed, a sound like nails rattling in a drawer.

"I'd look for a job, of course, too," I said. "I don't want to be a burden. Do you know, is there any kind of work for a lady in Graston?" I was operating on the assumption that anything my grandfather considered fit for a lady was doable without legs.

"Billy's had a 'Help Wanted' sign in the window of the market since Lela got herself in trouble," my grandfather said. *In trouble* meant single and pregnant, but I had no idea who Lela was. "How old are you now?" he asked.

"Twenty-six."

"Billy'd be tickled to have you show up. No one's come about the job so far but schoolkids and Negroes."

I stood there with the phone in my hand for a minute. Hearing casual bigotry from my flesh and blood was like turning over a rock in my yard and finding a swarm of white larvae. I felt filthy; I wondered how badly those mind-maggots had been gnawing away at my own thoughts of Tjuan, of Ellis and Inaya.

Inaya. My train of thought jumped to a new track and barreled right through the paralysis. My surge of hope wasn't enough to make me say what I should have said to my grandfather, but it was enough to make me fake saying "Hello? You still there?" and hang up on the old coot.

I had one more card I could play, and if I played it right, I might not have to give up on L.A., or Valiant Studios, or finding Claybriar, or any of it.

39

There was something exhilarating about finding a forgotten ace up my sleeve. The next morning, dressed in yesterday's clothes, with nothing on me but my wallet, my cane, and my prosthetics, I prepared myself for a magic trick that would make Vivian's Gotham Hall glamour look like Grandpa pulling a quarter out of my ear. I was about to re-create a life out of nothing. I was no fairy; I was no warlock; I was a *god*.

I also might have been having a manic episode.

I took a cab to the Target in Culver City, paid the driver to wait for me for twenty minutes, and withdrew some cash from a nearby ATM. Inside the Target I bought a backpack, as much food and water as I could fit into said backpack, and a prepaid phone. Next stop: library Internet to set up my phone service, print out a few Craigslist rental ads, and look up Ellis Barnes, PI.

"Hi there, old friend," I said brightly when he answered his phone. "I have some information for Inaya that will turn her world on its ear."

"What did you find out?"

"I said I have information for *her*, not for you, but I've misplaced her number. Set up a meeting between her and me, and if she isn't so blown away that she gives you a bonus, I will give you a hundred bucks out of my own pocket."

"That doesn't mean a great deal to me," said Ellis, "but I can tell it means something to you. I will speak to her and call you back."

I gave him my new number and browsed rental ads while I waited. I didn't have to be homeless. I just had to leash my Emotion Mind and look at the facts. If you can find a lonely old lady who's renting out a room of her house, she'll often skip the background check if you charm her and tell her your tragic story. Month-to-month leases can bite both ways, but they are lifesavers for people with shady pasts.

I jotted down several likely numbers and got halfway to the bus stop before Ellis called me back.

"Inaya wants to know where to meet you."

"West Hollywood." I gave him the address of the sushi place. "And tell her to wait for me if she gets there first. I'll be as fast as I can."

Most celebrities are not good at going incognito, but Inaya had it down. Her straightened walnut-brown hair was pulled into an unflattering ponytail that stuck out through the back of a baseball cap, and her cheap sunglasses were subtle enough not to scream "starlet in disguise." Standing there in baggy clothes with her back to the street, she affected a slouching posture that did nothing to advertise her curves. I almost walked by her myself.

"You must be Millie," she said, staring at my reflection in the window of the sushi place. To face me would have meant facing the throngs of people driving and walking by at midday.

I moved between her and the window so she could talk to me without turning around. She didn't back up to allow for personal space, so we ended up looking like a couple who'd been together long enough to quit dressing up for dates. Wouldn't that be something? A quick lunch, then back to her place, falling onto Egyptian cotton sheets, digging my heels into that smooth brown back. Except I didn't have heels, as if that were the least plausible thing about that fantasy.

"Good to finally meet you," I said.

"Who *are* you?" She lowered her sunglasses just enough to hit me with those smoky eyes. It took me a second to activate the language center of my brain.

"When we first spoke," I said, "I was working for the Arcadia Project. Now that they've fired me, I'm free to tell you all the stuff I wasn't allowed to tell you before. But first I need to make sure you're not recording or transmitting what I'm saying. There are very good reasons why the stuff I'm about to show you is secret."

"If it's secret, why are you telling me?" She pushed the sunglasses back up on her nose, looking skeptical.

"Because you are literally the last person left who can help me save someone I care about. Someone who's being held captive by people you trust, and might die."

"Are you pitching me a script?" she said. "Because I would read this."

"I'll keep that in mind for later, but no. This is real, as you're about to see. But you have to promise me that I can trust you."

"I prayed after Ellis called me," she said, "and Jesus gave me the green light. Whatever you have to say, I am ready to hear it."

I blinked. "Jesus . . . gave you the green light."

"You have a problem with Jesus?" She lowered the sunglasses again.

"Uh—"

"It's okay in this town to believe that crystals can heal asthma or vaccines cause autism or an alien overlord is going to give you special brain powers if you pay enough, but I say the *J* word and suddenly I'm crazy."

"I'm not the best person to give an opinion on that," I said. "But funny you should mention religion, because look where we're headed next." I pointed to the supposed Christian bookstore, so obviously out of place on a street dominated by drag couture.

Inaya looked at the bookstore. A delicate line appeared between her perfectly tweezed brows before she shifted her gaze across the street. "Oh, hey, is that a shoe store? You suppose they have any of those pumps in ladies' sizes?"

"Inaya, I need you to trust me, and just follow me into the bookstore, okay? Also, tell me right now, did you forget anything? Phone? Keys? Wallet?"

"Do I seem like the absentminded type to you?"

I started walking, and she followed me halfway to the entrance before stopping abruptly and patting herself down. "I— No, wait—I didn't forget anything. I just said that. Oh my God, are you a mentalist?"

"Just follow me, please."

"Ellis said you'd lost your legs," she said, eyeing my jeans, which concealed the prosthetics. "How did that happen?"

"We'll talk about it later."

"Can we go back to the sushi place? I *really* have to pee."

"There are bathrooms inside," I said. Actually, I had never

seen any, but I was also pretty sure Inaya West wouldn't show up to meet a stranger with a full bladder.

The ward was doing its tricks on me, too, of course, but once you've seen the structure of a spell and know what it's doing to your brain, you can kind of compensate for it. Just like a glance in the mirror after a dental procedure tells you that your lip isn't really three feet thick.

"All right," said Inaya. "But let me just pop over to that shoe store quickly first."

"You're trying to avoid following me. It's something the place does to you, a mind trick. My partner had to physically push me in the door."

"Don't even think about doing that."

"I have no intention of it. But that's why I need you to walk in under your own power, all right? By the time I count to ten, I need you to walk into that bookstore. If you do not, I am going to cause a public relations nightmare for you by pretending you pushed an amputee into the street."

"You wouldn't!"

"One . . . two . . ."

"I've always trusted my intuition," she said, sounding deeply unnerved. "But I honestly don't know what to do right now."

"Three . . . four . . ."

"Part of me is just *screaming* that this is some kind of trap, but another part of me feels like my whole life has been leading up to it."

"Five . . ."

She started to look panicky. "Do I sound crazy? I feel crazy."

I shook my head reassuringly but kept counting. "Six . . ."

"I'm not crazy." She straightened her spine and walked into

the dizzying technicolor splendor of the Seelie bar with me close on her heels.

Immediately she backed into me, hard, and her "Sweet Jesus!" was so loud that the patrons swiveled to look at us. One or two of them recognized me and looked wary; the rest just went back to their drinking. A glowering giant of a man with carrot-red hair approached the two of us, blocking our way to the bar and folding his bulky arms.

"You are not authorized," he said.

He used the word "authorized" with the same sort of childish glee that the Queen's messenger had. His facade had been designed with intimidation in mind; he looked as though he could reach out and snap our necks with one beefy hand apiece.

"I'm with the Arcadia Project," I lied. "Ask Baroness Foxfeather. And this is my guest."

Beefcake stepped aside just enough to let Foxfeather see us. She tossed her golden mane over her shoulder and gave the two of us a brilliant smile. "I know Ironbones," she said. "And her friend is familiar too."

"Seen any hit films these last three decades?" I joked.

"No."

"Oh."

"But I go to a *lot* of parties," Foxfeather explained. "It's a great way to meet humans."

"Would you excuse me for just a minute?" said Inaya shakily, and stepped out the door. I was about to hobble after her, but she stepped immediately back inside. "How is this even possible? How are you doing this?"

"Let's sit you down for a minute," I said. "You look woozy."

"She can't stay here," said the beefy guy.

"Let her stay, Craghorn," said Foxfeather. "Look how pretty she is. And she's with an Authority."

Craghorn grumbled to himself and sat down in a booth alone, continuing to glare at the three of us as I led Inaya to the bar and eased her onto a stool. Foxfeather stared raptly at her.

"So," I said to Inaya. "I am in no way supposed to be telling you this, but the reason this place looks like a bookstore on the outside is that it's magic."

Inaya shook her head firmly. *Oh great, one of those,* I thought. Admittedly she didn't have the advantage of glasses to see the spell directly, and for most people paradigm shifts are pretty rough regardless.

"It's not magic," she said. "There has to be some explanation."

"That *is* the explanation."

"If magic is real, then I am pretty sure it's the work of the devil, and I should be getting the hell out of here."

"Inaya, I hate to be the one to tell you this, but the world doesn't work exactly the way your preacher tells you it does."

"An atheist in Los Angeles," she said dryly. "I am *so* shocked."

"Look, I am not an expert on Jesus, or the devil, or any of that. I am not trying to tell you there's no God; how the hell would I know?"

"Then what are you saying?"

"I'm saying that magic is real. It's not native to this world, so maybe that world was made by a different God, or maybe your God made both worlds by different rules. I don't know. That's for people who care about God to figure out. All I know is that there really is a world where magic is common as dirt, and they've brought some of it here."

"Aliens?" One brow shot up toward her hairline.

"More like fairies. Though I think we're supposed to call them fey."

"You can call me Vicki Plume," the bartender interjected helpfully. "But at home they call me Foxfeather."

Inaya turned her poleaxed expression toward Foxfeather. "You believe you're a fairy?"

"I am a baroness of the Seelie Court," she said with solemn dignity. "I am the lowest rank of what some humans call the *sidhe*, or high elves, or 'fair folk,' or whatever."

"Vicki, honey," said Inaya with real concern. "If this is some kind of role-play thing that's fine, to each her own, but please tell me you don't really believe in this at your age?"

"Show her," said Foxfeather, bouncing on the balls of her feet. "Oh pretty please, show her, Lady Ironbones."

Since I couldn't think of a better idea, I reached out and grabbed Foxfeather by the wrist.

40

Gasps sounded all over the room, and Craghorn leaped up from his seat to come and beat me to a pulp or something.

"Craghorn, sit!" cried Foxfeather, all ablaze with rainbow glory, unfolding a pair of diaphanous wings.

Inaya sat rigid on her bar stool, and her wide, dark eyes suddenly overflowed with tears. Her lips moved a few times before words came out of them, and when I finally understood what she kept repeating, I went a bit numb from shock myself.

"It's you," Inaya was whispering. "The angel. It's *you*."

"Is it you?" Foxfeather asked in an equally awestruck tone. I let go of her wrist, and her human facade reached across the bar for Inaya's hands. When their fingers touched, both of them gasped and pulled back, and then they just stared into each other's eyes for a moment.

I had the sudden intense urge to disintegrate. "Third wheel" doesn't begin to cover it.

"How is this possible?" Inaya said, her voice raw as she continued staring at Foxfeather. "I stopped telling people about those dreams years ago, but I still have them. You're a fairy? I thought you were an angel."

"Maybe I am," said Foxfeather.

So this was what it was supposed to be like to meet your Echo. I was acidly jealous, of course. Jealousy is as hardwired into a Borderline as worry is into a mother. Inaya got dreams of angels and an A-list career; I got a phone number scrawled on a coffee-shop napkin.

I tried to focus on what I had come here to do, because this could really only help me. "Foxfeather is your Echo—kind of your fey soul mate," I said to Inaya. "Your muse. And if you want to think of it that way, a kind of guardian angel. Even without knowing her, you've felt her influence all your life. The two of you must have a very strong connection if she was able to reach you through your dreams."

"There are rules about this," Foxfeather said. "We are supposed to report this to the Authorities immediately."

"I'll take care of that for you," I said. And I would. Eventually. Once I was finished getting what I needed out of them.

"Obviously you can't tell anyone human about this," I said to Inaya, who was weeping and holding Foxfeather's hands. "Inaya, are you listening to me?"

"Yes," she said without looking at me.

"John Riven is also fey."

That got her attention. "I *knew* there was something weird about him."

"His real name is Viscount Rivenholt."

"He outranks me," said Foxfeather. "By a lot."

"He's used several different names and faces," I went on, "but he is David Berenbaum's Echo, just as Foxfeather is yours. David's been working with him for forty-odd years."

"Does Vivian know about this?" asked Inaya.

"She does," I said. I decided Inaya was coping with enough right now; the truth about Vivian could wait.

"She's one too, isn't she?" Inaya said. "Some kind of nasty one."

I sighed. "Let's not get into that right now. The point is, you need to know all this because this is the reason you've been feeling out of the loop lately."

"They've been doing . . . magic fairy stuff," she said, "and I'm the only one who doesn't know."

"They weren't allowed to tell you."

"Are they allowed now?"

I wasn't honestly sure. "I think we should keep your knowledge under our hats for a bit," I said. "Something odd is going on, and I need you to help me get to the bottom of it. If they don't know that you know, they might not be as much on their guard."

Inaya took a deep breath. "Okay, tell me what's going on and what I need to do."

I wanted to kiss her. Having something actually go better than planned was not a feeling I was used to.

"First, I need your promise that this stays between you, me, and Foxfeather. Not even the rest of the Arcadia Project needs to hear about this right now." At her blank look, I clarified. "The Project is an organization that regulates all the stuff that goes on between humans and fey. I will set you both up with them properly once this is all settled. But right now I don't know exactly who we can trust and who we can't."

Inaya nodded, her eyes glazing a bit. "Okay."

"Are you all right? Are you with me? The story gets kind of complicated."

"I'm kind of . . ." She flapped her hands vaguely. "Can you maybe give me a little while here to talk with Vicki? I can meet you later today to hear you out once I've had a chance to . . ." She looked at Foxfeather and crumpled. Somehow she managed to look beautiful while crying, which made me want to throw a drink in her face.

Foxfeather hurried around the bar to sit next to Inaya, taking the other woman into her arms as though she were a child. Perhaps she was a child, to Foxfeather; there was no telling how old the fey really was.

"We can meet at my place," Foxfeather said to me, lifting wet blue eyes to meet mine. "We can all talk there later."

"Inaya has my number," I said. "Have her call me when you're both ready." Awkwardly I turned for the door, leaving the two of them in each other's arms.

I'd kept the worst of my self-pity at bay up to this point, but seeing Inaya and Foxfeather's joyous reunion was sort of the last straw. I didn't have anywhere private to cry, so I settled for leaning against the wall in an alley between a game shop and a strip club and boo-hooing for a solid half hour.

Luckily, I had some useful distress tolerance skills at hand, and I used them as soon as I'd spent the worst of the storm. Distract, self-soothe. I visualized walking down a red carpet with Inaya. She was probably my friend for life now, and would be even more grateful to me when she knew what I had risked to take her to that bar. I wasn't sure what the penalty was for breaking the Code of Silence, but I had a feeling it wasn't a slap on the wrist.

It had paid off, though. I'd gone from a dim hope of Inaya's cooperation to a pair of grateful allies on either side of the border. I wondered if Vivian felt warm fuzzies at bringing her clients to their Echoes. Somehow I doubted it.

I thought of the man who might be my own Echo and almost certainly the sixth anomaly on the census. Ever since my conversation with Vivian, an unpleasant possibility had been nagging at the back of my mind. I needed an informed second opinion, so I swallowed a jagged lump of pride and dialed Caryl's number.

If she'd known who it was, maybe she wouldn't have answered, but she had no way of associating the new number with me, and so on the second ring I heard a husky hello. I surprised myself with a sudden flood of contrition that left me speechless.

"Hello?" she said again.

"Don't hang up; I have some very important information."

I heard a faint swell of baroque harpsichord in the background; clearly she hadn't disconnected.

"I'm fairly sure Claybriar's my Echo," I said, "and I think Vivian may have imprisoned him and some other fey to harvest their blood."

At last Caryl spoke. "Why do you think that?" she said.

"If you want to know the why, you're going to have to hire me back."

"I'm afraid that isn't possible. The Project can't afford to lose Berenbaum's cooperation."

The sound of his name was a punch to the stomach, but I soldiered on. "I think you're losing him either way. He's involved too."

"I have no particular reason to trust you, Millie."

Another stomach-punch. "Fine, then. Just answer this for me. If a fey bled out all his essence, he'd have to go back to Arcadia to recover, right?"

"That is correct."

"What if he were somehow caught between here and Arcadia, in both places at once? Would his essence still replenish?"

"In that hypothetical situation, yes, but we have yet to establish the feasibility of such a scenario."

"Forgetting about possible and impossible for a moment, just suppose there are half a dozen fey somewhere, trapped between worlds and with, like, IVs hooked up to them, drawing out their essence. How long until they'd be completely drained?"

"Hypothetically speaking again, I assume?"

"Yes, in theory, how long could you drain them like that?"

"Forever."

I sat there with the phone to my ear, one kind of horror transmuting slowly to another. "Forever as in . . . ?"

"Forever as in, as long as both worlds stand."

41

On the bright side, I had plenty of time to arrange a rescue, but I was a little too hung up on the whole "eternity of torture" thing to celebrate. I leaned my head back against the wall of the game shop, feeling dizzy. Across the alley, a gray patchwork of paint marked an ongoing attempt to cover graffiti on the side of the strip club.

"Millie," came Caryl's calm voice on the phone. "If you have information that can help us resolve this situation, withholding it benefits no one."

"It benefits me," I snapped. "I can find Claybriar without helping the people who threw an unemployed cripple out on the street."

"I do regret the way that was handled," Caryl said.

"You mean, the way you didn't handle it? The way you passed the buck to Song, someone I could actually hurt, because you couldn't be bothered to look me in the eye?"

"The reasons for my absence were sound, but you are not in the proper frame of mind to understand or even hear them. And I am afraid I need to end this conversation."

Fear of abandonment is one of the worst Borderline triggers, and I was already as unraveled as I'd ever been.

"Why?" I demanded, smothering panic with anger. "So you can go suck up to Berenbaum? The guy who dropped me on his driveway like a trash bag? I've tried so hard for you, and yet when I make one mistake, you—"

"Which mistake do you mean?" Caryl's words came out fast and inflectionless. "Do you mean causing thousands of dollars' worth of property damage and immeasurable personal insult to a man who has poured millions into the Arcadia Project? Or do you mean physically assaulting your partner on your first day? Perhaps you are referring to the addictive painkillers in your suitcase, or your act of self-injury while a guest on Project property, or trespassing in a client's hotel room, or posing as a licensed private investigator during an unauthorized phone call to a high-profile individual outside the Project's jurisdiction? Do let me know which of those was your 'one mistake,' as it will make an interesting footnote to the report I must give my direct superior when she flies in next week from New Orleans to determine whether my lapse of judgment in hiring you indicates that I need to be replaced."

Remorse is not something anyone feels easily. At heart, it comes from the recognition that you have done something beneath your worth. From a Borderline's perspective, nothing is beneath her worth, because she has no worth. A person with no worth can't hope for forgiveness, and so the only way to climb out of the purgatory of endless guilt is either to protest innocence or to drown out your own sins with the (invented if necessary) sins of your accuser.

I couldn't do either of those things. I wasn't innocent of the charges, Caryl had been doing her job, and there was no reason on earth that anyone should forgive me. I couldn't even kill myself, because I had learned how horribly that kind of violence ricocheted into the lives of blameless strangers. There was nothing I could do that wouldn't serve as further proof of my worthlessness.

Suddenly I wanted Monty. I wanted him like a child wants a red balloon now once its string has slipped out of her hand. I hung up the phone and slowly sat down in the alley.

Dissociation is one of the rarer Borderline symptoms, brought on by severe stress. It's different from person to person, but it had happened to me at Professor Scott's place, and it happened to me there again in the alley. I just left my body for a little while, the way you might leave a room when it's too full of smoke to breathe.

People walked by; I could hear them. One even commented to his companion about me as they passed.

I heard a phone ring, and absently wondered why no one was answering. Eventually, the ringing stopped.

A nicely dressed woman held out some money and said, "Here, sweetheart, get something to eat." I wasn't sure who she was talking to.

The phone started ringing again. It occurred to me that it was probably my phone, and I should answer it. I just had no concept of how to make that happen, how to move my arm, how to form words of greeting.

It was the chill that eventually brought me back. As the shadows deepened I started to shiver, and the movement of my muscles gave me context for my consciousness. I was sitting in something cold. It took me a moment to realize I had wet myself.

"Christ, Roper," I said aloud, words coming out drowsy and

slurred. "New low." I didn't want to get up. I didn't want to walk into the street with the kind of stains you usually find on a five-year-old. I didn't know what to do.

Dazed, I checked my voice mail. Two messages: a man trying to set up an apartment showing, and Inaya asking for a call back. Caryl's number didn't appear on my incoming call list, a fact that cut sharply. Pain was good, though; pain was *something*.

After somewhat drowsy deliberation, I tried Inaya.

"Hey, honey," she said after two rings. "I'm at Vicki's place."

"Inaya, I've had a sort of accident."

"Are you okay?"

"I have a condition. It's usually not serious, but I had an episode, and I need someone to come get me."

"Do you need me to call you an ambulance?"

"No, I'm physically fine. But it's just . . . I fainted, I guess, and I kind of . . . had a bladder mishap, and now I'm hiding in an alley in West Hollywood, too embarrassed to come out."

"Oh my God, you poor thing. I'm going to send Rosa, okay? She's really sweet; she's like your grandma. She'll take care of everything. Just tell me where you are."

As it turned out, Rosa was nothing like my late grandmother, which is to say she was not a racist alcoholic with brown teeth. She was not Latina, either, as I had embarrassingly expected. She looked Scandinavian. She didn't say much beyond hello at first, but she gave me a small blanket to wrap around my waist and escorted me briskly and compassionately to her waiting sedan.

"Thank you so much," I said miserably.

"Once," she said after a brief silence, "I got very drunk at a party and got terrible stomach cramps, so I ran to the bathroom and had a bowel movement, but I had forgotten to open up the toilet lid first."

I have no idea why that made me feel better, but it did.

I'd love go back in time and pay a visit to twenty-four-year-old Millicent Roper, maniacally optimistic UCLA film student, and tell her that in a couple of years she'd be wearing a pair of urine-soaked jeans into a fairy's apartment to meet Inaya West. She'd probably back slowly away with one hand on her pepper spray.

"I need a washcloth, a sink, a plastic trash bag, and some fresh clothes," I said in a brisk director voice as soon as I walked in the door, hoping to distract from how thoroughly pathetic I was.

"I'll take care of it," said Foxfeather, and scampered to a back room, possibly the same one she and her friends had been having sex in two days ago. She seemed strangely focused; was it her Echo's influence already?

I hung back near the front door, unwilling to inflict the smell of urine on a woman who had probably not walked her own dogs in decades. Inaya was sitting sideways on a love seat that faced the far window, looking over the back of it at me.

"Sorry if I interrupted anything, uh, intimate," I said awkwardly.

Inaya frowned. "Is it usually like that with people and their . . ."

"Echoes? I don't think so. But I figured you two would, what with you being so gorgeous and Foxfeather being so . . . Foxfeather."

Inaya shook her head slowly. "She sees me as a little girl, someone to protect."

"What a waste," I muttered.

"Pardon?"

"Nothing."

Foxfeather came out from the bedroom then with a washcloth and some sort of unidentifiable garment. She fetched a plastic trash bag from under the sink as well, proving that her short-term memory was functioning at an unprecedented level.

"Do you want me to help you clean up?" she said.

I glanced at Inaya, who raised an eyebrow at me, quelling my train of thought. Probably not a good idea to drag the good Christian's soul mate into the other room for a little interspecies fondling.

"I'll be fine on my own," I said, and awkwardly shuffled my way to the master bathroom.

One careful sponge bath later, I emerged back into the main room draped in a loose-fitting babydoll dress. It would have been stunning on Foxfeather, but it was a little ridiculous on me given the amount of titanium and scar tissue I was showing.

"So let's talk business," said Inaya, propping her pedicured bare feet up on the coffee table. Foxfeather, now seated on the love seat next to her, playfully mimicked her pose. I moved around to seat myself in a cushy leather chair that was placed at an angle to the two of them.

"I'll try to keep this simple," I said. "Best I can figure out, Vivian and David have a bunch of fey commoners captive somewhere and are draining their blood to work some magic at their new studio. I need your help to figure out where these prisoners are being held."

"No way," Inaya said.

"I beg your pardon?"

"David wouldn't do that."

I sighed. "I would have thought the same thing, Inaya, but he's not the man everyone thinks he is."

Inaya's spine straightened, and her face took on a haughty expression of bruised loyalty that made me crave better lighting and a camera. "I have known him for thirty years," she said. "I don't remember *not* knowing him. He would not torture innocent people."

"She said *commoners*, love," interjected Foxfeather, patting Inaya's arm. "They're not people."

"If one more person says that," I growled, "I swear to God I am going to go on a killing spree."

"Commoners don't have feelings," Foxfeather told me with patient condescension, as though I were worrying about my teddy bear getting lonely.

"Bullshit," I replied. "I've seen Claybriar's art, and he is up to his pointy little horns in feelings. Just because he's not as pretty as you, that doesn't mean he's not a person."

"David wouldn't hurt anyone," Inaya reiterated, hugging herself. Her expression reminded me of myself in the Berenbaums' garage right before I started smashing things, so I quickly groped for consoling words.

"I'm sure Vivian and Johnny have been feeding David the same bullshit about commoners that Foxfeather is feeding us right now," I said. It didn't excuse him, but I hoped it explained the seeming paradox enough that Inaya could accept it.

She just stared at me.

"All I know," I went on, "is that the three of them are involved in imprisoning these fairies, and I'm pretty sure it's to harvest their essence, their blood. Given how deeply you're involved in the studio, I thought you might have information that could help me piece things together."

Inaya caught her lower lip between her teeth and furrowed her brow in the sexiest display of intense thought I'd ever seen. "Is there any way this could involve diamonds?" she said after a moment.

I leaned forward. "You know something weird. Tell me."

"I'm the one who approves the expenses," she said. "A while back, David ordered a load of synthetic diamonds and some other weird shit, and when I asked why, he babbled about new technology and how it was complicated and time-sensitive and I should just give it my stamp of approval. Technology isn't my area, so I did. You have no idea how much I trust this man."

"No, no, I get it," I said. "After less than a week, I was ready to give him power of attorney."

Inaya put her head in her hands, slumping forward, and Foxfeather rubbed slow circles on her back. I pictured Claybriar doing the same to me. Then I pictured the steel in my body leaching the essence from his veins. So much for that.

"Synthetic diamonds and what else?" I said.

"Graphite, you know, the stuff in pencils? But in huge quantities."

Something clicked together in my memory. I stared out the window, barely noticing the hazy view of the Hollywood sign. "They're building a Gate."

42

A new Gate, on the Valiant Studios lot. Elliott would do a flip if I told Caryl, but I wasn't planning on talking to Caryl again in this lifetime.

"How is this possible?" I addressed my question to Foxfeather, appreciating the irony that she was the most reliable source of information in the room. "I thought the trick to building Gates was lost a hundred years ago or something."

"It was," she said, nodding like a bobblehead doll. "The last pair has been dead for ever so long. And they were one in a zillion."

I moved past the dubious statistic and repeated, "Pair?"

"Well, yes, you have to have one person on each side, Echoes, you know, because each piece has to go in the *exact* same place. They have to see through each other's eyes while they work."

"I take it not all Echoes can do that?"

"That kind of bond takes lots of time. Most humans find their Echoes too late and die too soon."

"Would forty years together be enough?" I asked. When Foxfeather looked blank, I clarified, "Half a human lifetime."

"Oh yes," she said.

"It's David and Johnny," I said. "Has to be."

This bugged me. Not so much the part about David being the lynchpin of an evil scheme—I had already tucked that away in the coping section of my brain—but the part where the guy at the head of this shiny new studio project just so happened to be the only human in a century who could construct a Gate.

"This can't be about the studio," I said. "Vivian wanted a Gate for some other reason. I think she came up with the studio idea to entice David into building it. Depending on how long she's been planning this, it may be why she went into entertainment in the first place."

Inaya rubbed her eyes as though they ached. "So what do we do?"

"I need you to help me figure out where on the premises this Gate might be, because I think Vivian found a way to use it to imprison the commoners. It's almost certainly glamoured like the bookstore, so you'll avoid it or not notice it. Is there any part of the lot you tend to ignore or shy away from?"

Inaya shook her head. "My dad's in construction, so I'm fussy; I was always inspecting every inch of the site to make sure the contractors David hired didn't screw things up. I can't think of any place I haven't combed over unless it's one of the soundstages."

"A soundstage would be a perfect place to hide a Gate," I said. "Plenty of room, easy to isolate and keep locked, easy to glamour so people think it's in use or whatever and don't go inside."

"There are a dozen of them," Inaya said, "and I don't have those keys."

I thought for a moment. "Crap," I said.

"What is it?"

"There's a really easy way to do this, but it's also the hard way."

"What do you mean?"

"I mean I'm about to eat so much crow I'll be stopping up toilets with feathers for a week."

I waited until dinnertime, when Caryl was most likely to be at the Residence. I paid the cabdriver extra and told him to leave if I wasn't back in fifteen minutes; my reasoning was that Caryl would either welcome me back or kick me off the property right away.

I knocked on the door, praying that the person to answer would be someone likely to let me in. When I saw Tjuan push aside the curtain, I sighed and turned back toward the cab. Just as I was heading for the porch steps, I heard the bolt come off the door. Tjuan opened it a foot or so and stood in the doorway, much as I had once stood to block Ellis.

"You have got balls of brass," he said in a way that made my palms sweat.

I kept a smile on. "Actually, that's one of the few metal bits they did *not* install when they were putting me back together."

He discharged a short sound that might have been a laugh.

"Can I come in?" I said. "I've pretty much solved this Riven-holt business for Caryl, and I want to tell her what I found."

"Bullshit."

"It's the truth, I swear on my Echo's life. Which is, by the way, being made unimaginably horrible in an interdimensional prison while we're standing here chatting."

"Also bullshit."

"At this point, wouldn't it be easier just to slam the door in my face?"

"I'm trying to find out what it is you're really after so I know whether I should beat you to death with your own leg first."

I looked at him for a long time and came to the tentative conclusion that this was humor. God but I hoped so.

I said, "How can I decrease my chances of such an outcome?"

"By laying off the bullshit and telling me what you really want. Think before you answer."

I battled righteous irritation for a moment. How was I supposed to convince Mr. Paranoid that something other than the truth was the truth, when the truth itself hadn't convinced him?

Then I realized he hadn't asked me why I'd come. He had asked me what I wanted. I cast around in my mind for the simplest answer, and when I found it a lump came to my throat.

"There we go," Tjuan said. "Spit it out."

"It doesn't matter what I want," I said. "I won't get it."

"That don't mean I won't enjoy hearing you ask. Make it good and I might let you in."

I stood on a precipice with only the dimmest idea of how important it was: not just to the case, but to myself as a human being. I felt the kind of fear I should have felt a year ago, looking down from a seven-story building. But this time I had to step forward. Some part of me had grown enough to know I wouldn't shatter, even if it felt like I would.

"I want forgiveness," I said.

I'm not sure who was more shocked, Tjuan by my answer, or me by his look of shock. I could have pushed him over with two fingers and walked into the house.

"What did you think I was going to say?"

"Hell if I know," he said. "Something in that suitcase of yours."

"Yeah," I said. "*Forgiveness* is the name of the romance novel I was reading. I'm dying to know how it ends."

"Get your ass in here," he said, stepping back and opening the door wider. "But if you want forgiveness, bark up some other tree."

"Why is that?" I said warily.

"'Cause I never really gave a shit," he said, and then disappeared into the dining room. I stood near the front door, listening to the sounds of eating and chatter, and wondered if Tjuan was about to announce my presence. I couldn't bring myself to go charging into the idyllic meal in progress. Damn it smelled good, though. My brain picked that moment to dredge up the look on Teo's face the last time I'd seen him.

Monty appeared from around the corner of the couch, arching his back in a tippy-toe stretch and eyeing me coyly.

"Hey, handsome," I said. "Missed you." He came over and butted his head against both of my prosthetics to declare me his property, then sauntered off with his crooked tail in the air.

After a few minutes I felt a familiar tingling shock as Elliott collided forcefully with my chest. I tried blindly to catch him, but by the time my hands moved, I could already feel him on my shoulder. I made a soothing sound, then saw Caryl leaning against the cased opening that led to the dining room.

"What brings you here?" she said, tugging on the cuff of one of her gloves. "I hardly give credit to Tjuan's enigmatic pronouncements about absolution."

"Vivian's having Berenbaum and Rivenholt construct a Gate somewhere on the new studio property in Manhattan Beach."

Elliot tumbled off my shoulder. "Go on," said Caryl.

"Probably on one of the soundstages, but it will take fey glasses to find out which one has been warded."

"I assume you are basing this theory on something other than your very fruitful imagination?"

"Shipments of graphite and diamond to the studio. I talked to Baroness Foxfeather, and she found it plausible that Berenbaum and Rivenholt might have been able to undertake the construction."

"Building a Gate without the supervision of the Arcadia Project is a violation of the Accord."

"Which means you're fully authorized to kick their asses. I'd really like to see that, but I understand if you don't want me there."

There was a long silence. Reading nothing from Caryl, I looked for Elliott, but of course I couldn't see him.

I looked back at Caryl. "I'm sorry if—"

"Don't waste time with apologies. I can feel stress fractures in the construct as it is."

"Sorry."

"You believe that Claybriar is your Echo?"

"He's the one who drew the pictures, including that one of me, and he seemed familiar to me the first time I laid eyes on him."

"Almost without exception, Echoes tend to be nobility, but we've had reason to believe Claybriar was a special case. If he is in fact your Echo, we will need you to accompany us, because you may serve as an additional help in locating him."

"Thank you," I said.

"Also, if he is your Echo, we will need to register you both properly."

She was all business, but from the feel of it, Elliott was now clinging to my neck. "For God's sake, Caryl, how am I supposed to just ignore your feelings?"

"In theory," said Caryl, "you could do what everyone in the Project seems able to do: recognize that if I wanted my emotions noticed and commented upon, I would wear them like everyone else. But as this concept seems impossible for you to grasp, I will remove myself and my familiar to another room. Given the current instability of our relations with Arcadia, it would be unwise for me to spend time there recharging from the loss if emotional overload causes a rupture in my spellwork."

"Well, for what it's worth," I said, "I missed you, too."

Caryl just spread her hands in a vague gesture of resignation, then turned and headed for the stairs. "Get a pair of glasses from Song," she called back as she walked away, "and tell Teo you'll be assisting us. When the two of you are finished fighting, come to your former room, and the five of us will discuss our strategy."

"Five?"

"Gloria and Tjuan will be coming as well."

"Caryl—" I began. But as usual, she'd already made her exit.

43

I figured of the two awkward reunions, the one with Song would be the least fraught, so I headed to her room with my most ingratiating smile. I found her sitting in a handmade rocker with her baby leaning half-asleep into the crook of her arm. I could have sworn he was twice as fat as the last time I'd seen him.

"Hi," I said.

"Hello," she returned quietly, glancing meaningfully toward the sleeping baby. There was a tense undercurrent to her usual passiveness that told me she'd put me in the "potential abuser" category. I couldn't feel particularly slandered; if the shoe fits, kick yourself with it.

"Caryl sent me here for a pair of fey glasses," I said, lowering my voice to match hers. At Song's dubious look I added, "I'm not hired back. I'm just helping with one last thing."

"They're in the top drawer," she murmured, pointing with her chin toward a dresser at the back of the room.

I moved as stealthily as my prosthetics allowed. "Your baby's looking healthy," I half whispered. "What's his name?"

"Sterling," she replied.

There was nothing I could reply that wouldn't reek of insincerity, so I just found myself a pair of glasses and tried out the fit. They pinched the bridge of my nose a little, but it wasn't as though I'd be keeping them.

"I'll bring these back as soon as—" My words dried up as I turned back toward the rocker.

The baby in Song's arms was *glowing*, and not just with contentment. The fey glasses revealed the swirling eddies of golden light that moved over his skin like vapor over dry ice. "Holy shit," I breathed.

Song turned and gave me a wan smile. "Oh," she said. "Yeah."

"Why is the baby—" I stopped, remembering that this household's mysteries had never been mine to know. "Right; it's none of my business."

Song gave a soft shrug, not meeting my eyes. "His father was fey. I didn't know about Arcadia then." She looked uncertain about saying more.

"You don't have to explain."

"Thank you," she said. She still wasn't looking at me, and she didn't say good-bye as I left.

Teo was in the kitchen, carefully wrapping up leftovers in foil while Stevie scrubbed pots. As usual, Stevie glanced at me and said nothing. Teo didn't see me at first, and I just leaned on the doorway, feeling a rush of tenderness for him that I knew would disappear the minute he opened his mouth.

I'd have to break the silence with something spectacularly lovable if I was going to survive the ensuing conversation, so I tried to quarantine my crazy away from the rest of me. Picturing my own little construct, I imagined stuffing my rage and lust and fear and self-loathing into it, leaving only the person I would have been if someone hadn't put my brain in backward.

"I'm sorry, Teo," I said, and bit down hard on my tongue before I could add all the explanations, the justifications, the mitigating circumstances that crowded into my throat at the sound of my own words.

"I don't care," said Teo, snapping the lid on a plastic container and taking it to the fridge.

"I'm still sorry," I said, trying not to be devastated at how little I had reaped from that massive act of self-mastery.

"And I still don't care," he said. "Either words mean something or they don't, and either way, you're fucked. You and I are done."

"Actually, we're not done, which is what I came to tell you. Caryl needs my help to wrap up this situation with Rivenholt and the census anomaly."

"I am not working with you again," he said flatly.

"Teo, I lashed out at you, and there isn't anything that will make that better. I'm not going to pretend I didn't hate you right then, but it's also not everything there is to know about how I feel."

"I really don't care how you feel." He turned around, leaning against the fridge. Stevie just kept right on washing pots. "I honestly was never into you," he said. "I don't find you attractive, and it's not just your scars or whatever. You're like, thirty, and your hair is too short, and you dress like crap."

"I'm twenty-six. And you kind of flirted."

"Who else am I supposed to flirt with? Caryl? That's like talking to a brick wall. I swear on my father's grave, you don't do anything for me. At all."

"I'm okay with that," I said. And I was, which was kind of weird, since I had always hung a lot of my self-esteem on whether or not men found me worthy of insemination. I didn't really have the time to look deeply into this breakthrough, because Teo still had more he wanted to unload on me.

"I don't mind people being crazy," he said. "I understand rage and depression and saying stuff you regret. But when I do it, I'm just a dumb dog snapping his teeth. What I don't like about you is that even when you're being nice, even when things are good, you're checking out people's weaknesses, storing things up to hurt them with later. You can't be trusted. Not ever."

"Maybe not," I said. "But for the same reason you can't trust me to be your friend, you can trust me to work out the weaknesses in a problem and solve it. Caryl wants everyone upstairs for a meeting when you're finished being mad at me."

"Don't talk about this like it's a mood swing," Teo said. "Sometimes things are just broken." He was calm in a way I hadn't seen before, and it gave me an uneasy feeling.

I opened and shut my mouth a couple of times, and then a little voice piped up behind me. An actual voice, not one of the many in my head.

"Shame on you, Teo!"

Oh, for God's sake. "Gloria, I didn't see you there," I said. Yeah, this time I was being an asshole.

Gloria seemed too focused on scolding Teo to notice. "Forgiveness is our duty as Christians," she told him.

"So is not stabbing people," said Teo.

"I know how hard it is to forgive," Gloria went on blithely. Apparently she'd recently armored over that weak spot. "But hon, the only way to be a better person than those who hurt you is to forgive them and show them kindness."

"Teo doesn't have to try that hard to be a better person than either of us."

Gloria turned her sleepy-lidded blue eyes up to mine and smiled with beatific sweetness. "God forgives you for the things you said to me," she said. "And so do I. And if Teo were half the man he thinks he is, he would be strong enough to forgive you too."

Teo snorted. "Fuck you, Gloria."

"Hey!" I snapped.

Gloria gave me a surprised smile, then turned back to Teo, looking ready to start into another lecture.

"Don't waste your breath," I said. "I forgive him for not forgiving me, okay? Now I think we're all wanted upstairs."

When I went up to the room I'd spent a few nights in, I was shocked to see that somehow in the past day it had been filled with new furniture. Caryl seemed in the process of converting it into an office space, all desks and bookshelves and filing cabinets. At the moment she sat writing in a notebook, her back to the door.

"Jeez," I said. "You guys wasted no time."

Tjuan shouldered his way past me into the room, nearly making my prosthetic knee buckle under the unexpected weight I threw onto it. "And who do you think had to carry all that shit up the stairs?" he said. "I guess it's always good to have a colored boy around to do the hard labor."

"Not to spoil another of your rants," said Teo, coming in behind him, "but I think maybe it had more to do with you being about eleven feet tall."

"How is that my fault?" he countered. "Maybe Gloria wanted to help move furniture. Did anyone ask her?"

"Ask me what, sweetheart?" Gloria was the last one in, perhaps on account of not being able to take the stairs quite as easily as Tjuan wanted us to believe.

"Get your lazy ass in here," said Tjuan. Gloria grinned at him like he'd called her gorgeous. Even if I'd had the dubious privilege of living here a decade, I seriously doubted I would ever understand these people.

We settled around a small table that had only four chairs. Caryl elected to stand, removing any awkwardness that would have arisen from one of the men having to give up his seat to me.

Closing her notebook with a soft snap, Caryl looked at us for a moment, then spoke in her usual bored tone. "We have reason to believe that the census anomaly is caused by fey that are being held in flux somehow via an incomplete Gate at the Valiant Studios construction site. We need to find a way onto the property, locate the Gate, and free the trapped Arcadian citizens."

"Are you going with us?" Teo asked Caryl.

"I am."

"Then the breaking and entering will be no problem, right? You can just make us invisible and do that thing you do to doors."

"I imagine the external gate to the property is made of metal, not wood, so I cannot decompose it. As for 'invisibility,' I'm afraid with my familiar in use I cannot afford the expenditure of energy required to cast a group enchantment."

"Do you have to bring Elliott?" Gloria asked.

"Without my familiar, I fear I would be more hindrance than help, due to the stressful nature of the enterprise."

"I can take care of getting us onto the lot," I said. Everyone turned to look at me. "Inaya can just drive us right in."

Caryl eyed me. "And just how exactly are you planning to explain to Inaya that you need access to her construction site in the wee hours of the morning?"

"I told her everything," I said.

"*What?*" cried Teo and Gloria in alarmed unison.

"Foxfeather met Inaya this morning, and apparently they're Echoes, so it's not like Arcadia is a big secret to Inaya anymore. She had information I needed, so I set up a meeting with her." I conveniently left out the order in which those events had occurred, but even so, Teo smacked a palm to his forehead, and Tjuan shook his head slowly with a look of profound disapproval.

"I will second Millie's 'relax,' believe it or not," Caryl said. "Her employment has already been terminated, and I am already due for disciplinary measures. We may as well be hanged for a sheep as a lamb, particularly when there is a chance to obtain some crucial intelligence about Vivian's plans. She's been building to something for years."

"Why's National pickin' on you, Caryl?" Gloria said, sitting forward in her chair. "You haven't done anything wrong."

"This is not the time to debate the responsibilities inherent in management," said Caryl. "Prepare yourselves for a bit of trespassing. The danger should be minimal; if we are somehow caught by their private security, I will recover my familiar's energy and enchant our way out of it. But let us hope that is unnecessary, as I will be dead weight after that at best. On a related note, can someone please get Martin's cat out of here?"

I wasn't sure how that was related, but Monty was indeed sniffing around a filing cabinet near the door. Tjuan obligingly rose and removed him, much to my disappointment.

"Be prepared to defend yourselves," Caryl went on, "in case I am unable to help you."

"Self-defense is not really my thing," I said. "I'm kind of pleased that I've mastered self-locomotion."

Tjuan sat back down, mumbling something that I was entirely sure I misheard.

"Huh?" I said in astonishment.

"I said I've got your back. Don't make it a thing."

"Actually," said Teo, "Millie brings up a good point. Isn't bringing her asking for, like, three kinds of trouble?"

"She is our compass," said Caryl. "She will likely feel drawn to Claybriar's location."

"Fey glasses," said Teo. "We just look around for a ward that screams 'keep out,' and we'll be fine."

"I'm going," I said flatly to Teo. "He's my Echo. You of all people should understand."

"Don't you say a goddamned word about my Echo," he said. "I understand fine; I just don't care."

Caryl cleared her throat. "If the two of you wish to bicker further, please do it after we've completed our objective. Teo, the advantage of having someone along who can direct us and potentially dispel wards outweighs the disadvantages of her physical and emotional handicaps."

"If she's going," said Teo, "I'm not."

"Very well," said Caryl. "You are dismissed."

I tried not to laugh at Teo's expression but didn't quite succeed.

Apparently I wasn't the only one amused. "Someone got his bluff called!" sang Gloria.

"Was that a bluff?" said Caryl. "I would prefer not to waste time with such things. If you delay us further with your griev-ances, Teo, I'm afraid I will have to leave you behind regardless of your preferences."

"I'll be fine," said Teo. "Forget I said anything. I'm fine. I'll go."

"I want you all to listen to me very carefully," Caryl said in a tone that brought me to full attention. "This rescue attempt must be done entirely by the book. Our book. We will break human laws if we must, but the laws of the Accord will not be bent, bruised, or in any way trifled with. I understand that in this country it is considered harmless, even admirable, to flout authority for its own sake, but when it comes to maintaining balance between two worlds, the rules are not arbitrary, and I am the authority here. I do not want to have to give an order twice, and I do not want to be questioned. Is that perfectly clear?"

A chorus of assent followed her question, though Teo's response was sullen. He was normally the first one spouting the rulebook at people too. I was going to have to find a time to figure out what was really eating him. Even I wasn't narcissistic enough to think that our argument could put him in this deep of a funk.

"When are we heading out there?" I said.

"Now," said Caryl.

44

"Now?" echoed Teo in disbelief.

"What did I say about giving orders twice, Teo?"

Teo scowled, rising from his chair. "Did it ever occur to you that some of us might have social lives or something? I gotta go make a phone call."

"Sit," said Caryl. "Your phone is in your pocket, and I don't want to waste more time herding stray sheep."

I took a cue from that and dialed Inaya, hoping she'd be as cooperative as I'd implied. I greeted her by name when she answered, glancing around the room to make sure everyone noticed. Teo wasn't paying any attention, of course; he had his own phone out.

"I need you to get us on the lot tonight," I said to Inaya.

"No problem."

"There are a bunch of us, so we might want a van or something."

"We have a van," interrupted Caryl.

"Never mind the van," I said. "We'll come pick you up, and then you can just deal with security and keys or whatever when we get there."

She replied something about private security, but I lost most of it because Teo's voice had risen to a distracting volume, as though he were talking to someone in a noisy bar.

"A bunch of people from my stupid job are going down to Manhattan Beach tonight," he was saying, "and they decided to drag me along. We'll have to have that drink later."

"Could you hold just a moment, Inaya?" I said as sweetly as I could, and then put my hand over the phone. "Teo," I said. "Can you lower your voice, please?"

Teo flipped me the bird.

I turned to Caryl, gritting my teeth. "Can we not just leave him here?"

Caryl rubbed at one of her temples with gloved fingertips in a long-suffering way that made it easy to forget she was the youngest person in the room. "I will keep Teo under control," she said. "Can I trust you to do the same for yourself?"

I wasn't entirely sure that I could, but I nodded. Act as if ye have faith, and all that.

"Sorry, Inaya," I said, putting the phone back to my ear. "You think you can get us past the security?"

"Oh, I can do better than that," she said. "Just relax and I'll show you some real magic."

Our ride was an unmarked white van with tinted windows—not suspicious at *all*. Inaya rode shotgun, and Teo made a point of squeezing between Tjuan and Gloria in the back bench seat rather than taking the more comfortable captain's chair next to mine. Poor Gloria got up with a sigh and took the chair instead. I watched Caryl calmly maneuvering the great white whale through evening traffic, and it occurred to me that when she had been appointed head of the Los Angeles Arcadia Project, she had been too young to drive without an adult in the car.

"Caryl," I said, "how dangerous is this, really?"

"I do not know what safeguards they have set up around the Gate," she said, "but if they are linked to Vivian's essence and you cannot fully dispel them, we will leave them be. I have no desire to get anyone hurt tonight, especially with National's eyes on me."

"Hope your probation works out better than mine did."

Inaya directed us to the studio's main entry gate; there was enough room to pull in out of the main flow of street traffic before stopping in front of the unmanned guard booth and drop arm. There was a smaller pedestrian gate to the side; as soon as we stopped, Inaya hopped out and pulled out a set of keys, trying one at a time in the lock. I carefully maneuvered myself into the front passenger's seat of the van so I could watch and listen.

An energetic young blond guy approached her almost immediately. "Ms. West," he said with a playful salute. "What brings you here at this hour?"

"Hmmmmm," she said, considering him. "Can you keep a secret?"

Caryl shifted in the driver's seat. "Millie—"

"Trust the lady," I said.

The guard was leaning against the gate in what I imagine he thought was a suave pose. "Keeping things safe is my job, Ms. West."

Inaya gave him a slow, sly grin. Foxfeather must have recently sprinkled her with fairy dust or something, because even from my angle, that smile set loose a cascade of butterflies in my stomach.

"I'm having a . . . private party for some friends here tonight," Inaya said. "But we might be doing some things that aren't strictly, you know—" She paused to make a puff-puff gesture with her elegant fingertips.

"Right," said the guard.

"I don't want you guys in trouble about it, so I'm giving you the night off, full pay. Can you radio the others? I want everybody gone till morning. That should give us enough time to clean up, and we can all just pretend this never happened."

The guard gave her another salute. "Sure thing, Ms. West."

"Can you lift up the gate for us?"

"That won't be necessary," Caryl called out to her.

Inaya looked confused but sent the security guard on his way. I retreated from the front of the van as she climbed back in. "Okay," she said. "What exactly are you planning to do with the van?"

"I was hoping you would drive it away for us," said Caryl.

"If you think I'm not going to help set those poor people free," Inaya said, "you are out of your mind."

From behind me, I heard a derisive snort from Tjuan. It was comforting to see that Teo was right; Tjuan apparently found *everyone* irksome.

"Inaya," said Caryl calmly, "I need you to drive the van away from here. It is huge and all but glows in the dark, and stealth may be required. We will call you when we need you to bring it back."

"Tell me you did not just Miss Daisy me."

Caryl and Inaya locked eyes. I could almost see the sparks of Inaya's steel striking Caryl's flint. If it had been a movie, they'd have lunged forward and started kissing, but instead Inaya sighed and threw up her hands.

"It's your show, I guess," Inaya said. "But you and I are going to have words later."

She let us through the pedestrian gate before climbing back into the van and driving away. We all slipped on our fey glasses and scanned the darkened lot.

"Teo, stop fidgeting," said Caryl dryly. "Millie, do you see anything? Feel anything?"

"I don't," I said.

"Then just start walking."

I sighed, vastly uncomfortable. The last time I had let my intuition guide me, it had guided me off a roof. At the moment I felt nothing in particular, so I picked a random direction.

"Squeak, squeak," said Teo.

"What?" I snapped.

"We're a bunch of lemmings headed for a ledge."

"Oh, I thought maybe my knee needed oiling."

"Are you seriously critiquing my lemming sounds?"

"Are you seriously making falling-off-a-ledge jokes?"

Caryl's gloved hand landed on the back of my neck, hard, and from the sound Teo made, I could only assume her other hand was on him somewhere. "Stop it," she said, and then took her hands away quickly. "If you persist in bickering," she said, "so help me I will give you both cancer."

I looked over at Teo in alarm and mouthed, "Can she do that?" He just nodded, eyes wide. We both elected to shut up at that point.

By luck or fate, my general direction turned out to be correct. As soundstages go, stage 13 wasn't particularly large, maybe a hundred by two hundred feet, and thirty feet high, topped by a gently peaked roof. Its main distinguishing feature was the intricate fractal web of Unseelie magic that pulsed and writhed around it. Even from a distance, even knowing what I was looking at, it took every ounce of my self-control to resist the siren call of Move Along, Nothing to See Here.

"Thirteen? Really?" said Teo.

"Most lots don't even have a Stage Thirteen," I said.

Caryl was studying Vivian's spellwork so intently that even without expression it was easy to read her admiration. "I think that's sort of the joke," she said absently.

"Can you unlock it?" Teo asked.

"If we can find an entrance with the proper amount of wood around the door latch, then yes. But I don't have enough power to rust metal unless I dissolve Elliott, and we all know why that's a terrible idea."

We circled the hangarlike structure until Caryl found a likely looking door at the top of a small flight of steps. She approached and gave it an exploratory touch with gloved fingertips.

All at once she recoiled with a cry and pressed a hand to her chest. She turned and staggered down the steps toward us, leaning heavily on the rail with the hand that wasn't curled into the fabric of her blouse.

"What is it?" I asked her in alarm.

She replied with a labored inhale, then released the rail just in time to politely cover a barrage of wet coughs. When she withdrew her hand, her glove was spattered with red.

"Oh, *fuck*," I blurted, backing up a couple of steps.

Teo, on the other hand, rushed toward her. In his panic he must have completely lost his senses, because he put his hand on the nape of her neck, where her tightly bound hair left her skin exposed. Her familiar had just a slice of a second to look terrified before flying into a thousand pieces.

"Elliott!" I called out stupidly as his fragments dissipated like smoke.

Caryl stumbled a few feet away from Teo, drawing in quick, shallow breaths. Then she sank down on the pavement and clawed at her chest. "Stupid, stupid, stupid . . . ," she gasped. "I shouldn't have touched it!"

Teo knelt next to her. "Carrie, it's okay. It's not your—"

"And you shouldn't have touched me!" She rounded on him, savagery lending her damaged voice a genuinely frightening snarl. This set off another paroxysm of coughing; this time both gloves turned gory. Teo stepped back, speechless for once.

"Well," said Tjuan, standing very still. "Now we're fucked."

"We are under no circumstances fucked," I said firmly. I took a couple of steps toward Caryl, who was struggling to take deep, even breaths. "Caryl," I said. "What exactly happened at the door?"

"Metaspell." She spoke urgently, snatching a breath between every few words. "I should have . . . seen the curse, but it was . . . it was lost in . . . all that warding. . . ."

"Don't beat yourself up about it," I said. "Are you okay?"

"No," she said, looking up at me with tear-filled eyes. "I'm going to die."

45

Terror tried to rise up in me like a tide of ice water, but I clamped down on it hard. I left my glasses on, hoping they would conceal what was going on in my head. "We're all going to die eventually," I said evenly. "Can you give me an ETA on your demise in particular?"

Caryl's gaze lost focus, as though she were searching inside herself. Her breaths were labored and shallow, and her lips were turning blue.

"Massive pulmonary embolism," she said. "Blood oxygenation dropping rapidly—I'd say—minutes, not hours."

I jumped to my feet and began to climb the steps to the soundstage door. "Is Vivian powering this ward?" I asked Caryl without looking at her.

"It seems to be . . . independent of her. But the curse—curses are always linked to essence."

"Is the curse still in the ward, or did you use it up when you touched the door?" I reached out.

"I don't know. Millie, *don't!*"

But I had already put my hand on the doorknob. I felt nothing, of course; one moment the soundstage was a seething mass of bruised magic making me want to look away—the next moment it was just a building, even through my glasses. I inhaled experimentally and found myself unhurt.

"Well then," I said. "We're good to go."

I turned to Caryl. When I saw her still struggling for breath, part of me crawled into a corner and died.

"Caryl," I said flatly, "before you expire, could you be kind enough to dispense with the lock?"

"*Millie!*" It was Gloria, her voice blurry with tears.

Caryl sat gasping in the middle of the pavement, pulling off her gloves and wiping her bare hands on her knees with an intensity worthy of Lady Macbeth. No one knew what to do, since the person who usually gave orders was busy imploding. I moved to Caryl again and crouched nearby, leaving a bit of distance between us. I stared at the discarded gloves where they lay limp and bloody on the pavement. "Caryl, I need you to unlock that door."

Teo advanced as though he wanted to choke me, but then stopped short, flexing his hands. "Millie, for God's sake, let's just get out of here before somebody gets killed."

"I'd say we missed that boat, wouldn't you?" I turned back to Caryl. "Are you sure the curse is lethal?"

"This is how . . . she killed Martin," Caryl gasped. His name fell from her lips like "Mommy" from a lost child's, and for the first time I realized the depth of her love for him.

I had to look away. It wasn't the blood at the corners of her mouth that got me, or the corpselike tinge to her skin. It wasn't even the grief for her mentor, or the fear that made her eyes look so young behind their dark liner. It was the trust mixed into it, the way she looked to me with irrational hope simply because I was the only person pretending to be calm.

"Vivian could undo the curse," I said.

Caryl shook her head. "She would have to . . . be here."

"We can call her."

"No," Tjuan interjected forcefully. "She'd kill all of us and have our bodies paved over."

"Also, she'd have to take the 405," added Gloria with a sniffle. "It's a parking lot this time of night."

Tjuan frowned. "Wouldn't she just take La Cienega?"

"Still, it'd be forty-five minutes at the very—"

"Shut up!" I snapped. To my surprise, they did. I turned, forcing myself to make eye contact with Caryl. "What do you want to do with the time you have left?"

She set her jaw, staring at the soundstage. "I'd like to . . . unlock that door," she rasped.

"That's my girl."

She looked up at me. "I'm your girl?" She didn't sound nineteen; she sounded nine.

"Damn right."

Caryl started to get to her feet, one hand positioned as though to keep her heart from bursting out of her rib cage. I reached to help her, hesitated out of habit, then remembered that the damage had already been done and gave her my hand.

Caryl gasped as she stood up straight. A deep gasp, a sweeping inhale of relief. It took me a moment to realize why.

"I fixed you!" I said breathlessly, my fingers tightening convulsively on hers. Her hand was as soft as a baby's.

She shook her head and laughed, tears glistening on her lashes. "No," she said. "It's like the facades. You interrupted the circuit."

An incredulous snort escaped me. "So you can live a long, full life, so long as I never let go of your hand?"

"Something like that." She actually *giggled*, giddy as a cheerleader.

"Well then, this will work out dandy until one of us has to pee," I said, just to hear her laugh again. "Come on." I tugged her toward the soundstage.

Even with all things considered, Caryl managed to pull together enough focus to rot the wood around the door latch, allowing her to force it open with a well-placed shoulder. I immediately tore off my fey glasses; the golden radiance of Seelie magic that spilled from inside the soundstage was like staring directly into the sun.

Something powerful took hold of us both, compelling us to cross the threshold and shut the door behind us. By the time I processed that it was yet another ward, it was too late to do anything about it. We both looked around, blinking, and then swore in unison.

The pair of us stood holding hands in the middle of a broiling desert, white sun beating down on us at the apex of a faded sky. Behind and beside us was nothing but jagged horizon; ahead of us stood the remains of a classic Western ghost town, bleak and picturesque.

"I know what this is," I said. I tried putting on my glasses again and nearly burned out my retinas for my pains. I slid them on top of my head, since the dress Foxfeather had given me had no pockets. "Bottom dollar says David painted the walls in here; this is a location from *Black Powder*. I just have to touch the—"

A sound behind me, like approaching thunder, made me

turn. Caryl crowded me, hanging on my arm, as we spotted a posse of a dozen men on horseback riding straight toward us. Black-and-white Appaloosas, skewbald pintos, bay mustangs, all gleaming with sweat under the desert sun and kicking up great clouds of dust as their riders spurred them into a frenzy.

"They're not real," I said, backing up slowly. "I'm eighty percent sure they're just painted on the wall behind us." But I was already adjusting the valve on my hydraulic knee.

"Millie . . . ," Caryl said, tugging my hand as the posse continued toward us. They clearly intended to ride us down. "Even if it's psychic spellwork," she said, "it will still *feel* like being trampled."

"Gotcha," I said. "Keep hold of my hand, don't pull ahead, and don't talk to me. Running is hard, so don't distract me."

"Millie . . ." A panicked note crept into her voice as we began to feel the ground tremble under us. One of the riders reached behind him to free the rifle that was slung across his back.

We took off, and I threw all my focus into movement. I hadn't gotten the valve setting quite right. The knee didn't bend fast enough, forcing me to sweep the leg around in an arc with each panicked stride. I focused my fear into the desperate energy it took to keep myself upright. With clumsy control I managed to gather some acceleration, but Caryl was trying to run faster still, starting to drag me forward in a way that promised to topple us both. I could actually *smell* the horses behind us now.

Caryl looked over her shoulder, which slowed us abruptly. I couldn't yell at her to keep steady; even taking the trouble to find words would have broken my rhythm. I just kept blindly flailing forward. Caryl was an idiot without her construct;

when she saw how close the horses were, she tried to pull me along faster, as though she could help, as though she could give me back my body whole. I cursed fluently as my steps stuttered.

At last Caryl seemed to see the problem, and she tried to release my hand. But then she'd be dead for real, so I crushed her hand in my grip, refusing to let it slip away. The effort broke my rhythm, and I stumbled.

We both fell to the hard, hot ground in a tangle of bones and titanium, and the posse rode us down.

I heard Caryl screaming in my ear, smelled blood. I felt my bones snap, the hot, bright pain of muscle tearing like raw chicken. I entered a slow-motion adrenaline dream, flashed back to falling, catching in a tree, things tearing and snapping and piercing, not knowing what was wood and what was bone. I thought I'd forgotten the fall, but there it was, fresh as new bread, and I was screaming, and my heart beat so hard it made a sound like a chair scraping over tile; I could feel it almost exploding in my chest.

Then the riders were gone, and I was alive.

I could feel my broken and bleeding body, but I looked down and saw that I was fine, except that my thigh had been jarred loose from the socket of my AK. Once I saw that I wasn't hurt, the pain faded. Caryl was curled in the fetal position on the ground next to me, gasping; her hand had slipped away during the fall. I reached over quickly to recapture it.

"Caryl," I said. "You're okay. Look at yourself. You're not hurt."

Her breathing slowed and she carefully sat up, wiping blood from her mouth and then feeling her own limbs experimentally. Dazed, she sat patiently and kept a hand on my arm while I forced my thigh back into the suction suspension. Without my powder, I couldn't get a comfortable fit. I settled for "not going to fall off in the immediate future," readjusted the hydraulic valve for walking, and then let Caryl help me to my feet.

"Shit," I said. "I have no idea where the wall is now, much less the door."

"I imagine that's the point of the horses," said Caryl. I still couldn't get over the unsteadiness in her voice, the expressive way her syllables rode the currents of her emotion.

"How are you feeling?" I asked her.

"Perfectly fine," she said, squeezing my hand.

"Well, I don't see a Gate standing around, do you? So if it's in here, it must be in one of those buildings." I pointed to the little town.

"Do you hear something?"

I did hear it. The white noise of ragged breathing and feet pounding on sand. We both turned to see Teo sprinting toward us, followed by a wild-eyed Tjuan, who had thrown Gloria over his shoulder. They were being chased by nothing we could see, other than their own dust clouds.

"Oh hey, guys," I said dryly as they barreled toward us, too panicked even to question our calm. "Those riders aren't"— they sprinted right by us—"real."

They managed to make it all the way to town and dive for cover on the porch of a dilapidated hat shop. Caryl and I eventually caught up to them, watching them recover their breath and turn their heads in unison to watch the nonexistent posse gallop by. Gloria winced and coughed as though the horses' hooves had kicked up dust in her face.

"John Riven, you are a genius," I muttered aloud. "An evil

genius I am going to personally throttle to death if I ever have the good fortune of meeting you."

The ghost town looked just as it had in the stills from Berenbaum's postproduction office: at the far end was the clichéd town square complete with an old stone well, a plethora of hitching posts, and a chapel with a decaying bell tower. Stretching toward us from it was a single dusty lane two carriages wide, with saloons and feed stores and mining supply depots and other shops whose signs were too cracked and faded to read.

"Everyone okay?" I asked my comrades as we approached the porch.

"I think my heart actually stopped for a minute," said Gloria, fanning herself with one hand. "My mouth tastes like an old penny."

"I fucked up my ankle," said Teo. "Didn't feel it till now, but *shit*."

"I broke a nail," Tjuan deadpanned.

"Okay," I said. "I think our best plan is for the three of you to search the buildings for the Gate while Caryl and I try to find a wall so we can dispel this ward and see what this place really looks like and where the doors are."

"What do we do if we find the Gate?" asked Gloria.

"Just shout," I said. "This place is big, but not as big as it looks, so we should be able to hear you just fine from wherever. Caryl will know what to do once we find the Gate."

Everyone looked to Caryl. She fidgeted, her hand tightening in mine. "Do as Millie says," she said, trying for her usual crisp tone and almost managing it. "I am placing her in charge until National arrives next week."

"Wha—" I spluttered, almost dropping her hand.

"Yes, ma'am," said Gloria quickly, the way you do when your boss has gone crazy. "Come on, boys, let's split up and search the place. And for love of the Lord, Teo, let someone else search the saloon; I don't want you getting distracted by some magicked-up lady of the evening." Her voice was too bright, too brassy, as she led them away.

I was still staring at Caryl, because with all this nonsense about putting me in charge, it had finally sunk in that she had every intention of dying.

46

The sounds of bickering faded as Caryl and I headed down the lane toward the town square, hand in hand. I shifted my fingers to interlace them with hers. "I kind of like hanging out with the real you," I said.

"This isn't the real me," she argued, as she had in the car after leaving Regazo de Lujo. Only this time with 90 percent more petulance.

"Now that you can't shut me up by saying I'll explode Elliott, I just want to say—I feel really bad for everything I put you through. You're a really good boss, and I enjoyed working for you, and I never meant to disrespect you in any way."

I don't know what I was expecting, but watching her completely fold in on herself and dissolve into tears wasn't it.

"Hey," I said, stopping in the town square, under the shadow of the ruined bell tower. "It's okay, shhh, it's okay." Which was bullshit, of course; I couldn't even find okay on the map. I tried to give Caryl a hug, but she cringed away, then immediately apologized.

"I panic if anything closes in on me," she said. "They used to put me in a box when I screamed too loudly."

"The Unseelie?"

"Let's just find a way out of here."

I squinted up at the sky, trying to find a seam, a difference in shading, something. But it went on and on smoothly for miles, the color of bleached denim. "Was it Vivian who kidnapped you?"

"Let's not talk about it, *please.*" There was such urgency in her voice that I reluctantly let it drop.

"All right, well, can we talk about why you put me in charge just now?" I said.

"Because I like you."

"I beg your fucking pardon?"

She made a spastic waving-away gesture with her free hand. "It doesn't matter. National will put someone else in charge when they get here next week. It was just . . . a gesture."

"Do you think it was a mistake to fire me?"

"I don't know. I can't think straight without Elliott." She tried to lead us out of the town square, but I pulled her up short.

"Yes, you can, Caryl; you just have no practice at it. It's not either/or. This is a thing they taught me. Emotion Mind and Reason Mind. They can work together. You don't have to get rid of your feelings, you just have to keep them out of the driver's seat. I'm not saying it's easy."

She gave a nervous, keening little laugh. "Very well then, I'll devote my remaining five minutes of life to the study."

"Apparently your sarcasm is intact. I find that weirdly reassuring."

She avoided my gaze. "If you find a way out of here, if you find out what Vivian is planning, National might let you stay."

"And if not, they'll want to kill me or something, right? Or wipe my memory?"

Caryl looked at me, aghast. "What makes you think that?"

"Otherwise what's to stop me from spilling your secrets and causing mass hysteria?"

She shrank a little and said nothing.

I suppose I should have put it together earlier. That's the problem with having a huge ego; you always assume that when you're chosen for something, it's because you're special, talented, better.

"*That's* why you hire from the loony bin," I said. "It doesn't have anything to do with sensitivity or creativity or anything like that. It's plausible deniability."

Caryl scuffed her toe on the dusty ground.

"And just mental illness isn't enough," I persisted. "They have to be the kind of people who would have a roomful of empty seats at their funeral. The kind of people with no one to vouch for them."

She looked up at me, eyes narrowed slightly. "I'll confess that's part of it. But if that were all, I could just scoop anyone off the street. Not all marginalized people are actually useful to us. Teo is dependable, lawful, and inventive. Tjuan is focused and clever. Gloria could get information from a gargoyle."

"And me?"

"You—" she said, looking away. "You, I liked."

I cleared my throat, laughed a little. "You keep saying that. But I kind of felt like I made a bad impression when we met."

"By then I had already made up my mind. When you made the news last year, I researched you. I saw your films."

"You're . . . a *fan*?" I barked a laugh. "Hey, guess what, you can run unopposed for president of the club."

"Don't make it sound like that," she said irritably, making as if to pull her hand away. I held on. "I saw *The Stone Guest*," she said. "It said things about growing up all wrong and too fast, things I didn't know how to say, or even really how to feel. You seemed . . . insightful. Complicated. Passionate."

"Holy shit. You have a crush on me."

This time she did manage to yank her hand away, but I caught it again. "I'm finished talking about this," she said, doing a damn good impression of her normal icy self.

"Caryl—"

"I want to find that Gate," she said. "Not only to save the prisoners, but because I want to know how Vivian did it. You have no way of appreciating how impossible it is to arrest something between worlds."

"Like falling halfway down a hole . . . but sideways!" I mimicked Foxfeather's lilting cadence, her little torso tilt.

"Just so," Caryl said dryly, and then stopped. Her grip nearly broke my fingers, and she stared at me with her mouth hanging open. No, not at me. Behind me.

I turned and found myself staring at the picturesque old well. As I followed her train of thought, my mouth fell open too.

"This is why you stopped here," Caryl said. "You led us right to him."

We approached the well and leaned over, looking down into its depths. It was darker inside than it should have been with the sun so high in the imaginary sky, as though here alone the glamour didn't penetrate. The bottom wasn't visible, but I could faintly see what hung at the end of the rope. Not a bucket, but a flat wooden platform, just big enough for someone to sit on. I tried to turn the crank, but between having only one arm to use and no good legs to stand on, I didn't get far.

"You're not thinking of going down there, are you?" Caryl said, squeezing my hand.

"Are you bonkers?"

Caryl moved to the edge, peering down. "Is anyone down there?" she called. Her rough voice reverberated against the smooth round walls of the shaft.

The staggered assortment of hoarse whimpers and moans that rose up to answer her made the fine hairs rise on the back of my neck.

"Millie?" came a faint voice then. I knew that voice.

"Clay," I said. "You bastard. Just hold on, okay? We're going to get you out of there. And then I'm going to kick your ass."

There was a long silence, and then he just said, faintly, "Okay."

"They've literally just turned it sideways," said Caryl, her voice soft with horror. "A tunnel they can't climb out of, and they're forced into continuous contact with it. If they were human, they'd have gone mad within a few hours."

"Fey can't go mad?"

"Fey are mad already."

"WE FOUND IT!" I shouted at the top of my lungs. "EVERYBODY GET YOUR ASSES OVER HERE!"

Caryl winced. "Is that how you address your film crews?"

"Whatever works," I said. As if on cue, all three of them came sprinting for the square, Gloria lagging behind.

"Where is it?" Teo asked, skidding to a dusty stop in front of me. Tjuan was close behind.

"They're at the bottom of the well," I said. "Vivian and

company built a Gate sideways, so there's no way out. They're *awake* down there."

They all peered down, as Caryl and I had done, listening to the pitiful moans from below.

Gloria started taking her shoes off. "Someone lower me down," she said.

"Oh hell no," said Teo.

"I'll have to bring 'em up one by one," she said, already straddling the lip of the well. "If they're awake, all I have to do is help 'em onto the platform. Tjuan?"

Tjuan glanced skyward, then moved to assist.

"Gloria," I said numbly. "Wow."

"Not doin' it to impress you, sugar."

The platform swayed sickeningly as Tjuan helped her settle onto it, and she let out one little "Whoa," before locking the rope between her thighs and giving Caryl a salute. "Let 'er down," she said with a cheery grin.

Tjuan reached for the crank.

"Wait!" said Gloria. "Teo, can I have your lighter? It's awful dark down there."

Teo hesitated, the bastard, but finally had the decency to hand it over. Tjuan set his teeth and began to turn the crank; it says something about me that even under the circumstances I noticed the flexing of his muscles.

"Everything all right?" called down Caryl after a moment.

"Yeah," answered Gloria in a thin voice. "I can see them. Yours first, Millie?"

"Please." There was really no fair way to choose, so I might as well not pretend to be impartial.

No sooner had I spoken than Gloria let out an earsplitting

horror-movie scream. The three of us not occupied in holding the crank flew to the edge of the well and peered down. There was not a hint of light; either Gloria had switched off the lighter or she had disappeared into a darkness that was impenetrable by ordinary means.

The screams didn't stop. Tjuan started to reverse direction, clenching his jaw, but then Claybriar called out hoarsely from below, just loud enough to be heard over Gloria's screams.

"Wait!" he said. Then after a moment, "Down!"

Tjuan glanced at me—oh right, I was supposed to be in charge. I nodded, a downward stab of my finger the best I could do at communication. Tjuan lowered the platform some more, and after a moment the screams faded to sobbing gasps. I heard Claybriar murmuring quietly, a soothing cadence, but I couldn't make out the words.

"Get us out of here," Gloria called up with surprising firmness.

Tjuan wasted no time, arms and back straining as he turned the crank, lifting them both up into the light. Gloria and Claybriar were clinging to each other, she straddling his lap in a way she would most likely have found unseemly under other circumstances. To make matters even more awkward, enough of Claybriar's essence had drained out of him that his facade was history, and I was looking at six and a half feet of faun.

Foxfeather's rendition of him hadn't been half-bad, actually, other than the vapid expression. He had crescent-shaped horns and powerful shaggy legs that bent the wrong way. His bare torso was well worth staring at, and his face looked almost like a caricature of the human version. But it was his eyes that took me aback when they locked onto mine. They were exactly the same. Why this made my scalp crawl, I don't know.

"You came," he said.

"I did."

Claybriar graciously accepted Gloria's help getting out of the well, though he was probably three times her weight. He approached me warily, his hooves soundless on the sand, as though I might bolt. "My sister," he said to me. "My sister's down there."

"She's the missing girl you were talking about?" I felt a tightening inside me that was at least two parts fear as he came closer. Something must have shown in my face, because Caryl squeezed my hand. Everyone was watching us.

"The viscount," Claybriar said, stopping in front of me. "He came to our glade, spoke to us." His ear twitched. "We weren't the first commoners he'd talked to. Something about needing volunteers for a rebellion. I got a bad feeling, so I told her not to go, but the minute I fell asleep, she slipped away."

I couldn't hurt him any worse, so I reached my hand out to him. When he touched it, his eyes took on a sharp focus.

"It's you," he said, in the same wondering way Inaya had. But to me, his hand just felt like a hand, albeit slightly fuzzy on the back.

"I'm your Echo," I said.

"I knew it as soon as you told me about your fall." Suddenly his words seemed to come fluently, lacking his former awkwardness. "It was obvious I had an Echo—I could do math, plan events, learn languages—they even let me assist at court. Then a year ago I just lost it. Lost everything. For months. I thought you'd died."

"I'm so sorry," I said. "But why didn't you just *tell* me the minute you knew?"

"You said you were friends with the viscount and his Echo. For all I knew you were part of their plans. I'm sorry. I should never have thought that."

"All righty!" Gloria distracted us by saying. Her voice was sweet and forced, like icing from a decorator's tube. "Back down I go!"

I pulled away from Claybriar. "Wait," I said to her. "What happened down there?"

"Well, honey, I had to get off the platform so Mr. Claybriar could get on. I don't have to tell you what that felt like; you've touched a Gate yourself." Was it the light, or was she a little pale?

"Are you sure you want to go back?"

"Who else is gonna do it?" she said. "Tjuan can barely lift the thing as it is."

"You are not wrong," Tjuan said, squeezing his own shoulder with a grimace.

"I'll get your sister next, sweetheart," she said to Claybriar with a wink. Claybriar gave her a lopsided smile that didn't come anywhere near his eyes. I was having a hard time looking at him.

Tjuan gave Gloria a lift back into the well, helping her settle onto the platform again. He gave the crank several turns, lowering Gloria into the shaft, then suddenly stopped. "Oh, shit," he said calmly.

"What is it?"

He was staring behind us, so we all turned to see what he was seeing.

"Oh, *shit*," I concurred.

47

Three figures approached, making their way briskly down the main avenue of the ghost town. The first to catch my eye was David Berenbaum, who for some reason was wearing classic Western sheriff garb, complete with gleaming star badge. His silvery-white Stetson shaded his face from the illusory sun. Next to him strode a blond Adonis with feathered braids and turquoise war paint, milk-white skin improbably bare except for his buckskin trousers. Viscount Rivenholt. Behind the pair of them, dolled up like a Wild West whore in bloodred satin and black lace, was Vivian Chandler.

It took me a moment to realize that they hadn't dressed for the occasion; my mind had dressed them. They were exactly as I expected to see them in this setting.

I waited for Vivian to give the obligatory speech about what fools we were for interfering in her designs, but she just kept marching toward the town square, a look of steely purpose in her painted eyes.

Just like that, Caryl bolted. She slipped her hand free and took off like a jackrabbit into the decaying chapel.

"Caryl!" I shrieked. "Have you lost your *mind*?"

"She's heading for sacred ground," murmured Claybriar. "Unseelie can't follow."

Not being Unseelie myself, I was about to take off after her when Vivian's words to Rivenholt pulled me up short.

"Toss the faun down the well, will you, darling?"

"Oh, hell no," I said, stepping pointlessly in front of Claybriar. I wasn't the ideal champion, but I had only just gotten him out of there.

Rivenholt started toward us, but David caught his arm with an *are you nuts* look.

"It's all right," the fey said. His voice was like satin sheets on a summer night. "The fall won't kill him."

"It'll kill *her*, though," said Vivian, flicking her long-nailed fingers toward the well. The rope holding Gloria frayed faster than Tjuan could move.

Gloria let loose the same free-fall scream of terror as before, but this one ended abruptly. It was echoed by the horrified shrieks of the fey still trapped in the well.

"GLORIA!" Tjuan's cry echoed down the shaft unanswered. When he turned back to Vivian, I saw the fires of hell in his eyes. I expected him to take off after her and die horribly to a snap of her fingers. But instead he backed away slowly, never taking his eyes off her.

It was Teo who went completely batshit.

"You said you wouldn't hurt anyone!" he screamed.

Vivian smiled. "I didn't hurt her. I hurt the rope."

I stood there like a poleaxed cow. Out of the corner of my eye I saw Tjuan take off toward the chapel. I should have too, but I was rooted to the spot.

"Teo?" I finally managed.

"Get Caryl, you moron!" he yelled at me, stabbing a finger toward the chapel.

"Teo, what is Vivian talking about?" Anger hadn't quite caught up with me yet. "When did she make a promise to you and why?"

"She just wanted me to spy for her! She didn't say anything about killing anyone!"

Vivian let out a silky laugh. "I should really thank you, Millie, for getting yourself fired and leaving him *all alone*," she said. "I almost peed myself when he called me, begging me to find his Echo. Which I will do, of course; I'm a woman of my word. Sadly, I never promised to *bring* her to him."

Teo stalked toward her and drew, of all things, a pathetic little pocketknife. Vivian did take an instinctive step back, though, at the sight of steel. She flicked her fingers in his direction, and I recoiled, expecting his head to explode or something. But he just stopped in his tracks and looked confused as Vivian sauntered past him, skirts swishing.

"Put the faun where he belongs, Rivenholt."

The viscount moved faster than my eye could follow. Suddenly he was behind Claybriar, making me look even stupider for trying to intervene. Rivenholt locked both arms around the faun's chest, pinning him. I didn't know what else to do but fling myself clumsily at them, digging my fingers into Rivenholt's forearm and trying to pry him loose. The viscount looked down at me in shock as his glamour dropped, revealing a creature of glass-feathered wings and blinding white eyes.

"I promised Vivian I would see this through," he said. "I'm sorry."

He released one arm from around Claybriar to try and

loosen my fingers, but then we were both distracted by Teo's gut-wrenching cry.

"What have you done!" Teo shrieked, staring with slack-jawed horror at his own left hand. He held it splay-fingered in front of his face.

"Teo, what is it?" A wave of dread made me dizzy.

"It's his hand," said Vivian cheerfully. "But good luck trying to convince him of that."

Rivenholt used the opportunity of my slackened grip to wrench free. At the same moment, Teo fell to his knees, brandishing his pocketknife and stabbing it into his left hand again and again.

"Get it off!" he screamed. "Get it off me!" Vivian burst into a cascade of delighted laughter.

I started toward Teo, but that bastard Rivenholt delivered a swift kick to my AK from behind as soon as I'd turned, making me fall back into the dust. I felt my suspension slip as my ass hit the ground.

Claybriar cried out my name but was quickly muffled by, from the sound of it, a punch in the mouth.

I twisted around just in time to see Rivenholt push Claybriar over the side of the well. I let out a growl and rolled over onto my good knee, dragging myself over to Rivenholt intending to—I don't know—bite his ankles? He saw me coming, snatched up my pricey prosthetic by the socket, and swung it in a wide arc, smashing it against my cheekbone. I saw a white flash, and my ear started ringing. I fell over onto my back with a moan.

The sky was so bright. David's white Stetson looked dark against it as he loomed over me, his face shaded from view.

Rivenholt appeared beside him. "I promised to see this through. You know I can't let her leave."

"I know."

"I'll do it. You shouldn't watch; I know you care for her."

David laid both his hands on Rivenholt's shoulders. "And you know how much I care for you, I hope," he said.

"Of course."

"Good."

And then David started to push Rivenholt, hard. I rolled onto my side; everything looked dim and disjointed, like a silent film. Berenbaum kept pushing his wide-eyed Echo back and back, a clumsy tango, until he sent the poor bastard toppling over the side of the well after Claybriar.

I must have grayed out for a second, because suddenly Sheriff Berenbaum was kneeling next to me—he smelled like Christmas and coffee—and trying to pick me up in his arms.

"What the hell are you doing, David?" Vivian's voice, sharp.

"The chapel," I murmured, slinging an arm around David's neck. "Vivian can't go in there."

"I'm sorry," David whispered. "I'm so sorry for all this. I just wanted to make great movies again; I didn't know they were *people—*"

"The chapel," I repeated curtly.

He lifted me, and Vivian called out to him again. "David, what are you *doing?*"

David ran as fast as a near-septuagenarian can run carrying a grown woman. I guess without my left leg I was lighter than most; it was still lying where Rivenholt had dropped it.

"This isn't a real chapel," I mused as we crossed the threshold. "How is it supposed to keep her out?"

"She didn't make the illusion," said David. "Johnny did. So it feels real to her."

Inside, a few beams of smoky sunlight from the decaying roof lanced downward to illuminate a dozen pews and a small altar. I didn't see Caryl as we entered, but I could hear her labored breathing somewhere toward the front of the room. My heart thrilled; she was still alive. David quickly helped me sit on one of the back pews.

"Find Caryl," I said. "Bring her to me."

For a man not used to taking orders, he responded with impressive alacrity. He helped Caryl up off the floor where she'd collapsed, and half dragged, half carried her over to me. The strain apparently wasn't good for her, because by the time he got her to the pew she'd stopped breathing altogether, and her face was turning corpse gray. I seized her hand and was rewarded with the sight of color rushing back to her cheeks, the sound of air flowing back to her lungs. She looked worn out, though; her eyes were at half-mast. David supported her with his arm, uncharacteristically silent.

"Well, that was a close one," I said. "What possessed you to run off without me?"

"What possessed you not to follow?" she countered weakly.

"Stuff like my Echo being thrown down a well and Teo stabbing a knife into his own hand."

"Oh."

"Look, Caryl. Vivian is here. All we have to do is lop off her head or whatever it takes to kill a fey, and you'll be fine."

"You can't kill her," Caryl said.

"She's immortal?"

"No, I mean, you *may* not kill her. Not until she has been

interrogated." As annoying as I found her argument, I was relieved to see her taking charge, returning to an adult state.

"I have some information that might help," interjected David, "but not much."

"Talk," Caryl said.

"Vivian promised not to cause me harm—in return, Johnny had to promise that he would do everything in his power to see the project through. That's why I had to, uh, take murder out of his power just now. Vivian was deadly serious about this project because she has some beef about the class system in Arcadia, and she said the studio was the first step in leveling the field."

"How, exactly?"

"Honestly, that's as much as she said to me. I assumed she just meant giving everyone equal access to inspiration. Is that such a bad thing?"

"Regardless of the end's virtue," Caryl said, "you can be sure you would not approve of her means."

"Just kill the bitch," I insisted. "Problem solved."

"It isn't just Vivian," Caryl protested. "We've known for some time that she's the head of a network, but we've yet to identify any of her conspirators."

"Other than David and Teo, you mean?"

David had the decency to cringe. Caryl blinked, and tears started to her eyes. "Teo?"

Right. She'd missed that bit. Also Gloria dying, but I thought now would be a bad time to bring that up. "Yeah," I said gently. "I think it was Vivian he was calling when we were planning this little trip."

"Teo?" she said again, faintly. "No. No, not Teo. He taught

me to play hopscotch." Her eyes took on a glassy look, and she slipped her thumb into her mouth.

"Aaand we've lost her," I said flatly. I looked around. "Where the hell is Tjuan? Didn't he come in here too?"

Still staring vacantly, Caryl took her thumb out of her mouth to point toward a place by the altar where the flimsy wood exterior had fallen away. It left a triangle-shaped gap just barely large enough for a person to squeeze back out into the desert.

"Why the hell did he leave you alone?" I wondered aloud. "All right then. David, help me and Caryl to the doorway."

"What for?"

"Just do it," I snapped. "I'm the director now."

David had the decency to shut up and let me lean on him so I could hobble one-legged to the door with Caryl clinging to my other hand.

"What's the matter, Vivian?" I shouted melodramatically toward the square. "Afraid of a little make-believe holy ground? Why don't you just haul Johnny back up so he can de-glamour it for you? Oh, that's right, because you cut the fucking *rope* just to hear someone die, you psychotic moron."

I could see her through the doorway as she strode onto the sagging porch. She stopped just short of entering but stood where I could almost touch her, one hand on her hip. Her satiny red skirts were dulled with dust.

"Is this where I charge furiously into the chapel because you so skillfully taunted me?" she said. "Instead of that, how about I stand here filing my nails while you starve to death?"

"If that was your Plan A, you'd be filing your nails, not talking. You want something from one of us."

"Well, darling," she said amiably, "that backstabbing geezer of yours seems to have pushed my GPS down a well."

I started to laugh. "Oh, this is fantastic. You don't know your way out of here either."

"So, what do you say?" Vivian batted her eyes. "Can we be pals? Let bygones be bygones? A fey's word is bond, and I will promise not to cause you harm if you will in return promise to dispel the ward on this soundstage and keep your cold little hands off me. Do we have a deal?"

Caryl popped her thumb out of her mouth and leaned into me. "Say yes," she whispered in my ear. I could smell blood on her breath.

"Promise to undo what you did to Caryl and Teo," I said. "Cause no harm to them, or Tjuan either."

"Bah," said Vivian with a little wave of her hand. "It isn't worth leaving four witnesses just to save myself a few days of trial and error. You have five seconds to take the deal I offered, or I am walking away."

48

Vivian actually started to count down. "Five," she prompted cheerfully.

I stood there, feeling anger clouding my higher thought. She'd killed Gloria, maimed Teo, broken Caryl. I hadn't gotten far enough in my therapy to swallow the bitter rage that rose up in my throat. "I'm not negotiating with you," I said.

"Four."

Caryl tugged my hand. "Do it, do it, do it!"

"Three."

"*Please*, Millie."

The childlike desperation in her tone almost undid me, but I violently shook my head. "She's asking me to let her kill you all—"

"She can't kill me," David reminded me.

"Shut up," I snapped.

"Two."

I didn't care. Nothing in this world, even fear of starving to death and rotting on a soundstage, could make me deal with her. But then I saw Tjuan approaching cautiously behind her, holding my prosthetic.

"All right!" I said to Vivian. "Stop counting. You have a deal. But first . . ."

"First what?"

Tjuan gave me a questioning look from behind Vivian. He pantomimed tossing the prosthetic to me and raised a brow.

I shook my head emphatically.

"*What?*" prompted Vivian irritably, just as Tjuan gave me a very similar look.

"Something just hit me," I said to Vivian.

"What?" she said impatiently.

"I mean, hit me figuratively, as in a realization. Not the way your friend Rivenholt hit me earlier with my own leg."

Tjuan got my message, and my prosthetic was subjected to its second round of abuse as he swung it with enthusiasm at the back of her head.

It's way harder to knock someone out than it looks in the movies, and that wasn't what I wanted anyway. What I wanted was for her to fall forward, and she did, right through the doorway.

I knew the pain was all in Vivian's mind, but that didn't make her screams any less chilling. Her eyes bulged; her whitened teeth stood out like marble as her lips drew back from them in anguish. She writhed, kicking at the floor, the heels of her hands thrust out, fingers curled into claws.

A twisted part of me wanted to just stand there and drink it in, but I had to take my advantage. If I couldn't kill her, I could at least take away her weapon.

With only one knee to bear my weight, I needed both my hands. I had to let go of David and Caryl. I scrabbled toward Vivian like a three-legged dog, feeling my BK prosthetic loosen as I did it, but I didn't care. I left my right foot behind me on the floor of the chapel as I lunged forward to grab Vivian's throat.

She was in too much agony to fight. I watched her glamour drop, revealing the horror underneath, some unholy hybrid of woman and mantis. Trails of red fluid seeped down her cheeks from the raw, sucking holes where her eyes should have been. Those holes were inches from my face; her teeth were like cactus spines in her too-wide mouth as she screamed. Given all that, I'll admit I started screaming a little too. But I held on to her throat, because I was damned if she was going to cast another spell today.

She started to shrivel, her white flesh visibly yellowing, creasing, sagging. That, I'll admit, I found slightly dismaying.

"What's happening?" I said out loud. Tjuan just backed away onto the porch, grim and silent. When I looked over my shoulder at David, I saw him leaning over Caryl. At first my unhinged mind thought he was kissing her, but then he sat back and started doing chest compressions, and I realized that she'd died.

"FUCK!" I said, bursting all at once into hysterical tears. And then I choked Vivian some more.

Because I knew what was happening. Like me, Vivian had no identity of her own, nothing at the core of her but a black hole. For centuries she'd been animated only by the stolen essence of other fey, and I was drawing that out now.

"You killed Caryl," I said, squeezing harder. Somehow even on that alien face I could recognize her fear. She faced her death with all the grace of a rabbit in a snare, bug-eyed, thrashing. I watched her skin desiccate and drop from jagged gray bones. I watched that flesh turn to dust as it fell, watched her bones crumble, felt my fists close tighter and tighter until there was nothing left in them but grit.

And then I just sat there crying, listening to the soft, desperate sounds of CPR behind me.

Tjuan came in and tried to hand me my leg, but I didn't move; I just stared at the pile of ruin that had been Vivian.

"You should try to get on your feet," he said. He glanced behind me, then out the door. "It's just us now," he said to the desert.

"Teo . . . ?"

Tjuan shook his head.

"Tell me he's going to be okay."

"I can't tell you that."

I fit my legs back into my prosthetics as best I could with shaking hands; Tjuan stood by, looking awkward and running his palms back over his hair. When I finished I reached up my hands, and he helped me get up off the floor. He let go as quick as he could; neither of us even tried for eye contact.

The AK was hopelessly broken. Sensitive electronic instruments don't take well to being used as weapons. The knee was stiff and unresponsive; I had to lurch out of the chapel and out into the square like a peg-legged pirate, past the well, to where Teo lay curled on his side in the road.

Blood had soaked the dirt beneath him, spreading out like a fallen hero's cloak. The boy had come damn near to cutting off his own hand with his pocketknife, driving the blade a surprising distance through bone before it had broken. The wound wasn't bleeding anymore.

I half sat, half fell onto the ground behind him, where there wasn't as much blood. I didn't reach to touch the body, didn't do much of anything.

"We were fighting," I said to Tjuan. My voice sounded strange.
"He knew you were sorry."

I just looked at the back of Teo's head. An illusory fly landed on the edge of his ear, so I shooed it away. Even over the wet, meaty scent of blood, I could smell that gunk he put in his hair.

"Asshole," I said, and laid my hand on his arm. All those old scars. His skin was cooler than it would have been if the sun had really been shining on it.

"Millie," Tjuan said, and something in his tone made me look up.

From the chapel, Caryl was making her way unsteadily toward us on Berenbaum's arm.

Joy did what pain couldn't; my vision blurred, and tears spilled hot and fast onto my cheeks. I wanted to get up, but I couldn't, so I just reached my hands toward her. Berenbaum helped her over to us, and she knelt down next to me. She looked at Teo, her eyes vacant and scared.

I pulled her to me and hugged her, not caring if she was okay with it. She stared at the body over my shoulder. I don't know how long we clung to each other, me shaking with quiet sobs, her limp and still.

"You killed her," she finally rasped. "I told you not to do that."

"You're alive, aren't you?"

She pulled back and looked at me. "They'll never hire you back now," she said. She reached up and laid her fingertips on the scar tissue at the side of my face. A maternal gesture, but her dark, colorless eyes were as lost as a child's. "What will you do?"

Berenbaum cleared his throat softly, and I turned to look at him.

He didn't meet my gaze, looking at Caryl instead. "I'll talk to Inaya. She's running HR for Valiant."

"There is no Valiant anymore," I said. "No blood, no magic."

"Inaya's got her own kind of magic." David smiled faintly, but with none of his old sparkle; he was like a wax model of himself. "Always has. She wants a studio; no power in the world's going to stop her. I'll make sure she finds a place for you."

"You see?" I said to Caryl with forced cheerfulness. "I always land on my feet."

Caryl's brow furrowed. She looked down at the stumps of my legs and then started to laugh, a wild cascade of husky giggles. Once she started she couldn't stop; the laughter shook her like a seizure. I wrapped my arm around her shoulders and looked at Tjuan; he was watching her too. He looked tired.

"You all right?" I asked him tentatively.

He turned his eyes to me but said nothing.

"I need to find some rope," said Caryl as she climbed to her feet, still giggling a little. "Or some cable. Something to lower down into the well." Her words were fast and bright as she turned her back on the body. Berenbaum reached out an arm, and she leaned on it. They walked off together, leaving me with Tjuan and Teo. It's hard to say who was warmer.

Tjuan looked at me, and I looked at him.

I hesitated. "Gloria was—"

Tjuan's eyes went hard, daring me.

I chickened out. "I need to try to find the wall so I can get rid of this glamour. Can you help me up?"

Tjuan's eyes released me, drifting toward the well. He didn't move.

"She was brave," I ventured. I waited for him to glare me

into silence, but he didn't. "She . . . always tried to do the right thing. She was . . ." I couldn't think of anything else to add to her eulogy.

Tjuan just kept staring at the well, and a muscle worked in his jaw.

"I'm not religious," I said, "but feel like I should go back to the chapel and say a prayer for her or something. Just . . . because." I let out a weak laugh. "She probably prayed for me all the time."

Tjuan turned back to me then, not quite looking at me. Slowly he crouched down next to me, gazing off over my shoulder. "You are not wrong," he said, and helped me back to my feet.

The ride back to Residence Four was about what you'd expect from a van with six traumatized fey piled in the back of it. One of them was apparently a banshee, based solely on the sounds she made the whole ride back. I would have tried to comfort her, only I'm pretty sure it was me she was screaming about. Once we arrived at the Residence, Caryl, Tjuan, and I did our best to put all the worms back in their can.

Tjuan took charge of arranging the fey's transport back to Arcadia while Caryl took Inaya aside for a private talk. My job—my last job—was to interview Claybriar and his sister. Back at the soundstage, David was busily creating cover stories for the deaths and arranging for proper burials. Except for Vivian. I think his plans for her involved a Dustbuster.

Claybriar's sister was called Trillhazel. The entire time I interviewed her, he didn't take his arm from around her or his eyes off her face. They sat on one of the sofas in the living room; I sat on the one facing them with Monty on my lap. The cat was clingy, as though he knew this was good-bye.

Trillhazel was lovely in a long-faced, feral way; she had delicate horns and was as bare-chested as her brother.

"I don't understand," I said to her. "If Vivian was trying to help the commoners, why did she have six of you imprisoned in a well?"

"Viscount, he—explain." Her English wasn't great. "He say— bad for good? Few hurt. Many better."

"You mean you were a sacrifice? You went willingly?"

Claybriar exchanged a few words with his sister in a musical language that made me feel as though I were lying in summer grass, watching clouds.

"Yes," Claybriar said then in English, still looking at his sister. The anger was back in his eyes, and this time the wounded edges of it were directed at her. "A sacrifice."

I shook my head slowly, running my fingers down Monty's spine. "Yet Vivian and the viscount managed to keep *themselves* out of that well, I notice."

Claybriar let out a short, mirthless laugh. "Nobles can't just vanish. But Her Majesty wouldn't have noticed a few missing commoners if one of them hadn't been my sister."

"How was harvesting blood even supposed to help the commoners?" I said. "I don't understand."

Trillhazel looked at me with haunted dark eyes; they were so like her brother's I felt a moment of vertigo. "I—before did not know," she said. "Please believe. Did not know."

"Know what?"

"She—want our blood for—use here. Destroy in Arcadia— land home. Home land?"

Claybriar clarified with her briefly in their native tongue. "Estate," he said, presumably to me, though he didn't meet my eyes. Then he said to her in confusion, "But her estate was already destroyed."

"No," said Trillhazel quietly, shaking her head. "Not her estate. Other noble. All, every one. Leave only the commons." Claybriar sat back like she'd slapped him in the face. Given that noble fey were more or less the entirety of the Project's clientele, I had a sudden certainty that Caryl was not going to be fired.

"It's all right now," I told them both. "Vivian is dead. She's not going to hurt anyone else."

Trillhazel looked at me as though she didn't quite believe me, and Claybriar leaned over to kiss her temple. My chest hurt, watching them, and I hugged Monty close.

"Go with the others," he said slowly to her in English. "Go get ready; we're going home."

She smiled up at him, then rose from the couch and headed for the stairs. Her hooves struck crisp, loud sounds from the wooden steps; I watched her, then turned back to Claybriar. His gaze was on me now, and I wished it wasn't; my skin crawled with bashful dread.

"You don't feel it," he said. His eyes reminded me of the well I'd found him in.

I shook my head miserably. "I'm sorry," I said. "I . . . care about you, and I think you're . . . amazing. God, that *drawing*, I can't tell you what it meant. But when we met, it wasn't—it wasn't like the thing I saw with Inaya and Foxfeather."

He nodded slowly, then dropped his head and stared at his hands. "I'm sorry too," he said. "I looked for you, for years. Felt you go west, and followed you. I was so close. But I didn't get to you in time. If I had—"

"No," I interrupted fiercely, staring in dismay at the top of his horned head. "No, it's not your fault. And—I was supposed to end up this way. You'd still be in that well if I weren't."

He looked up at that, and although he didn't make a move toward me, there was so much love in his eyes I didn't know what to do with it all.

"Why did you leave those drawings everywhere?" I asked instead.

"I've been doing it all this time," he said. "Like messages in a bottle. Everytime I'm stuck on this side waiting for anything, I make a sketch and leave it behind. I had to believe you'd find one eventually. And in the end fate puts you a few steps behind me, hunting the same guy."

I smiled sadly. All those drawings I'd never found, little slices of Claybriar I'd never see.

I thought of Officer Clay, with his gray T-shirt and his caffè mocha. He didn't scare me. I pictured sitting astride his lap, his hand curled around the scarred end of my thigh, his mouth soft against mine. But of course it couldn't be like that. He couldn't even touch me.

"I should go," he said, standing.

"Don't give up on me," I blurted.

He looked at me, startled, one ear twitching back. "Of course not," he said.

"You'll come back sometime?"

"Of course." He lingered a moment, then turned without saying good-bye. I averted my eyes from his hooves as he walked away.

I felt a twinge of guilt for judging his appearance—who was I to be choosy about legs—and it was that guilt that made me realize with a shock what had just happened.

When I'd imagined us together, he was the only one I'd changed. For the first time since my fall, I had imagined something beautiful happening with me in it. The real me, missing pieces and all.

Rivenholt was executed in Arcadia with great ceremony, according to an e-mail from David Berenbaum. When I tried to reply, my e-mail bounced back to me—no such account. The next day the trades reported that David had packed it off to some emu ranch in New Mexico with Linda, leaving Inaya West as the sole proprietor of Valiant Studios. As David had promised, she offered me a job as her assistant, and I accepted it.

Since Teo didn't legally exist, and Vivian was being treated as a missing person, only Gloria got an obituary. Gloria Day, freelance script supervisor and missionary to the needy, killed in a tragic accident, service to be held at St. Brendan Church. It wasn't until I heard the Latin hymns at her funeral that I realized why I'd never been able to find anything about her online. *Gloria dei* was more than likely not the name on her birth certificate.

I wheeled myself out of the service a little early—I still hadn't replaced my broken AK—and found Caryl lurking outside, leaning against the church.

"Well, hello," I said. "You're still basically human, you know. You can probably enter holy ground."

"Funerals make me uncomfortable," she replied evenly.

"Tjuan and Phil are up front; I don't think they saw me. But I'm sure they'd like to sit with you."

"I am only here because I didn't know where else to find you."

"I've got an apartment in the Marina; you can have the number if you want. I'm going to be Inaya's assistant at Valiant. How about you? Still have a job?"

Caryl was silent for a moment, then pushed off the wall and moved in front of my chair so I had to look at her. For some reason she'd cut off all her hair; it lay close to her head in well-groomed curls.

"National has put me on probation," she said. "Which means I still have the authority to hire you back, if you wish. Tjuan needs a new partner."

"Having employee turnover problems?"

"Millie." Her tone was flat, but I knew a rebuke when I heard one.

I sighed and ruffled my hair. "I can't imagine anything less fun than having Tjuan as a partner. And I have a roof now, and a job."

"But you're alone."

"I'm thinking of getting a cat. Seriously, I want to try living a normal life. If I come back, I want it to be because I chose it."

Caryl regarded me for a moment. "If you *choose* the Arcadia Project," she said, "you will be the first."

"Well, I'm pretty special."

"Yes, you are." There was no emotion behind the words; she must have had Elliott out. Still, it shut me up for a second.

"You know what they say," I said briskly then over the urge to cry. "If you love something, set it free."

Her mouth curved up in a bland little smile, and she reached out, giving my hand a single squeeze with her black silk glove before letting it go. "Good-bye," she said. "I'll contact you if we hear from Claybriar."

I watched her walk away down the sidewalk, and a little voice told me I wasn't going to be anybody's secretary for very long. Once you've seen the world through fey glasses, for better or for worse it never quite looks the same again.

ACKNOWLEDGMENTS

Because this book was begun with no expectation of success, it had a long, fragmented path to completion. Without a doubt, I've forgotten some of the people who made it possible.

A dedication isn't enough to acknowledge the contribution of Paul Briggs, who single-handedly led me through the first draft by dangling the carrot of positive feedback, two thousand words at a time. The world is dimmer for his unexpected loss, seven months before he could have held in his hands the book he helped to create.

A character namesake isn't enough to acknowledge Amanda C. "Dr." Davis, the first person brave enough to tell me why that first draft drove thirteen other beta readers into hiding. Without her, the book would still be in a drawer somewhere.

A paltry percentage isn't enough to acknowledge my agents, Russell Galen and Rachel Kory, for taking a chance on a newcomer and aiming higher than I'd have dared. And there isn't praise enough in the world for Navah Wolfe at Saga Press, whose perfect combination of fannish enthusiasm and surgical precision turned that stack of pages on her desk into a novel. In my wildest dreams I could never have imagined better synergy with an editor.

And Seanan McGuire! Good heavens. Still staggered by the unexpected outpouring of support from someone I'd only ever known as a name on my bookshelf. I think we're doomed to become either great friends or deadly nemeses.

There are many others who have made this book possible indirectly by propping me up when I faltered professionally or personally—too many to name, but I'll try a few. My husband, Matt, of course, everyday. Wren Wallis, partner in many things. Paul Park, Kim Stanley Robinson, Kenneth Schneyer, Shauna Roberts, Scott H. Andrews, Ferrett Steinmetz, Mary Robinette Kowal, Myke Cole, Joe Monti, Michael R. Underwood, Charles Coleman Finlay, Sunil Patel, Nate "Frog" Crowley, Jason Gruber, Sarah Goslee, Stephanie Gunn, Rachel Hartman, and Guy Gavriel Kay. (Some of you may not even know exactly why your names are on this list, because many of you are so in the habit of giving that you may not remember small gestures that, to me, meant all the world.)

Thank you, all of you, and to those I've forgotten: don't let me. Hound me, throw yourselves in my path. I'll find ways to thank you too.